Good Gifts

A Brenner Falls Romance

Kyle Hunter

Copyright 2022 by Kyle Hunter. All rights reserved.
Published in the United States by Monceau Publishing.
P. O. Box 40152
Raleigh, NC 27629
www.Kyle-Hunter.com

No portion of this publication may be copied, retransmitted, reposted, duplicated, or otherwise used without the express written approval of the author. Any unauthorized use of any part of this material without permission by the author is prohibited and against the law. The only exception is brief quotations in printed reviews.

This is a work of fiction. Names, characters, and situations are products of the author's imagination and are used fictitiously. Any resemblance to persons living or dead is entirely coincidental.

Scripture quotations are taken from the *Holy Bible,* New Living Translation, copyright ©1996, 2004, 2007, 2013, 2015 by Tyndale House Foundation unless otherwise noted. Used by permission of Tyndale House Publishers, Inc., Carol Stream, Illinois 60188. All rights reserved.

Cover design by Erika Alyana Sañga Duran.

ISBN 979-8-9856352-5-6

More novels by Kyle Hunter

Circle Back Around
One December
Postcard from Nice (A Novella)

The Provence Series

Prodigals in Provence
A Promise in Provence

The Second Chance Series

Marissa Rewritten (A Novella)
Julia Redesigned
Sydney Rewound
Eden Redefined

The Brenner Falls Romance Series

Good Gifts
Custom Made
Embracing the Broken
Mistaken Destiny

Good Gifts   *Kyle Hunter*

Good Gifts   *Kyle Hunter*

Now I will take the load from your shoulders; I will free your hands from their heavy tasks.

Open your mouth wide and I will fill it with good things.

Psalm 81:6, 10

Good Gifts *Kyle Hunter*

Chapter One

Nathan Chisholm watched through the smudged window of the Philadelphia commuter train as the landscape and unattractive brick apartment buildings sped by. He scanned the scenery for the familiar sign where he'd get out, even though the conductor always called the stop. Early evening clouds huddled in the sky in gray streaks as he joined the slow-moving throng through the station and out onto the street of his familiar suburb.

After a necessary stop at the grocery store with other exhausted shoppers, he arrived at his townhouse. Before he could unlock the door, the phone in his pocket rang. His arms were full, so he couldn't grab it. Maybe it was his best friend, Ben, who lived in Brenner Falls, the town where Nathan had grown up. He let it go to voicemail while he unpacked the plastic bags of food and preheated the oven.

He hadn't had time to do a single errand the previous weekend, thanks to overtime. Though he shunned the breaded chicken nuggets, cook-and-serve buffalo wings, and frozen pizza other harried employees ate, he *had* succumbed to frozen mac and cheese. He never thought his dietary habits would deteriorate so much, but over the previous five months, he'd indulged in that and worse. Even ordering takeout was no longer a rare event.

Back in the early days of his marketing job in Philadelphia, his first real job out of college, he'd committed to cooking for himself to unwind after work and stay healthy. He enjoyed trying new recipes and assuring the nutrition of what he ate. He used to invite friends and cook for them too. The same friends he hadn't seen in months. One of many activities he no longer had time for. What had his life become?

His schedule would lighten up in a week or two. At least that's what his manager, Jeremy, said regularly. Relief was in sight, with the completion of the advertising campaign for their biggest client. After that would be maintenance, which was its own load, but more predictable. Less crushing.

He headed to the bedroom and slipped on some sweatpants and a long-sleeved T-shirt he found on the floor. The room was a mess, another violation of his personal standard. Never leave the bed unmade. His mother had drilled that habit into him, and it made up part of his daily code. Until recently. His mom had given him a multitude of good habits, which were more useful to him than the material excesses she'd been unable to provide as a single mom. Those years of living on a tight budget, doing without, and putting on blinders to what other kids could buy or do. Seemed so far away now. He could buy what he needed and most of what he wanted. He'd worked hard and changed his life, leaving the cloud of fatherless shame behind.

He'd call his mom after dinner but would first check to see who'd called. The darkened screen of his phone brightened. His mom had been the caller but hadn't left a message. Unusual. Anxiety sprang up inside him. He tapped her number.

"Hey, Mom. It's me. Just got home. I was going to call you tonight."

"Nathan. . ."

Not *hi sweetheart*, as she usually responded. Instead, her voice broke, and she began to cry.

Nathan sank onto the couch. "What is it, Mom? What happened?"

"It's your Uncle Andy. He took a bad turn last week and went downhill so fast. I was going to call you sooner, but thought he'd rally. I'm sorry I didn't call." A sob caught in her throat.

"Is he okay?" A lead weight fell inside Nathan's stomach as he steeled himself for her response. Uncle Andy had been struggling for nearly two years with heart disease. The previous year, he'd cut back the hours he spent at Seasons, the dinner theater he owned, and had made a few other changes in his lifestyle. Despite his efforts, the disease continued to pursue him.

"No, he. . . he died this morning."

An invisible fist grabbed Nathan's throat and tears stung his eyes. "Died?" He'd heard her wrong, must have. "No, no!" Not Uncle Andy, who'd been like a father to him as he grew up. He struggled to breathe. A stab of guilt followed. He'd made trips home less often during the craziness of the last few months at work.

The last time he'd visited Brenner Falls, Uncle Andy had been pale and fatigued. He'd put on more weight and coughed frequently, but assured Nathan he was doing better and would beat the disease. He'd taken Nathan to lunch at Seasons as if he missed it. Nathan preferred going somewhere else but had indulged the older man. He'd called him a week earlier and Andy seemed to be holding on. But one never knew since Andy often minimized his suffering. "Oh, there are worse things," he would say, then turn the conversation to the other person.

"I'm so sorry, Mom. I'm so—" A sob sliced off the word in his throat. He and his mother cried softly for a moment.

"He was scheduled for hospice care, but never made it. He died at home." She stopped and blew her nose. "He slept a lot in the end, so I don't think he suffered too much."

Nathan swiped his wrist across his eyes. He stood to grab a napkin from the table where the box of macaroni still sat. "I'm glad he didn't suffer. I just wish I'd been able to talk to him or to see him one last time."

How could Nathan have missed the gravity of Uncle Andy's condition, the signs of the end? He might have known if he hadn't been enslaved to his deadlines, wrapped up completely in his own world. A world which had sparkled at the beginning, but quickly became a golden cage. Nathan's beloved Uncle Andy slipped away while Nathan was busy pushing marketing deadlines. How pointless it all seemed when he'd lost the one who taught him how to be a man.

They'd almost lost him twice before in the last two years. Andy hadn't complained. He merely said the Lord had given him more time.

"His service will be next Saturday. You can make it, can't you?"

"Yes, of course. I'll take an extra day or so. They owe me that with the amount of overtime I'm working."

"Good. I need to see my boy." Her voice wavered. "I need you, Nathan."

He needed to see her too. Suddenly, the longing to see his mother, to remind himself that he still had family, still had love and connection, crushed him from the inside. The pale walls of his townhouse only reminded him how alone he felt in that sterile place where he slept but did little else.

Fresh tears moistened his cheeks. "I'll be there, Mom. Don't worry. I should have been there for him before he was gone. I wish I had." Oh, how he wished he'd been there to hold Andy's hand as he slipped into eternity, to thank him for his love, for everything he'd done all Nathan's life. He would certainly be there for him now.

Though it was too late.

ଔ ଔ ଔ

Leah Albright slipped her arms into her cotton cardigan and slung her purse over one shoulder. Another long work week was at last finished, which flicked her drowsiness aside. Not that the weekend was an adventure waiting to happen. It was simply better than being at Smith-Fellows Insurance Company.

After arranging loose papers and to-do projects on her desk, she pushed in her chair and smiled at her colleague, Jenny, at the next desk. "See you Monday."

Petite Jenny peered over her round, dark-rimmed glasses. "You always look a little happier when you say goodbye on Friday than on any other day. I'm very astute. I notice these things." She let out a hearty giggle.

"You are *very* perceptive, Jenny. You should have been a detective."

"Ah, but the money's better here. Now you *know* I'm lying. I'll be right behind you after I finish this one thing. Do something *fun* tonight, Leah." Her voice became emphatic.

"Hmm. Wonder what *that* would look like. Something fun." Leah cocked her head in exaggerated pondering. "Dear Jenny, help me understand what you mean."

Jenny rolled her eyes. "Oh, Leah. You're pathetic! A date? Girls' night out? Streaking through downtown? I don't know. Be creative."

"Don't worry, I'll figure something out. You do something fun too, okay? And don't stay too late." Leah patted Jenny's shoulder as she passed her desk, then headed for the stairs.

Fat chance she'd do something fun. Laundry maybe. Ah, yes. She'd practice her flute. That was fun. Then she'd curl up with a book, Theo purring beside her. The previous evening, while she played a Chopin nocturn on her violin, Theo had closed his eyes, his whiskers twitching, as if mesmerized. Until she hit a bad note. His eyes had shot open, and he'd darted from the room.

She let out a chuckle at the memory as she took the steps two at a time and left the building. Living within walking distance from her job had its benefits. The six-block walk home was a favorite part of her day after sitting for hours, though in winter she bundled up like a mummy and often resorted to driving.

The day had ground on for what seemed like forever. Over the last six or eight months, her restlessness had become chronic. Her position at the company, like a stagnant pool, held little interest, little change, and little hope for either. But she still had a job. *That* was something, wasn't it? She wasn't hungry, out of work, or on her last ten dollars.

She turned to Market Street, across from City Hall. On the opposite corner sat Seasons, a historic dinner theater and landmark. Built in the forties, it stood like a proud society woman whose former beauty one could still imagine. A teal and brown Victorian style façade stretched across the front, with vertical spindles along the wrap-around porch. The back of the building squared into a more utilitarian space to accommodate the stage and the dining room.

Throughout the year, Seasons held periodic plays and musicals, whereas the restaurant was open all year. When she was a child, Leah and her family had looked forward to attending the annual Christmas show there. Several times, her dad even played a minor role in the chorus. And he'd been the one who'd painted the murals, one for each season, used as a backdrop for the stage between events. In high school, she'd had the chance to sing and play instruments for a couple of the events too.

Leah could still envision her family gathered around a table encircled with sparkling holiday décor, so magical to her child's eyes. Seasons had made a deep imprint on her early life, though it could still evoke a wave of nostalgia and pain as she thought of Dad. He'd died just before Christmas ten years earlier. And each Christmas brought an empty ache she tried to chase away with fake cheer.

A humorless chuckle erupted from her throat. Fake cheer was better than none, and usually ended up ushering in a portion of the real thing.

The late summer breeze licked her face and playfully ruffled her hair. She passed Warren Street, where lights still flickered in a row of three to five-story office buildings. Town residents teasingly called Warren Street the *business district*. Though the small town of Brenner Falls was hardly New York, it *was* growing as people discovered the rolling hills and sporting opportunities along a nearby branch of the Susquehanna River.

The new mayor who'd arrived two years earlier had promoted the town with numerous projects, and she saw the fruit of his efforts on every street. New restaurants, shops, and housing appeared. The principal streets and intersections now sported potted plants and flowers. Historic buildings got facelifts. In other words, the town was edging into the twenty-first century.

From the corner of Davis Avenue, she could see Johnson's Grocery Store, whose fluorescent lights spilled on to the sidewalk. Should she stop for groceries, or could she eke out the stale bread and bottled pasta sauce in her fridge for a day or two more? The seductive call of her warm slippers, or the rebuke of her empty fridge? Yesterday *and* the day before that, she'd opted for making do. Her stomach grumbled, so with a sigh, she changed her path and headed toward the store. This shouldn't take long.

Gathering the items on her short list was as quick as she'd predicted, but the line at the cash register was not. She smiled at a few people she knew. Her neighbor, Cathy. Mr. Robertson from church. While she waited, she pulled her phone from her bag to see what she'd missed during the final pressured hours of work.

Leah frowned. Four missed calls from Garrett, her only brother, three years her senior. The one who never called. Ever. But he'd called four times that day.

Unlikely that he'd called to say hello and he missed her. That would never happen. Their mother had moved to Delaware a few years earlier to live near her sister, Aunt Lindsay. If something were wrong with Mom, Leah would know it since she kept in touch regularly. And Garrett didn't.

As much as she craved getting into her slippers and sweats first thing after arriving home, she'd give him a call first. Hopefully, nothing was wrong. After that, she'd scrape together some dinner from the meager provisions she'd just purchased, and call her best friend Abbie, who lived a few doors down. *Then* she'd finally curl up in the armchair with Theo and sink into the novel she'd gotten from the library a few days earlier.

Leah picked up the pace as the house came into view. She could already feel the slippers cradling her feet, though Garrett's calls were still nagging at her. They weren't close, but he was her brother. She fumbled in her purse to grab her phone.

Good Gifts   *Kyle Hunter*

As she approached the rambling 1980s ranch house where she'd grown up, she spied someone sitting on the porch in one of the Adirondack chairs. The streetlamp hadn't yet turned on and shadows filled the space around the front door. Tension skipped down her spine as she squinted to see who it was. Couldn't be someone delivering a package. She hadn't ordered anything.

When she was about thirty feet from the covered porch, she recognized the intruder by his slouch and the thatch of unruly hair hanging in his eyes.

"Garrett! What are you doing here?"

He pulled himself up, his lanky frame topping her height by a foot. "Hello to you too, sis."

"I'm. . . I'm surprised, is all."

"You wouldn't be if you'd answered your phone today. Did you see I called a few times?"

There was an edge to his voice. As if she had deliberately ignored him. Which she might have, had she seen his call sooner. She waved her phone at him. "Yes, I saw your missed calls while I was in the grocery store. I was about to call you back. Did you leave a message? I didn't have time to check. You see, I work *full time*." The rebuke in her voice matched his own. "Did something happen?" *Why are you here?*

"I didn't leave a message. I wanted to talk to you in person."

Her mouth fell open and tension gripped her stomach. "Why, what's wrong? Garrett, tell me."

"Let's go inside first. It's getting cool out here."

Leah fumbled with the lock and pushed open the door. As she entered the darkened entry, Theo rubbed against her ankles and his loud purr rose to her ears. "Hey, buddy. It's good to see you too." She flipped on the lights and plopped her tote bag and purse on the bench of the upright piano against the wall.

She turned to Garrett. "Make yourself comfortable." Sounded strange to her ears, since he'd grown up in that house too. She'd moved back into the family home two years earlier, but lived alone, since Garrett worked in Pittsburgh in a tech firm. She noticed a suitcase sitting near the front door. Uh oh.

She slid out of her coat and sat in an armchair facing him. "What is it, Garrett? I'm sure I would have heard if something happened to Mom."

He shrugged from where he sat on the couch. "Probably so."

"Well, what's up then? Spill it."

The muscles of his tightened jaw seemed to crumble. He propped his elbows on his knees and buried his face in his hands.

"Garrett!" Leah straightened her shoulders. "What is it? What's wrong?" Her mind scrambled for horrible events, a terminal illness, a death threat, or worse.

He looked at her, misery twisting his face. "I got fired yesterday."

"What? You got fired?" Impossible. Her genius programmer brother, fired? "What in the world happened?"

"Well, um." Garrett took a breath. "Work has been light lately, so in my free time, I work on my own projects. I've been developing a game."

"On work time?" She toed off her shoes and tucked her feet under her.

"Only when I don't have something else to do. Or during lunch and most evenings. It's almost ready for testing."

"That's... good, I guess. I mean, that you're creating something like that."

"So, a few times, my manager saw me working on it. I told him I'd finished with my project, but I think he had it in for me. So, he fired me. I think they were looking for a reason to let some of us go. Last week, my buddy Quinn got let go for something minor."

"I didn't think that would ever happen to you." Garrett didn't have the best interpersonal skills, but he could code or develop pretty much anything.

"Maybe I should have asked first if it was okay for me to do it on work time, but they've always been cool about stuff like that. Like I said, they're looking for reasons to scale down."

"You'll find something else. You have a lot of skills." No doubt about that. But is that what brought him back to Brenner Falls from Pittsburgh? He hadn't even visited since last Christmas.

"Did you lose your apartment? Wait, you said it just happened yesterday. Garrett, I'm confused." *Why are you here?*

Garrett frowned. "There's another thing. Ginny broke up with me last week." His voice broke. He stared at the floor.

"Oh, no! Are you okay?"

When he didn't respond, an ache for him rose inside her. "I'm so sorry, Garrett. You guys were together so long. I liked her. Sort of. I thought there might be wedding bells soon."

"No wedding bells. Everything happened at the same time. Feels like too much." His voice had faded to a muffled blur as he turned his head to stare out the side window. "Gin said. . . well, never mind what she said. I had to get away. I wanted to see if you minded if I came for a little while."

"That's why you were calling today?" She gentled her voice.

"Obviously, I didn't wait for an answer. Just drove here this afternoon."

Leah nodded into the silence. "Um, yes, of course you can stay for a little while. It's your home too."

No, no! They had such different lifestyles. But she couldn't say no, not after what had happened. "Do you know. . . do you know for how long?"

"No. I need to clear my head. I'm going to let my apartment go. I'm just month-to-month right now."

Alarm shot through Leah. "You're letting it go? Isn't that extreme? You'll find something quickly. I'm sure of it. You have a lot of skills, Garrett."

That meant an open-ended houseguest. But she *liked* her privacy. Sometimes she even liked her solitude. Along with that, she and her brother had never gotten along.

"I need a break. Being here'll do me good, I'm pretty sure."

"It's just that we've never lived together, um, successfully before."

Garrett shrugged. "We're older now. We'll work it out. Anyway, it's only for a little while. I'll stay out of your hair, don't worry."

Leah swallowed. Her eyes panned her nest, one she'd decorated herself with cheerful reds and yellows, handmade throw pillows, a few unique finds from the flea market, and a shaggy, colorful rug to unify it all. The house her mother had insisted she live in after she moved away.

It was her mother's house, and Leah had no right to refuse to let Garrett stay. That was the other reason she couldn't say no. He was family, even though he didn't always act like it. Most of the time she felt like she had no family at all. She was lonely at times, but it had always been easier to stay at the house by herself. Especially after Michael.

"Of course, you can stay." Only for a bit.

Oh, boy. The moment she feared her life would forever stagnate, that didn't sound half bad.

Chapter Two

The sanctuary of the Brenner Falls Faith Community Church, or B. F. F. C., as members called it, looked more like a warehouse than a church. This may have made seekers more comfortable, but it didn't present a solemn setting for a funeral.

Exactly as Uncle Andy would have preferred.

Nathan slipped an arm around his mother's shoulder as a fresh sob escaped her throat. He drew her close, and they exchanged weak, teary smiles. Friends paying final respects to Andy Evans jammed the pews. Seemed the whole town had shown up. Many of those present shared memories and anecdotes that had evoked both chuckles and tears.

"I think I can speak for all of us," Pastor Frank said with both warmth and emotion lacing his voice, "in saying that Andy Evans made an indelible impact on this community. We will all remember that impact, even though we miss our brother. He completed the race God assigned him, and now stands in celebration and joy before our Father." He raised his hands. "Let us pray together."

Pastor Frank's prayer closed the touching tribute to Andy's life. Nathan's throat ached with piled-up emotions it would take time to traverse. He'd never forget his uncle's imprint on his life.

Susan Chisholm blinked away fresh tears. "I'm glad my brother's not suffering anymore."

"He's with the Lord as we speak." Nathan allowed that reality to sink deep into him, as well as hopefully comfort his mother. "He's in heaven coming up with new scripts for celestial theater."

He allowed an upbeat tone into his voice, though he, too, fought tears. During the drive from Philadelphia to Brenner Falls the day before, he'd broken down. Alone in his car, he let his tears fall freely as he rewound the memories of Uncle Andy. In his most poignant mental image, Andy had pulled Nathan aside at age six to explain that his dad was gone and not coming back. In a later memory, Uncle Andy showed him how to cook fettuccine primavera from scratch. And countless times his uncle had assured him he could do anything he set his mind to.

Uncle Andy had made Nathan the man he was. The good parts, at least. Through most of Nathan's life, Uncle Andy was the potent presence in the background, letting him know it would be okay. Now that presence was gone.

His mom turned and fell into the embrace of an older woman. They murmured and wept quietly together. Nathan turned at the touch on his shoulder, Ben Russo, his best friend from high school. Still his best friend. Like an oak tree, the roots of their friendship dug deep, and the branches reached far. Ben wrapped Nathan in a bear hug and held him in a tight squeeze. "I'm so sorry, dude. I know you loved Andy. We all did."

When they drew apart, Nathan met Ben's sympathetic expression. "Thanks, Ben. I should have come more often when he got worse. I didn't realize—"

"He knew you loved him, and he sure loved you back. He always talked about how proud of you he was."

"He did?" A warmer emotion swelled, penetrating the weight of his grief. Nathan swallowed the lump that ached in his throat.

"Yeah, like, all the time. Like you were his own son."

Despite Nathan's heartache, a half-smile slid across his face. "He was cheerful until the end. He always downplayed his suffering and joked with his home health nurses. I'd call to cheer him up, and he'd crack *me* up laughing. I haven't been here in a few months, but I called him every couple of weeks."

Ben's dark brown eyes found Nathan's. "How long are you in town?"

"Till Tuesday. I took a couple extra days to hang out with Mom. Figured she'd need some TLC. Can you get together?"

"Definitely."

The noise in the room rose as people stood, milled around, and slowly made their way to the gym where refreshments awaited. "I think everyone in Brenner Falls came today," Ben said. "There's Mayor Faulkner in the second row. Right behind him in the next row are some of the cast and chefs from Seasons." Ben pointed to clusters of people around the room. "Look over by the window. There's Brandon Cochran with Jonathan Zeppo from high school. Remember them?"

"Yeah, they were both in my biology class senior year. I'm surprised they're still in town."

"And there's Leah Albright. You remember her, of course. You guys were tight senior year."

Nathan's gaze slid across the room to a gathering of four women of various ages near the front of the sanctuary. "We were. Unfortunately, we lost touch after that." What had it been, eight or so years since he'd hung out with Leah?

Leah, his artsy but awkward friend from high school. Well, they were both awkward back then. They used to hang out in study hall and were in the same youth group at church. He could still picture her with long hair in a ponytail, glasses, jeans, and a pair of white Converse sneakers.

And here she was, years later, all grown up and looking pretty and self-assured. She wore a long navy-blue skirt that flowed around her calves and danced across her high heels. Her wavy light brown hair hung in layers that caught the sun as it poured through the skylight.

"She looks good." Ben echoed Nathan's thoughts. "She came back a couple of years after college and lives in the same house where she grew up."

"With her mom?" Nathan pulled his eyes away from her.

"No, I think her mom might have moved away. Leah lives there alone or maybe has a roommate." Ben sent Nathan a sideways stare. "Pretty sure she's still single."

Ben's words trailed out and found a foothold in Nathan's brain. Still single. "The first couple of years after high school, we got together during college breaks. I haven't seen her much since then, so I assumed she'd moved away." He'd catch up with her during the reception.

"She works for some insurance company in town. I ran into her at the park last summer."

Nathan and Ben joined the slow-moving crowd on the way downstairs to the gym, where refreshments waited. People stopped Nathan several times in the hallway and down the stairwell to share their condolences.

After what felt like a half hour, they entered the gym. Voices echoes in the cavernous space, which looked the same as it had when he'd played basketball as a teenager and the youth group had all-night lock-in retreats. The church was as much a part of his heritage as his Uncle Andy was. With a twinge, he knew his spiritual health had slipped into anemia over the last two years.

By the time Nathan reached the food table, he'd greeted and received sympathy from nearly everyone. He hadn't yet spoken to Leah Albright, though he'd kept her in his peripheral vision. She stood about ten people away at the end of the serving line. When Ben excused himself to talk to someone, Nathan slid out of place and found Leah further back in the line. "Alright Albright." He smiled at her, using his proprietary high school phrase for her.

She turned with a grin. "Nathan!" She slid one arm around his waist and squeezed. "I've been waiting my turn to talk to you. It's *so* good to see you." Her smile fell. "I'm so sorry about your Uncle Andy. He was a great man. Everyone in town loved him."

He'd forgotten how striking her light blue eyes were and, for a split second, didn't know what to say. "Thanks, Leah. I'll really miss him. It's good to see you too. How long has it been? Eight years?"

"I've lost count." She gave him a contrite smile. "After college, I ended up working near campus two more years then I moved back here." They inched forward in the line.

"You moved back to the same house where you grew up?" Ben was right, Leah had blossomed from the high school friend he remembered. She was downright classy. And beautiful. If only Nathan didn't live in Philly —

"I did. My mom moved to Delaware to be near her sister the year I graduated from college, but she left the house empty. She didn't really want to sell it, in case Garrett—that's my brother—or I wanted to live there. I would drive back once in a while for the weekend to check on things, then two years ago, I moved back."

Nathan snagged two paper plates and handed one to her. "I guess that means you found a job here?"

Leah gave him a weak smile and said, "Yes," but didn't elaborate. They reached the spread of tiny sandwiches, cut-up fruit, cheese chunks, and bowls of nuts.

An older man in line next to him touched his forearm. "I'm sorry about your uncle, Nathan."

Nathan didn't recognize the man, but his tone expressed sorrow, as if he'd known Andy well.

"He was a pillar of the community," the man continued. "And Seasons was our favorite place to eat. My wife and I, we loved the shows too. Such a shame. . ."

"Thank you. I agree, he was important to this town." Nathan struggled with appropriate responses. The effort was exhausting, but he appreciated the words from each person who expressed what Andy had meant to them. Often it involved Seasons, Andy's dinner theater. Many in the community likely wondered what would become of it. He did too.

"Want to sit over there?" Nathan asked Leah, gesturing his head toward a circle of chairs. He led the way, and they sat facing each other, balancing full plates of food on their laps. "I take it you don't love your job," he said.

"Can you tell? I work at an insurance company. Dullsville, but it's a job." She gave him a straight-tooth smile which still lit up her face as it always had. The faint freckles scattered across her nose and her smooth skin spoke of wholesome beauty.

He might be in trouble.

Nathan glanced away from her soft-looking cheeks. "What do you do there?"

She slipped a few blueberries into her mouth. "I'm an event planner-slash-human resource assistant, but that's a misnomer. I don't do much event planning since the budget keeps getting cut. I help the HR director with things she doesn't want to do, like payroll, IRA contributions." Leah made a face as if she were yawning.

Nathan laughed. "I thought you'd be on Broadway by now, or at least teaching voice lessons to little kids."

"I wish." She picked up a ripe strawberry with two delicate fingers. "Although teaching music is a good idea. I did some of that in college. Now I only sing at church and in the shower. And around the house."

"Me too. Sing in the shower, I mean. But don't tell anyone." Their eyes met and a series of electric sparks began inside him.

"What did you study in college?" he asked.

"Music and business. My mom insisted on the business, so I'd have something to *fall back on*." She made air quotes. "Turns out I needed that backup plan."

He popped a square of cheddar into his mouth, then another, unsure of what to say to that. "Still play a mean flute?"

Leah narrowed her eyes in fake severity. "Very mean. In fact, playing it for someone would be a mean thing to do to them."

He laughed, and she joined him. "I'm sure that's not true," he said. "In fact, I have memories of your exceptional talent at church and high school orchestra." The kind of talent that made it a crime for her to be hidden away in an insurance company.

"No, I'm kidding." She fingered the edge of the napkin spread on her knee. "I keep up with the flute and violin on my own. I play them at church sometimes. And piano."

"Do you still come here to church?"

Leah shook her head. "I did when I first moved back to town. Last year, B. F. F.C. sent out a team of volunteers to start a daughter church on the other side of town. It's called Real Faith Chapel. I joined the team, thinking I could help with music. It's. . ." she shrugged. "It's not doing all that well right now, but it isn't fully established yet. There's a young pastor who's well-meaning but a little disorganized. I'm giving it a chance before I come back here." She lifted one hand with the word *here*.

"A daughter church. That's pretty cool. It's great that this church wants to expand to other parts of town. Even a small town like the Falls."

"I agree. I wanted to be part of the team to contribute something I know, namely music."

"Didn't you play an instrument for a couple of the shows at Andy's place?"

"Excellent memory. In high school I did. That was my big break, so to speak. Which led to nothing, and I didn't expect it to. You can imagine how hard it is to make a living playing an instrument or singing. So, I kept it as a hobby."

A long sigh lifted her shoulders. Nathan thought he saw a curtain of sadness fall over her face. "A lost dream." He hadn't meant to say it aloud. He brightened. "But hey, life isn't over. There's always the future."

Leah laughed. "I'll be sure to let you know when my first album comes out."

Nathan grinned in response as their eyes met again. "I wonder what'll happen to Seasons without Uncle Andy."

"I was thinking the same thing," she said. "The restaurant stayed open, didn't it?"

Nathan nodded. "There's a full-time chef there. I think it's been the same one for years. He held things together during Andy's illness, but I don't know what'll happen now. Maybe it'll be sold." Nathan had spent a few summers working at Seasons in the kitchen. Andy hadn't had the income to do necessary upgrades, then his health went downhill. Sadly, the building would probably be torn down and replaced with a new, trendy shopping center or restaurant.

A man approached their circle of chairs. "Nathan, Pastor Frank wants to speak with you whenever you're finished." After a moment, Nathan recognized him as an elder at the church, Fred Bannister.

"Sure, Fred." Nathan turned to Leah, he said, "I'm surprised I remembered his name. It came back to me, so I saved face."

"It's that long-term memory archive, Nathan. I'm glad it served a purpose. Mine often doesn't." She looked down at her empty plate.

"I'll be back in a minute after I speak with Pastor Frank. Do you want a refill on anything?"

"No, thanks. I have to go now, unfortunately. It was nice to see you and catch up a little." She stood.

Nathan stood and hesitated beside her. He wanted to convince her to wait for him. But she had to go, and he lived in Philly. No point in that line of thinking. "I come here sometimes to see my mom. Want to exchange numbers? That way, I can look you up when I'm back."

Leah looked pleased and pulled her phone from her purse. "Great idea. That way, we won't lose track of each other for another eight years." He recited his number, and she typed it into her phone. "Here's a text with mine."

Nathan couldn't suppress a grin. "Talk to you next time, Leah."

She lifted her face from her phone. Her expression was sober, compassionate. "Next time, it'll be happier circumstances." She lifted her hand in a little wave and with a muted smile, left the circle of chairs.

He spied Pastor Frank speaking to an older couple. As he walked toward him, he cast a backward glance toward Leah. She disappeared through the exit door in a swish of blue skirt.

ଔ ଔ ଔ

"Garrett, please run over to aisle five to pick up some multigrain cereal and oatmeal, okay?" Leah said as she studied her list. "I'll get the produce, so meet me there when you're done."

"Yes, commander." He smirked. "How about if I walk instead of run?"

Leah rolled her eyes. "Whatever."

He'd been in the Falls for close to two weeks. Seemed like a month, but she'd gotten through it. He was her brother, after all. He acted less despairing about his job and failed relationship and had firmly settled into vacation mode. Meaning he wasn't looking for work or helping around the house. She hadn't brought it up, since wishful thinking had convinced her he wasn't staying long. She could treat him like a visitor if that's what he was, but he'd made no mention of leaving. In fact, the previous week he'd made an overnight trip to Pittsburgh to clear out his apartment. He'd returned to Brenner Falls with a rental truck full of furniture which now sat in the garage and filled one of the spare bedrooms. Leah had to park in the driveway and dreaded scraping winter frost and snow from the windshield in the coming months. Theo didn't know what to make of this tall, sullen stranger who had suddenly appeared and wasn't leaving.

Maybe Garrett would be gone by Christmas. She could always wish.

Leah selected apples and bananas then went to the wall display to choose romaine, arugula, and fresh spinach. Her thoughts seeped back to the funeral a few days earlier. It had been a fitting tribute to a man everyone had loved for his integrity, faith, and kindness to those he met, whether the mayor or the local garbage collector. She'd expected, even hoped to run into Nathan Chisholm. In high school, they'd been platonic friends and shared a couple of classes. Well, platonic on *his* side. She remembered having a mild crush on him back then. They went their separate ways after high school and years fell away without seeing him. Then there'd been Michael. Leah frowned. No use tainting a good memory with a bad one.

Nathan had hardly resembled the adolescent boy of her memory. He'd filled out, gotten taller. A man instead of a teenage guy with beginner whiskers and a naïve expression on his face. Now his square jaw and direct green gaze made her spine tingle as they talked together after the funeral. She knew he was only catching up with her after years of separation and silence, but she was still pleased he'd singled her out during the reception. He always had a way of making her feel important and seen. He did that with everyone, as his uncle Andy had done. The way he looked at people when they spoke, responded to them instead of only talking about his own interests. He was different, maybe because of the pain of his childhood when his dad abandoned the family.

She regretted having left the reception so quickly. He might have come back to continue his conversation with her. But then again, he might have been snagged by a half dozen more friends sharing condolences and she'd have been left there for who knows how long. It had been past Theo's dinner time and the service had lasted longer than she'd expected. Hopefully, he'd call her during one of his future visits. She sighed. It was a shame he lived in Philly.

"Is this what you wanted?" Garrett appeared beside her and held up the cereal. "I got this one for me. I don't like the ones you eat."

"Too many nutrients?" She grinned at him.

"Tastes like sawdust. I'd rather have eggs and bacon."

"You can make eggs and bacon for yourself whenever you like." Leah stared at him pointedly. "You'll contribute to the groceries, right?"

"Uh, okay. Sure. I have some money in savings."

Leah blinked. "Okay, sure? You were planning on coming for an undetermined time period without contributing *anything*?"

"No, of course not. I'll get a new job soon."

"And in the meantime, you have savings, you said."

Garrett grunted and he surveyed the aisles behind them. "This grocery store doesn't have much selection. My grocery store in Pittsburgh is huge. They have everything."

"This is a smaller town, as you know. You'll have to adapt." *And if you like your bigger store, go back to Pittsburgh.*

They got into line behind seven or eight people. "There aren't many cashiers working tonight," he said. "Look, they have seven, eight cash registers and only three people working. That slows everyone down after work when it's crowded." He looked around. "Looks like everyone in town is here in this store. It's gonna take us forever to get home."

"Maybe they have a labor shortage," she said lightly. The line budged in front of her, and they stepped forward.

"You have an answer for everything, don't you?"

Leah let out an exasperated sigh. *That* was why she didn't want to live with Garrett. "You complain a lot, Garrett. Don't you have anything pleasant to say?"

He frowned as if thinking of her question. "No. Not really."

"How about the fact that you're not on the street?"

"Yeah, right, okay. I guess I'm supposed to show gratitude that I can live in our mom's house. It's not even yours, Leah."

"I'm not saying you should be grateful to *me*. Just grateful in general. You're right, it's not my house. Be grateful you have a place to go instead of . . . since you, uh, lost your job."

"Thanks for reminding me, sis. Move up, it's our turn."

They reached into the cart and put their items on the black conveyor belt. The cashier gave them a cheerful greeting, despite the scores of shoppers she'd likely dealt with already that day.

Leah's brief conversation with Garrett left a bad taste in her mouth. Why couldn't they have normal interactions instead of sparring? Was it her fault? She could understand why Ginny had broken up with him. Hopefully, he'd find a job soon and move on and she'd get her privacy back. In the meantime, she should set some ground rules. No, as he'd said, it wasn't her house. They were both there at their mom's invitation.

The brick ranch house sat on a shady avenue three streets from the center of downtown, which made it practical to do errands by foot. That evening, she and Garrett had three bags apiece, more than she normally carried.

"Do you carry groceries home every time you shop? All the way to the house?" Garrett asked.

Leah shrugged. The handle of the heavier one dug into her hand. She shifted the bags to opposite sides. "I don't usually have this much. But there are two of us who eat and two of us to carry stuff."

"Huh. If you say so." Garrett groaned and shifted his bags. "Some of those houses are really run down. I hadn't noticed before."

The shadows deepened. Leah let Garrett's commentary pass and focused on the house that was now in view. Her new strategy with Garrett would be to ignore his negative comments. Then an idea came into her mind. "I'll tell you what, Garrett. I know you probably want to be more positive, so I'll help you. Every time you complain about something, I'll sing a couple of lines of a song. Maybe a Christmas song, or a Broadway classic."

"Maybe I'll avoid you, then."

"It's not like I sing poorly. It'll make you more aware."

They walked in silence for a couple of minutes. "It's freezing out here," Garrett groaned.

"It's beginning to look a lot like Christmas. . ." Leah sang.

He held up his free hand. "Okay, sorry. It's not cold, it's *seasonal*. It's invigorating."

"Ah, that's much better." She couldn't stifle a giggle. In the yellow light of the streetlamps, she could see a faint smile stretch his mouth as well.

The next Sunday, following the service at the small daughter church, Leah spent a few minutes greeting church members, including an elderly couple visiting for the first time, and her new friend Blair McCartney. Blair lived near the rented church building. She waved at some of the high schoolers who helped with refreshments but didn't stop at the table on her way to the door.

Leah emerged into the fall air and breathed deeply of her favorite time of year. The church met in a strip mall only about twenty minutes' walk from her house. Soon, the cold would arrive, and she'd have to drive instead of walk.

Leah tapped Abbie's number. She and Abbie O'Reilly had grown up on the same street, had gone through every grade together, and had been best friends for as long as Leah could remember.

"Hey, Abbie."

"Hey, girl. How was church?" Abbie's perky voice filled her ear.

"It was okay. Honestly, I'm not sure this little church is going to make it. I think Pastor Todd has good intentions, but he's not organized. His sermon was all over the place. Not sure he's gifted for it, but I wanted to support the church plant. But mostly, I end up frustrated."

"Hmm. That's too bad. It's so sweet of you to try to help, though, and be part of the core group. If he doesn't see his weaknesses, God may use you there to fill in some gaps."

Guilt stabbed at Leah. She should have done that *before* Abbie suggested it. . . try to help and fill in gaps rather than criticize and act like a consumer. "That's a good point. It's not about what I get, but what I can *give*." Wasn't that the reason she volunteered to be part of the founding team? To help? "I should pray about ways to help instead of comparing it with B. F. F. C., which may have started in the same way ages ago."

"I bet it did. I miss seeing you there, but I understand and support your desire to take part in the new one."

"I miss *being* there. But it'll be neat to see how this new one takes shape in the coming months." That is, if she can look for potential and not fill out her report card every week. Shame pricked at her.

"How are things going with Garrett?" Abbie asked.

Leah sighed. "You know we don't get along too well. But today's my day to recognize my faults. I haven't been the nicest sister to him. He's kind of negative, doesn't help enough. . . but really, a lot of our bickering goes way back. He was mean or indifferent to me when we were kids. But I'm the Christian, and I need to look beyond unpleasant behavior, right? I need to try to put myself in his shoes. He lost his job and his girlfriend in the same week and now has to start at zero after years in the same company. He's going through a hard time. But he's still not easy to be around."

"I'm sorry that hasn't been a smoother transition. Maybe if he gets some interviews he'll be encouraged. That may lead to a change."

"Huh. I doubt it. He's always been a glass empty kind of guy. Opposite from you, Abbs." It was true. Abbie's upbeat cheer seemed to be a constant. Leah didn't know how her friend did it. They had the same faith, but Leah's was so up and down. Being around Abbie was a steadying reminder to stay optimistic, to focus on freeing truths. Leah was usually optimistic in a general way, though occasionally, she faked it for appearance's sake as an ambassador of God. Usually, she felt like a fraud. In Abbie's case, it seemed to bubble up from an invisible spring somewhere inside her. All their years of friendship, and it hadn't yet rubbed off on Leah.

"By the way," Leah said. "I was at B. F. F. C. for a funeral a couple of weeks ago, for Andy Evans, who owned Seasons Dinner Theater."

"Oh, I'd heard he died. I didn't know him well, but he seemed like a wonderful man. Such a shame. What'll happen to the theater?"

"No idea. It'll probably get sold or torn down, since it needs a lot of repairs. That would be a shame. It meant a lot to our family." Melancholy puddled inside as she pictured the beloved Brenner Falls institution bulldozed and replaced by a strip mall. "The restaurant's still open, though."

She turned the corner, and her house came into view. "I saw a few people from high school at the funeral. Do you remember Nathan Chisholm? Andy was his uncle and a father figure for him. You know, after his dad left town."

"I do remember him. You and he were good friends back in the day."

A flush of warmth filled Leah's chest as she remembered her encounter with Nathan. "Yeah, he was a good friend. It was nice talking to him, catching up a little." *And he's turned out rather gorgeous.* No use in saying that to Abbie. Yet. The day of the funeral, they'd talked about her news more than his. She still knew nothing of *his* life. "He lives in the Philly area now working for some firm, I don't know what. He and Andy were so close, I was sad for him and his mom."

Leah climbed the steps of the front porch and flopped into the chair by the door, the same chair where Garrett had surprised her two weeks earlier.

"Yeah, that's hard, especially if Andy was like a dad to him. You lost your dad too, so you have that in common."

"I hadn't thought of that. Our conversation was cut short. Whenever I ever see him again, I'll bring that up. He'll know I understand what he's going through."

"His mom is still in town, right? He'll probably come back to see her."

An unreasonable spark of hope popped in Leah's mind. "Maybe he will. We exchanged numbers, so he knows how to reach me. Hopefully we'll stay in touch better." Even though Abbie was her best friend, it felt safer to keep her hopes down, her voice detached.

After they disconnected the call, Leah went inside to make a sandwich. She heard faint music from Garrett's room down the hall as she passed through the living room to the kitchen. He was slightly less grumpy in recent days. Maybe her singing did him some good. Leah laughed aloud. Definitely not. More likely, he was tired of squabbling with her. Some ambassador of God *she* was. If only she could be more like Abbie, with authentic joy and optimism.

Leah frowned. Not only was she wrapped in guilt from her attitudes toward her church and Garrett, but Christmas was coming. That required a huge effort to fake holiday cheer, as she'd been doing for years.

It was easy when her dad was alive because back then, it wasn't fake. She'd truly loved Christmas because he had, and he'd made it a magic season for their family. She could almost hear her own childish peals of laughter when he dressed up as the Grinch either at home or for one of the Seasons holiday programs.

With his buoyant effervescence, it was easy to get excited. It had been her favorite holiday of the year. Ever since his sudden heart attack and death, there was a void inside her like a burnt-out hole when she thought of the holidays. Christmas and missing her dad simply went hand in hand. As a result, New Years was her favorite holiday, because Christmas was over by then.

So, she compensated. Most people thought she loved Christmas, like her dad had, since she decorated the entire house, inside and out, always had a tree that touched the ceiling, and usually hosted a cookie exchange, an open house, or a dinner party. That year, she wasn't sure she could muster the interest in any holiday activity. If she didn't, her cover would be blown. Everyone would know that ever since her dad had died, she'd become a Scrooge.

Chapter Three

Nathan ended his thirty-minute call with his largest marketing client. The company rep had asked a deluge of questions about the campaign set to launch the following week. Even though the man had hired Nathan's firm to manage his account, he called often to ask questions, make suggestions, and keep a controlling hand on the campaign.

A growl sprang from Nathan's stomach. It was nearly one o'clock. He reached into his desk drawer and grabbed the sandwich he'd thrown together that morning, then took the stairs two at a time to the front door. City sounds engulfed him, and he breathed deeply of the fall air, barely laced with chill. His feet moved on autopilot as he started his daily walk two blocks from his office building along the crowded urban sidewalk to a small square of green behind a bank. There, he made a beeline for a bench next to a miniature pond.

Leaving the building lightened his spirits like being let out of a cage. He still had at least a month before fall temperatures coaxed him into a coat and gloves. Even in winter, he continued his lunchtime walks. The idea of eating at his desk, as so many of his colleagues did, made his stiff legs feel even more cramped. He slowed his pace, training his attention away from his annoying phone call and toward the green canopy over the pond's surface. Green and orange leaves encircled the pond. The full kaleidoscope wouldn't arrive for another month.

Time passed quickly, but he still had ten minutes before returning to the office when his phone vibrated in his pocket. He pulled it out but didn't recognize the number. "Hello?"

"Is this Nathan Chisholm?"

"Yes, it is."

"My name is Jason Abernathy, and I'm the executor and successor trustee of your uncle Andy Evan's estate. It's my responsibility to notify any beneficiaries implicated in your uncle's will or, in this case, the trust. That's why I'm calling you today."

"Oh, okay." Nathan hadn't thought twice about Uncle Andy's estate. He didn't have much to leave, probably his old Ford and clothing and his small home and its contents. Most of it could go to Goodwill.

"Do you have a few minutes?" the man asked.

"I have about ten minutes, then I have to go back to work."

"I'll be concise. Since Andy Evans didn't have children or a spouse, his estate has been divided among relatives, primarily you and your mother. Certain accounts will go to your mother, Susan Chisholm, and to you he bequeathed the Seasons Dinner Theater and his home on Acorn Lane."

Nathan's mouth dropped open. "What? Seasons Theater? He left it to me?" And the little Craftsman bungalow where Andy had lived for over thirty years. Both of which needed major maintenance, and neither of which Nathan wanted.

"And don't forget the restaurant, which is connected to the theater. Normally, this transfer of ownership would take months to complete in probate court, but your uncle took steps to avoid this inconvenience. First of all, before his death, he placed his assets into what is called a living trust with joint ownership. He named you as joint owner of his business and home."

"He did? When did he do that?"

"I have a signature here, that of Nathan Chisholm. He named you and you signed. You don't remember this?"

"No. Uh, wait." Did he? A few months ago, or maybe longer, Andy had him sign a form regarding insurance or something. He'd trusted Andy enough not to clarify what it was or pay much attention. It wasn't insurance. He'd named Nathan co-owner of everything even prior to his death. "I may have but didn't realize that's what it was." Which likely sounded stupid to the executor-trustee.

Nathan's head was spinning, not with the legalese, but the meticulous preparation by Uncle Andy, who wasn't disorganized after all. And the implications of all that legal planning. "I'm listening," was all Nathan could say.

"Of course, there are documents you'll need to sign in order to transfer his assets. The conditions of the trust cause everything to pass immediately to your ownership. I'll email you a summary of what the inheritance covers. There's an attorney in Brenner Falls, Charles Bittle, who is handling the legal aspects. How soon can you come to Brenner Falls to take care of the paperwork?"

"I. . . uh. Um, this is a shock, really. I'll have to let you know. I was just in town for the funeral a couple of weeks ago, so I'll have to arrange it with my work to be able to come back so soon. Let me check my schedule and talk to my boss. I'll call you back, Mr. . . ."

"Abernathy. Jason Abernathy."

"I'll call you soon, Mr. Abernathy. I have your number. Thank you."

Thank you for a big problem he now had to solve. It had never occurred to Nathan that his uncle would put him in his will. The man hadn't seemed that organized. And yet, he ran the dinner theater for more than a decade. Maybe two. That took some organization, and he'd employed a stage and restaurant manager. Were they still on the payroll? Had they kept it all running, or had it fallen apart along with Andy's health? Nathan had no idea. He'd called his uncle semi-regularly, but never had a reason to ask about the workings of Seasons. Once he'd left Brenner Falls, he hadn't kept in the loop with any of the happenings in town. And his uncle hadn't said a word about final wishes. Nathan always assumed he'd talked to his mom.

Andy's business. Andy's dinner theater. Now Nathan's dinner theater. He let out a long groan. He'd have to get rid of it and the house as soon as possible. They wouldn't likely bring much money, so it was more a matter of pushing these unwelcome meals from his plate.

Nathan's afternoon sped by with meetings and deadlines. He kept pulling his mind back to his job and away from the albatross that had been dropped squarely into his lap. Finally, the day ended and the questions he'd held at bay flooded his mind. While he was still riding the commuter train home, he dialed his mother.

"Hey, Mom. Did you hear from a Jason Abernathy about Uncle Andy's will?"

"I have a message from him, but I haven't called him back yet."

"He called me during work and told me that Uncle Andy had left Seasons to me in his will.

"He did?" His mother's tone spiked.

"And his house. He left some money to you, I think. I'm sure Abernathy will explain that to you when you call him."

"Oh." His mother's voice trailed to a trickle. "When he was sick and failing, I didn't question what would happen to the theater. I guess you were like his son, so it makes sense that he'd leave it to you. And you worked there a few summers, so you know a little about it."

"Ages ago. It's not like I'm planning to take it over and run it, Mom. I just want to get rid of it."

"It would be a shame to sell it, unless the buyer keeps it as a dinner theater. It's been in Brenner Falls for several generations. I don't know how old it is, but it's always been here. It's a historic building."

Right. He hadn't thought of that. The cultural value of the theater, even for those who'd never bought a ticket in their lives, was significant. A landmark, a sign of Brenner Falls's quaint history which began in the eighteen hundreds. Whatever. He couldn't keep it, and that was for sure.

"What else can I do? Do you think I'll move back and run the theater and the restaurant?" Nathan stifled an incredulous chuckle. No way. Out of the question.

"Of course not. I know you have your life in Philly, and you'd never want to move back here. Well, take it one step at a time and do your research. If you sell it to someone who can keep it as a theater, that would be the best option. Especially if they have the money to update it. As for the house. . . well, you can rent it to a young couple or sell it. I don't think you'd have trouble selling it. Though it *would* be nice to have you visit more often or even move back here. I have to be honest."

Yes, of course. He knew she'd be thrilled if he moved into Andy's house. Return home to the town he'd fled years earlier. But his mother knew he'd made a life in the city, hours away. He'd visit, take care of the sale, and return to his life. "No surprise there. Those are some good ideas, Mom. I'll do some research online tonight and try to wrap my head around this. Just wanted to let you know."

He was glad his mom would inherit some money. She'd worked hard all her life and had a meager retirement to live on. Somehow, Nathan doubted she'd get very much, unless Andy had been secretive about a fortune hidden away. No, he'd have spent it on Seasons if he'd had it.

That evening, Nathan sauteed shrimp in butter and garlic, topped linguini with the mixture, and roasted some Brussel sprouts. He'd begun cooking more after the last deadline had passed and he promised himself he'd keep it up, deadlines or not. So far, so good.

After he washed the dishes, Nathan settled in front of his computer. Where to start? He typed, *selling a business* into the search engine. Options scrolled down his computer screen. He chose the most general one, clicked it, and began reading. After nearly an hour, he knew he was in big trouble. He reached for his phone.

"Hey, Ben. Got a minute to talk?" He asked his best friend.

"Sure, bro. I just got home from the gym and out of the shower. What's up?"

Hearing Ben's voice settled Nathan's agitation. Though Nathan was known by many to be outwardly calm and unruffled, Ben alone knew how much Nathan stuffed inside and tried to handle by himself. This situation was way beyond him. He needed another heart and mind as a sounding board. A voice of wisdom.

"I have a situation. You ready for this? I just inherited Seasons."

Long silence. "Really? Andy's place? Oh. . ." Ben's surprised inflection dropped several decibels. "Yeah, I get it. He's gone, so of course, he'd leave it to you."

"Why *of course*?"

"Well, who else?"

Right. Who indeed? Nathan was the likely candidate. Andy had had a brief marriage to a woman whose name Nathan didn't recall. No offspring. "So, I need to sell this thing and I've been online for an hour reading about how to sell a business. They recommend hiring a broker if I want to get the best possible offers on the place. I have to get all the expenses and profit-loss statements in order going back three or four years. Then, it has to show a profit to get the best offer. I don't think it's had a profit in a while."

"The restaurant's still in business and running like normal, but the theater hasn't done anything for at least two years, since Andy got sick. He had a staff there, but he let go of the programming."

Good thing Ben still lived in the Falls and knew the status. That would be a help. "I was afraid of that. I don't know how bad it is. Maybe I should sell it to anyone who'll buy it. I need to get rid of it." Nathan got up from his desk and rubbed his eyes. Too much time staring at a screen. He walked to the living room, phone still at his ear, and flopped onto the couch against an overstuffed pillow.

"I know you need to unload it, Nathan, but I hope you'll be careful who you sell it to. It would be good to keep it as a dinner theater if possible, or at least not sell it to someone who's going to build an arcade or a strip mall on the property."

"I heard a similar sentiment from my mom when I told her I wanted to sell it. I know it's a fixture in Brenner Falls. But here's something else. The article I read recommended starting months in advance before selling. You know, to get everything in order, court the right buyers, yada, yada. I don't have time for all that."

"And the broker? Would he or she do some of it? Or all of it?"

"I don't know. That would cut into any profits if there are any, though I think it's worth it. A broker might turn it down. Lots of the brokers I saw online won't touch a business worth less than a million. We both know the Seasons is way below that."

"No doubt about that. I suggest you talk to one who accepts lower amounts. Or better still, maybe there's one who specializes in properties that need to be turned around."

"Like a flip, but for a business? They'd buy it dirt cheap, get it in shape, then sell it for a big profit."

"Maybe. Or someone would simply want to revive it because they see there's potential here in the Falls. You know, with all the growth, the tourists and all."

Nathan pulled himself up from where he lay on the couch. "You have a point. I can capitalize on that. Maybe I'll get some stats on the town, like projected growth, proposed projects, stuff like that, which can make up for the poor condition of Seasons."

"Make sure you look at all the numbers first. Could be that the Seasons isn't as bad off as you think or has potential for a comeback."

"You mean, with a new owner?"

"Not necessarily."

Ben's meaning rolled slowly into Nathan's brain. "Wait, I don't want to do it, Ben. It's not my thing and I already have a job."

His friend laughed. "Calm down. I'm not suggesting you change careers. But since you need to show some better numbers to a potential buyer, and since it may take a few months to even find said buyer, you could do some kind of, I don't know, special holiday program or something to up the numbers."

"I don't think a few months of profit is going to impress anyone. Why do you think they ask for the last four years?"

"Maybe before Andy got sick, it was profitable. Then he got sick, and it went down. Then nephew Nathan takes over and it's profitable again. Right before it's sold to another theater guy or gal who has some capital to put in, sees the potential in Brenner Falls for future development."

"Wait. Let me see if I understand what you're saying. Do a drama or musical or something? Like a full-blown production? And do it by Christmas?" Nathan couldn't help himself. He laughed aloud. "Sorry, dude, but you're plain crazy."

"Maybe so." There was an irritating smile in Ben's voice. "But it's worth a thought. Might not be as hard as you imagine. Special menu, a little entertainment. Only once. It'll be a test. See?"

He did. But it didn't make him want to run back to Brenner Falls and organize the comeback himself. "You have a point. A good one for someone else to tackle. Don't forget, I have a job."

"So you've said. Just think *and* pray about it. Start there, bro," Ben said. "But you'll need to come back at some point to look at all the numbers, regardless of what you decide. Even if you get a broker, get a buyer, then sell it cheap, you'll still need to set a price for it based on actual numbers."

There was no way around this, no way to make it go away in a matter of days. Nathan had to face it, to know the options. Learn how bad it was.

He had to go back to Brenner Falls.

ɔʀ ɔʀ ɔʀ

Leah rinsed the bowl sitting on the counter. Garrett's bowl. She opened the fridge and pulled out yogurt and flax seed along with some blueberries. Sharp autumn sunlight poured into the bay window, spilling across the table in the eat-in kitchen. Leah's favorite spot, sunshine or rain. She slipped into the chair by the window, her usual seat, and stirred her yogurt. Garrett came into the kitchen wearing a rumpled t-shirt and baggy gym shorts. His hair poked up at angles like a crooked crown and pillow marks lined his face.

"Morning." She kept her voice cheerful.

"Hi. Any coffee left?"

"In the pot. As usual. If there's no coffee, by the way, the fixings are in the cupboard over the coffeemaker." She'd been making the coffee daily because she got up first. It took her several days to realize she was sending the wrong message. That things would be ready when her brother got up, as if he were at a bed and breakfast.

"Did you sleep well?" she asked.

For a moment Garrett didn't answer, aside from a grunt. "Went to bed too late."

"What do you do so late? Watch movies? Or work on your game?"

She hadn't seen him actually *work* on his game yet, the one that led to his being fired.

"Nah, I was playing games, though. There's this one that's real addictive and I always stay up too late with it."

Leah frowned. That was the longest sentence he'd uttered prior to ten a.m. "I guess that's therapeutic." She wasn't sure it would get him back on track emotionally. Might be more of an anesthesia. *You're not his mom, Leah.*

"Have you. . . have you talked to Ginny?" She said to his back as he poured his coffee.

His shoulders sagged slightly. A wave of regret hit her. "Sorry, didn't mean to bring her up. I was wondering if you guys were trying to work things out."

"Not at the moment we're not." He hadn't turned to her.

"Sorry," she said again. "I'm not trying to pry. I'm here if you want to talk."

"Okay, I'll keep that in mind. I'm actually trying to forget. That's why I came here. To get distance from everything."

"Got it." She stood. "Okay, I'm off to church. You can come anytime you want. Let me know."

Garrett slumped into the chair with his cereal. "Yup, you told me that last week too. Have fun."

"Put your dishes in the dishwasher when you're done. Not on the counter. 'Kay?"

"Yup."

"Oh, and my friend Abbie from down the street is coming for dinner tonight. You remember her, don't you?"

"Think so. But I haven't seen her in ages."

"You're welcome to join us, of course. Just wanted to let you know."

He grunted again and stared into his phone.

Leah sighed as she left the kitchen. Reminder to self. . . don't invite Garrett to church anymore. If he wanted to come, he'd come. In fact, avoid the urge to mother, cajole, encourage. She was probably annoying him as much as he annoyed her. Second reminder to self. Don't expect substantive conversation in the morning.

They'd gotten through three weeks so far. Might get better. Or worse.

After church, Leah extended her walk home by making an extra loop through downtown. Felt good in the brisk air stretching her legs in the afternoon sun. The weather was a perfect balance of balmy and slightly crisp. At least she could still hike and walk. Soon, it would be too cold to do that too.

When she returned to the house, she sank onto the wicker couch of the porch. She dialed Abbie. "You're still coming tonight, right?"

"Absolutely. What can I bring?"

"A salad would be nice. I warn you, Garrett will be there."

Abbie laughed. "Leah, he may be going through a hard time, but he's not the town criminal. Why the warning?"

"Like you said, he's going through a tough time. But he wasn't easy even before that."

"It'll be nice to see him again. It's been years. See you at six."

Leah stood and went to the front door. It was unlocked, which meant Garrett was still home. She'd given him a key and encouraged him to go out for exercise or visit the library. Anything to move him ahead. Anything to keep him from becoming a permanent fixture in her house. One that didn't help or pay any bills.

As she was finishing a toasted ham sandwich, he came into the kitchen. "Hey Garrett. I'm going to rake a few leaves and I'd like your help." She'd been tempted to ask him if he wanted to help her but decided a more direct approach was better.

"Um, sure. After I eat."

A pleasant surprise. She'd expected resistance. "Okay. Meet me in the backyard when you're done."

Leah sang a couple of Broadway tunes while she raked and bagged leaves. She also watched the back door for Garrett. Her singing lost gusto as her irritation mounted. Thirty minutes later, Garrett appeared. She bit back a retort about how he didn't hurry himself, did he? Or that she'd almost finished the job by herself. Since when had she become such a shrew? She threw him a grateful smile. "I'll rake and you stuff bags, then we'll switch."

They worked for another hour. A row of black plastic bags lined the wooden fence like a platoon of chubby soldiers. "We can call it a day. What do you think?" She propped the rake against the shed as Garrett finished tying off a bag.

He ran his wrist across his forehead. "We're not supposed to work on the Sabbath, are we?"

Leah sat on the concrete back step. "Surprised you know about that."

Garret sat beside her. "I'm not as much a heathen as you think."

Leah raised her brows. "You're not? I mean, I never called you a heathen."

"I remember a couple things from Sunday school. Dad made us go for, like, years."

Leah handed him a bottle of water. She took hers, and they both drank a few greedy gulps. "Raking leaves makes me miss Dad." Fall and winter in their entirety made her miss Dad. "He used to make a game out of it."

Garrett offered a rare grin. "It was his way of tricking us into doing leaves."

"Maybe so. Thanks for helping today."

"No problem. It was kind of fun. Got me out of my head."

A moment of silence passed. She took another deep sip as several golden leaves swirled down from the trees. Many more would fall in the coming weeks, but at least they'd gotten a head start. A slight bite of cold laced the air but felt refreshing after her exertion.

"Sorry I mentioned your ex today," she said. "I won't bring her up again."

He shrugged. "That's okay. It hadn't been going well for a few months. She wants to be married, but apparently, not to me. I'm not ready for that either. We started arguing about it." He stopped, as if realizing he'd said more than he intended.

"Maybe she's not the right one for you. Did you want to marry her?"

"I wasn't ready to marry anyone. I should have let her know sooner. But then, she started getting all demanding, like she wasn't happy with the person I am. She wanted me to change. Be husband material or something."

Leah couldn't stifle a laugh. "That's funny. Maybe she's been reading marriage books, and you didn't fit her picture."

Garrett sighed. "Guess not. Maybe it's true, I'm not marriage material. At any rate, I'm not ready to think about marriage. Look at me, I don't even have a job now."

Leah's heart ached for him. Despite how annoying he could be. He was opening a small window to her. "You will. I'm sure you'll get something. Or else your game will become a viral hit."

A look of doubt passed over his face. "Need to get back to it. But then what will I do with it? Sell it?"

"Start a company? I don't know anything about tech. Music's still my jam."

"If that's true, you're way off course." He looked at her. "As much as I am," he added softly.

More leaves fell, clumps of them, then a few one by one. Winter might be severe if it was this chilly in early October. The swirling motion of the rogue leaves held her attention as she rewound Garrett's words. It was true, she was off course. But what was her course? Two years earlier, she thought she knew. Her life was traced out. Her life with Michael. But that ship had sailed. No, it had crashed into a barrier reef and sunk to the ocean floor. Took her a year to clean up the wreckage and she was still trying without success to rebuild a foundation of hope in her heart. Still trying to rebuild. . . something. She had no idea what.

"Have you started on Christmas yet?" Garrett's mouth twisted with humor.

"It's only October."

"You know how you go overboard every year. I thought maybe you'd already started."

"I will soon. Got to plan menus, gifts, decorations. . ."

"You're trying to keep up with Dad."

His words hit her with a thud. Was she? Is that why she felt the need to fake Christmas cheer every year? "Yeah, I guess I am. He made Christmas so wonderful for us every year." She blinked. "I know it's not the same." Not at all. Her efforts didn't spring from a well of joy and holiday spirit. No one knew that, though.

She understood why she did it. It was a frantic effort to ward off the inevitable depression that came every year as she considered the holidays that were no longer there. That would never again be there.

Was it possible to get it back without Dad? Their mother apparently hadn't thought so. She'd never even tried to create a holiday spirit for them. She'd been even more devastated after his death and unable to fake it. Eventually, she moved away to start over. Maybe she'd come for Christmas this year if she ran out of excuses not to.

It was up to Leah to do it for the family, though family always felt like only her. Why did she even bother? Because it was better than the alternative. Remembering.

So, she pushed on. Made cookies. Put up lights. Pretended to recapture the joy they had when Dad was alive. At times, it was fun. When her friends were there, and they laughed together during parties. That felt a little like a family. But the effort she put in was only partly successful at creating the real thing. She was always relieved when Christmas was in the rearview mirror.

Chapter Four

A week after the fateful phone call from Jason Abernathy, Nathan found himself driving once again from suburban Philadelphia, northwest to Brenner Falls. The second time in a month, a Thursday afternoon. The following day, he'd meet with Charles Bittle, the attorney. After that meeting, he, Nathan Chisholm, would be the legal owner of Seasons Dinner Theater. Like it or not.

His boss had been understanding about his dilemma and waved away Nathan's apology for taking off more time. Nathan would continue his efforts to sell Seasons on weekends, online, or by phone. He felt slightly less overwhelmed after his conversation that morning with Carley Romano, his new broker as of last week. She'd already found three prospective buyers for Seasons. He was happy to pay her commission if she could help him unload his inheritance.

Prior to emailing Carley, he'd researched the tourist draw for Brenner Falls, since that was likely the only way she'd agree to work with him. She'd seemed annoyed by his complete lack of numbers or facts about the business. He improvised by exaggerating more than a little about the town's potential as a tourist magnet and haven for watersports. It wasn't a total bluff, given Brenner Falls' upward growth over the last three years.

The impractical side of him wanted to see Leah again during his weekend visit. Impractical for a couple reasons. Every moment was scheduled, so there wasn't much time for socializing. Yet after their brief conversation at the funeral, he'd thought of her too many times, trying to ignore the swell of attraction. The practical side kicked in with a rebuke. No point in starting something long distance with her.

A few poignant memories of her which brought a smile to his lips convinced him that he was being a dope. Their friendship was a treasure in the past and could be again. Renewing that friendship didn't take him down the aisle. But the other day when his insides ached with loss, their brief conversation comforted him and reminded him of all they'd had. All that was still there.

So, he texted her. Said he was coming to town, and he had news, but would tell her when he saw her. Cryptic, yes, but the whole thing was too huge to even contemplate, let alone explain in a text.

Soon, his mother's lemon-yellow ranch house came into view, along with a surge of nostalgia. He'd grown up in that house, remembered when the sugar maples were small. Now they arched over each side of the small home like a picture frame of stunning orange and red leaves. He parked behind her old Honda on the double strip of concrete that made up the driveway.

He opened the door, likely left unlocked for him, even though he had a key. "Mom, I'm here." He entered the familiar living room with its plaid couch and contrasting wing chairs and set his small suitcase on the floor. One of his mom's two cats snoozed on the ottoman.

"In the kitchen. Follow your nose!"

He did, happily enveloped by the tangy aroma of tomatoes and cheese. When he entered the kitchen, his mother was pulling a Pyrex pan full of lasagna out of the oven. She set it on the stovetop. Her brown curls laced with gray crowned her flushed but smiling face. The enticing aroma engulfed him. His hollow stomach rumbled.

"You didn't have to do that, Mom. Lasagna's a lot of trouble."

"I don't get you here that often, so I made one of your favorites." She put down the potholders and folded him in her arms.

"I'm not complaining, just so you know." He pulled away. "Can I help with anything?"

"All done. I hope you're hungry." She untied her apron and hung it on a hook in the pantry.

"Starved. I didn't have anything before hitting the road." And he'd eaten little during his lunch break, which was taken up by his call with Carley.

Nathan sat at the table, already prepared with plates and silverware. His old spot where he'd eaten for almost two decades before leaving home. The same vegetable print curtains topped the window over the sink. Outside it, darkness had fallen. He prayed for the meal, then his mother slid a slab of lasagna onto his plate, a puff of steam billowing over the table. He closed his eyes and took a whiff as his stomach let out another protest.

His mother peered at him over her fork while she blew on the hot mixture. "You said you'd bring me up to speed. Is this a good time, or would you rather talk tomorrow?"

"I don't mind. The facts are still rolling in, so I don't know what to think yet." He stirred dressing into the salad leaves and took a bite. "So, I have what they call a broker. Her name is Carley. She's supposed to look for interested buyers for me. Like a real estate agent, sort of, but for companies. She's found three potential buyers."

"Three!" His mother's eyes widened. "That's wonderful. So quick too. Who'd she find?"

Nathan braced himself for her reaction. "The first one is a developer. He'd probably tear everything down and build something like an apartment building."

His mother's smile fell. "Oh. That might not be the best for the town. Brenner Falls *is* growing, so there might be a need for new housing or stores. But we'd miss our old theater."

"I know. I haven't even talked to the guy yet, so don't worry. There are lots more people who'll respond, you'll see. If three showed an interest in the first week, I imagine there'll be a lot more. I'll find the right buyer."

She looked relieved. "Who else did she find?"

"The second one has a chain of restaurants. Not sure what kind. I'll get a lot more info if it gets serious, and of course, I'll meet the people on top of my list. The last one has the most potential for me because he's interested in keeping it like it is. Apparently, the guy has a few dinner theaters already and is open to buying another one. Carley said he liked the concept and would keep it the same. The thing is he wants to see all the numbers. Well, they all do, but especially him, because he wants to make sure it'll be profitable as a dinner theater. I guess the others won't care as much, as long as the land is in an excellent location." Which it was.

His mother shrugged. "Seems to be. It's near the center of town, across from City Hall. But we wouldn't want just anything going in there. The townspeople, I mean. Both Seasons and City Hall have a certain historic look about them." She laid one hand on his arm. "But that's your decision, Nathan. You're the new owner and you should do what's best for *you*. You won't be able to cater to everyone's wants."

"I know. I don't want everyone to hate me either."

"Impossible! They'd never hate you for any reason. You're Andy's boy. They know that." She grinned, and he found his smile.

Andy's boy. If he could ask Andy what *he* wanted him to do, Nathan could guess what he'd say. He'd want him to work there himself, take up the mantle, continue the vision. But that wasn't possible. Surely, Andy had known Nathan would be obligated to sell it. He'd encouraged Nathan several times over the years to come back to Brenner Falls. *There's something wholesome and satisfying about living where you grew up*, he would say. Maybe he thought inheriting the theater would draw Nathan back. He could still hear his uncle's voice. *I know you like the big city, but Brenner Falls is growing. It's expanding, modernizing. I'm sure you see the progress every time you come for a visit.*

Nathan did. But that didn't mean he wanted to return. Why would he want to settle in the place where people knew him as the boy whose father had deserted him and his mother when he was six and ended up doing time? Even though he had no memories of his father, he remembered plenty of cruel words from kids at school. Those words remained etched in his mental archives, as if it were his fault his dad hadn't stayed in town. Fortunately, by the time high school rolled around, they'd either grown bored with the taunts, or found themselves in a similar situation. Nathan's athletics, grades, and friendships all helped fill the gaps. And Uncle Andy. Those things helped him forget. Mostly.

And now the fatherless kid was the owner of Seasons Dinner Theater. Life was strange.

"What about Andy's house?"

Nathan wiped his mouth with a paper napkin. "That was good, Mom. Uh, yeah, the house. I'll have to go over there tomorrow and check it out."

And ransack every room to see if he could find financial records, employer records, debts, bills, anything, and everything that he'd need to present to a potential buyer. Made him tired just thinking about it.

Then he'd visit the restaurant and look over the entire building. Ask about the status, as if he even knew what to ask. He'd worked there as a college student not that long ago. Okay, it was over five years earlier, but he remembered a bit. Paul Duchamps had been the manager and head chef for as long as Nathan could remember. The restaurant maintained a loyal clientele, which explained why it was still in business despite losing Andy. Paul was still there keeping it alive, even though the theater had been dormant since Andy got sick. Paul was likely waiting to see what would happen next, who the next owner would be, and if he and his staff would still have jobs.

Nathan said goodnight to his mother soon after they cleared the dinner dishes. It had been a long day already, and tomorrow would likely be surreal. He flipped on the light in his old bedroom, where he stayed each time he visited. In the last year, it hadn't been often. His mom had updated the room, but some of his teen artifacts still graced the shelves and dresser. Photos of him with Ben in football uniforms, a photo from the senior prom with a girl whose name he didn't remember.

He washed his face and brushed his teeth quickly, ignoring his grimace in the mirror. Fatigue washed across his body as he fell into bed, though his thoughts still pinged off the inside of his skull. Though loving and well-meaning, Uncle Andy hadn't done him any favors.

"Lord, I need to give all this to you. I need your wisdom and your help." He spoke aloud as his eyes searched the darkness, then gradually adapted, making out the corners of the room and the edge of his suitcase. A silvery light from the window outlined the desk by the wall, streaking its surface. He'd developed a bad habit of thinking through his problems alone and praying later. Ben had mentioned the importance of prayer in their phone call. The urgency of not taking it on solo, as he usually did. Always the kid alone. He wasn't that kid anymore. He was an adult with a responsible position in a top marketing firm. But to God, he was still a kid who'd *never* been alone, but who'd always assumed he was.

Nathan sighed. Knowing the facts didn't make it easier to open the firm shell he'd developed over the years. God was still there to take the burden, if only he'd let him.

ᘓ ᘓ ᘓ

The canvas tote bag biting into Leah's left shoulder would lighten considerably once she'd returned the six library books inside. Four of them had been for Garrett, to encourage him in his job search, which he hadn't begun. The other two were novels for her private escape into the life she'd never have. Of course, the characters in the books always had huge problems before they reached their state of happily ever after. Not necessarily an encouragement.

Her thoughts bounced away from Garrett and her dull life, which had become more promising in the recent month. Instead of deadweight inside, butterflies zipped around in anticipation and a touch of nerves. Nathan was in town. He'd texted her Thursday. He'd wanted to meet at Sophie's Coffee Shop Saturday morning.

She hurried into the library on Summit Street and slid the books into the slot at the entrance. The one book she selected was for her this time, not Garrett. She did too much for him as it was and hadn't seen him do a lot for himself in the month he'd been home. October had arrived with no visible sign that he planned to move out or return to Pittsburgh.

Abbie had come for dinner the previous Sunday and, unexpectedly, she and Garrett had hit it off. Before her eyes, sullen Garrett came out of his shell and charmed Leah's best friend. Leah still didn't know how Abbie felt about him, since she'd later said things like, *he's nice,* and *he's not as bad as I thought.* Of course, Abbie was a committed Christian and Garrett was committed to nothing, not even his own game invention, so she could safely guess it wouldn't go anywhere.

Saturday morning shoppers bustled in the street. Seeing the town vibrate with weekend activity along with the faint chill biting the air flooded Leah with well-being, aside from her coffee date with Nathan. She loved autumn, and she loved Brenner Falls. Even with its recent modernizations, it exuded a comforting familiarity. She belonged. Her four years at college were fun and different, as were the two years after that, but she'd been glad to come back.

Sophie's came into view and Leah's pulse jumped. Nathan her old friend. Her new preoccupation. *Stop it, Leah!*

He'd settled at a café table for two next to a steamy window near the back. There he was in person, not in her imagination or high school memories. Saturday shoppers filled the popular café. Noise and the scent of chocolate and cinnamon permeated the crowded space.

Leah wove through the clusters of customers and slid into the chair across from him. "Hi, Nathan. Good to see you again so soon."

She met his eyes and smiled. My, but he looked good. A faint rosy pink stained his freshly shaven cheeks and dark green sweater intensified the color of his eyes.

"Hi, Leah. I'm glad you could come. After we saw each other at the funeral I was kicking myself for losing touch with you. I was determined not to do it again."

"I always knew you were smart, Nathan." She winked.

He gave a small bow of his head. "And you're smart for knowing *I'm* smart." They laughed.

She folded her hands on the edge of the table. "Well, I lost touch with you too. Don't want to do that again. I mean, who else have I known forever and who was such a great friend? We have history."

"Yes, history." Their eyes met. "And lots of catching up as well. Do you want something to drink?"

"I love Sophie's hot chocolate but I'm in the mood for tea."

"Me too. I'll get it. Earl Gray, okay?" She nodded and he rose to join the short line at the counter. A few minutes later he returned and placed two mugs and a teapot, fragrant with Bergamot, on the table. "There should be enough tea in here to keep us going today."

He poured the tea for them. Leah took a sip. "When you texted, you said you had news." She was glad to have an opening, though doubted they'd have any trouble in conversation despite the gap of years. "Don't keep me in suspense."

Nathan let out a long sigh. Didn't seem like *good* news.

His eyes met hers. "Uncle Andy left me Seasons in his will."

She couldn't stop her mouth from dropping open. "He did? Oh, Nathan. That's. . . I don't know. Is it good news? I'm not sure what to say."

He laughed. "You're the first one to question that. Not many people know about it, but those who do think it's great for me. Wonderful news. Believe me, it's a headache."

"I can imagine. Not the inheritance you would have chosen, probably." She gave what she hoped was a sympathetic smile. "Do you know what you'll do about it? Will you come back to run it? I know you have a job in Philadelphia."

"No, I don't plan to run it." His voice held the weight of finality. "I'm mostly here to determine its condition so I'll know what to do next. I hope to learn more about my options by the time I go back home."

"I'm sure you will. I noticed the restaurant stayed open, even after Andy got sick."

"Yes, fortunately. This afternoon I'll go over there and meet with the restaurant manager, Paul Duchamps. He's a good man and good at what he does. It's a relief he's been there through the transition. The theater hasn't done any shows in a couple of years and the whole building needs major renovation."

Leah took a slow sip of the hot beverage. "I see why you call it a headache. Along with the fact that you live somewhere else." She brightened. "But Seasons is still a treasure, don't you think? Such a heartbeat of the community."

Nathan frowned. "You think?" He looked into his tea as if searching for wisdom there.

"I know it needs some work, but with time and gradual renovations, you could take it in an upward direction. You know, modern and vibrant again." She stopped. No, he said he wasn't going to run it. "You said you wanted to know what to do next. What are your options?" She braced herself for his response.

He met her eyes. "You haven't said anything I haven't thought about, Leah. I know the town residents really care about the historical value of the place. But selling it is the most logical thing to do."

"Maybe so." Her voice was quiet, but inside something screamed. Not Seasons, where she could still picture her dad singing in the chorus of one of the holiday events. Where his murals still stood on the stage. "But it's a landmark and a reference, though many more restaurants in town are more popular. Is that the only option you have?"

He lifted his hands, palms to the ceiling. "What else? If I can't run it myself—and by the way, I have no experience doing that—what else can I do? If someone local can buy it, someone who wants to keep it a historic monument, that would be great. It's a business, and you can't run a business on people's nostalgia and good feelings. Salaries have to be paid. Renovations cost money. It's a big thing."

Of course, it made sense. Sadly. "It's sad, but I do see your point. Have you started looking for buyers yet?"

"I'm working with a broker. As much as I want to get it off my plate, I think about what it meant to Uncle Andy. I'd really love to find a buyer who's like-minded, you know? Someone who'll keep its purpose but make it better."

"That would be perfect. Anyone like that on the horizon?"

"There may be one guy the broker found. He's got a few dinner theaters and is looking for more. But he wants to see profit. We don't have much of that." He let out a laugh. "My buddy, Ben Russo, suggested I do an event to increase the profit and show the potential."

"That's a great idea, Nathan. I'll help. I don't have tons of time, but I'm pretty organized. I was in a couple of shows before. I can help with music if there's any music involved."

Nathan grinned and reached out to squeeze her forearm. "Thanks, Leah. You're sweet to offer and I know you'd do what you could."

He pulled his hand away. Her arm still tingled from his touch. "But it sounds like you're not considering it."

He shook his head. "I'm not. Well, let me rephrase that. It's not a bad idea in itself, since it would be a barometer of whether or not it could be revived, but since I don't want to keep it, it's kind of pointless to think about. Even if I wanted to do it, there isn't much time before Christmas."

"I see." She didn't know what else to say.

He fell silent, his eyes not leaving her face. A flow of heat seeped up through her neck.

"What about you?" he asked. "Fill me in on your life. We got cut short at the funeral."

"As I recall, I did all the talking. I'd like to hear about *your* exciting life in Philadelphia."

He gave her a wily smile that melted her insides. "But I asked you first. So, be polite and answer my question, please, Leah."

They laughed. And suddenly, it felt almost as comfortable as it had in high school when they'd been close friends with open communication, trust, and tons of teenage self-esteem issues.

"Okay, then," she said. "I already told you about my current exciting job. So, I'll back up. I think I told you I stayed and worked in College Park for about two years after graduating." She'd hated those jobs, but was dating Michael, who was working on his master's degree. "

"And you moved back two years ago, you said. You live there by yourself?"

"And Theo, my cat. He's a good roommate. For the moment, my brother Garrett is staying there too. He's between jobs."

"I remember Garrett, though I don't know if I'd recognize him. I vaguely remember where you live. What made you decide to leave your other job and come back to the Falls?"

Leah hesitated. Nathan had been honest with her, so she could tell him her sad story. "During my senior year, I was dating someone. He was doing a master's in chemistry. When he finished it, we got engaged, but he moved to Michigan to begin a doctorate. I came back to live here for a few months until the wedding. But we broke up, so I stayed."

Nathan frowned. "I'm sorry. That must have been hard."

"Yeah, especially since he broke it off two months before the wedding. But I guess it was for the best."

"You don't sound sure."

Leah shrugged. "If he wasn't sure, I didn't want to build a life with him. I offered to move to Michigan and get a place there until we could be married. I also suggested we postpone the wedding if he wasn't ready. He may have gotten cold feet, or realized we weren't right for each other."

"Did you ever see him again?"

Leah shook her head, ready to change subjects. "We spoke on the phone a couple of times." Long, agonizing phone calls full of doubts, accusations, and apologies. Calls that resolved nothing. "Not sure why I'm telling you all this." She let out an awkward laugh and glanced out the window. She felt his eyes still upon her.

"Because I asked?"

"And you're easy to talk to. Always were." *Which is why I had a crush on you in high school.*

"I hope so." Nathan's face brightened, as if he were uncomfortable with her compliment.

"So, what else do you have to do this weekend?"

"I went to see the attorney this morning. Signed a bunch of papers. I'll go over to Seasons this afternoon then I'll need to rummage through Uncle Andy's home office to see if he left any paperwork there that'll be useful in the sale."

Leah couldn't help it, the heavy thud inside at the word *sale*. "Any other visits with old friends? Or is it all business?"

"I'll get together with Ben tonight for dinner. You remember him, don't you?"

"Of course, I do. He was in our youth group, and he graduated with us. I always think of him as having big ideas. Remember when he organized the camping trip for the whole junior class? I always figured he'd run for public office one day."

"Maybe he will. Right now, he's working as an engineer in town. He never wanted to leave the Falls."

"I did once, then I couldn't wait to get back." Leah drained her mug.

"I couldn't wait to get away. Another reason I can't run Seasons."

Her smile fell. "Do you still feel that way, after all these years?"

"No, not really. I feel fine now. But there are some bad memories here. Time helps. I actually enjoy coming back for visits."

"That's good. You need to keep in touch with your old friend Leah." She grinned. "It's a shame we didn't run into each other sooner."

He returned a silent nod and the ghost of a smile. "But now, we have." He glanced at his phone. "I'm meeting Paul at Seasons in a few minutes. Do you happen to be walking that way?"

"As a matter of fact, I have to pick something up at the dry cleaners. It's at the end of Summit nearly to Market Street."

"I remember. We can walk part way."

They stood up and left the café. It wasn't a long walk to the intersection where their paths would divide. Unfortunately. "Please keep me posted on your discoveries and decisions. I'll be a good sounding board."

His face looked care-worn, but he mustered a smile. "I'll need one, that's for sure. It was great seeing you, Leah. Talk to you soon."

They hugged and he turned to the intersection at Market Street.

"I hope so." She spoke to herself as she watched him cross the street.

Chapter Five

A late September breeze stroked Nathan's face as he left Leah on the corner of Summit Street. As he headed across the intersection toward Seasons, her smile was what he saw etched on his mind. Whatever else happened that day, he'd spent an hour or so with Leah Albright, his high school pal, now an alluring adult woman. She'd looked fresh and cute wearing a sheepskin jacket, unzipped over a red t-shirt. A knit beret perched on her head at an angle and her flushed cheeks made him think of an Irish lass out for a walk on the highlands. They'd slipped into conversation so easily that one would never believe they hadn't seen each other in years. He'd had trouble taking his eyes off her simple, pure beauty and eyes so blue he could swim in them forever. "Be careful, Nathan," he muttered aloud. His heart pounded just remembering their magical hour at Sophie's.

One aspect was less magical. Leah clearly had strong attachments to Seasons, which would make his inevitable decision that much harder. His mom had advised him to do what was best for him. He couldn't please everyone, she'd said. But Leah? Of all the people he didn't want to disappoint, she topped the list.

Brenner Boulevard vibrated with activity. He didn't recognize many of the pedestrians he passed. He'd been away too long. The triangular intersection now had a fountain in the middle, still flanked by geraniums. Must have been a new addition thanks to the Brenner Falls beautification effort that had begun a couple of years ago. About the time the new mayor arrived. *There* was a man with a vision. Nathan wondered what *he* thought of his neighbor, Seasons Dinner Theater.

Before crossing, he surveyed Seasons from the opposite curb. It had the potential to be an attractive building. Though tired looking, it already was, with a Victorian façade and a long, elegant front porch. But it would still take a lot to turn the ugly duckling into Cinderella ready for the ball. Lots of people would love to be in his shoes, so why was he feeling grumpy and trapped? Was there any way this wouldn't be a long-term pain in the neck? He'd find out soon.

He hadn't been to Seasons in over a year when he'd lunched there with Andy. Nathan had wanted to take Andy out for lunch, but Andy had preferred eating at his own restaurant. He knew the menu, knew what he liked. And eating there, he'd claimed, allowed him to experience it like a customer instead of the owner. Nathan didn't have time to do the same that day. His priority was to get an overview through observation and a meeting with Paul, the chef manager.

Nathan pushed on the glass door. *My restaurant. I'm the owner. Of this restaurant.* His mental reality pinch didn't take effect.

It was early afternoon, so no dinner customers filled the square tables. That was what Nathan had in mind. He didn't want to survey the place nor meet with Paul amidst the distraction of customers. Paul wouldn't have been available during the dinner rush, anyway. The last thing Nathan wanted to do was put Paul under pressure, even though technically, he was now Nathan's employee.

A lone waiter stopped at each table and laid sets of silverware wrapped in a paper napkin at each seat. Cheerful yellow paint on the walls lightened the atmosphere. Artificial trees woven with tiny white lights filled the corners of the room. Rows of tables fanned out in a semi-circle around the stage, now filled with artificial plants and wrought iron sculptures in front of the closed curtain. As a camouflage, it could have been worse.

"Can I help you with something, sir?" asked the waiter from a few tables away.

"No, thanks. I have an appointment with Paul." The man nodded and was about to walk away. "Wait, please. Can I ask you a few questions?"

The young man stopped and stood attentively.

"I'm... I'm Andy's nephew. Andy, the owner. The late owner, rather."

The man's expression slid into a solemn frown. "I'm so sorry for your loss. We all miss Andy."

"Thank you. I miss him too. I wondered how the restaurant is doing overall, you know, with Andy's sickness and since his passing. Has it been affected, do you think?" Probably sounded cold to the man for Nathan to ask about customer count in the wake of his uncle's death. He couldn't explain the situation or how little time he had to investigate his new predicament.

"I've only been working here about six months, but it seems the same, thanks to Paul. He's held everything together. You may know that the theater aspect hasn't been open in over a year, maybe more. That's what I heard, anyway."

"Yes, I was aware of that. I'm glad it hasn't affected the restaurant too much. I was curious. Would you say it's a popular restaurant?"

The young man cocked his head. "There are newer restaurants that are more popular. We rarely fill up. It's steady with regulars, though."

"Oh, that's good. I was curious. Thanks."

"Sure thing."

As he expected. Seasons was a fixture in town, but an old one. Every few years, Andy would do some minor updates, but the place needed an overhaul. It still looked old-fashioned to him, and over time, it might please the original residents of Brenner Falls, but not the newcomers. Even if the food was still good.

Nathan glanced at his watch. Almost time for his appointment. He'd called Paul to schedule the meeting, saying only that he was the new owner of the Seasons. The less said the better.

"Hey, Nathan." Paul approached, wearing a stained white apron. His graying hair was neatly combed back and held in a stubby ponytail by a rubber band. He stuck out his hand and Nathan shook it.

"Hi, Paul. Thanks for meeting with me. You probably don't have any down time on a given day."

Paul chuckled. "You're correct about that. But this is the best time of the day to talk. Let's sit down." They chose a nearby table. "I didn't get a chance to speak with you at the funeral. I wanted to express my sympathy in the loss of your uncle."

"Thanks, Paul. I know it was a loss for you too." Nathan knew Paul had worked for nearly a decade managing the restaurant for Andy. "Seems you've done a good job of keeping the ship afloat through everything."

"Thanks, I appreciate that. And now, it's all yours. I'm eager to hear what you're planning."

Nathan had always liked and respected Paul. His straightforward manner of talking and his integrity in his work were both a comfort. The man loved the restaurant and was faithful to it, though he could have had a more illustrious career elsewhere.

He owed Paul an honest answer. "Paul, I'm going to be straight with you. I have a job in Philly and a life there. This all fell in my lap and was a big surprise. I'm considering selling it but haven't made any definite move or decision yet."

The man stiffened. "Can't say I'm surprised."

A thought floated into Nathan's mind which, for some reason, hadn't occurred to him before. "Would you be at all interested in buying it? I can't give you a price yet, but you'd certainly be a better buyer than anyone else I can think of."

Paul laid one hand on Nathan's arm. "It means a lot that you'd say that, Nathan. Honestly, I'm not a young man. I've been in this business for going on thirty years. Trust me, this line of work ages a man more than some others. I can manage another five or so years, barring anything unforeseen. I'd be happy to keep managing Seasons if you keep it, but owning it is more than I want right now."

He pressed his lips together. "So, I'm wondering, of course, where that leaves me and my staff when you sell it."

Nathan looked at the tablecloth as he considered his words. "Fair question. Honestly, I don't know." He met Paul's gaze. "I'm not sure what to tell you, Paul. Right now, I need to learn as much as I can about the numbers. I need to know the performance and future potential before looking for a suitable buyer. Though I can't promise, I'll do my utmost to find someone who will not only keep it a restaurant, as opposed to tearing it down, but also keep you on staff."

"Whoever buys it may have his or her own manager, though I'd be happy to stay too. I can go elsewhere or take an early retirement. Move to Florida and fish every day." His smile was half-hearted.

"That's the spirit." Nathan smiled at him. "Sounds like you have a good plan. I'll do my best. I'm only beginning the process, though. What about the theater? I've heard nothing's going on there."

"Yes, that's true. It's been nearly two years. At first, people missed it. Then, they got used to it being closed. Andy didn't really have the money to do the shows like he wanted to, then figured low quality was worse than no theater at all."

As he spoke, Nathan's gaze wandered back to the stage. "It's a shame. Maybe the stage can be converted into more seating for diners."

"We don't have a need. We don't even fill the dining room."

Nathan returned his attention to Paul. "Would you say the restaurant is struggling?"

"It goes up and down. I've tried some new menus, specials, prix fixe, things like that. Moderate success. I think it's the décor. A bunch of new trendy places have opened in the last year. Open concept, tall ceilings with pipes sticking out and all that."

"Yeah, it's a bit outdated here. Nowadays, good food doesn't compete with a trendy atmosphere in people's minds." Nathan had observed that in his own suburb. "And that would take a boatload of money."

"Yes, it would. Andy knew that. He wanted to do some renovations but didn't have the capital to do it right. So, he made little changes here and there, but it still looked dated. The food was good, so the regulars kept coming. But fewer new people. That's my impression."

"Good food's important. Apparently, you have that here." Nathan wasn't sure what else to say, since Paul had confirmed his fear.

"But it's not enough." Paul glanced toward the kitchen, where he likely had hours of work waiting for him. More servers had filtered into the dining room to prepare for the dinner opening.

Paul's attention returned to Nathan. "I have some legers and other documents for you in the office. We'll pass by there on the way out."

"Hope I can make sense of it, since this isn't my wheelhouse."

"Your buyer will understand it. And you'll understand more than you expect."

"I hope so. Thanks, Paul." Nathan stood. "I appreciate your taking the time to talk."

"Probably won't be the last time." Paul gave Nathan a reserved smile. For an instant, Nathan could see working with Paul in some capacity, as he had during a couple of summers years earlier. He chased the image from his mind. He had a job. He didn't need another one.

They stood, and Nathan followed Paul to the kitchen. It looked the same as before, but Nathan considered it from his new perspective as the owner. For now.

"Is all the equipment in good working order?" he asked to Paul's back as they left the kitchen and went down a short hallway.

"This is my office in here. Currently, everything works. Andy replaced a few pieces of equipment before he got sick. I have all the receipts and service documents on everything."

"Great. I'm glad all that's available. Sounds like you're organized."

Paul opened a deep drawer and pulled out a massive notebook and two thick file folders. "Most of these are originals." He placed them in Nathan's hands.

"I understand. I'll take good care of them." He looked at the documents in his hands as though they were ancient and fragile maps of hidden treasure. He almost laughed at the thought.

A treasure? Not in a million years.

It was nearly four o'clock when Nathan arrived at Andy's house. Nathan had always liked the house, a Craftsman built in the fifties. A raised porch with a white railing extended across the front. Chunky columns flanked either side of the front door, and two more held up the corners of the overhang. Looked like Andy had painted the siding in recent years, so that was one thing less to do before selling the house. He didn't have time for a thorough examination. His priority for that weekend was to get all the paperwork and facts he needed so he would look more savvy to buyers and less clueless with Carley, who he needed to call. Both objectives would save him money and expedite the whole thing. Theoretically. Besides, he'd eventually have an appraiser and inspector give their reports when the time came.

He stood on the porch for a moment and let it sink in, the fact that this house he'd known all his life was *his* house now. A flood of memories washed over him, so many hours of his childhood spent on this porch, in the yard, in the house. The rocking chairs where he'd passed hours with Uncle Andy drinking lemonade as he plied young Nathan with questions about school, about the bullies who taunted him, about what he was learning and how he shouldn't give up. . . Those chairs were still sitting on the porch, needing a coat of paint, but in solid condition. Nathan's throat tightened and his eyes stung. Couldn't believe Andy was gone.

The sun still hung high in the autumn sky, so he sat on one of the rocking chairs to call Carley. He'd neglected contact with his broker for a week or so and didn't want her to forget about him.

Maybe she'd have a couple new prospects lined up. "Hey, Carley. Hope it's okay to bother you on a Saturday."

"No problem, Nathan." Her alto voice, complete with a sharp northeastern accent, filled the phone. "I was actually going to call you myself this afternoon. What have you learned about the condition of your uncle's business? You said you'd get more details while you were there this weekend."

She didn't waste any time or allow him to soften the ugly truth. He cleared his throat and considered where to start. "I did learn a few things about the business, although I am not a businessman and can't speak in detail." He sighed. No use painting a pretty picture. Carley might resign from his case, but he had to risk it. And she'd be more helpful if she knew what they were up against. "I'll be honest, the business is struggling, from what I can tell. It's bringing customers, but not like before. There's been competition with new restaurants opening. But the concept is unique. A dinner theater is a dying breed, but one that's valued in this community. I'm interested in finding someone who will see its potential, be willing to invest in an overhaul, and make it profitable again."

"You may be dreaming, Nathan," Carley said in a clipped tone.

A staccato laugh devoid of humor erupted from his throat. "Tell me what you *really* think, Carley." She was no-nonsense, but maybe that's what he needed. A slap in the face to wake him from a stupor.

"I don't know what else to say. I haven't had any new bites since I gave you those three. They're still interested as far as I know, but that's it so far. My advice is to sell to the one who gives you the best deal and don't worry about what they do with it. This is business. You can't please everyone in that town."

"Yes, I've thought of that and heard it too. I know I can't. But I grew up here and I know what Seasons means to everyone. I'm still wide open to all three prospective buyers. What will it take to get an offer from one of them for me to consider?"

"They'll need to visit, of course. The developer doesn't need to see the stats for the business because basically he's only interested in the land. Did your uncle own the property or rent?"

"He owned it. I own it, I guess."

"If that town is growing and attracting new people like you say, that's your best money right there. Let them tear it down and build something that'll fit in with the new generation that's coming. Dinner theaters are old school. There aren't but a few left in the country, primarily in the Midwest."

Nathan wasn't so sure of that but recognized the wisdom of her words. If the best price was all he was concerned about, the decision would be easy, unless there was special zoning that would limit what could be built there. The lump came back to Nathan's stomach as he envisioned a bulldozer taking down Seasons, leaving a smoking hole where a town landmark once stood. Andy's landmark. His legacy.

She was saying something. "Excuse me? I didn't hear you."

"I said I need to run. Keep doing your homework and send me an email once you finish. Then maybe we can arrange some visits."

"Could you send me more information about these potential buyers in the meantime? Something more about the kind of work they do?"

"Sure thing. I sent you website addresses, but I'll see what else we have on them. Talk to you soon."

"Bye, Carley."

He stared at the phone in his hand for a long moment before rising. He felt like an old man. Old at age twenty-eight. He turned to the front door, opened the screen, and fit the keys into the lock and deadbolt. As he entered the great room, a musty odor enveloped him, since the house had been closed for a month. Nathan pushed down the rising grief, which felt like a small animal clawing inside his chest. His eyes stung. *Keep it together. Andy's in heaven. He's happy, even though I miss him. Focus.*

The furnishings looked the same as he remembered. There were a few magazines scattered on the coffee table and a coffee cup under the lamp, as if Andy had been there only that morning. Nathan caught himself. Best make this quick. He strode through each room, reigning in his sadness. He disciplined his eyes too, since it would be far too easy to stop and look at photos, wonder what books had interested his uncle, all the things he hadn't noticed in the last decade. Too late now.

After a quick glance at each of the three bedrooms, he identified what must be Andy's home office. The piles of paper stacked on Andy's desk triggered a rising panic in his chest. It would likely take hours to go through them, and he was already feeling overwhelmed again. An optimistic voice inside told him at least there *were* documents, along with a large filing cabinet, that would provide facts about his new business. That and Paul's information would be a big help. But it would take a while to go through it all.

His mind went back to the stack of folders and legers Paul had given him, which he'd tucked in the trunk of his car. He had plenty to do with that alone, and it was only Friday. He'd take one thing at a time. Yes, maybe *that* he could do.

Later that evening, Nathan slid into the booth at Pizzarama across from Ben. "Hey, bro." The tang of cheese and tomato sauce saturated the air.

"Nathan, good to see you." He clasped Nathan's hand across the table. "Bet you need a break after all your sleuthing around town."

"You got that right." Nathan thrust his fingers through his short hair, feeling the stress unwind like a released slinky. "I just spent the afternoon at Uncle Andy's house, and I'm overwhelmed all over again. The business, the house."

"You don't have a hurry on the house. It's paid off, right?"

Nathan nodded. The one thing in his favor. Dealing with a mortgage would have pushed him to sell the house first. "Next to Seasons, the house'll be easy. I'll definitely make a profit on that."

"Or you can rent it for monthly income."

"Maybe. How's Colleen?" Nathan asked of Ben's long-term girlfriend.

"She's good. She's on a trip for work all this week. Chicago. She travels a whole bunch on her job. I hardly see her anymore." Despite Ben's statement, he didn't seem disturbed by it.

"Guess who I spent time with today." Nathan waited until Ben looked up from the menu. "Leah Albright." He was gratified when Ben's face broke into a grin.

"Way to go, Nathan. Quick, too. How'd that come about?"

"I caught up with her some at the funeral and we exchanged numbers. I'm not trying to start anything, Ben. I wanted to rekindle the friendship we had. I can't pursue her when I live in Philly."

"Not sure why. Well, start with the friendship track and see what happens."

"Yeah, I will." Nathan pulled open the menu to block any further speculations about his relationship with Leah. And he'd try his best to keep his thoughts about her in line with his statement about friendship. He was failing at that already.

They spent a few minutes going over the menu and decided to split a medium pizza with sausage, pepperoni, and mushrooms. "I can smell it already." Ben lifted his face and pretended to inhale pizza aromas. "I've been fixing a section of my roof all afternoon, so I worked up a big appetite."

While they waited for the pizza, Ben talked about his job and a new car he was considering buying, as well as supplying news on changes in town.

"Hello Ben, hello, Nathan."

Nathan looked up and saw Fritz and Eleanor Sutton, an older couple he'd known for years who he'd seen recently at Uncle Andy's funeral

"Hi, Mr. and Mrs. Sutton." He straightened and smiled at them. "How are you this evening?"

"We're fine, out on the town just like you two. We had some excellent pasta." Fritz chuckled then sobered. "I'm sorry about your uncle Andy, Nathan. I hope you're getting along okay in spite of how sad it all was."

Some people did remember, even after more than two weeks. "Mom and I'll get through it. It's hard, but he's with the Lord."

"Keep thinking of that, Nathan." Eleanor Sutton touched one hand to a string of large beads around her neck. "I wondered if you knew what would become of Seasons."

He took a breath. "I'm not sure at this point. I'm overseeing Seasons for now. I mean, I'm not living here, but hoping to find someone who can take it over."

"Oh, that's a relief. I was so afraid it would be torn down. They seem to be doing that to all the older buildings as the new housing and restaurants come in." She shook her head as if to say it was a shame. "It'll change the whole personality of the town, if they get their way."

"If who gets their way?" Ben asked.

She waved the air. "Oh, you know. The builders, the developers, all of them. They'll change everything. We go to Seasons every Thursday night and it's delightful. Of course, we'd welcome the theater if it comes back. I hope it will. That was always a nice evening of good entertainment. It was always clean, too. Andy made sure of that." She searched her husband's eyes for confirmation, and he nodded.

"At this point, we don't know what will happen. It's too soon to say." Nathan's lips tightened. Maybe they'd go away now.

"Yes, that's understandable. Well, enjoy your dinner." Fritz Sutton gave them a little wave. He took his wife's elbow and led her toward the front door.

Nathan stared at Ben. "See what I'm dealing with?"

Ben laughed aloud. "You couldn't have been more vague. You're *overseeing* Seasons? Is that what you said?"

Nathan frowned. "What was I supposed to say? I own it now and I'm looking for ways to dispose of it?"

"Not as raw as that."

"It's called self-protection. Suppose I told them I'm going to sell it. What would they think? *I* don't even know what'll happen to it."

"No, you gave a good response. I can imagine this is overwhelming. Did your broker give you any ideas?"

Nathan snorted. "She basically said don't dream."

"About getting a buyer who will keep it as a dinner theater?" Ben paused. "I think she's right."

At Ben's words, Nathan's shoulders fell.

"But the one thing she doesn't know is what it means to this town. I think if it's bought by someone else, they need to know the history."

Nathan met his gaze. "Like that'll make a difference? No, I get what you're saying. She's speaking as someone who works in black and white business transactions. Sell to the developer. He'll pay top dollar and I'll be happy."

"Medium pepperoni, sausage and mushroom pizza?" The voice came from a perky blonde ponytailed waitress.

"This is the place." Ben bestowed a broad grin on the attractive woman. He peered at her name tag. "Thanks, Emily. I'm sure you're an excellent cook."

She gave him a grudging grin. "Let me know if you need anything else."

The conversation roved to other things as they ate their pizza. "So, what's the next step?" Ben asked when they'd finished.

"Good question. My gut tells me I'm going to sell to the highest offer. It's called progress. Old stuff gets torn down so new stuff gets built. They'll get over it." But as he spoke, his stomach tightened, and the faces of Fritz and Eleanor Sutton flashed in his mind.

"Ha! You're too soft for that. You care too much."

Nathan bowed his head. "You're right." If only it weren't true, all this would be easier.

"Here's an idea." Ben leaned forward, his dark eyes animated. "Out of your three potential buyers, you'd like to sell to the guy who wants to keep it a dinner theater. Didn't you say he's got a couple in the Midwest?"

"Southeast, I think. He knows how to run them and can make it work. He might even have a bunch of capital to renovate it. But he wants to see a profitable one here. That's not the case. Not by a long shot."

"Okay, here's my idea. Don't shoot it down yet. See if you can come to Brenner Falls until the New Year. Get a leave of absence or work remotely or whatever."

Nathan opened his mouth to protest but Ben held up a hand. The New Year? Was Ben crazy?

"Just hear me out, Nathan. Then you can pray about it and take some time. So, I was saying you come here till the New Year. You learn what's happening at the restaurant, first. You've spent, what, thirty minutes or an hour over there? I don't think it's possible to really understand what's happening in an hour."

"You're right, but I'm not planning to run it. I'm going to *sell* it."

"Okay, but suppose you need to learn more and study it before you do either one, keep it or sell it? You give it that time, then you put on a Christmas event to make some money and show the town what they've been missing. Remember, I mentioned that before. It'll give you an idea if it's even worth it to try to salvage Seasons, as well as give you some cash in the meantime to show to the buyer."

Nathan stared at him. "That's your idea? To pull off a Christmas play in two months' time?"

Ben nodded smugly. "You can dig up the actors that were involved in it before, sing a few Christmas songs, do up the décor. There are Christmas programs you can buy that aren't too difficult. It's a win-win."

"Spoken like a man who knows nothing about theater. It takes months to prepare something like that."

"Maybe not, if you get experienced people, use the Christmas classics that everyone knows, shouldn't be as much work as a new play no one's done before. Don't do a scripted thing, do more of a dramatized *concert*. You can get away with that at Christmas. In the meantime, you can get the little house ready to sell, if that's what you want to do. In your place, I'd live there so you can get to know it better and see its selling points. Wouldn't it be better to be knowledgeable before you try to sell these things? Uncle Andy would want you to at least make that effort."

"Not sure about that. But I tell you what. I'll think and pray about it, okay? About coming back, I mean." It did make sense to spend more time instead of shotgun weekends here and there. Plus, he'd get to see Leah more often. And his mom and Ben, of course.

"That's the first thing you should do. Don't sell it without asking God for his guidance. See what he says. Ask him what he wants you to do."

Nathan nodded. He'd fulfill his promise to Ben to pray about it as well as examine all the angles. But the idea to do a Christmas production within two months—with no actors, musicians, or anything—was plain preposterous. He could come back a few weekends. Maybe he'd be able to work remotely.

But even with all of that, he sensed the outcome was only a matter of time.

Chapter Six

Leah's violin was cool under her chin as the melodic notes closed out the final song of the church service. Violin had always been her favorite instrument to play, but she'd done little with it, aside from church services when she had the chance. The sound was pure beauty, slicing the air, heavy with meaning. Yes, she was a music nerd.

"That was wonderful, Leah," said Blair McCartney, Leah's new friend. Blair had recently moved to Brenner Falls with her six-year-old son, Jake.

"Thanks, Blair. How are you two today?" Leah looked down at Jake, an adorable tow-headed imp she fought the urge to cuddle.

Blair sighed and her gaze landed on her young son. "Jake didn't want to go to kids' church today and fidgeted next to me for the whole service. In spite of all his distraction, the sermon blew me away."

"Yeah, me too." Leah had to agree. Pastor Todd had been focused, linear. Like a hammer, his points hit home. Something was different, as though he'd himself had a revelation about delivering truth with power. His message described how God built believers into a living temple for his glory. A gathering of humans, warts and all, but bound by their common faith. "It's so amazing to think of us. . ." Leah gestured toward the two dozen or so people in the room. ". . . as a temple of God. He's building something, even as small as this." It was too stunning to grasp. It stirred her in her depths as she saw the little congregation with new eyes.

Blair's hazel eyes glistened behind her glasses. "It helps to remember that when things get hard. God is building something in each of us individually and together." She looked back down at Jake, who was busy moving the limbs of a stuffed dinosaur he held.

"Is everything okay, Blair?" Leah asked, sensing a fragile disquiet in her friend.

She gave Leah a quick nod and what seemed to be a forced smile. "Just some new behavior issues I'm trying to figure out. Along with the fact that we're still adjusting to a new town. It's all good, though."

Leah felt a surge of compassion. Alone to raise a child in a new town. It couldn't be easy. "I'm sure it's tough to move and have everything to do, and not know people. Jake'll settle down once he gets used to things, I bet. Give me a call sometime and we'll have dinner or meet for coffee." Leah tried to make her voice inviting. There was no reason Blair had to go through her adjustment alone.

"I'd love that. Thanks, Leah."

Blair's words stayed with Leah as she shuffled along the sidewalks, kicking fallen leaves. She'd give Blair a few days then call her to see how things were going.

As Leah walked, more golden leaves swirled like dancing fairies from the branches above. The hot summer gave way to mellow days barely laced with a crisp edge that couldn't yet be called a chill.

Along with wonder at the truths presented that morning, a thread of guilt pinched her gut. Since arriving at the little gathering nearly a year earlier, her attitude hadn't been great, as she caught herself sometimes comparing it to the established church she'd grown up in. Why had she volunteered to be part of the core group? To serve, not to criticize. Weren't most church plants messy in the beginning? Wasn't an imperfect but sincere desire to start new churches precious to God?

Leah blinked away the hot tears that pricked her eyes. *She* was an imperfect, broken member of an imperfect, broken church. She fit right in. "Oh Lord, I'm sorry," she whispered. "Your church is a beautiful thing, no matter its size or how it functions. Let me be a blessing to this living temple. Let me serve and make it better, not sit in judgment." The ache of inner chastisement blended with the joy from the truth of Todd's sermon. It was as though she glimpsed God's heart for a moment as he smiled at his imperfect children struggling to create a part of his kingdom on earth. Maybe Blair would find a family there and feel less alone.

Leah blew out a breath of air and rounded the corner to her street. She'd pass six houses before reaching hers, enjoying each step and the gentle breeze blowing like a caress. She'd never longed for the big city and wondered how Nathan and Garrett were able to adapt there. At the thought of Nathan, she couldn't suppress a smile. She'd rewound their coffee date several times in her mind, savoring it like a secret. She hoped he'd visit the Falls often.

From one house away she could see Garrett on the porch with someone. Abbie. As she approached, she saw them sitting across a small table from each other, playing chess. Their laughter spiraled up into the lazy day. Garrett and Abbie? Why wasn't Abbie in church? And why were they playing chess together?

She mounted the steps. "Hey you guys. What a surprise." She smiled to mask her questions.

They both looked up, as if pulled away from intense concentration.

"Hi, Leah." Abbie grinned at her. "Garrett is soundly beating me. I think you need to have a talk with him."

"Not me." Leah shifted her weight. "Didn't know you guys liked chess." Didn't know they liked each other enough to play chess. She hoped for an explanation, not that they owed her one. It was just so . . . weird.

True, they seemed to have a magical connection at dinner the other night.

"I thought it was a great morning to sit out here and play chess, so I took a chance that Abbie was available and willing to get beat."

Garrett's face was less sullen than usual. His smile made him handsome in a boyish way.

"Temperature's just right," he said. "It won't stay that way for long." He still eyed the chessboard, a piece in one hand. He thumped it onto the board with a grin of triumph. "Ha! Gotcha."

"Oh, no!" Abbie fell back against the chair. "I'd say you can join as a spectator, Leah, but I think we're done. I've lost. For now, anyway." She narrowed her eyes at Garrett. "I'll get you later."

"That's okay," Leah said. "I'm hungry. Enjoy your game." She went inside, still wondering. Abbie and Garrett? Were they only friends? It would surprise her if it were more than that since Garrett was far from having any kind of faith. Like Leah, Abbie was holding out for a likeminded man.

Leah cooked a grilled cheese sandwich and reheated the vegetable soup she'd made a couple of days earlier. The scene on the porch still gnawed at her, but why? She placed her meal on the table and stared into her soup bowl, lost in the question. She was feeling. . . left out. As if Abbie, her best friend, had taken sides with Garrett and Leah had been pushed aside.

How ridiculous. They were simply playing chess. Why was she making an issue of this? She didn't understand what was going on, either inside herself or between them. As soon as she did, she'd feel better, right? She'd ask Abbie later and it would all be clear. But the connection she'd seen between them also sparked a wave of longing.

It had been years since she'd felt that with someone. Was that why she was so hungry for Nathan's company? Partly, though she couldn't deny her attraction to him. The way she felt comfortable with him, even after so many years apart. She was thankful for their renewed friendship, even if nothing else came of it. But she dearly hoped it would. Long distance or not.

Leah cleaned her dishes, but her mind was far away, embroiled in Nathan, in Garrett and Abbie, and weighing the wonder of Todd's message. What a jumble of emotions. Was it that time of the month? Had she slept poorly?

Garrett was right about one thing. It was a gorgeous day with a spotless blue sky and leaves tinged in orange. She returned to the porch, where Garrett was folding the chess board and Abbie stood, preparing to leave.

"Going for a walk, guys. See ya soon." She gave them a wave.

Abbie's face showed concern. "I'll call you later."

"I'm free all evening."

They'd clear the air. More exercise would help her untangle her wad of thoughts and troubling emotions. One bedrock of her disquiet was her relationship with Garrett. He'd landed on her doorstep—literally—a month earlier. Though they'd never been close as kids, due to a three-year age gap and the fact that he'd never included her in anything, their current living arrangement might yield a chance for them to become closer.

But his presence inconvenienced her. He'd upended her quiet, controlled existence. When she returned home from work each day, instead of anticipating a calm evening alone with Theo and her books and instruments, she was aware of his presence in the house, and her stomach tightened. Her comfort was gone. He'd invaded her peaceful nest.

Did she subconsciously believe he'd stay indefinitely if she made things too comfortable for him? She'd been blaming him for his snarky, negative attitude, but she had her own to deal with. Maybe he felt more relaxed with Abbie because Abbie didn't judge him or pressure him to get a job. Of course, he needed to contribute somehow, but if he could do that without working, who was she to nag him? He was her brother. An adult. He could do what he wanted to but had to live in fairness and consideration with her. That was his sole responsibility.

Leah sucked in a breath of cool air as she approached downtown. It felt good to walk with no particular purpose. What felt less good was realizing her crummy outlook. "I'm so messed up," she said aloud. Several of her attitudes needed revising. She pressed her lips together. She'd have to talk to Garrett.

Her steps took her down Swanson Street, connecting Summit and Warren. There, the boutiques were just opening their doors on the Sunday morning schedule. The mood remained calm, sleepy. She turned left on Warren and faced Market Street, where Seasons dominated the corner. It reminded Leah of an elegant epoch when people dressed up and went to Seasons for the Friday night show. She didn't envy Nathan in the decision he had to make, though she fervently wished he'd change his mind. She couldn't picture him leaving his life in Philly to move back and run Seasons. Yet, it would be a shame to see it reduced to rubble, replaced by a strip mall or block of condos. Maybe he'd find the likeminded buyer he sought, someone who'd update it to its former glory and provide the shot of modern adrenaline it so needed.

Leah retraced her steps and returned to a quiet house. Theo snoozed on a sunlit armchair in the living room. A faint noise from Garrett's computer floated from his room. She dreaded her conversation with him but couldn't bear to continue with the way things were. She understood *her* part in their silent feud. Not a feud, really, but it could be better.

She took her phone and returned to the front porch, chillier than a while ago. She slouched onto the couch. "Hey, Abbie. Is this a good time to talk?"

"Yeah, sure. I was about to call you. Are you having a good day? How was church?"

"Church was really good. I know I haven't said that in a while, but I think there's a change brewing. And a change in me too."

"Oh?"

"Yeah. I realized I was being critical, instead of being there to serve. To be part of the family of Christ. His living temple."

"Wow. Well." Abbie's voice was low, breathless.

"It was cool. I felt convicted about my attitude." She paused. Swallowed. "So, is something going on between you and Garrett? Can I be nosy for a minute?"

Abbie laughed. "Leah, you're my best friend. You can be nosy anytime you want. There's nothing going on per se. . ."

Leah's scalp prickled. "But there might be?"

"No, we're just friends. But he seems, I dunno, relaxed with me and even asked some questions about my faith."

"Really? That's great. How did that come up?" Leah pulled her knees up under her chin.

"He asked about church. I guess when he was a kid, he went to the same one I do, right?"

"Yes, we all did as a family. He stopped going in junior high, then left his faith. If he even had any. Not sure about that."

"So, I told him a little about what church was like now but made sure to say that faith wasn't about church, but about a daily relationship with the God who loves us."

"Way to go, Abbie. What did he say?" He'd never asked Leah those questions, but the fact that he'd asked Abbie filled her with elation.

"He didn't respond to that, but it seemed like he was thinking about it. We'll see."

"I'm so glad. He doesn't ask me any questions about it. I thought he was closed."

"Sometimes it's easier for people to talk with a friend than a family member about spiritual subjects. They think their family member will harass them about it. Not that you would. It's harder with relatives."

"I hope I wouldn't harass him, but I probably would," Leah said glumly. "I haven't been very user-friendly since he arrived. I guess I was annoyed that he moved back in. Another thing God convicted me about today." She let out a heavy sigh. "Growth is good but hurts sometimes."

Abbie made a sound of agreement in her throat. "Rest assured, I have days like that too."

The conversation drifted to other topics. Leah never had trouble talking to Abbie about everything on her mind. Or almost. "Abbs, I didn't tell you. I had coffee with Nathan Chisholm yesterday. He was in town this weekend but he's probably on his way back home now."

"He's such a great guy. You're renewing your friendship?"

"Yeah, I hope so. We exchanged numbers at the funeral, then when he came back this weekend, we got together."

"And anything else?" Abbie's voice prompted Leah.

"I admit, I like him. A lot. But he doesn't live here. Not sure where that'll go."

"So? It's a start. I'm glad. You better keep me posted."

"I will," Leah promised, then quickly changed the topic. There was simply nothing further to say on the topic of Nathan Chisholm. She wouldn't divulge to Abbie Nathan's dilemma with Seasons since it was shared in confidence.

Abbie and Leah chatted for another twenty minutes. The wall of confusion between them, in Leah's mind, at any rate, had disappeared. Now she needed to talk to Garrett. At dinner.

"What's the occasion?" Garrett asked as they sat at the eat-in kitchen table. Between them sat a platter covered by a steaming roast chicken surrounded by baby carrots and sauteed sliced potatoes.

"It's Sunday dinner," Leah said lightly. "It's also a peace offering."

"Why?" His brows gathered. He shifted in his chair.

Leah crossed her arms on the edge of the table. "I don't think I've been very welcoming since you got here. I want to ask your forgiveness."

"You don't have to do that."

"Yes, I do." She swallowed. Before she lost her nerve, she'd spit out her confession. "Specifically, I've tried to act like your mother. I've been critical either verbally or in my thoughts. I've lived here alone so long, I started thinking it was *my* house and you were invading my privacy. So yes, I need to ask your forgiveness. None of those things is true. It's your house too."

A half-smile crooked the corner of his mouth. "You *can* be a pain sometimes. I forgive you."

She grinned. "Thank you. I'll try to be a nicer sister. I need to think of it as we're roommates sharing our mom's house. We each do our thing, but we have a relationship too. I'm not your mother, I'm your sister. Equals."

"That sounds good to me."

"And as equals, there is another side I need to mention."

His frown returned.

"I need you to help more around the house and not act like a hotel guest. Act like you did in your own place in Pittsburgh. We're here together for I don't know how long. So, that means I can't foot the bills for everything, like utilities and food. I can't do all the housecleaning either. I'm not the maid, not the landlady. I'm your roommate. Okay?"

Garrett blinked back at her. "That's fair. I'm sorry too, Leah. Guess I was kind of a slouch. I didn't think I'd be here this long. I needed a place to escape my, uh, ordeal."

"You need a plan, even if you need to escape for a while. I don't know if you've been looking for a new job, working on your game, or whatever. I don't know what you do in your room every day. I'd like to know because I'm interested. But I'll stop nagging you and hinting that you should look for a job. As long as you can pay your part of the bills, it's not my business. Okay?"

"I don't mind telling you. I've been looking around town some. It's nice to be back, to tell you the truth. But nothing in IT is available here right now."

"Um. . . what about other types of jobs, you know, just to make some money in the meantime and get out with other people?"

He shrugged.

"They need help at Seasons in the kitchen," she offered. "And some other restaurants in town. The grocery store might need help with stocking. Any job is a worthy job, Garrett. For now, I mean. Employers need extra help at holidays."

He rolled his eyes. "Stocking shelves?" He paused. "Yeah, I guess you're right. Any money is better than none. At least I don't have rent anymore on my place in Pittsburgh. That'll help."

"You don't plan to go back?"

"Don't know yet. For now, I'm here. Maybe after the New Year."

"The New Year?" Leah's voice trailed off. *Remember, Leah, it's his house too. He's your roommate, not your problem.*

She looked up at him and forced a smile. "Okay. Be a good roommate, and you can stay. Meanwhile, help yourself to some chicken."

Nathan rinsed his breakfast dishes and put them into the dishwasher. Andy's dishwasher. No, *his* dishwasher. He'd arrived the day before with a suitcase of winter clothes. His boss had surprised him by complying with his request to work remotely until the New Year. Maybe he'd imagined Nathan would have to quit otherwise, in the face of his sudden task of disposing of Seasons. Nathan was grateful to still have his job and be on site in Brenner Falls to untangle the mess Uncle Andy had left him.

He'd wasted no time putting the plastic trash bin to good use with all of Uncle Andy's old magazines, expired coupons, worn-out cookware, and all the other clutter he spotted in every room. Even if his brain told him to get to work on Seasons first, he had to organize the little house if he wanted to be able to think straight. His aim was to declutter as well as better suit it to his tastes, since it would be home for several months. Call it a compulsion, but he felt calmer and more in control of his new reality once he'd neatly arranged his clothes in Andy's dresser and his own sheets were on the bed. He'd begun stuffing Andy's clothes, coats, shoes, and other personal items into garbage bags to take to charity later. Doing so triggered a fresh wave of grief, but he stuffed it down. There was simply too much to do, and he had to stay focused.

During the week, Carley hadn't called with any new prospective buyers. The more time that went by for those who had shown interest, the more likely they'd be to find something else. He was antsy for a visit and an offer. Of course, he was rushing things. He knew in his head selling a business took time, possibly years. He'd have to accept that as a possibility and have plan B in his back pocket.

Leah. The decision to stay in the Falls, at Ben's inspiration, had happened so fast, he hadn't let her know. He pulled out his phone to text her. *Hi Leah, guess what? More surprises from your old friend. The weekend trips weren't cutting it to handle everything, so I'm here until the New Year working remotely. I'm living at Andy's. Hope to see you.* He hesitated. Erased that last line. *If you have time, want to take a walk tomorrow?* The next day was Saturday, so she might be available. It likely wasn't a great idea to call her the moment he set foot back in the Falls. She might take it exactly how he felt. . . that he was interested in her. He couldn't stop himself because even after only a week, he missed her. He clicked *send.*

His gaze flitted around the cozy, sunlit kitchen. Eventually, he'd replace the outdated curtains and repaint the walls. Wouldn't take too much to make this little house an adorable first home for a newlywed couple. While he was there, he could do small cosmetic improvements and repairs on the house. That and keep up with his full-time job and manage or sell Seasons. Nathan shook his head as a sarcastic *huh* slipped out. Maybe occasionally, he'd also manage enough time to sleep.

His cell phone rang. Likely his mom, to check on how he was settling in. Of course, she'd been pleased he was staying in Brenner Falls until the New Year. Less pleased that he wasn't planning to stay permanently.

His mom's name wasn't displayed on his phone, nor was it anyone he knew. "Hello?"

"Is this Nathan Chisholm?" An unfamiliar female voice asked. "This is Brenda Mosley from Mayor Faulkner's office."

Nathan stilled. The mayor? "Yes, it is. Good morning, Ms. Mosley. What can I do for you?"

"I understand you are the new owner of Seasons Dinner Theater. Is that correct?"

"Yes, I inherited it from my uncle, Andy Evans." Word got around.

"Mayor Faulkner would like to meet with you to talk about your plans for Seasons. He's involved in new city planning projects and wants to know what you have in mind so he can include that in his plans. Could you come in for a brief meeting sometime next week?"

"Uh, sure. I should tell you I don't know exactly what I'm going to do yet with Seasons. It's a little early for me to talk about that in detail."

"That's not a problem. He'd just like to meet you and discuss what his vision of the town is for the near future and learn more about your options for Seasons."

"I see. So, maybe his vision is something I can keep in mind while I research my options?"

"Exactly. Maybe think of it as a collaboration of sorts. Of course, he won't influence what you do, but he'd like to be in the loop."

"I understand. I'd be glad to meet with him." And hear more about Mayor Faulkner's ideas for Brenner Falls. Yes, that could be ideal timing to get solid information from a reputable source—no less than the top—about where the town was headed. Perfect. "I can come whenever it's convenient for him next week. I'm living in the Falls for the time being."

May as well not say too much.

"Wonderful. I'll let him know and I'll call you back to schedule an appointment."

Mayor Faulkner's vision for the town may go a long way to make up for the Season's lack of profitability. Maybe things were starting to work in his favor.

The following morning, Nathan waited on the corner of Lansbury Street, where Leah lived. He saw her approach, and despite the crushing pressures on him, a whoosh of joy and lightness filled his chest. For an hour, maybe two, he'd push everything aside and live in the moment.

Leah reached him. "Hi, Nathan. Welcome back. I'm glad you can stay for a couple months." A genuine smile lit up her face. Her long hair was pulled back in a ponytail, giving a full view of her creamy skin and sky-blue eyes. She wore a navy-blue hoodie and faded jeans with a hole in one knee.

"Me too. I needed more time on site, like I told you. But there are other advantages, like taking a walk with you." He grinned.

"Where do you want to go?"

"I was thinking of the river. Might be nice there this time of year." At her eager nod, he started walking and she fell into step beside him.

The temperatures almost touched seventy with a light breeze. They walked along a broad avenue lined on either side with ranch homes cradled by sweeping willows and white oak trees.

She shot him a sly glance as they approached the river. "Bet you miss the fishing," she said.

Their eyes met as a thousand memories infused his brain. "You remembered." He shook his head, the grin stuck to his face like paint. "You remembered and I forgot. Now that you mention it, I did miss it for a while when I went to college. I spent a lot of summers down here on Joe Sullivan's boat." Those summers catching catfish and flatheads. And tires and shoes. Under the merciless sun but laughing so hard it didn't matter to them. He took a breath, savoring the brief mental movie from the past. "Then I became an urban boy." Something deep and wordless grabbed at his chest. It spoke of loss, of confusion.

"No more thirty-pound flatheads? That doesn't tempt you at all, Urban Boy?" Her smile taunted him as they continued to walk.

Nathan laughed. "If I thought about it, I'd miss it. Miss *this*." He spread his hands in the air to indicate everything he'd run away from. The lure of stunning orange maple leaves in the fall. Fluffy green and red foothills on the horizon. The river valley whose beauty never failed to render him mute with awe. Had Brenner Falls gotten less toxic, or had he healed from it all? Become different, immuned?

"Maybe the urban thing is a phase." His words slipped out so quietly, he wondered if he were speaking to himself. Was it a phase? The closer they got to the river, the more he wondered.

As they walked another ten minutes, he plied Leah with questions about the church plant. Why had they decided to start one? How did it begin? What was the first service like? She answered his questions, but her tone became electrified with enthusiasm with each response.

"Last week something hit me." She tapped his arm. "It was after a sermon on how we all form a temple for God's glory. The temple in the Old Testament was so important they made a movable one for the trip across the desert. But *we're* that temple now. You and me. And all believers. Isn't that cool?" She was practically jumping.

"Yes. It's amazing." And how he'd missed that community or been unable to see it amidst a highly programmed weekly event involving two thousand people. No less a modern-day biblical temple, though.

The river came into view as sunlight glinted off the surface of gently flowing waves. Being near the river expanded his lungs and lifted his emotions beyond any cares he'd had that week. "Just as beautiful as ever. I'd forgotten."

"I walk here a lot when it's nice out. Lately, I've been walking in town and in my neighborhood." She chuckled. "I guess I do a lot of walking."

"That's good exercise. What else do you do for fun?"

"In the outside category, I love to kayak and hike. Sometimes bike."

He patted her shoulder. "That's how you stay so trim." And regal, and elegant. And adorable. Did those qualities go together? In Leah, they did.

"And in the inside category, I play my instruments and I like to read."

Nathan sighed. "I just go to the gym most days after work, unless it's crunch time, then I don't." At those times, he went home and crashed on the couch.

She tilted her head in sympathy then pointed ahead of them. "Here we are. There's the trail we used to take when we were processing our lives. Let's go there."

He laughed. "Is that what we were doing? I guess we were. Figuring out adolescence together. I was full of angst back then. I wanted badly to get out of Brenner Falls and I finally did." He shrugged. "Now, it doesn't seem so bad."

"It was circumstances but mostly, the way you viewed them."

"You think?" Nathan thought about it. "You may be right."

"You felt persecuted because of what people said about your dad, so you wanted to leave." She squinted at him, and a smile tugged her lips. "But you turned out okay."

"I'm glad you think so." Their eyes met and they were both smiling. Heat rose in his neck. He looked away in case she could see a pink flush inching up his cheeks.

They took the trail that snaked alongside a narrower section of the river. Though the Susquehanna was the longest river on the east coast, it had many personalities, lazy, wide, or rushing, depending on where it was.

A metallic bridge in the distance glinted in the sunlight. They walked in silence for a few minutes. "Want to sit there in our traditional spot?" He stretched out a hand toward a grassy bank between two clumps of low trees.

"Yes, absolutely. We spent hours here, didn't we?" She settled with a contented *ahh* onto the lush grass, and he plopped beside her. "It's a perfect day."

"Yes, it is."

They fell into silence, each likely lost in memories created long ago in that very place.

"How did you decide to come back until New Year's?" she asked. "You told me there was too much to do for weekends alone, so I get that part."

"Yeah. I was unrealistic about what it would take and thought I needed to learn more about what I was dealing with. My friend Ben suggested asking at my company to work remotely for a while. Lots of people in my field are doing that now. So, surprisingly, they agreed. Now the challenge is to do my job like before while still having enough time to deal with Seasons."

"That doesn't sound easy. I already told you, but I'll say it again. I'm glad you're back."

The sunlight blazing from the river's surface glinted on her hair and sparkled in her eyes. Nathan swallowed, sensing dangerous ground. "Me too. Gives me a chance to hang out with my old friend Leah." He slipped an arm around her shoulder and gave her a squeeze. A friendship squeeze that she wouldn't misinterpret. He wished it could be more. Wished he could pull her into his arms and brush her soft lips with his.

The moment splintered when she said, "Have you given more thought to a Christmas program at Seasons?"

He couldn't stifle a groan. "Not a lot. Ben thinks I should do it, and I guess you do too. Am I right?" He could tell by the sudden intensity in her eyes.

"Listen, Nathan." She pressed a hand to his chest, likely unaware that it burned a brand into him. "I don't want to pressure you at all. I do think it'll be a good idea, and if you decide to do it, I'll help. I participated twice in shows at Christmas, so I remember a little bit of how it worked."

"Do you even have time for that?"

Leah frowned, as if realizing she'd overcommitted herself. "I'll make time. I do music at my church, but that doesn't take too much time."

His eyes narrowed with doubt. "You sure? You work fulltime too. And I'm not committed to this thing yet."

"I understand." Leah's sweet grin was almost enough to convince him, though his brain told him to run away from the idea as fast as he could.

"What do you remember from the times you were part of the program there?" he asked.

She linked her arms around her knees. "We did a lot of music. I played and sang a few songs. We had a small orchestra, mostly community people. There was a stage manager. What was her name. . . Olivia. That was it. Maybe we can reach out to her. Can't remember her last name. I didn't get to know her, really, but she seemed efficient. Another woman oversaw the actual music part and Olivia oversaw *her*. Did Andy leave you any phone numbers or information about Seasons?"

"I'll confess, I haven't had the courage to go through the office. I've been meeting with people here and there, but I have to tackle that eventually."

"I'll help you. Next Saturday? I'll come over and we'll go through everything together."

"That doesn't mean I'm doing the program, you know. But seeing what's there may help me sort out the options." *Keep it vague, don't commit, Nathan.*

"Whatever you decide, I'll support and help."

"Thanks, Leah." He bestowed a grateful smile. Was he ready to jump into this crazy idea, just to spend more time with her?

She returned his smile and bumped his shoulder with hers. "Of course. What are friends for?"

Chapter Seven

"*Your love, your love, it's so good to me. . .*" Josiah, a high school guy on the worship team, strummed the chorus of the new song he'd just taught the tiny congregation.

With her flute poised, Leah waited to come in at the instrumental bridge. She watched the congregation, the upturned faces of people worshipping, as tears slipped out, as hands were raised. Her own eyes stung, and her throat tightened. Was God waking up her passive heart? All week she'd pondered the message of God's living temple. Here they were, his temple, in jeans, in sweatpants, with green curls, tattooed, covered with wriggling infants, or topped with white hair. They were all part of a living temple. An imperfect but precious one.

As she played, she listened carefully to the lyrics. How many times in the previous year had she only gone through the motions? Her efforts were imperfect, but her heart was making baby steps.

The service ended with smiles, tissues, and a rumble of conversation as people stood. Todd's wife, Janelle, took center stage and waved at the congregation. "Can I have your attention for a moment?" Dark bangs framed her enthusiastic expression. "We'll be having a Christmas program and we plan to invite the whole town. We're renting the multipurpose hall near the Outdoor Adventure Depot. We want it to be an outreach to Brenner Falls, but also introduce people to our little church. Our theme will be *God's Good Gifts*, the main one, of course, being Jesus. So, we'll have a fifteen-minute meeting right after the service as a first step, then have a longer meeting Thursday evening at our house."

A Christmas program. That might be a way for Leah to exercise her newfound sincerity and offer her music abilities to the little church. From the heart, for a change.

During the meeting, Janelle jotted a list of volunteers for each of several sub-committees, including refreshments, music, decorations, and publicity. "Some of the teens are preparing skits and we have some amazing dancers among us as well." Janelle's eyes panned the small group. "I appreciate your excitement and commitment. We'll meet at our house Thursday evening at seven. We'll have dessert together then do some serious planning."

Leah left the church and walked to her car, buttoning her wool cardigan almost to her neck. Temperatures had dropped overnight but the memory of her walk with Nathan the previous day flooded her with giddy warmth. Their walks by the river would be cut short by the cold, but their friendship had been reestablished. Her winter would be less dreary by far.

During the church meeting, she'd volunteered to head up music for the Christmas program. Hopefully, she hadn't bitten off too much, but music was the primary way she could promote her little church. She'd have help from Josiah and other members who'd volunteered for the music team. She'd been glad to see Blair sign up to help with refreshments. That would help her get to know people better and feel more a part of the church.

Once at home, Leah pulled a bowl out of the kitchen cupboard to heat some soup she'd made the day before.

Garrett entered the kitchen and went to the fridge "I saw your car. Don't you usually walk to church?"

"I was running a little late," Leah said. "And it's getting cold. Any luck with the interviews you told me about?" Leah pulled open the door to the microwave and gave the soup a stir. She added thirty more seconds.

Garrett had scheduled a few interviews for programming. "Yeah, I have a phone interview tomorrow morning. They're not hiring yet but wanted to talk about my skills. The one from Friday says they're interested in talking to me, but they don't have an opening either. Maybe after the New Year."

"See, I told you people would want to snap you up as soon as they knew what you can do."

"Huh." Garrett pulled two slices of bread from a plastic bag. He crossed the kitchen to the fridge and pulled out cheese and deli ham. "I don't think I'm being *snapped up* yet, but they've got my resume. Maybe they'll call when they have a position open."

"Something'll turn up. Think you'll want to stay here in the Falls?"

He shrugged. "Maybe. I like it more than I thought I would. For one thing, it's a lot quieter than Pittsburgh."

And then there was Abbie. Something was developing there, but Leah didn't dare ask her brother too many questions. He'd clam up for sure, and they were barely beginning to get along well for the first time in their lives. The conversation they'd had the week before had apparently proven to him she wasn't his critic or his antagonist. She was trying, at least. He'd responded by helping around the house, once she'd created a division of labor, and pitching in with the bills from his savings.

"I filled out an application at the grocery store. I kind of liked your idea of stocking shelves."

Leah stopped and turned to him, a look of exaggerated surprise on her face. "Wow, Garrett, I'm proud of you!"

"They said they needed someone. It's an evening shift, so I can still look for jobs and work on my game during the day."

And get him out of the house. Perfect. Her day just got better. Even though their relationship was far more peaceful than it used to be, she missed her calm evenings alone with her books, instruments, and Theo.

After she finished lunch, put food away, and wiped down the counters, Leah called Abbie. "Ready to walk?" A few days earlier, she and Abbie had agreed to walk once during the weekend and at least twice during the week until it got too cold.

"Yes, let me get my hoodie and I'll meet you on your porch."

Leah waited on the porch for Abbie. Beyond the wooden overhang, a canopy of yellowing leaves glowed like a golden tent around her. Who knew things could be so much better with Garrett? He wasn't even complaining as much anymore, though she still sang whenever the mood struck her. And now, he might leave her a few evenings alone per week. Her own involvement with music would intensify, given the looming date of the church Christmas production. She didn't do music halfway. She'd do the best she possibly could, and that would require time. At least some of her newly quiet evenings would be filled with practice sessions.

"Hey girl. How are you doing?" Abbie's presence pulled Leah from her reverie. Her thick dark hair hung in a ponytail under a baseball cap. She wore her favorite ratty canvas high top sneakers and a thick college sweatshirt. "You looked intense in thought."

Leah laughed. "I was. You startled me. This morning at church they announced a Christmas program and of course, I signed up to help with music. Well, to *head up* the music. I'm looking at a lot of evening rehearsals between now and then." The two of them left the porch and walked side by side down Lansbury Street to complete two loops through the neighborhood.

"I think it's a great idea." Abbie kept up a brisk walk next to Leah. "People can learn about the church. And at Christmas, people who aren't thinking about God or Jesus are more likely to be open. My church is doing something too, but I'm not sure what."

Leah chuckled. "Sounds weird to hear you say *my church*. It used to be mine too."

"I saw Nathan Chisholm there this morning. Do you know he's here until New Year's?"

A tingle and a smile began at the mention of Nathan's name. "Oh, Abbs, I forgot to tell you. He texted me Friday and told me he'd moved back, so we went for a walk yesterday."

Abbie's dark brows gathered. "And you didn't tell me? Leah, I'm your best friend."

"I'm sorry, Abbie. I was going to tell you today. So, I guess since you talked to him, you must know he inherited Seasons."

"I didn't know before church today. He said he's working remotely and living in his Uncle Andy's house." Abbie was still staring at Leah. "The other day you said you liked him. Do you think it goes both ways?"

Heat flooded Leah's face as they started walking again. "I don't know. Might be merely renewing friendship for him. But he's doing a good job keeping in touch." Maybe that meant something.

Abbie laughed. "Your secret's safe with me. He *did* look awfully good. All grown up and sophisticated with his stylish clothes and all. And he's always been such a sweet guy, and thoughtful, polite, honest, not to mention good-looking. I applaud your choice."

"Oh, stop. It's not my choice. I'm glad he'll be around for a while. But he lives in Philly."

"But he's here *now*." Abbie waggled her eyebrows and nudged Leah with her elbow. "Maybe one day, he'll come back to stay. I wouldn't want you to go to Philly, though."

"Whoa, we're jumping ahead a bit fast. One day at a time, okay?" Leah pulled her mittens from her pockets. "Time for these." And time to change the subject. "Did I tell you about the program at church?"

"Yeah, just about five minutes ago." Abbie let out an annoying giggle.

Leah smiled.

"I think you're changing the subject, but that's fine. We have months to talk about Nathan Chisholm."

Only if something promising happened, which was no guarantee.

"The church music program sounds right up your alley," Abbie said. "What are you planning?"

"I don't know yet. I have four or five people on my committee. I'll have to choose music according to the theme."

"Which is. . .?"

"They're calling it, *God's Good Gifts*. Shouldn't be too hard to find good Christmas music to go along that."

"Sounds great. Perfect, in fact." Abbie grew silent for a moment. "Good gifts. There won't be enough time to talk about all of those. I'll come. Maybe Garrett'll come too."

"Good luck with that. I invited him to church a few times then gave up. But you're working your magic on him, so maybe he'll come."

Abbie grinned. "Not *my* magic. We haven't talked much lately about spiritual things, but he's softening in some ways. Anything good that's happening isn't because of me."

"He's easier to live with, I can tell you that. I told you about that talk we had. He was surprised to hear me apologize." Leah cringed when she remembered how judgmental she'd been. "I was so critical and intolerant of him. I thought *he* was the irritating heathen and all the while I was the one."

"I don't think you're irritating. You've made efforts and it shows. You seem more content."

"I am. Outside of work, life is better."

"Any chance of finding something else? A different job?"

Leah shrugged. "I don't know what I'm qualified for."

"You have a college degree, so you can do a lot of things. People will train you. Just find something you think you'd like."

"That's the problem. No one will hire me to sing and play the violin. I'm not good enough for the philharmonic."

Abbie laughed. "You're very good, but the philharmonic would be tons of pressure and require you to travel everywhere. You wouldn't like it for long."

"I remember the day I finally accepted the hard reality that I couldn't make a living doing music. It was my junior year of college. The music field is so competitive. My mom was overjoyed with my disappointing discovery, because she was afraid I'd end up destitute. A starving musician. Anyway, my job is good enough. Some people don't have jobs at all. At least I have benefits."

"Oh, there you go again." Abbie shook her head. "Good enough. I should call you Miss Good Enough."

"What do you mean?"

"Let's sit on that bench. I'm thirsty." Abbie fell back onto a wooden bench near the sidewalk. She scraped her sneakers through a pile of leaves strewn under the bench and took a long swig of water.

Leah burned with curiosity and waited for Abbie to explain.

"You're at work eight hours a day. You don't really come alive until you get home and can play music or see your friends. You've told me that. Why do you think you have to settle for something only *good enough* when it comes to your career?"

Leah frowned. Abbie was right. Corporate work sucked her artist's soul dry. It felt like she died a little bit each day. "I don't know what would make me happier among jobs that I could actually get. I've kind of gotten used to just—"

"Just settling. You've done that for years now, Leah. Don't you think God wants you to have more? He promised an abundant life, after all."

"That's not really a guarantee for everyone. Jesus said he *wanted* us to have that, but not all of us will. All you have to do is look around you to see that."

Abbie gave an exasperated groan. "It starts with believing he can do it in his timing. And asking for it, of course. I'm not saying name it and claim it. I'm saying if you settle, you stop looking for it. If you believe God wants to give good gifts to his kids, you'll be more expectant."

"Hmm. I'll think about it." Good gifts. Her mind went back to the church Christmas program.

"I was thrilled to hear you like Nathan, because it means you're finally getting over Michael."

Leah's head whipped to face Abbie. "What? I've been over Michael for years."

Abbie lifted one eyebrow. "Really? Is that why you haven't dated anyone since then and spend every evening at home with your cat?"

"Who is there to date, Abbie? And Theo is actually an excellent boyfriend. He's very attentive, doesn't argue with me that much, and gives good hugs."

They both laughed.

"Yes, I know he tickles you with his whiskers and always admires your music."

"Not always." Leah chuckled.

"I think. . ." Abbie's voice softened, and she grew solemn. "I think you've forgotten how to dream."

Abbie's eyes looked sad as she spoke. Like she thought it was some kind of tragedy that Leah had stopped dreaming. Leah's throat tightened as she felt a small crack open inside her. Out of it leaked a trickle of longing.

"I'd like to see you with an outrageous dream that you'll ask God for." Abbie sat up straighter and lifted both eyebrows. "Do it and see what happens."

Leah smiled indulgently. She used to have dreams long ago. It was safer not to. Safer to be realistic. "Oh, Abbie. I love you. You can dream for me, okay?"

Abbie frowned and looked up at the trees. "Lord, please help her see." She threw Leah a sneaky smirk. "Maybe you'll marry Nathan Chisholm. *That's* what I'll dream for you."

Leah swatted Abbie's arm. "Let's go. Enough bench time."

They continued walking, but Abbie's words circled in Leah's mind. When had she stopped dreaming? When she was young, she'd had endless dreams, projects, lists.

She'd stopped dreaming when Dad died. Part of her heart died with him, and the future bled out a few shades until it looked gray. Her hopes for a life of music died somewhere in her junior year of college. Then Michael came along during her senior year. She'd put her hope in him, in their future together. He had many of her dad's good qualities, his humor, his playful side. His commitment to follow God first. Until they both realized, he wasn't a thing like her dad. He was distant, moody, and convinced she'd learn sooner or later she'd made a mistake. So, he broke it off before she could.

After him, she knew she couldn't handle another gut-wrenching round of pain.

And her job? The best quality of her job was that it was better than nothing. She knew that wasn't saying much. But at least there was no drama. It coated her life with a predictable sameness that she both loved and hated. As Abbie had said, Leah put in her hours *then* began her life.

Maybe Abbie was right, and Leah was settling for far less than she was meant to have.

ಋ ಋ ಋ

Nathan was almost six feet tall, but he felt small behind the massive wooden desk shining under the fluorescent lights of Mayor Faulkner's office. Brenda Moseley brought them glasses of water. The smooth chill of the glass against his hand helped settle his agitation. The meeting could be a blessing. Or a trap.

Mayor Dennis Faulkner's full head of black hair was streaked with gray and combed back in a way that reminded Nathan of a mafia boss. He hoped the resemblance stopped there. Nathan had expected the man to be in a suit, but he wore a long-sleeve gray polo shirt. Despite Nathan's mental Godfather image, the man's casual disposition and friendliness put him at ease right away. He'd even told Nathan to call him *Dennis*.

"So, in the three years that I've been mayor, the town population has grown about fifteen percent."

"What do you think accounts for that impressive growth?" Nathan asked, though he knew at least some of the reasons.

"The river is a big draw. People from the nearby cities, Philly, Reading, even up in Jersey, like coming here for the rolling hills and river sports. You grew up here, Nathan, but it's not the same place. You get what I'm saying?"

"I've noticed it's more progressive." That must have been a good response because Mayor Faulkner almost preened.

"That was a deliberate strategy. There was already a good quality of life here, but it's small-town. Not that there's anything wrong with that, don't get me wrong. I'm not trying to make it into a theme park here. But we have a lot to offer and right away I saw the potential."

His dark eyes were lit with energy and his voice rang with animation. His hands splayed as he emphasized certain words. "What I really want to see here is an artful blend of trendy innovation with valued traditions. Some of our downtown buildings are from the late eighteen hundreds, and others are from the early part of the last century. Lots of the homes are Craftsmans and mid-century, which have timeless popularity. We have charm, we're not cookie-cutter. People love those traditions. Traditions in architecture and in events throughout the year. Stuff we're known for. But there's room for modern spaces people love. You get what I'm saying?"

Nathan nodded again and suddenly understood where the conversation was going. Tradition. Seasons. He braced himself. "Yes, the modern alongside the traditional." Or maybe he got it wrong. Maybe the discussion was about to pave the way for a different type of restaurant to replace Seasons. More modern. Or even a condo complex, as a modern space to accommodate the newcomers. He waited.

"Exactly. So, I'd love to hear some of your ideas about Seasons. Of course, it's a fixture in Brenner Falls. A landmark."

Hmm. The landmark argument again. "A tired one," Nathan ventured, noting the mayor's face. It revealed nothing. Now it was Mayor Faulkner waiting for Nathan's vision of Seasons. A vision he wouldn't want to know.

Nathan took a breath. "I'm aware that Seasons is a traditional structure in Brenner Falls, one people are used to. They don't necessarily frequent the place, but certainly know it. My uncle poured his heart and life into it." Hopefully, the mayor would understand that warm feelings around tradition didn't meet the bottom line of a restaurant and numerous salaries.

Tread carefully, Nathan. "I've inherited it, but never expected to." He added a smile.

The mayor grinned and nodded energetically in response, possibly understanding that Nathan was *glad* to be the new owner of Seasons.

Nathan swallowed. "I mentioned earlier that I live in the Philadelphia area and have a job there. I'm here temporarily to, uh, to investigate options."

"You plan to sell it?" The question was abrupt but fair.

"Yes, probably. The question is to whom."

The mayor's cheerful grin dropped at the corners. Nathan thought he saw concern in the man's eyes.

"I'd love to hear some of your ideas. Options," Mayor Faulkner said.

A new thought crossed Nathan's mind. There would be zoning regulations that might dictate who he could sell to. Might rule out a block of condos anyway. He wanted to sell it, but not necessarily for an apartment block. "Of course, there are developers who'll want to build a shopping complex or condos on the site."

"But of course, you wouldn't sell to *them,*" Mayor Faulkner blurted. His eyes searched Nathan's and his voice dropped. "Would you?"

"That's only one option. I don't know what the zoning is. I take it that wouldn't work with your vision of Brenner Falls."

Mayor Faulkner leaned back in his chair and steepled his fingers. "I'm sure we'll need more housing and shopping areas, but I envision those more on the outskirts of town, not in the central square. Pretty sure it's not zoned for that anyway, but it can be changed, of course. The more important point is that the location of Seasons is right downtown. Its legacy fits with the historic flavor of the town, don't you think?"

"Possibly." Nathan didn't have as much emotion tied into historic buildings as a lot of people, but Seasons was different. *His* history was tied up in it. And though a developer might be the most lucrative buyer, selling Seasons for an apartment or mall would pull out part of his heart. He couldn't do that to Uncle Andy. "I think the best buyer would be someone who'd keep the Seasons' purpose the same, but with updates in both the building itself and the entertainment it offers."

"Yes!" Mayor Faulkner slapped the desk and Nathan jumped. "Is there such a buyer?"

"There might be. I've had three parties who've shown interest. One of them has two or more dinner theatres already. I don't know much about them. He'd likely be interested in keeping it the same. He'd be my top choice but hasn't come to see it yet."

"Ideal. You can sell it to *him*." The man paused. "Or do you prefer to keep it and do those improvements yourself?"

Nathan shook his head. "I don't think I'm cut out to run it myself. I did work in the restaurant for a few summers when I was in college. But I'm not planning to move here."

"You're here now so you can sell it to the buyer you mentioned? But you said you're staying here."

"I'm here temporarily. I need to. . . If Seasons shows a profit, the buyer will be more interested. It's not that profitable currently, so it'll be a tough sell. It's been suggested that a Christmas program of some kind could generate a spike in revenue—"

"Marvelous idea!" Mayor Faulkner almost jumped in his chair. "You can count on all the support you need from my office. We'll come alongside and promote it if you need help with that."

"Oh, that's very kind." And he was very *stupid* for talking about it. Now he *had* to do it. "I'm not sure about it yet. There's a lot to consider and I don't have a background in that kind of thing." Not to mention the expense of putting a Christmas program together. He'd likely end up spending a wad of cash on a dog and pony show, then break even with the sale. Net result, a total waste of his time.

But Andy would have been pleased, along with Mayor Faulkner and tradition-loving residents like the Suttons.

"Of course, it would be *perfect*," the mayor crooned. "I mentioned our traditional events in town, remember? But the Seasons Christmas program used to be one that people looked forward to all year. Of course, there were other types of productions that your uncle put on at other times, but the Christmas show was special. Along with events like the tree-lighting and the Christmas market. Remember when we used to have those?"

"You don't have them anymore?"

"Yes, they've been revived. We didn't have them for a few years, but we started again last year. So, your Christmas program at Seasons will fit right in with the Christmas spirit. You get what I'm saying?"

Nathan could only offer an agreeable smile. He'd done exactly what he hadn't wanted to do. He'd painted himself into a corner.

Chapter Eight

Nathan peered into a wide wooden bin filled with eggplants. He selected a large, firm one without blemishes and added a head of cauliflower. The farmer's market hummed with conversations and mid-week shoppers. He'd been elated to learn that a bi-weekly market existed in the town park on the west side of Brenner Falls. He planned on being a regular customer during his stay in the Falls, even though temperatures would soon tumble.

Since returning to the town the previous week, he'd gotten back into the habit of cooking proper meals for himself and found renewed joy in his nearly forgotten practice. The previous evening, he'd cooked thick bone-in pork chops with a thyme-balsamic glaze, curried roasted carrots, and garlic mashed potatoes. Seemed like too elegant an effort for only himself, but the enjoyment of eating the finished meal equaled the therapy of preparing it. One day, he'd have friends he could invite. Or even cook for a family of his own.

That thought triggered a brief flash of longing in his chest, a wave that surprised and shook him. Then, as if to torment him further, a family of four came into his line of vision. They perused a flower stand together. He watched them for a moment as the mother bent over to show her toddler a bouquet of carnations. The little guy swept tiny fingers across the curly surface and giggled while an older child poked at the grainy center of a giant sunflower. The father took the bouquet, paid for it, and presented it to his wife.

A scene that could take his mind and heart to places of loss and solitude. No. Focus. He had produce to buy. And a restaurant to sell. Nathan sighed. His life had become complex. Despite his newfound complications, the peaceful vibe of Brenner Falls lapped against him like a calm lake. Its small-town comforts like the farmer's market and the revered traditional buildings. . . A chuckle escaped his throat. He knew he wasn't immune to the charms of small-town history. But he never thought he'd be held hostage by them.

Okay, onions next. He selected a few white ones to add to his collection. Oh, and fresh basil. And parsley. The dried thyme he'd used on the pork chops was okay, but a fresh sprig would have added some zing. If it weren't winter, he could plant some in the backyard.

Except that he wasn't staying. A minor detail he'd be wise to remember.

His phone buzzed in his pocket with a text message. He put in his code to look in case it was from work. It was. A colleague had texted. *Hiya Nathan. Hope remote is working out. Don't know if you heard, but the company is entering negotiations for a possible merger or buyout for early spring. Don't know which one. Not sure what it means for all of us, but I wanted to give you a heads up. Don't have too much fun out there.*

Fun? Creating a holiday event without enough time was stressful, not fun. But seeing Leah again was fun. An odd combination, but there he was. The news he'd just received should have ruffled him, but oddly, it didn't. A lot could happen before next spring. And he didn't have enough room in his brain to handle worries about a possible layoff on top of everything else he was juggling. His colleagues, his boss, his work environment, it all seemed so distant to him. He struggled to even picture it in his mind.

The previous evening, he'd found a recipe for cauliflower crusted pizza topped with white sauce and roasted eggplant. He couldn't wait to make it, maybe over the weekend. Once he got home, he had some investigating to do in Uncle Andy's office, a task he dreaded. He'd consciously detoured the messy little room a half dozen times already. But since he'd obligated himself to putting on a Christmas pageant, he'd better dig in. Or should he wait for Leah? She'd promised to help him on Saturday. Together they could brave the mess. Her company could make even that task enjoyable.

With a stab of guilt, he remembered he *also* had a full-time job he'd agreed to do remotely. He'd been squeezing in an hour here, a couple hours there. He'd need to put in some hours that afternoon too, but it wasn't nearly as appealing as puttering around the farmer's market on a golden, cloudless day.

"Nathan, here we are again."

He turned. Leah. An unreasonable flush of pleasure coursed through him. He grinned at her. "Yes, we are. What a pleasant surprise." He observed her canvas bag with a few ears of corn sticking out of the top. "Did you take a day off today?"

At his question, he thought he detected a shadow creep into her eyes, though her smile remained.

"Sort of. I had a dentist appointment this morning and my boss told me I could take the rest of the day off. I'd thought about taking it anyway as a vacation-slash-mental health day, but they offered it."

"They sound very generous."

She let out a staccato laugh. "Believe me, they're not. I have to almost beg for a cost-of-living increase each year at my review. This makes me suspicious, but it *has* been slow lately. It comes and goes."

Nathan listened attentively as she spoke but couldn't help staring at the spark of sunlight glinting off her gold-streaked light brown hair, with long silver earrings gleaming through. She wore it stylishly layered to fall in curls around her shoulders. It was probably soft and full, but he didn't dare test his theory.

"Well, then. You should fully enjoy the day off if they're giving you one," he said. "They might not even dock you for leave."

Leah shrugged. "With them, one never knows." She paused. "Oh, look, there's Blair, from church. You probably don't know her. She's a clothing designer and sells her work here once in a while." Nathan followed her pointed finger and saw a blond woman talking to a customer.

"I'd introduce you, but hopefully, she's making a sale."

"That sounds like a hard line of work. About like you trying to make a career out of music."

Leah's gaze returned to her friend Blair maybe fifty yards away. "I think she has a day job too. Like many of us artists." She grinned at him then cast a pointed glance to his plastic bag of veggies. "And what is that *you* have there, veggieman?"

"I'll have you know," he declared in a theatrical tone. "I'm making a cauliflower crusted pizza with roasted eggplant. *And* a garlic white sauce."

Leah's eyes widened. "Wow, I think my stomach just let out a growl. You probably didn't hear it. I'm *much* too ladylike to growl in public." They both laughed. "But it sounds awesome. I didn't know you were a chef." They meandered through clusters of shoppers.

"It's kind of a hobby for me. I have a high-pressure job, and it's therapeutic to get in the kitchen and mess with food. Though until I came here, I found I was too tired to do it on most days."

"So, no therapy until you came back to the Falls."

"I'm still trying to get myself organized," he said. "It's like I've been deposited into a different world, and I have all these new tasks to do. I'm still trying to figure it all out." Felt good to verbalize his feelings, his confusion to another person, especially Leah.

The previous day at the mayor's office, he'd slipped haplessly into a commitment he didn't want, planning a Christmas extravaganza at Seasons. He didn't have that concern with Leah, even if she wasn't neutral on the topic of Seasons. "I've, uh, sort of promised Mayor Faulkner I'd do the Christmas show. Everyone's thinking of the old days. All along, I was against the idea, but then I go blurting this out to the mayor." He shook his head, still angry at himself. "He was so hyped about it, I feel like I need to follow through."

Leah scrunched her shoulders then dropped them with a sigh. "I know you only came to tie up loose ends and now you're getting all this pressure to do a show. I want to help, not pressure. But it might be fun to do it, and you wouldn't have to do it alone. When

Andy was alive, he had Olivia run the theater part of things. Remember, I mentioned her the other day when we were walking. Andy didn't do all of it himself, and you shouldn't either."

She had a point. He felt the weight lift ever so slightly. "That's true. The other day I told you I'd been avoiding going into Uncle Andy's office, but I should. There are probably notes to guide me and maybe some names of people I can contact. Maybe I can delegate the planning and then just oversee it."

"Does the mayor know you plan to sell it?" Leah stopped to inspect some vine tomatoes. She selected a cluster of five. She put them into a plastic bag and paid for them.

"I mentioned the possibility. I told him the same thing I told you. The guy who wants to keep it as a dinner theater wants to see a profit first. If I can show the potential of profit, he might buy it and keep it as a dinner theater. That's the strongest argument for me in favor of doing this program. That way it's a win for the community and hopefully leads to a sale." Might be wishful thinking.

Leah seemed to consider his words as they passed in front of a Mediterranean sandwich stand. Tantalizing aromas of kabobs and roasted garlic rose into the air.

"Last time I came to the farmer's market, there were only a few fruit and vegetable stands. Now, they have all this. It's like a mini festival." Nathan breathed in the aroma. "Smells wonderful." He looked at Leah. "Have you eaten lunch? My treat."

"No, I haven't. Thank you."

They stood in line behind two other customers at the food stand. Nathan had finished his shopping but was compelled to prolong his time with Leah. He bought them two gyro sandwiches, a small container of hummus, and a side of stuffed grape leaves. "Have you ever tried stuffed grape leaves? They're amazing," Nathan said as they walked away from the stand toward a picnic table. "I'm surprised to see them here in provincial Brenner Falls."

"They're really grape leaves? From a grapevine?" Leah's face showed a trace of apprehension.

"You'll have to try one and see what you think. They're more appetizing than they sound. They're real leaves but they've been marinated and filled with a rice mixture along with lemon, onions, and dill, then rolled up and cooked. Are you an adventurous eater?"

"I think I am. Though mostly I default to what's easy. Grilled cheese, soup, stuff like that. Maybe I can learn a thing or two from you."

She smiled at him, and a tingle spread through in his chest. "Okay, if you're game, I'll teach you." He pointed to an empty table under a tall gathering of pine trees. "Let's sit over there."

Nathan slid onto one side of the picnic table. His gaze panned the park-turned-farmer's market, remembering when it was only a sparse gathering of local growers. "Did all this change when the new mayor came along?" He gestured to the busy park.

"I'm not sure of the timing. It's been like this for about two years. I agree, it's an enormous improvement. I enjoy coming here but can usually only make it on Saturdays."

He had to admit, Mayor Faulkner's improvements were appealing. Now the market met twice weekly and displayed many other types of food, flowers, textiles, cooked meals, and even artisan breads. The addition of picnic tables encouraged residents to gather and order picnic takeout from local restaurants. Smart guy. Maybe his offer to help promote the Christmas show at Seasons wasn't an empty gesture. His support might make a vast difference in the turnout.

Nathan slid the grape leaves over to Leah. "I've made these before and they take a chunk of time, but I think they're worth it. Try one."

She bit into the small green roll. Her eyes widened and she smiled. "I like this. It's really good. I can taste the lemon. Okay, you have to show me how to make these too."

"You got it." It made his day to help Leah discover a new taste experience. Maybe she'd help him sample the cauliflower pizza too. He gave her one of the gyro sandwiches and set the hummus and flatbread between them.

"So, tell me more about the church plant you're involved in. Did they ask for volunteers to start the new church?"

"Yes. About that time, I'd been wondering if I could do anything bigger in my faith than sitting on the pew. My life was so comfortable. I started praying for something to challenge me. Not long after that, they announced a new daughter church on the other side of town. A core group of about twenty-five of us went to the new location, which is a storefront in a strip mall over by Outdoor Adventure Depot. I may have told you, I help with music."

"Perfect. Music is your thing, Leah. I remember you play the flute. And violin too?"

"Good memory. And voice and piano. I've kept those up, fortunately. I mostly do music for church and the occasional wedding."

"You're contributing in an important way to the new church. No one said it had to be paid work, right?"

"Yeah, that's true." Sadness slid across her face. "I never thought I'd only do music as a hobby or a ministry and do something I don't like as a job."

Nathan furrowed his forehead. "You don't have to stay in a job you don't like. And you can probably find a job you'd like that doesn't involve music. Isn't there something else you'd enjoy?"

"You sound like Abbie now."

"I've known Abbie for a while, though not well. You guys have been friends since forever."

"Yes. She tells me the same thing about a job. I don't know what else to do. But with both of you cheering me on, I guess I'd better think more about it."

"I'll cheer you on anytime."

"Thanks. I'll need it."

Her eyes connected with his. "I have a thought," he said. "Since you have the rest of the day off from work and you were going to come by this Saturday anyway, do you want to come now? We can tackle Andy's office together without any more delay."

"Great idea. I'll be your investigative partner. We'll figure out what Uncle Andy had in mind."

ॐ ॐ ॐ

"I don't think I've ever been inside the house," Leah said once they arrived at Andy's place. Didn't look like he spent much time out there. Other than a couple of worn-out rockers on one end, the porch was empty and swept clean. "Looks nice and neat. Probably because of you, right?"

"Andy was neat too, but not as much as I am. You remember a lot about me." Nathan unlocked the door. "I am a neat and tidy man." His smirk was full of humor. "In addition to being urban man and veggieman."

She laughed. "I need to stop giving you nicknames. Or else, find one that's perfect." She considered him. "Hmm. I'll have to think about that."

They entered the darkened house. She slipped out of her jacket and hung it over a chair.

"Want something to drink? Cold or hot?" he asked. "I mean, before I put you to work?"

"I'm ready to slog through the office with you. Are you making tea? I'll have some if you are."

"Coming right up." He disappeared into the kitchen just beyond the living room.

Leah slipped her hands into her pockets as her eyes brushed across the space. It looked comfortable in a worn but attractive way. Perched on a beige slip-covered couch sat four bright turquoise cushions. Matching curtains hung on small windows that flanked either side of a white brick fireplace. On one end of the mantle, two earthenware pots spilled trails of ivy, reflected in an antique mirror.

"Don't know how you had time to decorate the house along with everything else you're doing, but it looks nice," she said when he returned with two mugs.

He shrugged, looking sheepish. "Thanks. I didn't do much. I got rid of some of Andy's junk and bought a few pictures and matching stuff. I like things to look coordinated." He paused. "How'd you know I was the one who decorated?"

"Intuition. It seemed like something you'd do. I like the cushions. They add a nice touch." Said a lot about the man, and it was all good.

"Your intuition was correct. Thanks for noticing." He still held the mugs. "Follow me into the cave of despair. Only then will I give you your tea."

She giggled and followed him into a shadowy hall which led to a bright office. A large wooden desk sat bathed in light under a double hung window. Papers covered the surface, but a closer look revealed neat piles with labels on each one.

Nathan stood beside her and surveyed the surface of the desk. He set the mugs down. "This isn't the unholy mess I've been afraid of." He exchanged glances with her. "It makes sense now. If he wanted to pass the baton to me, he'd leave instructions."

Leah couldn't stop a grin. "Andy left you a treasure hunt. Let's see what's here." She pulled a chair beside the desk.

Nathan sat beside her and began to shuffle through the stacks. "Look at all this. This'll make things a lot easier."

"Look, Nathan. There's an envelope with your name on it."

He reached across the desk and took the envelope. He took a breath and opened it. His concerned eyes found hers. "I'll read it aloud."

"Are you sure? It's personal. Maybe you should read it yourself first."

He did. She watched his eyes skim back and forth as moisture gathered in them. A sad smile tugged at the corners of his lips. "I'll summarize. He told me how much he loved being my uncle and like a dad to me. Said it was the most rewarding role of his whole life." Nathan's voice broke. He sniffed and swiped tears with one wrist. "He says he knows I wasn't planning to run Seasons but in case I changed my mind, he wanted to make it easy for me." He kept reading silently. Tears rolled down his cheeks.

Pain radiated in Leah's throat as she watched him, and her chest filled with compassion and a depth of emotion she couldn't name. Her eyes burned as she waited in silence.

"I'll read this part if I can get through it. He says, *I hope Seasons and its purpose will carry on, whether you take the helm or someone else does. Just know that I believe in you, Nathan, and trust you to do the very best thing. It's out of my hands now. By the time you read this, I'll have forgotten all those pressures. And even the joy it brought me has been overshadowed by a much greater one.*"

When he looked up from the letter to Leah, they were both crying quiet tears. He swallowed. "I still have doubts about all this." He waved the letter in the air. "But this letter makes me want to give the program my best shot."

She found a tissue and handed him one and used another one to mop her face. "Shall we?" Her words, thin and full of emotion, creaked out.

Nathan dried his eyes an picked up one of the stacks. "This is what I need. It's a list of phone numbers. Olivia's is right on top. I vaguely remember her from the funeral. She introduced herself and expressed condolences. If I'd known then how much I'd need her, I'd have gotten to know her better."

"Want to call her now?"

He smiled and reached for his phone. He tapped Olivia's number.

"Hello, is this Olivia Stevens?" He put his phone on speaker so Leah could hear. "This is Nathan Chisholm calling. Andy's nephew."

"Oh, hi Nathan. How are you doing with the loss of your uncle? I'm so sorry."

Leah's toes tapped on the floor in nervous anticipation.

"Thank you. It's still hard, but with time will be easier. He's kept me busy, I guess you could say."

"Really? In what way?"

"Well, that's why I'm calling you. He left me Seasons in his will. I'm back in town for a few months to sort it all out."

"Oh, that's a big thing for you." Solemn surprise laced Olivia's voice.

"Yes, it is. So, in an effort to revive Seasons, I'd like to do a Christmas show, like we used to do every year in the past. I wonder if you'd consider helping with that just for Christmas." He waited.

"I'd like to hear more," she said after a long pause. "I think I may be interested in that. Just for Christmas."

Nathan shot Leah a jubilant expression. A flush of joy coursed through her.

"Yes, that's all I've projected for now. It should give Seasons a little boost and help me with the next step."

"Let's talk more about it," Olivia said. "Do you have a cast in mind?"

"You're the first person I'm talking to about it. I gotta tell you, I know nothing about putting on a dinner theater. I don't know if the previous cast was made up of locals or a traveling troupe, or what. But there is this list of names on Andy's desk, and it appears to be cast members for different programs over the last few years that shows were done."

"Good thing you have that list. That'll make our work much easier," Olivia said. "Many of the actors and musicians who were regulars had other jobs but enjoyed theater or music and it was a side thing for them. They received some payment, but they didn't live from that. That means many of them will still be in town."

Leah's heart pounded and she'd slid to the edge of her chair as she clung to every word of Nathan's conversation with Olivia. This was *very* good news.

"Oh, that's good," he said. "I know we only have a couple of months to pull it together, but we can do mostly well-known Christmas songs with cool décor and some dance numbers, whatever they have done in the past. Do you think that'll work?"

"Yes, I do. We can do a lot of the same pieces we did last time, because not only are Christmas tunes traditional and people would expect them, but the last time we had a Christmas show was at least three years ago. We'll need musicians, though. Do you have ideas for that?"

Nathan sent a pointed look to Leah. "Yeah, I might know someone." He winked. "Maybe some of the people on Andy's list are musicians. I haven't looked through the names yet. I don't yet know how the payment part will work. I'm thinking everyone would have to wait until after the show to be paid. Is that okay?"

"It'll work fine for me. In fact, I'll donate my time. Can't promise that for the others, but if it's a one-time show, I don't mind doing it. My youngest just went away to college, so I'm looking for something useful to do. I enjoyed working with Andy and I've missed it."

Nathan grinned. "You don't know what a blessing you are, Olivia. Picture me getting all this dropped into my lap."

Olivia laughed. "Yeah, I can imagine it must be a lot for you. One day, you're living your life in another city. The next, you're the owner of a struggling dinner theater. I'm sure you'll rise to the occasion."

"Without your help, I'd flounder rather than rise to anything. But thanks for understanding."

"You have a regular job there too, don't you?" she asked.

"I work in a marketing firm in Philadelphia. Right now, they're letting me work remotely. I'll need a lot of help here in the coming days."

"Well, you have mine. But you need an entire cast plus musicians. Let's meet as soon as possible. Text me a photo of that list. We can split it and call people and try to have a meeting this Saturday to see who's available. We have to get our cast first. Then I'll fill you in on what I know about the theater part. Keep your ear to the ground."

"Absolutely. We can meet at Seasons on Saturday. Let's make it a lunch meeting on me. Noon."

Before Leah's eyes, she saw Nathan's shoulders straighten as he dove into the situation that had intimidated him a few minutes earlier.

"Okay. I'll let everyone know and we'll see who we get," Olivia said.

"Thanks a million, Olivia. I'll text you the responses I get too. See you Saturday."

He disconnected and turned as he and Leah both leaped up from their chairs. They let out a whoop and fell into an embrace. Nathan's arms were warm around her and he swayed her side to side. It felt wonderful, like she could stay there forever.

He released her and for several seconds, their faces were only inches apart. She felt his breath and saw a line of afternoon whiskers close-up. Her pulse went wild. Nathan blinked and stepped back.

"Why am I celebrating, Leah?" he asked with a grin. "I didn't even want to do this." But he laughed and she joined him. "I feel like a hundred-pound weight has rolled off my chest. Of course, I still need to see it through, but having someone who knows the ropes is priceless."

"I told you I'd help too." Leah's heart still pounded from their physical closeness, and what seemed like an almost-kiss. She swallowed, her thoughts still spinning. "Apparently, there's a need for musicians."

"But you have the church program too. Won't that be too much?"

"I'll figure it out." She didn't know *how* she would, but she would.

Maybe God was giving him a hand after all. And she was part of the answer.

Chapter Nine

Leah's mind wandered from the figures on the computer screen in front of her. She'd pulled her attention back a dozen times from her uncharacteristic wool gathering. Usually, payroll made her want to doze off but that day, her thoughts were quite awake, though focused on a different topic. Her day with Nathan, from their chance encounter at the farmer's market to the jubilant and intimate moments in Andy's office. Pulled along on a cloud, she was helpless to slow down her emotions. She didn't know how he felt or why he so often pulled back from her. Maybe it was his way of gently letting her down, keeping her from getting hurt again. He must have seen her feelings for him and wanted to rein them in before they went too far. That prospect dropped lead weight into her pleasure, making it muddy.

He was so easy to talk to, she'd slipped back into their close friendship of adolescence. She'd even shared her deferred dreams with him. Abbie had pointed out, she'd forgotten how to dream, but against her better judgment, she allowed Nathan to reawaken them.

She glanced at the bottom of her computer screen, where the tiny clock seemed to advance slowly. It was almost time for a meeting with her boss, Bradley. They had meetings from time to time, but usually not on a Thursday. He'd emailed her that morning and asked for some time in the afternoon.

Her extension rang three minutes early.

"Leah, Bradley is ready for you now." The receptionist chirped into the phone. The woman always seemed to be in a cheerful mood. If it was real, Leah envied her that. Often, Leah was too, but when she wasn't, she faked it so she wouldn't be inconsistent with her portrayal of a joyful Christian.

"Thanks. I'll be right in."

She closed her document and, after a light knock on Bradley's office door, went in. "Hi, Bradley." She sat across the broad metallic desk from him and perched her notebook on her lap as she waited.

Instead of launching into a new project, he drew his chair toward the desk, a solicitous expression on his face. He folded his hands.

A sudden ribbon of dread snaked through Leah's gut.

His smile looked forced. "Leah, you may have noticed lately that there have been fewer projects for you to do as well as fewer events to plan, and even Cheryl doesn't need as much help as before."

A wave of understanding fell over her like a soiled curtain. She could predict what he would say next. Panic wrestled inside her along with something else she didn't immediately identify. Relief? Wait, she was about to hear terrible news.

"As a company, we're behind in our projections compared to last year. We have some competition, and with less traveling, recovering from Covid and all that, well, we're going to have to eliminate your position. I'm sorry, Leah."

Leah sat motionless for a moment, though her brain scrambled to reorganize, to absorb the implications of his statement. "When?" Her simple and quiet reply seemed to take him by surprise.

"At the end of the month. The thirty-first."

"I understand. Times are. . . hard."

Bradley pressed his lips into a line. "Thanks for taking it so well, Leah. Of course, I thought you would. Not to say it's good news. No one likes news like that, but I'm glad you're not crying or screaming or anything." His voice trailed off.

She offered a weak smile. "I don't usually cry or scream. Well, sometimes I cry, but in a different context." Yes, she'd cried plenty during the devastating losses of the last few years. If she could survive those, this would be bearable. It could always be worse.

"We'll give you a small severance and an extra month of health benefits. Make that two, to take you to the end of the calendar year."

"That's generous and kind of you. I appreciate it, Bradley."

He'd expected her to cry or rail, but that was far from her mind. She would have to regroup. That was for sure. Abbie had told her to dream. Maybe God was forcing her to do just that. But to be honest, survival was the first thing on her mind. Food, gasoline, heat.

"Do you have questions for me?" Bradley asked, still looking worried.

"Only one. Since my last day is Halloween, do I have permission to wear a costume that day?"

His open mouth froze in place for an instant before he burst into nervous laughter. "Of course. As long as it isn't indecent."

She forced a chuckle. "No Lady Godiva costume, you mean? No problem. Thanks for everything, Bradley. I know it's difficult, I mean with the company and in lots of places. We all feel it."

"You're very kind, Leah. Not everyone would be so understanding. We've had to cut four other positions, so you're not the only one." His shoulders lifted with a sigh. "It's never easy to lose good people. Of course, I'll give you a good reference for your next employer."

She rose and tucked her unused notebook under her arm. "Thank you, Bradley. Not sure yet who my next employer will be, but a reference is always a good thing."

"And not a hard one for us. You've been an excellent employee. Good luck, Leah."

Leah gave him a tight-lipped smile and walked back to her desk, not betraying any bad news on her face or in her posture to her fellow employees. She sat at her desk and remained motionless. *What am I going to do?* God was steering her in a new direction. He'd provide. Presumably. Time to exercise the faith she claimed to possess.

She wasn't good at unknowns nor at waiting. Well, no one was. She understood better what Garrett was going through. But he had more skills than she did. His were marketable, but even he could only find grocery store work stocking shelves in the evening. What were *her* options?

Abbie could help her brainstorm. Abbie. She quickly dialed her friend's phone, hoping she wasn't in a meeting with the mayor or another higher up in the town hall office.

"Mayor Faulkner's Office. Public Works. Abbie speaking."

"Abbie, it's Leah," she whispered.

"Hey, Leah. Is everything okay?"

"Sorry to bother you at work, but I have to ask you something. Have you been praying that I'd lose my soul-sucking job?"

Abbie's laughter rang out, then halted. "Wait, Leah, no. I haven't. Did you lose your job?"

"Yup. Just today."

"Oh, that's great news! I mean—I'm sorry, Leah." Her response degraded into a mumble.

Leah couldn't stifle a snicker. "Yes, I lost my job. I'm not feeling like it's great news, because now I don't have one. But since you knew I didn't love it, I thought you were praying for a forced transition. You know, so I'd seek my dream or whatever you called it."

"Well, you said it, not me. Yes, I wanted you to dream a little bigger, and your job was a kind of security blanket that I thought stood in your way. That's the only reason I said it was good news. I'm sorry. I shouldn't have said that."

"It's okay. But you need to help me brainstorm. I need income. Benefits."

"Yes, gladly. Over dinner? Your house?"

"Garrett won't be there. He's working."

"No, silly. Not for Garrett. For my best friend. For *you*."

Something soft unfurled inside Leah at Abbie's words. Tears stung her eyes. "Yes, come at six. I need your input." And a good Abbie hug.

"You'll have it. And I'll bring homemade apple crumble for dessert. And pumpkin spice decaf."

Okay, maybe she'd get through this. Despite the tears that threatened to pool and spill over, Leah smiled.

Good Gifts   *Kyle Hunter*

෴ ෴ ෴

On Saturday morning, Nathan tackled the cauliflower crust, but with one eye on the clock. He'd have to do it in stages, since he had a lunch appointment with Olivia and the cast in an hour.

With smooth, regular strokes of the butcher knife on the wooden cutting board, he diced the cauliflower into florets. Regret weighed inside him. He'd planned to invite Leah so they could prepare the cauliflower pizza together. She'd shown interest when they'd talked about it over lunch at the farmer's market. He enjoyed cooking with friends. But he also craved her company. The moments they'd shared a few days ago in Andy's office hadn't left his mind since then. He could still feel her in his arms and envision her wide blue eyes as their lips almost met. Right before he pulled away.

And why did he do that? It had taken superhuman strength to pull back from her. For one thing, he was going back to Philly after this mess was resolved. It wasn't feeling so much like a mess anymore, though. More like a work in progress.

For another thing, he didn't know if she felt something for him. He couldn't assume anything based on their friendship, the past version or the present one. He could simply ask her, couldn't he? That's what grownups did, didn't they? What if she shook her head and said, *I'm sorry, I love you like a friend*? He might damage their friendship if he brought it up with her.

The previous day he'd been on the verge of calling her for a pizza cooking class and he stopped himself. Was he sending the wrong message or did it fall into the same category as working in the office or walking by the river? He loved her company, but he'd momentarily forgotten the bigger picture. If he were staying in the Falls, he'd pursue her in a heartbeat. Cooking together was an ideal pretext since she'd given him the perfect opening. Yet, anything he started now would hurt more later. And Leah had already been hurt badly by a man.

So, he hadn't called her. And there he was alone in Andy's kitchen pulsing chunks of cauliflower in the food processor until they were pulverized into tiny bits. Usually, he enjoyed cooking, but being alone when he could have been with Leah made him grumpy.

The day after he'd gone through Andy's office with Leah, he'd had made another visit to Seasons to tell Paul that he'd be staying until the New Year. Paul welcomed the news and seemed eager for Nathan's opinions and suggestions to the menu. His willingness to include Nathan in those decisions both surprised and humbled him. Clearly, the man wasn't territorial. Maybe he was simply exhausted and happy to have some input and backup.

When Nathan spoke about the Christmas program, Paul broke into an enthusiastic grin. "We're back! Took a while, but we're back." Nathan tried to point out that it was a one-time holiday show, and he didn't quite know what would come afterward, but the man's excitement had taken over. "I'll get started on the Christmas menu and we can talk about it next week." To this, Nathan simply nodded. Like it or not, he was already swept along by a current beyond his control.

Suddenly restless, Nathan left the vegetables on the counter and wandered to the back window. He hadn't prayed much or asked for help when Seasons had fallen into his lap. Or onto his head, more like it.

A voice inside told him he had nothing to prove, but he knew better. Proving himself had been the thread that had structured his life practically since he could walk. His journey hadn't always been smooth, but now he stood light years away from the shame-filled kid with no dad. He'd overcome a lot and now people would say he was successful. Settled. On the outside. He had a secure job with a marketing firm. Well paid but routine. Interesting sometimes, but not exciting. As he thought about the thirty or so years until retirement. . . well, he couldn't.

How could he prove himself *now* in a business he'd never wanted or had any experience running? It seemed impossible.

Pastor Frank would say it's a perfect scenario for God to show up. Might be a good time to test that theory.

Since settling back into the Falls, Nathan had attended his home church again. While he was at home in his Philly suburb, he attended one, but a chronic tug inside reminded him he'd lost his heart. The operative word was *attend*. Like visiting, but regularly. He warmed the pew, made the appearances, but wasn't sure at what point his passionate spirit had dried up and settled into the cracks of life. The eager teen believer had become the do-it-yourself adult. Faith had become a social statement and not a lot more.

Nathan stared out the back window at the yard framed by a tall wooden fence. A few fluffy bushes squatted in front of them. The crisp blue sky overhead spread a sheet of light that stirred hope inside. *Lord, you knew all this in advance, and I know you have a plan. I need to depend on you, not myself. It's hard since that's what I've always done. It's all I know. I hope to change that, Father. You're giving me the chance to do that now.*

He closed his eyes a moment to allow his declaration to settle in. He wanted to mean it. Do things differently.

He spent a few more minutes in peaceful silence then it was time to get ready for his appointment. A meeting that would tip the scale for or against the Christmas show at Seasons. With Olivia's help, they'd meet with interested former cast members. Hopefully, the free lunch he'd offered would bring a bigger turnout.

By the time Nathan arrived at Seasons for the meeting, his stomach was wound tight. How would people respond to the idea? How much should he tell them? No more than necessary. Same as he'd done with Olivia, although he probably owed her more.

Olivia was already seated at a long table next to a wall adorned with a giant mirror. He slid into a chair next to her and smiled.

Her dark hair streaked with strands of gray was pulled into a barrette. Lively blue eyes engaged his from behind metallic glasses. "Ready, boss?"

He laughed. "I'm the boss of no one. Not even myself. In other words, I have no idea what I'm doing."

"Not to worry. You've got the right partner." She gave his arm a maternal pat.

"Gosh, don't I know it." Nathan rolled his eyes with a long sigh. "You're the perfect person to be on my team. A real lifesaver." He jerked his head toward the door where a cluster of people stood scanning the room. "Look, here come some of our cast."

Olivia knew everyone, of course. "Hi, Paula. Great to see you. Jim, Sean. Janice," she called to the new arrivals who sat near them.

Nathan surveyed the small group. Jim was middle aged, while Sean and Janice looked to be college students. Paula, he guessed, was in her mid-thirties. A good start. That is, if they agreed to do the show. And it looked like more were coming in the front door.

"Everyone, this is Nathan," Olivia called to the group. "He's Andy's nephew and the new owner of Seasons."

Something about the way Olivia said *owner* and the deference shining from the eyes of some of them gave Nathan an odd mixture of puffed self-esteem and dark certainty he was a fraud.

Within ten more minutes, they were nine around the long table, plus Olivia and Nathan sitting near the middle so everyone could hear them. A quick glimpse of the dining room revealed a half-full restaurant for a Saturday lunch. He would soon pose the dreaded question. What was an average crowd on a weekend? That would come later. For now, the group watched him as they waited for him to speak. He'd hoped Olivia would handle the basics, since she knew them, but it *was* his theater and his idea. And he hadn't prepared.

"Um, thanks for coming, everyone. It's nice to meet you all." He projected his voice in what he hoped was a friendly way. "Why don't we order first, then I'll outline my ideas and see what questions and suggestions you all have." That would put things off a bit and give him a chance to break the ice with them.

They ordered their meals and beverages. Then it was time to dive into the meeting. May as well get it over with. It would get easier with practice. "Can everyone hear me?" He looked toward both ends of the table. Everyone nodded. "Good. As you know, our beloved Andy passed away last month. I know we all miss him. I sure do." He hadn't planned to say that. It just popped out. He blinked away the sudden burn in his eyes. He noticed the faces of Sean, Paula, and several others grew soft at the mention of Andy's name.

A knot had formed in his throat. He swallowed it and took a breath. "He appointed me as the new owner of Seasons in his will. I'm not sure what direction it'll take, but I thought it would be a good boost if we had a Christmas program, as Olivia has told you. For now, it's a single event and we thought we could do two showings, two Saturdays in a row in mid-December." He looked at Olivia, who was ready for her part. "Olivia will tell you more about the show itself."

Olivia sat up straighter and addressed everyone like she'd been doing it all her life. "All of you here today participated in the Christmas show three years ago. Your memories may be fuzzy on details, but you might recall that we did a series of traditional Christmas songs along with a few that were new. Candy Warren, who has since moved away, created a choreography with human snowflakes, adults and kids. You all remember that? It was amazing!"

Nathan hadn't heard that part. *Sounded* amazing. This might be fun after all. Olivia continued to summarize to the group the content the two of them had discussed the previous day on the phone, or rather, the things he agreed on that she suggested. She was the pro, and he let her run with it. She mentioned another choreography involving a sleigh and people strolling through fake snow under bare trees. He could picture it vividly, even though he'd never seen it. Were the sets still available somewhere? That would be a huge help. Where could they get a sleigh? Nathan jotted a note in his phone.

As the meals arrived, so did the questions. It was Nathan's turn to describe the conditions. That might lose a few of them. "We have about six weeks to put this together. You would need to follow the rehearsal schedule that Olivia sets up. You'll be paid for your work, of course. I don't know the exact amount, to be honest, but it should be in the range of what you've received in the past for a single show. Also, you won't be paid until after the shows are finished. The amount you receive will also depend on the amount of your involvement. If you're excited about this event and willing to be flexible, I'd love to have you help bring Christmas back to Seasons."

A few people cheered, some grinned, while others scowled. Still, Nathan felt a small victory having gotten through the meeting at all. With Olivia's know-how and a program in mind, along with a few willing cast members, maybe it had a fighting chance of working. No one would be more surprised than Nathan.

ෆ ෆ ෆ

It was a typical Saturday night in some ways. Leah had spent part of the day cleaning house and grocery shopping. At the grocery store, she'd stocked up on staple items as if a hurricane were coming, since she'd soon be without income. After a light supper, she practiced her church Christmas pieces on her violin and made several notes about the program. Theo seemed to approve, since he stayed in the living room the whole time, his eyes closed and whiskers flicking.

In the backdrop of Leah's mind hovered two thoughts. She wondered how the next months would unfold without employment.

And she wondered about Nathan.

He'd texted her Thursday to thank her for her help in Andy's office. It had been short and platonic. Then he texted her Friday to let her know that he and Olivia would be meeting with potential cast members Saturday at lunch. He hadn't invited her to that meeting. Maybe there was no need. And he'd asked for her prayers. No text message to tell her how it went. Hopefully, it wasn't bad news.

What to make of this new friendship with Nathan Chisholm? Should she pray, as Abbie had suggested, for something in the dream category? Wouldn't hurt, even if her expectations were low.

At seven fifteen her phone rang. Nathan. A call, not a text. A smile curled her lips. "Hi Nathan. I was just thinking about you." As if she thought of anything else. "I wondered how the meeting went today."

"Hi Leah, I meant to call you sooner. Thanks for praying. I thought the meeting went well. I met everyone and Olivia outlined the idea for the program. Seems most of them are ready to be involved." His voice sounded buoyant.

"That's wonderful. You have a cast already."

"We gave them until Monday to let us know for sure whether or not they're *in*."

"How are you feeling about everything? Any less pressured or nervous?"

He chuckled. "I have to say yes. I feel calmer now, first finding Uncle Andy's notes and names the other day. You were such a big help, Leah."

She heard kitchen noises in the background. A knife cutting something. The ding of a microwave.

"I didn't do anything. You found the names."

"But you were willing to go in there with me, and that was the first step." His voice softened. "You gave me the courage to try. To know it was possible."

She didn't know how to respond. "I'm glad. What are friends for?" A dumb statement since it would probably send a *just friendship* message to him. The last thing she'd wanted to do. *Way to go, Leah.*

"So, what's the next step?" She was feeling left out already. Watching from the outside when her heart burned to be involved.

"I have another meeting with Olivia Tuesday or Wednesday. We'll talk about things from the stage and production side of things. We're not talking about music per se yet. But when we do, that's where you come in. If you have time, that is."

"You keep saying that. Not only was I already willing to *make* time but listen to this. I got laid off Thursday."

Silence filled the phone. Then, "Thursday two days ago? I'm sorry to hear that." A pause. "Should I be sorry? Or maybe glad? I have no idea."

Leah laughed. "That's the same thing Abbie said. You guys are funny. Either you're twins separated at birth, or you both know me really well."

He chuckled. "I don't think we're twins. She has black curly hair."

"You're silly. Anyway, that's a valid question. Aside from having no income, it's great to be free from a job I barely tolerated."

"Although no income isn't a good thing."

"No, not at all."

"What *is* a good thing is you'll have more time to devote to the program at Seasons, and something tells me you'd really enjoy that. Am I right?"

"Yes, absolutely. Which proves my point of how well you know me. I'd love it."

"Okay. You're hired. Well, there's not a lot of money in it and you won't get it till after the program, but you will be paid."

"Even better. I think I'd do it for free, just like Olivia. But if you're paying, I won't say no."

"I'll keep you posted about the next part, the part where you come in."

"Can't wait."

"So, when's your last day of work?"

"The thirty-first."

"Halloween. I wonder if that's some kind of omen."

She laughed. "I think it's called a blessing in disguise. Garrett is making me a website so I can start teaching kids music. I did that some in college. You mentioned it at the funeral, remember?"

"Yeah. The funeral seems like years ago. It's like, *before Leah* and *after Leah*. I mean, after I saw you again."

Hmm. Did that mean she was on his mind too? And that running into her again had made an impact on him? She'd choose to believe it did. Positive dreaming in practice. *Look at that, Abbie!*

Leah and Nathan talked for so long, she lost track. She laid back on the couch for a while then sprawled on the floor for a while as time went by. They talked about his schedule and how much he was skimming by at work, hoping to stay under the radar. About some ideas he had for Seasons. She talked about her plans for teaching, and possible songs for the Seasons program. About the fun summer activities in Brenner Falls and upcoming events at church. So many subjects linked together like a beautiful daisy chain.

"Well, I've worn you out, Leah," Nathan finally said. "You need to get some rest before church tomorrow."

"Oh, I'd almost forgotten. I enjoyed talking to you."

"Me too." His voice was gentle. "Sweet dreams."

She'd just spent her evening with those.

Chapter Ten

Wednesday morning brooded overhead, foggy and moist. After his morning tea and a toasted bagel with smoked salmon, Nathan hurried to Seasons to meet Olivia for a follow-up meeting after their lunch with the cast the previous Saturday. They had to get down to serious business.

Nathan pulled into the parking lot at ten o'clock. Only the employees' cars were there since they wouldn't open for lunch until eleven. Olivia told him they should meet on site, since they had to access the theater and plan out the event. They settled at a table far from the front door and requested coffee from the kitchen. As the owner, Nathan had access to the restaurant anytime, but he took little satisfaction in that fact.

They settled around a two-seat table with coffee. "What did you think of the meeting Saturday and where do we stand with the cast?" Nathan asked.

He'd spoken to her on the phone Monday night, but not everyone had decided yet. Then Olivia had a family commitment which lost a day, so they met Wednesday. Nathan had been on pins and needles until then. If he'd had more confidence and experience, he'd have called everyone himself, but deferred to Olivia. She knew them, she knew the terrain. And she wasn't terrified.

Olivia, who never looked ruffled about anything, pulled out a steno pad and shot him a glance. "You get right down to business, don't you?" She offered a calm smile. "Relax, Nathan. You're not going to your execution today, are you?"

He let out an awkward chuckle. "Why do you ask? Do I look pale or something?"

"No, you look anxious. It's going to be fine."

"Is it that obvious? I'm regretting I agreed to this circus."
She frowned.

"Okay, poor word choice. Sorry. I mean, you're great, Olivia. It's that there are so many moving parts. I had no idea. As we were talking about it, I realized we have choreography, music, costumes, décor, actors, invitations, ticket sales—"

"Yes, there's a lot that goes into it. But you personally don't need to do it all. We'll delegate. Andy had people doing all those jobs for years, but during his illness, many of them found other jobs or moved away. But we can find others. Seasons has a website, so we can set up ticket sales there. We'll post the menu and take reservations and money. We can already get an idea of how profitable this will be."

Nathan let out a breath. "That's good news. One role less. But what about choreography?"

"We can do without. We'll do something simple with a bit of stage blocking. Of course, the snowflake dance is another story, but we already have choreography for that, as long as we can find the notes and people remember it."

"Three years later?" Nathan's voice emerged louder than he'd intended. "Sorry, I'm trying to control my stress level."

"You'd better. Unless you want to have a heart attack." Her eyelids fluttered. "I'm sorry, I shouldn't say that after. . . after Andy. Anyway, it'll be fine."

Nathan relaxed his fingers from gripping his cup handle. "I'll be okay. So, how many confirmed cast members do we have?"

"We have seven yeses. That's not very many, but we can recruit. Luis, who was at the meeting, decided not to do it, and Peggy got an increase in her work hours, so she won't have time." Olivia examined her steno pad with its neat lines and columns. "We need a couple of female vocalists. The principal and a secondary."

He needed to pull together one event. Just this once. After that, it would become someone else's headache. The buyer, who he had yet to hear from. He'd call Carley later that day.

"What about promotion?" Olivia looked up from her notebook. "Don't you think we should start now, since it's in a month and a half?"

"Um, yes, it would be good to start early, I guess." Once they started promoting it, they'd have to do it, whether they had enough cast, dancers, musicians or whatever. "I wondered if it was premature to market since we're missing so many elements. You know, like musicians, dancers." And almost everything else. He could almost feel his blood pressure spike. What if they started selling tickets and didn't have enough cast members? Or musicians or costumes? What if the show flopped? They'd already have sold tickets, so would have some numbers, but people would go away with a bad taste. Then the second show would flop even worse, because word would get around.

"What are you thinking about, Nathan? Are you trying to win a frowning contest?"

He snapped back to attention. "I'm imagining a disaster or two. That's all."

Olivia chuckled. "Let's get back to work."

Clearly, she wasn't about to reassure or counsel him.

"The main thing we need first is people. People to do different things. Let's focus on that. Who can you get?"

"I don't even live here, Olivia. I don't have much of a network anymore."

"You grew up here. You must know *someone*."

"I know one musician. She has a lovely voice and a background in music. I think you know her. Leah Albright."

"Hmm. Name rings a bell. I think she was in one of our shows, wasn't she?"

"Yes, or more than one. She's good, but she's only one person. Maybe *she* has a network." Nathan pondered. Who else? Ben, his mom, a few people from church. Maybe Pastor Frank knew someone. He hadn't even asked them, but he could.

"Call Leah. Ask her who her contacts are."

"Are you always this, uh, authoritative?"

Olivia grinned. "How do you think I was able to pull this thing together for six years? I don't know what Andy did before I came along. Yes, I do, he floundered. He had this well-meaning college girl running everything, and she was a disaster." She waved at the air. "Anyway, I'm off track. It's my thing. What can I say?"

"So very glad," Nathan muttered. "Without you, I wouldn't even attempt this." So, she saw all the challenges, understood the risks, and was still in the game. He needed to stop whining and do the same. "I have some questions for you."

"Shoot."

He'd brought his own notepad and flipped several pages to the one he'd marked. "How many shows per year did Andy do in the past?"

"Four. One per season." She gave him a pointed look. "Hence the name *Seasons*."

"Oh. I get it. Just never made the connection before. What did they do in between those four shows? Was it a regular restaurant?"

"Yes. Andy wanted to do more shows and have the seasonal shows be the big, special ones, but he didn't have the staff or profit for that. Then, he started getting sick a lot. He should have left everything to his staff, and we'd still be running, but he wanted to stay involved. I think he loved the theater part more than the restaurant, to be honest. So, his absence eventually led to the theater shutting down. But to answer your question, the fact that most of the year it was a restaurant enabled it to continue once the theater stopped doing events."

That made sense. "Was there profit with only four shows a year?"

"No, the theater side wasn't profitable. And the restaurant was just average. Together, they'd be good if they could gain traction." She made a face. "Not sure this event's going to do it, though." She drained her coffee cup. "It's a lot to keep up with. It's easy if you have staff. But to have staff, you need profit. And to have profit, you need staff."

"A vicious circle."

"Yes, indeed. Then, when there are only four events a year, people go elsewhere for entertainment. Of course, now we have lots of options in town. Dinner theaters are a bit out of fashion, but here in the Falls, people have a sort of reverence for Seasons."

Nathan shifted in his chair and glanced around the empty room. "I noticed. But that should work in our favor." And maybe people would be more forgiving if it was a bust.

"Then, with fewer shows, it doesn't provide enough income for people to want to stick with it, unless we get part-time people who do it as a hobby and have regular day jobs. Do you understand all that?"

He understood perfectly. He understood that, after this event, he'd have no choice but to sell Seasons. He'd walked into a crumbling, out-of-date nightmare. One that Leah happened to love.

A slight pain throbbed in his temple. "What about décor? Sets?"

"There's some stuff in the basement under the theater. We'll go see, and it may cheer you up."

"I need it."

They rose, and he followed her toward the stage. On one side was a small door, almost invisible, since it blended with the color of the wall. Olivia flipped a light switch, and they went down a narrow concrete staircase, musty and forgotten.

The stairway opened to a large room Nathan guessed had the same dimensions as the stage above them. Olivia pointed to some trunks stacked along one wall. "There are costumes in those trunks that belong to Seasons. Sometimes Andy rented costumes if he needed something special. For a while, he had to get them from a place in Reading, but now we have a rental place here in town. To save money, though, he often had people wear their own clothes, but in certain colors or styles, if they had them."

Nathan looked at the trunks, guessing that the contents were his property. He felt like he'd entered a different world from the restaurant above them. "Anything in those trunks we can use for Christmas?"

"Yes, certainly. I'm not sure how many costumes there are. Might not be enough. We might be able to find a willing seamstress who can help us with a few more."

"It's a start." Nathan's attention wandered to the far wall where he saw two Christmas trees with clear plastic bags over top. "There are some trees. We'll need those for sure."

"But we need lights for them." Olivia approached one trunk and set her hand on the corner. "The snowflake costumes are in this trunk if I remember correctly. There are different sizes for adults and some for kids."

"Can we do the snowflake sequence? That sounded nice."

"We could, but don't have enough people."

"I can picture little kids dancing in snowflake costumes across the stage. People would love that."

Olivia's eyes widened. Her serious expression stretched into an animated grin. "Nathan, you're brilliant! I don't know why I didn't think of this, but we have a children's theater in town. I know the director. She'd love to help us out. She always liked Seasons, too, so I know she'll be supportive."

"Perfect. That'll guarantee at least their parents will come see the show."

"You said you know Leah. Does she also dance?"

Nathan shrugged. "I can ask. Does she have to speak Portuguese, juggle flaming swords, and do handsprings too?"

She cocked her head, a half-smile forming. "Yes, of course." They both laughed. "I'll come back tomorrow when I have more time and check out what costumes we have. Most people will simply wear seasonal colors, maybe scarves and hats, and that should do."

They climbed back up the staircase.

"What about musicians?" he asked her once they were again seated.

"I'm still trying to get in touch with some of the old gang. I have the pianist, so that's a big win. But that's all she does. She can't coordinate all the music. If we don't find anyone else, we'll at least have piano music."

"I bet Leah can coordinate music," Nathan offered, a warm spark igniting inside at the thought of her. He hadn't seen her in a week due to mutual schedule craziness, but they'd texted. A lot. "She's already doing that at her church for a Christmas gig. I'll ask her."

"Excellent. One thing we can do after people have eaten is have a singalong."

Nathan grinned. "I guess you can only do that at Christmas." Lucky for him, it was a Christmas show and not a spring or summer themed event. "Is there a music school in town where we could borrow some musicians? Or a school band?"

"Maybe. Good idea."

"Excuse me for disturbing you," said a male voice. Nathan and Olivia looked up at a middle-aged man standing next to their table. "I heard you're the new owner of this place and that the Christmas show is coming back," he said. "Just wanted to tell you my wife and I are so happy about that. We're planning on getting tickets as soon as they go on sale."

Nathan gave the man a tight smile. "That's great, sir. We look forward to seeing you here."

"Well, I'll let you finish your conversation."

He wandered off, and the sinking feeling began in Nathan's stomach. "Well, I guess we're obligated now."

"Guess we are." Olivia's apparent pleasure at this truth matched his dread. She glanced at her watch. "Gotta run, Nathan. My book club meeting starts in a half hour. See you soon."

She disappeared through the front door.

Nathan buried his face in his hands. "What have you gotten me into, Uncle Andy?"

ଔ ଔ ଔ

"So, what costume did you wear to work today, since it was your last day?" Garrett had emerged from his room-cave. He snagged a bag of potato chips from the kitchen cupboard and slid onto an armchair. Leah sat on the couch with her laptop open and a sleeping Theo curled against her thigh.

She looked up from her laptop. "I decided to wear a jester hat, you know the kind with metal balls on the corners. I was going to go all out, but mentally, I'd checked out by then." She'd dragged herself through those final days, glad it was nearly over.

"Know what you mean. It wasn't a great job, Leah. I've been telling you that."

"I've known it for a while, but like Abbie said, it was security for me." She watched her brother's face as she said Abbie's name, but he revealed nothing. Leah still didn't know if her brother and her best friend only maintained a friendship or if something deeper was brewing in the nearly two months since Garrett had come back to Brenner Falls.

The day Leah learned about the end of her employment, she'd brainstormed with Abbie and decided to start teaching music to kids in the community. Leah had done some teaching in the past, but the unpredictable income hadn't been ideal. She hoped to do better this time.

She scanned the new website Garrett had created for her music business. On the homepage, Garrett had made an attractive banner that included a small circular photo of Leah in the upper left corner and a list of her skills and background. He'd even created a small form where interested parents could request a phone call or an email response for more information. She'd supplied her brother with the text and the result had been sleek and professional. She and Abbie had both told him he ought to start a web design business, to which he had answered with a grunt.

In any case, it was about time Leah put her music skills to good use, as Abbie had pointed out. The only reason she hadn't taught music sooner was that she needed health benefits. A full-time job anywhere seemed more secure than teaching the occasional music students. What a myth *that* had proven to be.

If she were honest, she'd admit she looked forward to managing her own time, having more of it, and investing in music for more than her own enjoyment. She'd already begun choosing Christmas songs and recruiting volunteers for the church program. She'd had one planning meeting and one practice session and had loved both.

Once she decided to start teaching music again and the website was complete, Abbie helped her put up flyers around town—at the library, grocery store, in shop windows when possible, and in mailboxes. She had two students so far for flute and one for violin. It was a start. She played the piano too, but it wasn't her strongest instrument. On her website, she offered flute, beginner piano, violin, and voice. Abbie assured her she'd soon be in demand for musical instruction.

The doorbell rang. "Your turn," Leah told Garrett. "I've been doing it for the last hour."

Garrett pulled himself up from the chair with an exaggerated sigh and opened the door. He was met by a youthful chorus of, "Trick or treat!" He reached for a bowl of candy sitting on a table by the door and a handful of half-sheet flyers announcing Leah's new business. He'd suggested it might generate some action. Leah grudgingly admitted it was a stroke of genius.

"Thank you!" The childish voices cried in unison before Garrett closed the door.

Her relationship with Garrett had improved after their talk at the kitchen table weeks ago. His job stocking groceries took him out of the house several nights a week. *That* had certainly improved Leah's mood. Starting the next day, she'd have to find a new rhythm. Her students would come in the afternoon after school, so she'd have to find something to do during the day. But she could hardly support herself with a few hours of teaching each evening.

Ten minutes later, the doorbell rang again, but Garrett had disappeared into his cave. How convenient.

She set her laptop beside her and went to the front door. She didn't mind the Halloween kids, but rather enjoyed seeing and talking to them. "Trick or treat!" This time, there were two children, Spiderman and a fairy princess. The princess had glittery wings and a sparkling crown and seemed to be about four years old.

Leah feigned amazement, touching her hands to her cheeks. "Look, it's Spiderman! Right on my front porch! And who's this? Are you a *real* princess?"

The little girl giggled. "No, my name is Christine." Another giggle.

"Well, you look like a real princess to me. I bet you both want some candy." Leah took the bowl and squatted to the little girl's height. "Pick whatever you want. Take two if you want." She looked at the boy. "I bet you'd like some too, wouldn't you?"

"Yes ma'am," he said as she extended the bowl to him. His mother had taught him manners.

She raised her eyes and saw a familiar-looking woman hovering protectively a few feet behind them on the porch. Leah gave her a small wave. "Hello. I recognize you, but I don't know your name."

The woman approached the door and pulled her quilted jacket closer around her. "I'm Ellen from two streets over. We've been in the community for about five years now, but I guess our paths haven't crossed."

"Good to meet you, Ellen. Your kids are really sweet."

"Thank you." Ellen smiled fondly and ruffled the boy's hair behind his Spiderman mask. "I guess they'll get even sweeter when they get some candy into them."

Both women laughed. "I'm sure you're right about that," Leah said. "Then they might need dentist visits, but that can come later."

"First, it's Halloween, then Thanksgiving, and then Christmas. We can hardly catch our breath."

"At least it's all fun." As a child, Leah had so loved the fall season for all the fun events and the change in the weather. Now, she mostly faked it and let out a sigh when it was all over.

"Speaking of Christmas," Ellen said. "I just heard Seasons is planning to do a Christmas show. First one in three years. My husband and I went twice in the past when Andy Evans was alive. This year we're thinking of taking the whole family." Ellen offered a wistful smile. "We've missed it. And we miss Andy too. Apparently, his nephew is taking up the reins. Might be expensive for all four of us to go, but it'll be a good family event."

A family event. Yes, it certainly was. Leah had gone with her family back in the day, with her ever-jolly father insisting they stir up a little Christmas spirit.

"Oh, for sure. You should definitely go, Ellen. I've been a few times in the past. It launches the Christmas season in a great way."

Leah said goodbye to Ellen and the children, but not before handing her a flyer. "In case you are interested, I teach music to children. Voice, piano, violin, and flute." Leah's neighbor accepted the paper with a smile and waved a goodbye. "Happy Halloween. And Thanksgiving and Christmas too."

"You too. Hope to see you again before then, maybe in town."

Leah's grin faded as the woman and her children disappeared into the night. The street had become quiet as Halloween wound down and finished for another year. One holiday down, two to go.

After Nathan's second meeting with Olivia, he'd called to recruit her to help with music. No, to head up and completely supervise the music. A big job, but she wouldn't dream of saying no and not only because of Nathan. Despite her happy and sad memories of her dad and Seasons, she couldn't wait to once again be involved in a musical production.

The next day, she'd meet with Olivia to organize the program. Not a moment too soon. They had a month and a half.

Chapter Eleven

Brenner Falls didn't have traffic jams. Nathan couldn't use that as the reason he was late for his lunch appointment with Ben. He'd simply lost track of time as he reviewed the list of songs Leah had suggested in her email. Losing track of time wasn't something Nathan Chisholm did. Ever. But since arriving in the Falls and diving into everything Seasons, he'd been distracted, or maybe drawn in.

Leah had made brief notes after each song title, offering ideas for choreography or instruments that might go along well with them. She was gifted and had expertise, that was clear. Yet she presented her thoughts as mere suggestions, giving him the final say. *And* she'd given him the entire list within forty-eight hours of their phone conversation when he'd begged for her help.

The light changed and Nathan advanced through the intersection. He'd texted Ben, who'd said *no worries*, he'd hold their table. Ben's tastes were more hamburger and pizza, while Nathan preferred sushi and farm to table restaurants. But given the lack of time for both of them that day, burgers it would be.

Nathan's phone rang. He groaned when he saw the name on his screen. His high-maintenance client whose call he'd avoided not once, but twice. Not that he wanted to jeopardize his job. He hadn't had the time or mental bandwidth to deal with the man. He absolutely had to answer. "Hey, Chuck. I was just about to call you." He forced cheer into his voice. "Look, I apologize for not being able to call sooner. How have you been?"

"Right now, I'm irritated, Nathan," the man blustered. "I called you twice yesterday and didn't hear back from you. This was going to be my last time before I talked to your boss."

Nathan bristled. On one hand, he'd have to do better if he wanted to stay under the radar and continue working remotely. He couldn't afford for something to go wrong with the arrangement. On the other hand, if Chuck wanted instant responses to his phone calls, Nathan was no longer that guy. Unfortunately, he'd trained the man to say jump and Nathan had.

He stifled a patronizing sigh. "I'm sorry you're frustrated, Chuck. I was blocked all day yesterday but was going to call you today. What's up?"

Chuck recounted his concern in a petulant voice. Nathan half-listened, sighting George's Burger Shack ahead. Just as he'd predicted, his client only wanted to have the comfort of vocal contact, not because there was new information or a specific question, but to reassure himself that Nathan was working continuously on his account as if he were the only client. Nathan would be relieved when this campaign finished. There were too many Chucks in his life, and he was losing patience with babysitting them. Especially when he had a new business he had to figure out.

Nathan sat in the parking lot long enough to let Chuck finish whining, knowing he was getting even later for Ben, but felt helpless. Finally, he disconnected from the call and dashed into the restaurant, an airy place with a vaulted wood panel ceiling and a large, enclosed grill space in the center. The earthy smell of barbeque and meat filled his nostrils. Suddenly, he was hungry. He spied Ben at a booth near the window.

"Sorry, bro. I was already running late, then a client called me, and I couldn't get away." He slipped into the seat across from Ben and relaxed his tense muscles.

Ben waved the air. "No worries, like I said. I started with a drink and looked over the menu." He laughed. "Not like I don't know it by heart. George's is my go-to burger place."

"Yeah, so you've told me."

After they ordered, Ben sipped his drink. "So, what's happening? Haven't seen you in a couple weeks."

Nathan summarized the myriad of responsibilities involved in reviving Seasons and the progress he and Olivia had made. "As I complain about all there is to do, I should also say that I've been blessed with a couple of smart and hard-working women who are lightening the load considerably."

Ben's dark eyebrows lifted, and a smile teased his mouth. "Go on, I'd like to hear more about these women."

"First, Olivia, who was the stage manager, or I should say *everything* manager, when Andy was alive. She knows everything about this business, at least on the theater side. She agreed to work on the event as a volunteer. Thank goodness she has a very organized mind."

"And she used to do it, so she has all that experience."

"Yeah. It's a huge help. I feel like a little kid following the teacher around."

"We all have to start somewhere. You've never done this before, but you're learning fast."

"When I saw all there was to do, I wanted to quit. But we met last weekend and again this week, and she threw me a life raft. Then we needed a vocalist and I thought of Leah Albright."

"Ah, cute Leah. Perfect."

Nathan smirked. "Don't start matchmaking, okay?"

"Just saying. You like her, I can tell. Your face changed a little when you started talking about her."

Nathan narrowed his eyes at his friend. "For an engineer, you certainly are observant. Something's wrong with that." They both laughed. "Yes, I do like Leah." He liked Leah a *lot*. "But I live in Phila*del*phia." He emphasized the city's name.

"Oh, please." Ben waved the air. "Like you'll always live there, and she'll always live here. It's the twenty-first century, pal. People move around. Who knows? She might be dying to move to Philadelphia." He paused and gave Nathan a wily grin. "And eventually, you'll be dying to get out. Mark my words."

"What makes you so sure?"

Ben could be annoying in his certainty *and* accuracy, and the way he picked up on signals Nathan hadn't even known about himself. Like the way he was starting to enjoy being in the Falls. Away from the pressures of the daily train into Center City, as it was called by the locals. Distanced, to some degree, from people like Chuck.

"Speaking of Philadelphia," Nathan said, "I got a call from my boss yesterday afternoon. He told me my company is negotiating a merger with another firm. I'd already gotten a heads-up from a colleague, but it's more serious now. It may lead to some layoffs."

"Are you worried?"

Nathan shook his head. "Not really. First, it's not for sure we'll merge and there will be layoffs. Second, if I'm laid off. . ." He lifted his hands palms-up. "I'll find something. Marketers are marketable, I guess you can say."

"There may be an opening at Seasons." Ben grinned.

Nathan laughed. "You think? I don't know if they'll match my salary."

A waitress arrived with plates heaped with tall sandwiches and home cut fries. "George's gourmet quarter pounder for you, and the turkey melt with avocado for you, right?" She placed their orders on the table, then left.

"So, you were telling me about Leah and what she brings to the project." Ben opened his mouth wide to bite into his multilayered hamburger. "Aside from beauty, talent, and potential romance."

Nathan wanted to throw a napkin at him but ended up stifling a laugh. "Turns out she's very organized along with what I already knew. She's an excellent musician. The entire program is based on Christmas music, and she's taking it on like a champ. She also sings and plays three instruments."

"Wow, looks like you struck gold with her."

Gold in a multitude of ways. Warmth pooled inside him as he considered the calm he felt when they talked either in person or on the phone. "I did. She's going to help a lot. And she has the time. She lost her job a couple of weeks ago." He wiped his mouth and glanced at his watch. "She's meeting with Olivia right now so they can get to know each other and go over all they've planned so far."

"Women are *so* efficient," Ben said. "Whenever we have a family thing to plan, we give it to my sister Sarah and my mom, and we know it's going to be fantastic. They think of every detail."

"As soon as I leave here, I'm going to Leah's house. That's where they're meeting. They'll bring me up to date and we'll figure out the next step."

Ben smiled like the Cheshire Cat and sipped his soda. "Just want to tell you, it doesn't have to be perfect, this Christmas Extravaganza. People are gonna love it because they love Seasons, they love Christmas, and they loved Andy. So, lighten up. It sounds like you have a great team. And the Christmas show at Seasons is symbolic for people. They'll just be glad it's happening." Ben took a dramatic tone and gestured with splayed fingers. "Like it's rising from the ashes."

Nathan shot him a grateful smile. Ben was right. He had a good team and people were eager to come back to Seasons. He didn't want to disappoint them. He'd always been a perfectionist though it hadn't always served him well. He was realizing the self-reliant make-it-happen spirit wasn't the strength he'd always assumed it was.

"So, have you ever, even for five minutes, entertained the idea of keeping Seasons? Running it yourself? You have some experience from summers in the restaurant. And you have a lot of strengths that would fit."

"Ben, you see all the angst I'm having by doing just one show. Keeping it? I can't wait to unload it." Nathan swiped a napkin across his mouth.

"Not even five minutes? Think of it, Nathan. Suppose the show's a success and people love it. Suppose *you* even start liking it? Then you've got Olivia and Leah on your team. Olivia wouldn't need much prompting to get her old job back. Leah, as you said, is unemployed and a great musician. She'd probably love a music-oriented job where she can use her skills. Between the two of them alone, you've got a recipe for success."

Nathan folded his hands and stared at Ben. Ben who was starting to make sense. "Even if all that's true, it would cost tens of thousands of dollars to refurbish Seasons and bring the building into the twenty-first century instead of, well, the mid-forties or fifties. The town is growing and there's all kinds of new money and new families and all that. But who's going to frequent an old-style restaurant with an outdated menu and an occasional music show?"

Ben steepled his hands on the table. "Well, there are these people called *investors*. They might take a shine to Seasons and love the vision and potential enough to pour in some money." His eyes were wide, his face animated as he waited for Nathan's response. "Or you can get a loan. There are ways."

"I have a job."

"Do you love it?"

Nathan impaled Ben with a stare. "Do you love yours?"

Ben laughed. "I see this conversation's going nowhere. No problem. I still love ya, bro."

"Thanks for your ideas, Ben. They're good ones. It's just that I'm not really looking for them. I need to sell it. That's my goal, whether I live in the Falls or stay in Philly."

"Fair enough. Just wanted to give you food for thought."

"Thanks. You're a good friend." He grinned at Ben, who looked relaxed as always. "And I *do* feel better about the whole Christmas thing, thanks to you. And the women on my team."

"Those women, bless them!"

"Yes, and I have a meeting with those blessed women right now."

ଔ ଔ ଔ

Leah brought the carafe of boiling water to the dining room table. "Here's some more water to refresh your tea, Olivia."

Olivia chuckled. "Any more of that and I'll jump all the way home instead of driving." Though truthfully, the cups of tea had grown cold as the two women talked and planned. Outside, rumpled gray clouds hung low in the sky, making it look later in the day than it was. Might rain or even snow, but Leah didn't care either way. She'd adjusted quickly to working at home, happy to be in her slippers at her dining room table instead of at the office.

She'd known Olivia in a superficial way when she participated in a couple of shows. But once they really got down to discussion, she felt an immediate connection to her. The older woman's personality was no-nonsense, her way of thinking systematic. Yet, she had a wry humor and optimistic perspective that put Leah at ease while assuring her of having a competent mentor for her new role.

"What time is Nathan getting here?" Olivia asked.

"Should be here any minute. He had a lunch appointment and said he'd be right over."

There was a rap on the front door. "That must be Nathan." Leah couldn't smother a tiny spark of pleasure at the thought of seeing him. It had been several days. Of course, it was important that he hear what they'd planned and give his approval. By his own admission, Nathan was in over his head. She and Olivia could probably do whatever they wanted, and he'd agree.

"Hi, Nathan." She smiled and met his gaze. She thought she saw an appreciative flicker in them, but certainly it was wishful thinking. "Come on in. I haven't been out yet today. Is it cold?"

Nathan came in and rubbed his hands together. "I'd say *yes*. There was frost on everything this morning." He handed her his coat and unwrapped a blue scarf from his neck.

"I heated water for tea. Want some?" Leah hung his coat on a row of hooks by the door.

"Thanks, that would be great." He followed her to the dining room. "Hi, Olivia. Have you ladies had a productive morning?" He pulled out a chair facing her.

"Hi, Nathan. It's been very productive. I wish I'd gotten to know Leah years ago. She's a genius. We knew each other, but it's strange that we've been in the same town for ages and never crossed paths, except maybe at the grocery store."

Once they were settled with fresh cups of tea, Nathan looked at the women expectantly. "So, bring me up to speed."

Olivia slid what looked like a typed list across the table. "Here's a chronological order of the evening. We'll have people eat dinner first, but there will be attractive holiday décor already on the stage and Christmas music playing through the sound system. The wait staff will be dressed like elves, which is what we've done in the past."

He glanced up from the list. "Do we have elf costumes?"

A sly smile spread across Olivia's face. "A couple of days after we met, I went back to the supply room and went through all the costumes and props. I found a lot more than I'd remembered. We still have elf costumes, enough for many of our servers. Oh, by the way, you need to have Paul hire some more of them for the performances. We'll need more help."

"I have a friend from church who's a clothing designer," Leah said, glancing from Olivia to Nathan. "Her name's Blair and she's new in town. She can make us more costumes if we're running short. It'll be nice to get her involved."

"Great, call her." Olivia didn't look up from her list. "Let's see. . . once the meal's finished, we'll have the first part of the program, which Leah will explain to you, Nathan. During intermission, the guests will have their dessert and coffee. Then the program will continue, finishing with audience participation of four Christmas carols." She looked at Leah. "Your turn. Didn't want to steal your thunder."

Leah grinned at her. "You were brief and to the point." Unbelievable how much fun the morning planning the event with Olivia had been. It almost felt like. . . well, like her perfect niche.

In an instant, Abbie's words came back to her about having a job versus a passion. Had she ever felt a passion when working in a job? She marveled at the impact of what she now had. What a difference it made.

She pulled Nathan's copy from her stack and handed it to him. He looked at her with curiosity as he took the paper, probably wondering about the delighted expression she must have on her face.

He skimmed down the page. "This looks great, Leah."

"In all, there will be three solos, two quartet numbers, two duets, and three pieces involving the whole cast. Then we finish with the four carols with audience participation. We'll end with Silent Night and dim the stage, so it's solemn. The wait staff will light candles and stand around the edges of the room during that piece."

"Like human sconces." Olivia grinned. "That was Leah's idea." She turned her head toward Leah. "Well, *all* the program was your idea, pretty much."

Leah's face heated at Olivia's compliment and the look of awe on Nathan's face. "The waiters can distribute a sheet of lyrics for the carols with dessert." She pointed back to the list. "There on the list you see the order and movements, décor, and any kind of dance associated with each piece. For instance, there will be eight children from the children's theater who'll do the snowflake dance. I thought we could end right before the carols with a duet couple in costume with the sleigh."

Nathan's head shot up. "You found a sleigh?"

Olivia laughed. "I'm trying to find a real one, but my son and husband are both pretty psyched about building one from wood."

Nathan shook his head. "You two are amazing. You've really planned everything. It's so. . ." His eyes met theirs, one woman at a time. Swallowed and blinked. "It's an answer to prayer, is what it is."

Leah held back a sudden urge to throw her arms around him. "I'm so glad." Her voice cracked. Why was she so emotional that day? Her world had just opened, for one. And Nathan sat close to her at the table, a winter flush tinting his handsome face, while he shared the vision of the Christmas event.

Olivia wore a contented smile. "We're glad to be helpful," she said briskly. "And it's fun to be involved in the Seasons Christmas show again."

"Have you thought about publicity?" Leah asked Nathan.

"I've *thought* about it. I'm a marketing guy, so I do have a couple of ideas. The Seasons website is outdated, but we can put something there about the show." He looked at Olivia. "I didn't see where people can order tickets online."

"Andy wasn't very tech savvy so, honestly, I don't think it occurred to him. The hostess at the restaurant also did box office if you want to call it that."

"Garrett can update the site," Leah offered, sitting straighter in her chair. "He's a whiz with all that. You should see what he did for my teaching website."

"Will you ask him?" Nathan's pleading gaze held hers. "Of course, I'll pay him. I can also contact Mayor Faulkner about what the city can do for publicity. He was supportive about the event when I met with him."

"When I started my business, Abbie and I covered the town with flyers." Leah pushed her papers aside and leaned on her elbow. "We can do the same thing for the Christmas show."

"I can recruit my friend Jane's kids," Olivia said. "They're younger and still at home. They love stuff like that. My son may help, but he's the oldest and has a job in town. And we can borrow a couple of costumes from the theater and dress a few kids up as elves. They can hand out flyers downtown on Black Friday. Who'd refuse to buy a ticket from a cute elf?" They all laughed.

"Fantastic!" Leah clapped, a spurt of joy rising within her. "Garrett can put a QR code on a poster, and people can scan and buy tickets on the spot."

"Ah, the beauty of marketing mixed with technology." Nathan grinned, seeming caught up with their enthusiasm.

"I can mention it to my book club members," Olivia said. "Their kids can help too. We'll make a team activity. Call it *Team Seasons!*"

"See what a little teamwork will do?" Leah looked at both of them. Nathan looked as though he'd gone from a pressure cooker about to explode to a man on vacation. He nodded and held her gaze for a long moment.

"Well, I need to go now." Olivia gathered her papers and notebook under one arm. Maybe she wanted to leave them alone. Fine by Leah.

Olivia stood and pushed in her chair. "What's your next focus, Nathan, now that the program is on track?"

"I'd like to spend some time with Paul at the restaurant. He's asked for my input for the menu and I'm eager to suggest some things. I'm talking about the Christmas menu as well as the regular menu, which needs some changes."

"I think you're right." Olivia turned to Leah. "Your next step, of course, is to schedule rehearsals. You can do that either here or borrow a room at the school or a church. We usually close the restaurant two or three evenings during the week before the program, so we can rehearse on stage with the full cast and musicians."

"Got it." Leah rose and accompanied Olivia to the door. "We'll work it out, I'm sure. I've already contacted the people who said they'd do the show."

"Wonderful. You're right on top of things, Leah. It'll be a pleasure working together."

Leah returned to the dining room where, she was glad to see, Nathan still sat as if he weren't planning to dash out the door to his next appointment.

She sat and crossed her arms on the table. "Well, what do you think?" She couldn't stifle a grin. "It's going to be great, Nathan." She reached out and squeezed his forearm.

As she drew away, he grabbed her hand and squeezed it. "Thank you, Leah. I don't know what to say." Slowly, he released her hand.

"I'm. . . I'm happy to do it. Really. Not only for your sake, you know, to help out with Seasons, and for Andy, but I'm realizing this is what I love doing. I never had the chance before. So, I should thank *you* for giving me that chance."

"I just thought of a way to say thank you." A mischievous glint sparked from his green eyes. "How about I teach you how to cook grape leaves?" He laughed. "Or, whatever you want to learn."

"I'd love to. Now that I have more time, I want to learn more about cooking and a few other things. I never had time before. Now I have time *and* a food mentor." Two mentors in one day, including Olivia. And her other mentor was gazing across the table in a way that heated her blood. And had asked her over for a cooking lesson. Kind of a date. Almost.

"Saturday?" he asked. "The cauliflower pizza turned out pretty well, so we can do that, or I'll find a different recipe."

"Anything's fine. I have a lot to learn in the kitchen. I'll bring dessert."

"Deal. Well, I better go now." He stood and gathered the copies of the program Leah had given him. He slid them into a folder.

She walked with him to the door where his coat hung. He put it on and pulled a knit hat over his head. "Ready for the tundra."

Leah smiled. "Better you than me. I'm comfy here."

His eyes grew serious. "Thanks again, Leah. You and Olivia, I can't say it enough." He pulled her into a long hug that flooded her senses and caused her heart to thump against her ribs. As he pulled back, he surprised her by pressing his lips against hers. The kiss was quick, and when he stepped back, he too looked surprised. She simply stared at him, unable to react, though her lips tingled.

Nathan looked embarrassed, as if he hadn't intended it. "Well, goodnight." He slipped through the door without another word.

Chapter Twelve

Nathan lived only a neighborhood away from Leah, so it didn't take him long to arrive home after the meeting with the women. As he drove, his mind tangled with the question: *Why had he just kissed Leah?*

Kind of a stupid question, when he'd been longing to kiss her for the last two months. But why then, so sudden, so unprepared? He'd been overtaken by gratitude for what she'd done. But naturally, there was more. Every time he saw her it was as though roots were growing under the soil of their history, binding them together. He didn't know if she felt it. What *had* she felt when he kissed her out of the blue? He saw only shock on her face. He had no idea if the kiss was welcome. Or not.

He'd have to either pretend it didn't happen or talk to her about it. Say it was an impulse. Ben would think he was crazy to backpedal after kissing a woman he liked so much. But Nathan hadn't come to Brenner Falls to fall in love. He'd come to accomplish a purpose and go back to his life. Hadn't he?

That's why kissing Leah had confused him, or rather, disturbed him. He could have easily prolonged their kiss. Could have spent the entire afternoon kissing her. . . Nathan shook the alluring thoughts from his head. He was about to lose his way and go completely off course.

Though it might be too late.

Not only was he falling hard for Leah Albright, but Brenner Falls was beginning to feel like home. And Andy's house was as well.

As he unlocked the front door, he let out a breath of air, a cloud of vapor in the cold. Home. After a full month, he no longer hesitated to use the term. In his first week, he'd spent a day or so making it cozy according to his standard, but it ended up being more than a temporary shelter. He appreciated returning to a house that felt more *his* than Andy's. No longer a squatter in someone else's house.

It was as though there was a quiet conspiracy to make him stay in Brenner Falls.

He'd had his mail forwarded to Andy's house for the time being, so there wasn't any pressing reason to return to his townhouse in Philly to check on anything. No pets, no plants. Static furnishings with no soul. He'd hardly thought about it in a month.

Along with his thoughts of Leah, his mind and emotions flooded over with the blessing he'd just experienced. His homegrown pit of self-effort, of shouldering responsibility, was cracking. In the previous month, he'd suffered from anxiety, sleeplessness, and stress, all from taking the load on himself.

He could have prayed more, given the burden to God. A pinch of guilt needled him. In recent years, he'd taken on the habits of dropping into that relationship when it was convenient. He'd made God an accessory to his life instead of his foundation. A mixture of shame and awe swilled inside him. Awe at how his burden had lightened when he hadn't even properly asked. He'd been submerged in need—drowning—and God provided through other people.

That day, two women who *enjoyed* putting events together ferried away his biggest nightmare. He had to admit, as long as the full burden wasn't on him, he kind of enjoyed it too. Teamwork, Leah had said with a magnetic sparkle in her eyes. Being on a team with Leah was worth all the. . .

Nathan stopped himself. Leah. He'd impulsively invited her over for a cooking class. Given the heady chemistry that was zipping around the room a few minutes earlier, he hadn't been able to stop himself from wanting to be with her more. And kissing her. She'd surely considered it a date, the beginning of a deeper relationship. He had too, for a moment. Until, too late, he realized he was again making a promise he couldn't fulfill.

What to do now? He couldn't cancel with her. Didn't want to. One thing he could do is invite his mother, hitting two birds with one stone. He winced at the idiom, not because of the birds, but because Leah wasn't a project or an item on his ever-growing to-do list. His mother either. He'd neglected his mom over the last week and had intended to have her over for a meal. He and Leah could make the meal, then his mother would arrive, and they'd eat together. Leah might be less likely to interpret romantic intent on his part. *And* he'd still enjoy the time with her.

Nathan wasn't completely comfortable with his decision, but knew it was the better alternative.

"Hey, Mom," he said when she answered the phone.

"You must be up to your ears, Nathan. How are things going with Seasons and all you have to do? Did you find a buyer?" Concern filtered through her voice.

"I think it's about to lighten up." His mom didn't know the latest. "I don't know if I even told you we—I decided to do a Christmas show, like the one Andy used to do. My idea was to have an event to show that Seasons could be profitable since my best potential buyer wanted numbers. Not only numbers for one program, of course, but potential for others in the future. To see if Seasons can be revived and if people will get behind it."

"I'd heard there was going to be a Christmas event," she said. "I didn't know if you were putting it on or if the new buyer was."

"Yeah, I'm sorry I fell off the radar. There was so much to do, and of course, I have all this plus my regular job."

"You can't keep doing that for long, son. You'll wear yourself out."

He explained to her how Olivia and Leah had agreed to help and had taken the entire program off his plate. He still had trouble absorbing it. "You'll never believe how. . . how God intervened. " It had been on his tongue to say *how things worked out*. But he knew better. It had been a long time since he'd used those terms, but he couldn't deny it.

"That's wonderful, Nathan. Seems like he wants to show you that you can count on him. God can provide in any way he wants to, but often, he uses other people."

"Yeah, I was thinking the same thing." Nathan flopped onto the couch and stuffed a cushion beneath his head. He filled her in on the details of the program and what they'd accomplished so far. "I had a vision of the whole thing going up in flames, figuratively. But Olivia and Leah came along just in time. I wasn't sleeping enough and felt like I was running in all directions trying to do two jobs. Even though there's still a lot to do and not a lot of time to do it, it's like a load has been lifted."

"That's wonderful, Nathan. But you're still planning to sell it."

That question again. "Mom, I. . . I don't really know what I'm doing. I haven't focused on the possible buyers or even talked to my broker in a few days. I've been absorbed in all the preparation for this program. Now I need to switch gears and work more on the restaurant angle for the event."

"Are you enjoying anything in this process?" His mother's voice was soft.

He paused. "Uh, despite the stress, which I brought on myself because I thought I had to make it perfect—" His mother's chuckle stopped him.

"What's funny?"

"I'm not surprised, Nathan. You've always been like that. Ever since you were little. Not only a perfectionist, but not wanting help from anyone, as though you had something to prove. No wonder you had to take anxiety pills in high school for a little while. Not that there's any shame in that if it's needed."

He cringed at the reminder. But it was true. He could barely cope back then. He'd been so determined to outpace his childhood reputation by light years that he'd nearly put himself in the hospital. Thankfully, he'd found a better rhythm along with stronger faith during his junior year in high school. In fact, Leah's friendship had been instrumental in his survival back then.

Leah. The memory of her soft lips floated into his mind. He stifled a groan.

"So, back to my question, Nathan. Are you enjoying it at all? You were saying despite the stress. . ." She prompted him.

He couldn't block the smile that crept across his face. His mother knew him well and had a point to make. She saw from a distance what he couldn't see in front of him. "Yes, I kind of enjoy it. The stress and expectation I put on myself was a problem, but the idea of putting something together to make people happy at Christmas makes me happy too."

"And it would have made Andy happy." She paused. "Maybe you shouldn't try too hard to sell Seasons until *after* Christmas. Then you can take stock and have actual life experience to help you decide what you really want to do."

"How'd you get so smart, Mom?" Nathan laughed. "I called to see if you wanted to come over for dinner Saturday. I invited Leah so we can cook together, then we'll serve you our creation. What do you think?"

"I run into Leah from time to time. Such a lovely young woman. I'm glad you're renewing your friendship with her. I'd love to come over, though I'd certainly understand if you wanted to spend time alone with her. I don't want to crash your evening together."

"You and Ben. You both want to fix me up with Leah."

Soft laughter erupted on the phone. "So? She's perfect for you. Could you ever imagine liking her as more than a good friend?"

He already did. Nathan let out a deep sigh. "Where could it lead, Mom? She lives here and I live in Philly."

"But you do like her?"

"Yes, I like her. Happy?"

"Very. Now I know how to pray."

"Suit yourself. I'll see you at six-thirty Saturday."

ଔ ଔ ଔ

Leah checked her hair for the second time. *Not a date. Not a date*, she practically chanted to herself to keep the fluttering in her stomach in check. She'd dressed in neat jeans and a long-sleeve Henley and added gold dangle earrings that complemented her hair's gold highlights. She added light eye makeup, which brought out the color of her eyes, and soft pink lipstick. The look wasn't messy, but not overdone, either. They'd be cooking, after all.

Then his mom would arrive, and they'd all eat together, making it a *non*-date. Although Leah liked Nathan's mom, she couldn't deny a wave of letdown when Nathan called to ask if she minded him asking his mother to come for the meal. After his impulsive kiss, she'd assumed he would take a next step, which would, of course, be a date. Then he invited his mother, as though he were setting Leah straight about his intention. Just friendship. He'd explained he hadn't seen his mom in a while, and it would be a chance to share the meal together. Leah had cheerfully agreed. What else could she do?

Each time she'd spent time with Nathan over the previous two months, the stirring of attraction and the sense of belonging with him only increased. At its foundation lay the years she'd known him as a friend and understood his heart and integrity. Then the adult version had all that plus was manly, handsome, accomplished. And still single.

If she were honest, she'd always liked him. Seeing him again raised hopes and fears at the same time, and fear muffled her expectation. Fear of hope, of thinking that something could finally work out for her. After losing her dad, then losing Michael, she feared another episode of agony. It was often easier to renounce hope and striving, simply living in the margins. Like she'd done in her job for years. Though she'd allowed her heart to grow passive, she couldn't snuff out the longing that spilled through like a faint light under a darkened doorway.

The turn of events had thrilled Abbie, both the kiss and the cooking class. When Leah told Abbie Nathan had invited his mom, she advised Leah to relax and give it time. Time? Leah had frowned at her advice since Nathan planned to leave town in just over a month.

She took a selfie and texted it to Abbie for her input. "Look OK?"

Seconds later, she received Abbie's reply. "Beautiful and appropriate! Take your apron with you."

Oh, good idea. Nathan might not have one, let alone two. And she didn't want to spend the whole evening with stains down the front of her shirt. Having promised to bring dessert, she'd made an apple cobbler that afternoon. Seemed a fitting treat for the fall season with salted caramel ice cream to dollop on top.

Leah knocked on the door of Andy's house, now Nathan's, at four thirty.

The door opened and Nathan appeared with a wide grin. He wore a lime green polo with long sleeves pushed up to his elbows. "Right on time." He opened the screen door, ushered her into the entryway, and took the casserole dish and ice cream from her hands. "Mmm, what's this?"

"Apple cobbler with ice cream." She unzipped her jacket and slipped out of it.

His eyes widened, and he exaggerated licking his lips, which reminded her of Theo after a meal. "I love it. Good choice. I'll put this ice cream into the freezer. The kitchen's back here." He gestured with his head.

Leah followed him through the living room into a wide galley-style kitchen with an island in the center and an eat-in area just beyond.

"This is a nice kitchen. Perfect for a chef man."

"Is that my new name?" He turned to her with a smile. Then the smile slid away. "Leah, about the kiss. I was excited about everything and of course, I feel so close to you. I hope it didn't bother you."

Her mouth fell open. "Um, bother me? No, Nathan. I. . . I liked it. I mean, I liked your enthusiasm. And I liked the kiss." Her words were quiet, honest. But her hopes wilted like shriveled rose petals.

Did his statement mean it hadn't meant anything to him? Or was he feeling awkward because he'd wanted it and gotten carried away? She had no idea how to take his apology.

Nathan seemed at a loss for words. "Okay, good. Uh, me too." He paused as if he was about to say something else. "Do you want something to drink?"

"Just a glass of cold water." She forced a smile. At least she knew now before her unrealistic fantasy had gone too far. Unless he was simply fighting his feelings. He *did* say he'd liked it too.

No, she would *not* spend the evening analyzing. It was still possible that he liked her but had other reasons for backing off. Before he headed back to Philadelphia in January, she'd simply ask him. For now, her goal was to enjoy his company and be a good friend. That, she could do. "What are we making?"

"I thought about Osso Bucco, but then decided on chicken paprikash."

"Do I need to learn a new language to cook with you?"

He grinned. "Probably wouldn't hurt. But I don't know either Italian or Hungarian. The ingredients for the chicken dish are easier to find and the meal is less time intensive than the Osso Bucco."

"Sounds like a good choice. I know how to cook in general, but like I told you the other day, due to time constraints, I've slipped into the habit of making simple stuff. Baked fish, salads, soup. Wholesome, but nothing fancy. Looks like you're going to teach me fancy."

"No, not too fancy, but interesting. The recipe's new for me too. It's nice to do something special for yourself or friends or your mom. And I don't mind experimenting on them." He pulled a long black apron from a hook in a pantry closet.

"I brought my apron." Leah pulled hers from her purse and slipped in on.

"I'm impressed. You're prepared. Ready to be my sous chef?"

She tied the apron strings around the back and stood at attention. "I'm ready. What do I do first?"

Nathan set Leah up at the butcher block kitchen table to cut green peppers, tomatoes, and onions while he stood at the island and carved a whole chicken into serving pieces.

"How did you develop an interest in cooking, Nathan?" Leah carefully removed the membrane and seeds from the sliced green pepper. She pushed them to the side and began peeling the onion.

"When I was a kid, I was over here all the time." Nathan went to the sink to rinse chicken goo from his hands then fished a large, covered pan from one of the lower cupboards. He returned to the chicken to wrestle the skin off the parts. "Andy was like the dad I didn't have."

As Leah watched, his hands went still and he bowed his head, likely remembering the gravity of his recent loss. She kept silent as an ache radiated in her throat and down to her chest. She was still his friend and she understood. Grief could ambush a person in a vicious attack.

Nathan turned and snatched a paper towel from the counter. He pressed it against his pinkened eyes. "It'll take a while. Sorry."

"No need to be sorry, Nathan. I've been there. And it *does* take time. You can't rush it."

Nathan cleared his throat. "So, often I'd come here after school while my mom was still at work." He piled the skinned chicken pieces into a large bowl. "Andy had more flexible hours, so he'd arrange to be here when I got out of school, and we'd cook dinner together. On those days, my mom would come over, and we'd all eat together like a real family. Well, it *was* a real family."

"It certainly was. I bet it was great to have meals together. Your uncle Andy taught you to cook, then?" She'd suspected as much.

"He taught me, but also gave me an appreciation for it. Now, it's my hobby. De-stresses me. I never wanted to be a chef, but it's nice to cook for friends and for my mom. And for myself." He fell silent as he finished skinning the last piece and set the bowl on the counter. "Done," he said as he threw the oily skins into the trash. "I hate that part, but it reduces the fat content in the sauce and eliminates the need to skim it off later."

"Smart thinking." Leah finished cutting up the peppers and the onions, thankfully. Last was tomatoes. Then she'd receive further instructions.

"This morning, I met with Paul, the manager at Seasons. He wanted my input on the food, including the special Christmas menu. It was a productive meeting. We came up with two primary choices for the event. The ticket price will include a meal with four courses and the show. I thought having only two choices, plus a kids' choice, would simplify things and allow for volume preparation."

"I'd like to say, *smart thinking*, but I think I already said that." Leah grinned at him. Abbie's words came back to her. *Relax, give it time*. Her sadness loosened and comfort at his presence took over. "You're really a natural at this, Nathan. What did you decide about the rest of the Seasons menu?" And why did he care about the menu if he was going to sell the restaurant?

"Honestly, lots of the menu items were old-fashioned. Like meat loaf. Who orders meat loaf at a restaurant? I guess that's how it got the reputation for home cooking instead of fine dining."

"Depends on your goal for the place. Nothing wrong with home cooking if that's your brand."

Nathan laughed aloud. "You sound like me. I'm in marketing and I use that term all the time. You're right, don't want to be off brand." He shook his head, finding it funnier than she did.

"Are you aiming for fine dining? In that case, yes, you'd need to change everything about the menu."

"Well, not everything since we'd lose much of our current clientele. Some people have been regulars for decades. I suggested taking out the things that don't sell well and are too ordinary and replace them gradually with some upbeat choices. Can't change too much at once. It might be a good idea eventually to stay open only for lunch during the week, if lunch is the most popular time. Then we could focus more on dinner when we have an event." He reached down to pull a Dutch oven from the cupboard and ran water into it.

"Looks like to me you've really thought it through. Sure you're planning to sell it?"

He paused. "Still planning on that. I want it to be as attractive as possible to a potential buyer."

"Not my business, but you seem to like food-oriented things and you have an obvious ability with management. How does that match your job in Philly? You said you do marketing, right?"

"What do you mean when you ask how it matches?" He turned to her and swiped his wet hands on his apron. "In what way?"

"Your passion. Are you passionate about marketing?"

Nathan let out a chuckle. "Is anyone?"

"Well, yes. If you're choosing a career where you spend eight or more hours a day, you ought to enjoy that profession, unless you really can't find anything else. Which I doubt would be the case for you."

"Says the girl who spent how many years in an insurance firm."

"Point taken. The thing is, I've recently seen the difference between boring job security and what I'm doing now, which matches my passion and gifts. I'm *enjoying* finally being involved in music. And planning the Christmas program at Seasons is like the event planning part of my old job, which is what attracted me to it, but ended up being only a tiny part of the job."

He crossed his arms and leaned against the island. "Though you can't make a living at what you're doing now. I'm glad at least you love it. Can't pay the bills with that, but I'm glad for you." He smirked then reached to an upper cupboard to pull down a bag of egg noodles.

"I don't have anything handy to throw at you now, Nathan." Leah narrowed her eyes in a fake grimace. "Only this knife, but I won't do that. I might get arrested."

He laughed. "I'm sorry, I don't mean to tease you. Not much, anyway. My job is interesting, with measurable results. I like that. It pays well. On the negative side, I'm working for someone else. Don't quite like that. There are periods when I work a lot. A *whole* lot. But then, there's some flexibility. For example, I'm currently working remotely."

Leah shook her head in amazement. "How are you able to keep up with it, considering all the other stuff you're doing?"

"Barely, that's how." He took the plastic cutting board from the island and slipped it into the sink. "I'm barely doing my job. I'm finding it's almost an afterthought, and that's a dangerous spot to be in." He snagged a rag from the sink and began to wipe down the island. "I'm starting to have difficult discussions with my boss and some of my clients. I need to do better, or they'll decide the remote arrangement isn't working and yank me back."

"Yikes. What will you do? You have to put that first, don't you?"

"Theoretically, though it feels less urgent than Seasons. Not sure why I thought I could do both."

"Maybe you thought Seasons was a matter of getting the right buyer at the right price, signing a few papers, and scooting out of town. Is that right?"

"At first, that's what I thought. Then—" He shrugged one shoulder. "I wanted to make it *better*, so I could find the right buyer."

"Because of the selling price?"

"Not really." A pensive expression crossed his face. "I want a particular buyer, a buyer who's likely to keep it a dinner theater instead of tearing it down. I'm not sure why I decided to go all in instead of doing the minimum to sell. I think it was for Andy's sake. His heart was all in and this is his legacy, you know?" He paused and blinked, as if caught by the thought of Andy.

Leah nodded. A mental image of the family dinner scene Nathan had just described flashed into her mind. This was no mere business transaction for him.

Nathan crossed the kitchen and pulled a colander filled with something green from the fridge. "Ben Russo, he's my best friend, he's the one who first encouraged me to do the Christmas show. It seemed like a good way to spike revenue. But it also seems like an insane idea, when you consider how little time we have before Christmas. I went for it but saw too late how much it required."

"Do you regret it?" she asked softly, placing her tomato juice covered hands on the table in front of her.

"I don't. It sounds. . ." He let out an awkward laugh. "Well, it doesn't make sense. But your help and Olivia's make all the difference. I'm eager to see it through."

"Before you leave us all here and return to your pressured marketing job." She pulled an exaggerated sad face. She shouldn't have said that to him. She had no right to question his reasons for wanting to return to a job that he seemed ambivalent about. He hadn't invited her in that far.

Nathan didn't respond but seemed to either consider what she'd said or how to object. He brightened. "So, the next step is to sauté the onions and peppers. Too much talk about work is making me nervous. Let's cook."

Gladly. The atmosphere would have been tense if it had been anyone besides Nathan. She'd stepped over the line, but maybe he needed a little nudge to question what was best for him. As if she knew. Selfishly, she'd love him to move back to the Falls. Was that desire behind her questions? Her selfish desire to develop a romance with him?

She joined him at the stove.

"This is a step you likely know," he told her. "But since it's a cooking class, I should give you your money's worth."

"Yes, chef. Because I paid so much for the class, it nearly broke me." She smirked and bumped his shoulder with hers. He bumped back and a flush of pleasure snaked through her previous sadness.

"We brown the chicken in the oil then put in all the goodies you've just chopped up along with the Hungarian paprika." He gestured to a square container on the counter. "Or you could put the veggies in first to give them a head start. The chicken can simmer for about forty minutes. At the end, we add in sour cream and boil the egg noodles. They'll be great with the sauce."

"Yum. What time is your mom coming?"

"Six-thirty. So, we have time to argue some more while the chicken cooks." He winked at her.

Relief softened Leah's concern. At least Nathan hadn't been offended by her pointed questions, though she had a hard time imagining him angered by anything.

"Seems like a pretty easy recipe," she said.

Nathan put the chicken on simmer. "Let's take our drinks into the living room." He removed his apron and set a timer.

They sat on the couch about two feet apart and placed their glasses on the coffee table. Leah turned to him and tucked stocking feet under her. "I want to hear more about your current life going way back to when I last saw you. I don't mean the funeral. I mean college. I don't know any of that."

He blew out a whistle. "Eight years is a lot to summarize, but I guess it won't be hard if I say I went to Temple University, which you may remember. I loved being near the city, got a job in Philly and stayed." He splayed his hands. "See? Not much to say. I live in a suburb close to Center City and take the train in. Sometimes, I work from home."

"That leaves a lot to the imagination." She joined her gentle rebuke with a crooked smile. "You're sure I'm the only one who leads a dull life?" She paused. "Sorry, Nathan. I'm just teasing you."

He waved the air. "Of course, I've developed a few friendships. I found a church I like, but it's kind of big and easy to get lost there."

No mention of a girlfriend.

"I remember in high school you were intense and focused," she said. "A high achiever. We used to talk about that, remember?"

"Yeah. Walking around the halls when we were supposed to be in study hall. I went through that period of anxiety I couldn't shake for a while. It got better, and you were a supportive friend."

His gaze slid to the coffee table where he watched a flame dance atop a fat white candle. Leah hadn't noticed it before.

"Did you ever learn the cause?" she asked. "And what finally helped you overcome it?"

The candlelight caught in his green eyes and cast a glow on his cheeks. "When I was little, some kids made fun of me because my dad had left. I think you know that part. Then somewhere along the way, I internalized this drive to rise above that. To prove to people I was my own self-made person, worthy of their respect regardless of what my dad did." He pressed his lips together and swallowed. "That's enough to make anyone anxious, I guess. Living for others' opinions. I met God around that same time, and that's what helped me the most. I attended church before that but didn't really understand that he wants to take the burden. Once I understood I could lean on him, I was able to get off medication and feel better about myself and my life."

Leah remained silent. She hadn't realized he'd taken medication for his anxiety. At his vulnerability, his trust, a hidden place inside her opened, as if her heart were reaching toward him. She fought the urge to lean into his arms. "God came through."

His eyes met hers with an intensity that stole her breath. "He did. You were there for me when a lot of people weren't." He held her gaze for a moment longer then glanced away. "I hate to say I've lost some of that connection with God in the last couple of years and, guess what? The anxiety has come back."

"Not surprising. Staying connected moment by moment is important. None of us does that perfectly. I sure don't. But you also need to address the lie that you have to *prove* something to the world. That's the thing, Nathan. You have *nothing* to prove."

She reached out and laid her hand on his forearm. With his other hand, he covered hers. The heat of his skin on hers prickled all the way up to her wrist. "You're a wonderful man, just the way you are. I saw that in high school, even before you became Mr. Big City Marketer, top chef, great athlete, and so on, and so on." She'd probably said too much but couldn't help it. She longed for him to see himself the way she saw him.

He listened intently to her words, staring down at their hands.

"In other words, you've accomplished a lot, but that's not what makes you special and worthwhile."

He lifted his face and gave her a stunning smile, relaxed and sincere. "Thanks, Leah. I know that in my head. The old voices are loud sometimes. So loud that I don't even hear them, I just believe them." He pulled his hand from hers and rose from the couch. "Need to go check on the bird. I'll be right back."

Topic closed, but that was okay. He'd trusted her enough to share his failings with her. Leah shook her head as rich and multilayered emotions engulfed her. Nathan may have filled out, gotten more handsome, succeeded in the world's eyes, but his heart hadn't changed. The thing she'd loved about him before was still there, maybe even stronger with years and confidence.

The doorbell rang. Couldn't have been two hours already. "Should I get the door, Nathan?" she called.

"No, I've got it. You know my mom, but it would be more polite if I answered and let her in."

Susan Chisholm had always been a familiar face, since she'd worked for years as a secretary at the high school where she and Nathan had both attended. Her dark wavy hair curled close to her neck and her rounded face gave her a youthful appearance. Nathan must have gotten his square jaw and light brown hair from his missing dad. "It's so nice to see you again, Mrs. Chisholm."

"Yes, it's nice to see you too, Leah. But please, call me Susan."

"The meal isn't quite finished, but pretty close," Nathan said. "Come into the kitchen with us as we finish the sauce. Leah's been a great sous chef."

"Ha, I haven't done much at all, but I sure learned a lot," Leah said as Nathan's mom slipped into a chair in the eat-in kitchen. "Nathan's a pro, as I'm sure you know." A stack of plates which were not there before sat on one end of the counter. Nathan must have been multitasking while he checked the chicken.

He added sour cream to the pan and gently stirred it through the simmering gold-red liquid. Leah spooned the sauce and chicken into a ceramic bowl as Nathan assembled the green beans, noodles, and salad he'd somehow prepared when she wasn't paying attention. She was functional in the kitchen, whereas he was gifted. Or else had supernatural powers to make things appear with a snap of his fingers.

As the meal progressed, Leah observed how relaxed Nathan acted with his mother and how easily they discussed and teased. They'd been through a lot together. The next hour went by as quickly as Leah's time with Nathan had. A lively discussion ensued around the table as they talked about the topic of the hour, Seasons.

"Sounds like you've found your niche, Leah, with the music lessons and the show at Seasons," Susan said after she wiped her mouth and pushed away her plate. "That was delicious, you two."

Leah and Nathan thanked her in unison.

"Glad you liked it, Mom. It's a new recipe for both of us." Nathan winked at Leah.

Both of us. His words warmed her, and his wink turned it into a small bonfire.

"Nathan has told me what a blessing you and Olivia have been. You two are like the dynamic duo."

Leah laughed. "I hope so. Like Nathan, we'd love to see Seasons revived at Christmas. The people of Brenner Falls will love it too, I'm sure. And Andy would have been ecstatic."

Susan's expression softened. "Yes, he certainly would have been. *And* proud of you both." She looked at her son and touched his shoulder. "He's watching from heaven and cheering Nathan on."

"That must be why I'm led to do this. Uncle Andy's up there pulling strings." He grinned. "It's for him, it's for Brenner Falls. Maybe it's for something we don't even know yet."

Chapter Thirteen

The glass door of Seasons chilled Nathan's hand as he pushed and entered. On the front door, he'd placed a small sign that stated, *During November and December, Monday through Thursday, Seasons Restaurant will be open only for lunch. We apologize for any inconvenience.* When Paul informed him that the weekday lunch crowd was larger than at dinner, they'd both agreed to the change. One clear advantage was the availability of the stage for rehearsals.

He hovered inside the doorway for a moment, silently observing the stage. Leah stood near the back curtains playing her flute while a couple sang a duet near the front. She wore a flowing calf-length black skirt, black heels, and a red blouse, and had tucked her shoulder length hair behind one ear. Her elegance never failed to draw his attention.

With embarrassed regret, he recalled how badly he'd botched his kiss apology. He'd likely left her with the impression that for him, it had been nothing, a mistake. Though it had been impulsive and poor timing, it had *not* been meaningless. He'd been haunted by the memory of her lips against his ever since.

A woman Nathan had never seen before played a grand piano on the stage. He could hardly believe they'd only begun rehearsals the week before. He was no musician, but thought they already sounded almost professional.

No light beamed from the small window into the kitchen, and only a dim glow filled the corners of the dining room. Nathan slipped into the kitchen and flipped the switch, immediately blinded by the fluorescent lamps overhead. He only wanted to see it empty, without the flurry of activity normally present. Gleaming and clean, quiet, and still. It was a thing of beauty, really, a professional kitchen. One could do so much, not only with the profusion of equipment, but with a full staff.

A flashback entered his mind, one of a half dozen or so white-clad cooks darting around the space, shouting orders, or receiving them, cutting, cooking, plating like bees in a hive or mechanical parts to a machine. He'd both loved and hated it those several summers he'd worked there while he was in college. Now he owned the place.

Nathan simply shook his head. The subtle pressure from Ben, Leah, and his mom had nibbled away at him for the last few days, weakening his stated resolve to return to Philadelphia as soon as he could. Since the dinner with Leah, one question tugged relentlessly at his mind, conscious and not. One question that spawned two dozen. What if he kept Seasons? What would be his role? He wouldn't want Paul's job nor Olivia's. What if everything started working like a well-oiled engine and the crowd returned to the old establishment? Would he be able to make a living? Should he call off Carley?

To add to the arguments in favor of staying in the Falls, he considered Andy's passion for Seasons and the trust he'd placed in Nathan in passing him the mantle. Honoring Andy and doing what would please him wasn't a meaningless afterthought in a decision that grew more impossible each day.

Another option would be to sell Seasons to the dinner theater mogul and move back to the Falls anyway. He could plead with his boss to stay in a permanent remote position, even though he'd had made it clear the arrangement was temporary. Or Nathan could get a different job or start a marketing business of his own. A cascade of viable options flowed through his mind, choices that might enable him to see more of his mom and Ben. And pursue Leah.

"There you are." A voice broke into his memories and questions. Olivia. "I saw a light on in the kitchen and came in to investigate."

"Just looking." Nathan smiled at her, but embarrassment crept up his neck, since he had no other explanation. "It's so different when it's closed."

Olivia chuckled. "Quite. It's like a madhouse in here during the day and on weekends. I've seen it once but forget the reason I was even here. But now, *you* are. But you're the boss, so I guess that's fine. I just came to catch the rehearsal."

"Me too. Sounds great so far, but I just got here." He'd put in a full day at his desk, attempting to catch up on his real job and placate his boss and his clients. He craved a change of environment from his home office and felt strangely relaxed as soon as he entered Seasons.

"Well, take a seat and enjoy. Pretend you're one of the Christmas dinner customers." Her manner was brisk and efficient, but warm.

"Good idea. I will." He followed her out of the kitchen and turned out the lights. He walked toward the stage and sat at a table nearby. The cast was between songs. Leah held a clipboard and wrote something on it then spoke to the couple who had just sung. They sang a few bars a cappella, and she nodded.

"That's much better," she said to them. "I like going to A7th instead. Then you can resolve to D and finish strong." The couple appeared to agree with her decision.

Leah turned and spotted him at the table. She grinned and added a small wave. It caused a nest of butterflies to soar inside him. He waved back.

Next up was a mixed quartet followed by a male solo. Both pieces were traditional Christmas songs, but with creative elements added, as other cast members acted out the song lyrics or did a dance sequence on the opposite side of the stage. A lit Christmas tree adorned one side of the stage while a second one took a central place in the dining room.

Nathan's ears fully enjoyed the music, but his eyes kept searching out Leah, like a missile locking on its target. After the male solo, she stood still and composed behind a microphone in full view on center stage. She hitched her head toward the pianist, who played an introduction. Leah began to sing softly. At the chorus, her voice rose and filled the room. As he listened, his throat tightened, and tears pricked his eyes. He blinked, surprised by his own reaction. She sang out in a clear, steady, and soulful tone, not overly high, but rich and strong. He knew she sang well, but he had no words for what he now heard. Her voice and the sweeping melody she sang cut him to the core. "Wow," he murmured as he blinked multiple times.

During the rest of the rehearsal, he strove to keep his emotions in check. Only a few of the pieces were sacred, but nearly all of them stirred him by their melodies and messages. Leah frequently interrupted the musicians to have them repeat a phrase or chorus, try it a different way, or return to another part of the song. Some cast members showed more talent than others, but overall, their abilities were clear, especially Leah's. She appeared to be a pro in the music realm. And she knew how to lead others, efficiently yet with encouragement, to the desired goal.

The rehearsal ended at nine o'clock. Leah called out to those assembled on the stage, "Good rehearsal, everyone. See you on Thursday evening, same time. Please study your sheet music, especially the changes we made tonight. And don't forget to practice the movements and gestures we talked about. Have a good night."

Conversation among the cast members as they put on their jackets and prepared to leave raised the noise level. Leah came down the stage steps to his table. "Well, boss, what'd you think?"

"First, I'm not the boss. You are." He grinned up at her and gestured to the chair across from him. She pulled it out and sat. "Second, I can see it's going to be fabulous. I know you're just in the rehearsal phase and haven't been at it that long, but I'm already very impressed. A few more practices, and you'll be like Broadway."

"Not Broadway, exactly. But thank you. That means a lot." Her smile seemed shy but sweet.

"I'm totally serious. And you have an incredible voice, Leah. Wow, you could be professional. I can tell you enjoy it too. When you sing, it's like. . . the real *you* comes straight out of your heart." He gestured with one hand from his chest outward.

She rested her chin on her folded hands, a wistful softness in her eyes. "That's *exactly* how I feel. Like my real self pours out of me when I sing." Sadness lingered in her eyes. "As opposed to the rest of the time, or at least some of it, when I'm putting on an act."

"An act? What kind of act?" He linked his fingers across his stomach, intrigued.

"Well, if I'm feeling unhappy about something. . ." She stared down at her fingernails. "I'll still act happy because I want to make a good impression for God." She raised her head and met his gaze. "You know, Christians are supposed to be joyful, right? Then at Christmas, I make tons of effort to be festive, but inside, I'm really sad because I miss my dad. I miss him most at Christmas because during my childhood, he made it so perfect. And he died shortly before Christmas." She lifted a delicate hand toward the room. "One reason Seasons is so meaningful to me is that my dad used to perform here sometimes." Her gaze returned to him. "So, I spend a good deal of time being completely fake. But when I sing. . ." Her luminous blue eyes glistened. "I'm not."

He frowned. "I didn't know. I don't think you've ever been fake with me, past or present." Which was what he loved about her. Her expression seemed broken by regret or shame. His throat tightened. "I haven't seen you much over the years, Leah," he said softly. "But I'm pretty sure fake joy isn't what God wants for you."

He was a fine one to talk since his relationship with God was gathering dust in the corners of his life. Though, recently, he been driven to run to him and admit his need.

Leah didn't respond.

"Not that I know from personal experience," he added with a shrug. "I think God is nudging me more than usual."

She slipped a lock of hair behind one ear. Her dangling earring glinted in the muted light. He felt like running a finger down her smooth cheek, letting it linger there to feel the softness but also to express understanding. And desire.

Nathan's eyes darted toward the stage.

"I know God wants more for both of us, Nathan. And I'm glad he's nudging you. He's nudging me too. Abbie told me I didn't desire enough. I was too easily satisfied. Well, not satisfied, really. Fearful. Fearful of wanting more. More of him, more from life. When you don't risk anything because of fear, you don't see God come through in a big way. So, when I lost my job, it wasn't so much a courageous step of faith. I was literally shoved out of the nest."

He grinned. "And he caught you. And led you to Seasons so you could sing your heart out."

She didn't speak, though her eyes glistened with unshed tears. She swallowed then blinked. "Yes, he did. Did you walk here tonight?"

"No, I drove. Would you like a ride home?" *Wonderful.* An opportunity to extend his conversation with Leah, as raw and vulnerable as it was.

"Yes, that would be nice. It was a good, brisk walk on the way here, but by now it's probably gotten cold."

As they walked to his car, her phrase echoed in his mind. *When you don't risk anything because of fear, you don't see God come through in a big way.* Did that describe his life too? Were his current risks motivated by his need to avoid disappointing people, or did he really trust God?

The drive to Leah's house didn't take long. It would have been a long, dark walk for her through town, so that was another reason he was glad she'd asked. He pulled into her driveway and waited.

"Would you like to come in for a cup of tea or hot chocolate?" she asked.

"Yeah, sure." He'd *love* to. He shouldn't because he was far too attracted to her and he lived in Philly, not in Brenner Falls. But he couldn't stop himself. Nathan cut the engine and followed her inside.

While she prepared tea for them, he surveyed the cozy colorful living room, imagining where she'd likely put a Christmas tree. A large bay window in front would be a nice showcase for tiny colored lights, along with a holiday display of some kind on the window ledge.

She joined him. "Tea is steeping. I made orange cinnamon herbal. Hope that's okay."

"Sounds perfect."

"What are you looking at?"

"I want to help you and help myself recover the true spirit of Christmas." He shot her a sideways glance and walked to the window. "Where do you put the tree? Here? In front of the window? What about lights?"

Leah stood beside him. "Let's get through Thanksgiving first, but yes, I do put the tree here. Garrett puts a string of lights across the roofline and often we have a smaller plastic tree lit up on the porch. Inside, there's usually a ton of stuff. Little snowmen, lights on the mantle, stuff hanging from the ceiling, every doorway, chandeliers, candles." She sighed and crossed her arms. "Thanks, Nathan. I'm ready to stop mourning each time Christmas comes around."

"Good, I'm glad. Your dad would want you to stop being sad for his sake." His voice was emphatic. He enjoyed the Christmas season each year, mostly because his mom and Andy had made it special. And the spiritual importance had always been deeply present. Could he help Leah rediscover it? "The central idea is that God's gift to us in Jesus is ours eternally, not just at Christmastime."

"That *is* the main thing," she agreed. "So, we need to have joy in him all year, and it takes on a special additional. . . zing at Christmas."

Nathan chuckled. "Yes, exactly. I like the way you expressed that. And you need to *own* your Christmas spirit. Instead of riding on fumes of past holidays. They can be good memories but shouldn't dictate every Christmas forevermore."

"Or *condemn* every Christmas forevermore."

She pursed her lips. His gaze drifted there.

"You're right," she said. "I allowed myself to be sad for too long instead of remembering the good times and knowing the present can be just as good or better."

He grinned. "That's my girl." Too late, he realized what he'd said. It was the intimacy of their conversation that made him feel unreasonably close to her, as though she *were* his girl. Like he could tell her anything. Like he didn't want to leave her side. Ever.

Heat flooded his face at his realization. "Do you think the tea's ready?" His question was abrupt but useful.

"Oh, I forgot! Well past ready." She hurried from the room.

During their conversation, Nathan hadn't missed Leah's expression, which he'd describe as soft wonder. Maybe she was already thinking of how different Christmas could be.

Her smile was genuine. She wasn't faking anything.

ଔ ଔ ଔ

"Hi Mom, it's nice to hear from you," Leah said in a cheerful tone. Her mother hadn't called in a while, though Leah reached out to her every couple of weeks. That's how her mother knew the latest about her life and Garrett's. Losing her job, her involvement at Seasons, Garrett's job search, along with the weather and town events. Ever since moving to Delaware four years earlier, their mother had gradually transitioned from a parent to a distant friend in the lives of her adult children.

"Will you be coming for Thanksgiving this year, Mom?" Leah asked after they'd caught up on the main news. It wasn't a given. Leah's mom had developed a new social life in her sister's and her own circle of friends.

When her mother hesitated, Leah knew she'd made other plans.

"I planned on coming, but then Phillip invited me to visit his children for Thanksgiving."

"Phillip?"

Her mother let out an awkward chuckle. "I guess I didn't tell you yet. I'm dating someone. His name is Phillip and he's very nice. I want you and Garrett to meet him sometime."

"So, did you *forget* to tell me you were dating someone, Mom?"

"I thought I'd told you, but I guess not. It's only been a few weeks, and I didn't know if it would develop or not, so I was on the fence about telling you."

"Oh-kaay. And you'll spend Thanksgiving with his kids, not your own."

"Well, I was with you all last year, honey. And I came in the spring to visit. I don't want to miss the chance to meet Phillip's kids."

Leah took a breath. She should be used to this. But it was alright. "That's true, you were here fairly recently. I'm happy for you, Mom. I hope he's a nice guy and you're happy with him. And it's about time."

"Thanks for understanding, Leah."

"No worries. I hope you all have a great holiday. Now, tell me more about Phillip. How did you meet him and what do you like about him?" Leah pushed aside her annoyance at being passed over by her mother at the holidays. Her mother's voice became animated as she described her new relationship.

Garrett walked in the front door as she ended the call. "You just missed Mom. She told me to tell you hello and she'd love to hear from you sometime."

He snorted. "Phone works both ways." He shrugged out of his jacket and hung it on the hook by the door.

"True, but she's your mother," Leah called after him as he disappeared into the kitchen. She found him rummaging in a cupboard. He took a bag of tortilla chips and began stuffing some into his mouth.

"She's not coming for Thanksgiving this year. She's met a man named Phillip and she'll be going to see *his* kids instead of us."

Garrett shot her a look as if to say, *So?* He proffered the bag to her.

She took a handful. "Guess it's just us, bro."

"Is that a bad thing?" With a loud crunch, he chomped down on a mouthful of chips.

"Absolutely not." Her words were sincere. There had been a seismic shift in her attitude about the holidays since her discussion with Nathan, and another shift a couple weeks earlier in her relationship with Garrett. She no longer minded his presence and had grown to appreciate him more. Acceptance had led to healing. "We can invite some friends over."

He narrowed his eyes. "Are you trying to do the fake holiday cheer thing again, Leah?"

She couldn't stifle her laughter. "I didn't know you knew it was fake. But no, I'm trying something new. I had a good talk with Nathan and realized holidays were good on their *own*, without hanging onto the past. Each holiday is a new thing. I want us and our friends to enjoy it. Period."

A flush of joy flowed through Leah as she mentioned Nathan's name, though she tried to keep her face stoic for Garrett's sake. No sense in giving him ammo for teasing her. They'd gotten closer, but he was still an annoying older brother at times.

She'd detected, she hoped accurately, that something in Nathan's eyes and gestures had changed toward her, despite the fumbled kiss. Maybe he had wanted to but not then. And it still seemed as though he were sending her an invitation rather than a warning. She longed to see him again, to test whether it had been in her imagination, her wishful thinking. Her feelings for him were growing deeper, but also held a thread of anxiety. It could all go up in smoke if there was even anything there. Her hope could simply drive back to Philadelphia in January, and she'd have to heal all over again.

"I've known it was fake for years." Garrett interrupted her thoughts. "And the other day you talked about it while we were raking leaves. Glad you're getting with the program. I want to invite my friend Pete."

"You have a friend? That's great, Garrett."

"Very funny. I have a friend from the gym named Pete. Then there's Abbie. She could come."

"Yes, of course. Her parents may want her with them, but she can come here too. I can invite Nathan and his mom."

"That's six people."

"Great, it's a party!"

"You mean that? You're happy about it?"

Leah crossed her arms and cocked her head, enjoying a wholly different emotion. Anticipation. Making the day festive, not to ward off sadness, but to bring joy to her friends. "Yes, I think it's becoming real. I just had to let go of a few things."

Garrett grabbed more chips from the bag. "Like our parents. I mean, we don't absolutely need parents to have a great holiday, Leah, if they can't be here. Have you noticed we're adults now?"

"That's *true*. I had *not* noticed." She spoke to him as a second-grade teacher would but was smiling. "We can enjoy it when she's here and also when she's not. I want Mom to have her own happy life. She's been alone for ten years and now she's met someone. And I want to treasure Dad's memory, but not let it make me sad every year."

Garrett just stared at her. "It's about time, Leah. By the way, *I'm* your family."

"Yes. And I'm yours." Her voice softened. She could hug him for his statement. Then she did. She stepped forward and threw her arms around his neck. He stumbled back then his arms went tentatively around her to return the hug.

"Now, what should we have?" Leah asked when they pulled apart. "Do you want traditional or nontraditional for Thanksgiving dinner? How should we decorate? Should we get pumpkins and dried corn wreaths, stuff like that?"

Garrett waved the air with both hands. "Whoa, that's your department. I'm just here to inspire you." He grinned and left the room.

She grinned too.

Good Gifts   Kyle Hunter

☙   ☙   ☙

Nathan had put in a good morning's work in the small home office of Andy's house. Now that the Christmas program was in such good hands with Olivia and Leah, he could focus on his real job in addition to marketing the Seasons Christmas event. At least marketing was an area he understood and felt competent doing, unlike everything else he'd encountered in Brenner Falls.

No more news regarding the reorganization of his company. Maybe it had all fallen by the wayside or been delayed. He wasn't planning to ask.

Garrett had revamped the Seasons website and designed a page for online registration and payment for the evening, as well as a method of selecting meal options. The guy was a genius as well as a Godsend yet was working at Johnson's grocery store stocking in the evenings. Maybe Nathan should have a talk with him about how much potential he had to work for himself or an up-and-coming local company.

For the Seasons campaign, Nathan had used the slogan, *Christmas at Seasons: Santa is Back* to capitalize on the nostalgic attitude people seemed to have about Seasons. He'd set up social media sites and automated announcements.

True to his word, Mayor Faulkner put city money behind some community billboards around town and in the local newspapers. Why the man had such a strong interest in the success of a private business, Nathan wasn't sure, but he admired the man's vision for what Brenner Falls could be.

Nathan went to the kitchen to make a light lunch of salad and broiled fish. He'd throw in a load of laundry while the fish cooked. He wore his sweats and sheepskin slippers. He didn't miss the daily commute on the train to Philly. At first, he'd loved the energy of the big city, but very quickly, it had worn thin, especially on days when he had to work late, and it was past dark when he arrived at his townhouse, only to tumble into bed and do it again the next day. Climbing the ladder was more exhausting than he'd been told.

As he ate, he thumbed through the string of emails on his phone. The phone rang in his hand. Carley. He hadn't spoken to her in over two weeks. He'd been caught up in everything else and had hardly thought about his broker. She'd been silent too, which he interpreted as lack of interest from current and new potential buyers. Apart from the first three bites he'd gotten early over a month ago, no one had surfaced. Not at all surprising.

"Hi, Carley. I was just thinking about you yesterday. We haven't talked in a while. What's up? Anything new?"

"I have to say, I'm used to clients who are more involved, but I also appreciate not being texted daily about possible buyers."

"Oh. Well, I've been busy trying to put together an event so I can show better numbers to the potential buyer who already has a dinner theater. What's his name again?"

"That's why I'm calling, Nathan. His name is Brian Prokovich. He wants to come right after Thanksgiving to see the place."

"Uh, no, Carley, that's too soon. I wanted to have some numbers to show him after the holidays. We're doing an event in December two consecutive Saturdays, and we're hoping for a good crowd. That'll do a better job of showing him the potential of the place. Can he wait until after Christmas?"

"No, he can't. He said this is a good time for him because he'll be in your area. He said you don't have to have all your figures together yet. He wants to get an initial impression to see whether he should move forward with an offer. After he sees the financials, of course."

Whether he should move forward. This guy was Nathan's only hope. Without any numbers to show potential, the man wouldn't move forward. He'd laugh and walk away when he saw the physical and fiscal condition of Seasons.

"Maybe after the New Year, you'll get a few more bites from other buyers," she said. "There hasn't been any interest except the first three. I don't even know if the other two are still in the picture."

"I haven't heard from any of them either. If Brian is determined to come, there's nothing I can do to stop him." The man would get suspicious if Nathan tried too hard to delay him. "But if there's any way you can put him off until after the show, that would be helpful, Carley. Better still, he can come to the show. He'll see the place in action. We have registrations pouring in already."

"Tell him that. He'll see the potential, Nathan. If he likes what he sees, he can come back after the New Year and may make you an offer."

Nathan sighed. "Thanks, Carley. Sounds like there's nothing I can do to persuade him to wait." May be just as well. Nathan could get the bad news without losing any more time.

Chapter Fourteen

Leah's bank account was shrinking fast. A month after losing her job, the meager severance she'd received was nearly gone. Already, she was digging into her savings. Though her spirits soared while she was immersed in music projects, discomfort hovered around the edges of her mind as she viewed her balance and calculated upcoming expenses. She'd have to ask Garrett if the grocery store was hiring.

She'd applied for unemployment benefits, but the wheels of government moved at a predictably slow pace. Maybe she could get holiday work in the meantime.

She now had six students. Between rehearsals for Seasons and practices for the church program, no time remained to recruit more. Once the New Year arrived, both holiday events would finish, and she'd be able to devote time to finding more income. She'd have to be frugal until then or continue depleting her savings.

Blair's son Jake had begun beginner piano. Blair had humbly suggested he might have a gift. Not only was Jake cute and precocious, but Leah agreed that, even at age six, he demonstrated an unusual aptitude for music.

Despite the dire shape of her finances, Leah's focus zipped from a new song idea to a key change to an alternate ending for one of the carols as she drove across town to the church. With a cold snap typical of late November, she'd begun driving, even to church. That evening, she had a rehearsal for the church holiday outreach on site instead of in her living room. Then tomorrow evening, she'd welcome eight children on the Seasons stage to practice the snowflake dance, which she eagerly anticipated. Nathan had told her he wouldn't miss *that* for the world.

Then Thursday, she and Garrett would host Thanksgiving for Nathan, his mother, Abbie, and Garrett's friend, Pete. Instead of dread and fake cheer, Leah anticipated the event. Especially since Nathan was coming early to help her prepare the main course.

She'd see Nathan two days in a row. A smile curved her lips and she let out a small squeal.

As Leah parked in front of the church rental space, she noticed light already streamed from the small storefront. She carried her violin and flute inside. "Hi, Josiah, hi, Katie." Two faithful members, high schoolers, had already shown up.

"Hi, Leah. How many people are coming tonight?" asked Katie, a cute pony-tailed eleventh grader tuning her guitar.

"I think everyone except Steffy will be here. She had a time conflict, but we'll be able to have a full rehearsal."

Leah was glad that Josiah had joined the team. A senior, gifted in voice and guitar, he added a lot to the team. His shaggy mop of blond hair almost covered his eyes, and he usually wore an affable grin.

"Leah, I wrote a song this week," he said. "I thought of the theme being God's gift, so wanted to write a song along those lines. Want to hear it? Maybe we can do it for the program. That is, if you think it's good enough."

"Sure, I'd love to hear it. Most people aren't here yet, so you can play it for me now if you want."

"Okay. You'll see that for the chorus, each line ends on a phrase that begins the next one, so it has, like, more emphasis."

He seemed bashful at first as he strummed his guitar and sang in a solid tenor voice. He arrived at the chorus. "*All the world was waiting in darkness for a sign. A sign that God was with them in the fullness of time. In the fullness of time, the greatest gift arrived. God's gift was a baby who'd give us all new lives.*"

As Leah listened to him, her throat tightened as the truths of Josiah's words flooded inside her. God's gift. Announced centuries beforehand but given in the fullness of God's time. She'd known for practically her whole life that Jesus was God's gift to mankind but had gotten used to the traditions. She'd gotten callous to the glory of what God gave and how it had changed everything for her. Christmas wasn't about her dad and lights and gifts. It wasn't about holiday cheer, or food, or friends. Those things were icing, extra pleasures that served only to elevate the primary essence.

Josiah scrutinized his own fingers and strings, so he didn't notice that tears streamed down Leah's cheeks. When he finished his song, he saw her face and frowned. "Are you okay? Was it good?"

Leah swiped her cheeks with her wrist. "It was perfect."

ཪ ཪ ཪ

Nathan couldn't remember a better Thanksgiving in years. Candles sputtered from a holiday centerpiece laden with artificial berries and leaves, and tiny white lights framed the frosty window. With an uncomfortably full stomach, he considered the assorted guests around the dining room table—his mother, Abbie, Garrett, Pete, and Leah. As different as they all were, they'd spent the day telling stories and laughing together. When at Leah's urging, they all shared something they were thankful for, even Garrett expressed gratitude for his new friends and rediscovering his hometown. And he added he was thankful Leah was bugging him less, and that drew laughter from everyone, including Leah.

A far cry from the previous year, when Nathan and his mother had celebrated with Andy, who'd spent most of the day nestled in an armchair and covered by a blanket, as his health seeped away. They'd known they were losing him a little at a time. The holiday ended up a solemn occasion, despite their valiant efforts at fake cheer, which would have rivaled even Leah's.

Early that morning Leah had put the turkey into the oven since it would take several hours to cook. She'd scheduled the meal for two in the afternoon. Nathan came over at noon to help her with the sweet potato and vegetable dishes. They'd agreed on traditional vegetables with a nontraditional twist, settling on coconut curry sweet potatoes and an Asian mixed green vegetable casserole with ginger and cashews. Nathan's mom and Abbie brought desserts, pecan pie and chocolate cream pie, while Garrett and his friend Pete supplied an assortment of beverages.

During the food preparation, Nathan was grateful for another chance to cook with Leah. Being next to her in the kitchen allowed him to breathe in the scent of her hair and enjoy her sense of humor. He savored simply being with her. A new facet of Leah was emerging before his eyes. Unfurled, less tense, even playful. An inviting sparkle glinted in her eyes, and her laughter bubbled like uncorked champagne. With which, he knew, he was quickly becoming intoxicated.

Leah rose from the messy table and collected the dessert dishes. Nathan hastened to help her.

"Tea or coffee, anyone?" She scanned the faces of those at the table.

Everyone declined. Nathan's mother rose from her chair. "Let me help you with the dishes, Leah."

"No, really, Mrs. Chisholm, I mean Susan. Please relax and enjoy yourself. I'm going to do these later anyway."

"If you're sure. I do have to get home to feed my cats."

"Go ahead, Mom," Nathan said. "I'll help out here."

She smiled at him, though he detected more to her smile than gratitude. He knew his mother well, and she was pleased to leave him alone with Leah. Nathan almost laughed. In fact, that idea wasn't far from his thoughts, either.

Leah fetched his mother's coat from the guest room, where they lay in a pile on the bed. His mother hugged Leah, then slipped into her coat. "Thank you for a lovely day, Leah. Everything was just wonderful."

"I'm so glad you could come. It was great having you."

After she left, Nathan continued clearing the table while Abbie and Leah got started in the kitchen. Hardly seemed fair that the women always ended up cleaning the holiday mess. Meanwhile,

Garrett and his friend disappeared into his room, so Garrett could show him the video game he was developing. Nathan had never heard Garrett's tone so animated as when he was discussing programming. About the time they'd finished cleaning the kitchen and dining room, he and Pete emerged. Pete thanked Leah and told everyone goodbye.

Abbie finished wiping down the counters. Garrett hovered in the doorway. "Want to go for a walk, Abbs? Work off the pie?"

She turned to him and grinned. "I guess you need some air after all your hard work, eh?"

He shrugged, as if her gentle rebuke pinged right off him. But of course, it would. It was Abbie and for him, she could do no wrong.

"You're all so efficient. You don't need me in here underfoot." He turned a pointed gaze to Abbie. "Wanna go?"

"Okay. I'll need my scarf and gloves." Abbie hugged Leah and followed Garrett outside. Soon, Leah and Nathan were the only ones left in the house.

"Another Thanksgiving come and gone." Leah let out a satisfied sigh. "Want to sit in the living room for a bit, or do you have to go?"

"No, I can stay." Was she hinting? He didn't think so. Just in case she was, he'd play dumb.

"Do you want any more pie? Or tea?" she asked.

Nathan groaned. "I can hardly move. How about some tea?"

A few minutes later, they settled on the couch with steaming cups of cinnamon tea. Leah's cat, Theo, lay curled in a ball in the armchair like a cute, furry cushion with twitching white whiskers.

"Is something going on between Garrett and Abbie?" Nathan peered at Leah over the rim of his teacup as he took a sip.

Leah had slipped out of her shoes and curled her stocking feet under her on the couch. She cradled her tea in both hands and blew into the cup. "At the moment, they're friends, but I think there's some chemistry there. Garrett isn't a Christian, and Abbie's working on him. But I think she likes him too."

"Hmm. Is she making any progress?"

"Not sure yet. He likes her, so maybe he'll listen. *I* sure can't get through to him. I've invited him to church a couple times. Of course, I know it isn't about church. It's about relationship with God. But hearing Pastor Todd might inspire him."

"I'd like to visit your church plant one day." He himself needed that inspiration.

Her face brightened. "You would? Yes, come. Anytime you want."

He took a sip. The tea was cool enough now not to scald his lips. "How about this Sunday?"

"Perfect. I play music there for the worship team. It's small, I warn you."

"I like small. Seems kind of, I don't know, grass roots." Before it had the time to become like a corporation or a show. If the little church could inspire him, he'd be there. He had to get back on track in his spiritual life. *And* bolster his courage for his upcoming meeting with Brian Prokovich, the potential buyer for Seasons.

At the thought of selling Andy's lifeblood, a heavy weight sank in his stomach. It wasn't the pecan pie.

"Are you alright, Nathan? You seemed really sad just now." Leah's brow furrowed. If only he could capture the concern beaming from her blue eyes and tuck it inside. "I, uh. I have a buyer coming this week to look at Seasons."

"Oh." Leah seemed to visibly deflate. "Are you. . . do you feel ready?"

"For sure, no." His voice came out louder than he intended. "I mean, I'm trying to go slowly in courting buyers. I kind of forgot about selling Seasons because I've been so absorbed in the Christmas program. Then my broker calls out of the blue and says one of the possible buyers wants to come this week. I tried to put him off until after Christmas, but he's in the area, so it's convenient for him to drop by. I won't have any profit numbers from the show to help persuade him." He looked down at his knees where he rested the mug of tea. "And now, I'm feeling a little shaky about selling it at all. I wonder if I could make a go of it. Most of the time, quite honestly, I don't see an alternative to selling."

"Because it needs so much work?"

"That's a big part of it." His eyes lifted to meet hers. "Do you understand why it's risky?"

"Yes, I think I do." Her voice was soft. "It's an outdated concept, yet the people here like the tradition of it. That doesn't mean they'll frequent it, though. And then there's the cost of overhauling it, changing the menu, bringing in new talent to run the theatre. It's a big thing."

Despite his growing dread of his meeting with Mr. Prokovich, Nathan grinned at her. "You've really been listening, Leah. I'm impressed."

"Of course, I have." She cocked her head and gave him a half smile. "I've listened to you and sympathized, but also imagined myself in your shoes. I don't know much about business, but I can see how big a challenge this is. As you said yourself, you can't pay bills and salaries with nostalgic loyalty to Seasons."

"You've hit the nail on the head. It seems crazy to even consider keeping it, but I have."

"Why have you considered it? People's pressure?" Her voice dropped. "My pressure?"

"No, you haven't pressured me. I know you love Seasons, and you told me your dad was involved there. But well-meaning suggestions got the wheels turning. Then there's Andy. It was his dream, his business. He might have left it to me because he had no one else, but I believe there was more to it. I know Andy's heart. He thought I'd get a heart for it too."

"Did he have a reason to believe that?" Her voice prompted him.

"He thought I was gifted at it."

"Maybe you are." Leah unfolded her legs and stretched one arm across the back of the couch.

Nathan had never told Andy's words to anyone before. Andy had observed him all those summers he worked for minimum wage in the kitchen. True, Nathan had proposed a few good ideas back then, ways to streamline the kitchen process. Suggestions of new menu items. Andy had told him he could easily see him running Seasons one day. Nathan had laughed.

"Nathan, you don't have to be nervous about this guy coming, because what's supposed to happen will happen. And once it does, you'll know your next step."

"You think I will?" He sure hoped Leah was right.

"Sure. Either way. Right now, you say you're on the fence because of Andy and maybe you're starting to like the idea of keeping it. So, if this guy makes an offer, nothing will happen immediately. Certainly not before Christmas. You can pray about it and after the holidays, you'll know more about whether it can be revived or not. If he's not interested, you'll know that too."

"I'll be back to square one."

"Not really." She fingered the paper tab of her teabag. "If you do the Christmas event and people respond, keep going. Do a few changes and see what happens. If the light stays green, go with it. If it's not working, you can say you tried and do something else. You can stop and sell it *anytime*. You don't have to do it now."

Nathan studied her lips as she spoke. Not just a pretty face, but a sharp brain too. "That's a good point. But what about the renovations? I can't afford all that."

"Maybe a little at a time? Or take out a loan? I don't know, Nathan. Just giving you food for thought. I'll be honest, I'm glad it's not my decision. I will pray for you, though."

"Thanks, Leah. I've talked to my friend Ben about it too, but he thinks I should keep Seasons. Might be because he wants me to move back to the Falls."

She gave him a soft, shy smile. "I do too."

Nathan didn't know what to do with that as his eyes met hers. Did she mean what he hoped she did? "I have to admit, being back in town is growing on me." Leah Albright had already grown on him until she was almost all he could think about. "It's calm and peaceful compared to my life in Philly."

"Which, if I can say it, you don't seem to love all that much."

Nathan frowned. "I get so busy, I don't know if I love it or not. I have no idea most of the time."

"I used to have a job like that."

"But now, you have no job. Don't you worry about that?"

"Yes. Often." She dunked the teabag into her cup several times. "I have some savings since my expenses were low over the last two years. But I can't bring myself to look for something similar. Not unless I get desperate."

"Maybe you won't have to. If Seasons survives, you can work there. And if I keep it, I'll hire you." He grinned. "I'm totally serious. You're amazing."

Leah laughed. "Thanks. That would be great. But I'm not sure Seasons could afford to hire me."

"Probably not. Not yet, anyway."

"A girl can dream."

After a pause, Nathan rose. "I should get going. Most people are off tomorrow, but I have a lot of work to catch up on, so I'll get up early."

"I'm sorry about that." Leah stood and set her mug on the coffee table. "Try to do something fun too. And don't work all weekend."

He smiled. "I won't. And I'm coming to church with you Sunday. That'll be fun." They stood facing each other. He didn't want to leave. He didn't have to, really, but thought she might want to relax after the long day they'd had. "Thank you, Leah."

"What for?"

"For listening and caring." His tone grew soft. He lifted one hand to run a couple fingers down her arm. "For understanding what I'm going through and the decision I need to make. Makes me feel less alone."

She didn't answer but stepped toward him and slipped her arms around his waist. A familiar gesture of friendship, though he felt nothing like a platonic friend to her. His arms circled her shoulders, and he pulled her into him. She rested her head on his chest. He held her for several seconds, as his heart pounded, and his need for her engulfed him. Her heat seared his torso like a healing balm. He couldn't let her go.

Finally, he loosened his arms and faced her. Her head lifted, maybe to speak, maybe inviting more. Her face was so close, he could see the velvet texture of her skin. His own breath became ragged as his heart pounded against his ribs.

Nathan tipped his head forward and gently brushed her lips with his. The touch electrified him. He kissed her more deeply then, pressing into her, groping her lips with his own. She melted into him and lifted her arms around his neck. As she opened her lips to him, she tasted like cinnamon, felt warm and soft, like he'd imagined she would.

He didn't know how long he stood kissing her but knew he could easily stay there forever. Nathan pulled away from her but kept his arms around her small waist. "I've wanted to do that for a long time," he whispered.

"You have? Why didn't you, after that first time?" Her blue eyes widened, and a flirtatious lilt entered her soft voice.

He *loved* it.

Her eyes lowered. "I. . . I thought you regretted kissing me that time."

He shook his head vigorously. "No, not at all. I regretted the way I handled it but that's another matter. I mean, I was so confused about what to do, not do. I was dying to kiss you, but I kept thinking about having to go back to Philly. I thought it wouldn't be right to start something when I knew I was leaving, like it was unfair to you. But now I don't *know* which way I'm going."

Truer words he'd never spoken. At that moment, he thought he'd never go back. Not when his arms were around Leah Albright who'd just kissed him like she meant it. Like she sang, in fact. From the deepest place in her heart.

"Did you know I had a crush on you in high school?" she asked.

"No, I didn't. I was kind of a nerd back then."

"No, you were not. Maybe in junior high, but you were, um, quite attractive by the time you were a senior."

"You had a crush on me?" A small grin stretched his lips.

She nodded. "I still do, Nathan. Even more than before."

His eyes searched hers. "Yeah, me too. I'm humbled and happy that I ran into you. That we reconnected our friendship. I just don't know where all this is going." He traced her smooth cheek with one finger. "This, meaning my life. And us. All I know is I really like you."

"That's enough for us for now. We don't have to have all the answers tonight."

"You're right." Her words untangled the anxiety that had formed in his chest. Her soft tone spoke to his fear. She seemed good at living in the moment and not overthinking the future. A skill he needed to learn. Maybe with her, he'd learn it too.

Nathan touched her forehead with his own. "You're so wise, Leah. You calm me. You always did. You told me that in high school and you're still saying it. One day at a time." His eyes roved over her smooth face, so calm, so beautiful, then to her full, pink mouth, then back to her eyes. "For now, I just want to kiss you again."

"I hope you will." Her voice, soft like flower petals, caressed him deep inside, drawing him. He slid his fingers through her soft hair and drew her head forward to kiss her again. As the intensity of their kiss increased, a quiet groan emerged from his throat.

Several minutes of ecstasy passed, and Nathan reluctantly pulled back from her. "Want to discover a new restaurant tomorrow night? It'll be fun to be together, but we can also do some undercover menu investigation." He raised his eyebrows to invite her.

"To get new ideas for Seasons?" She giggled. "I like that idea. We can be spies together."

"Exactly. See what the competition is doing."

"I'll be your research partner anytime." Her voice was gentle, breathy, like angel feathers swirling around him.

After a final kiss—or several, who was counting?—he drove back to Andy's Craftsman bungalow. His chest and mind hummed with energy close to exploding. He could still feel Leah's lips on his, her arms around him. His life was up in the air, his future hanging on so many different decisions tangled together.

Despite all that, he could honestly, for the first time in a long while, call himself a very happy man.

Chapter Fifteen

"Want to go pick out a Christmas tree today?" Leah sat across the breakfast table at Garrett, who'd finally made himself some bacon and eggs. He seemed to enjoy them so much, he didn't respond to her except with a grunt. Or maybe it was because he was scrolling through his phone and hadn't heard her.

"Earth to Garrett. Christmas tree?" She gave him a hopeful grin.

Finally, he glanced up from his phone. "Sure, as long as it doesn't take too long. We don't have to, like, cut it down or anything, do we? I have to do some work this afternoon."

In the previous two weeks since the new Seasons website went public, Garrett's website expertise became known, and he'd received two requests from people in town to design and create websites. At Leah's suggestion, he planned on starting a business after the New Year. It had been a good week for her too, with the addition of two music students.

Leah laughed. "No, brother of mine. We won't trek into the snowy tundra with our hatchets in tow to find the perfect evergreen. There's an empty lot next to Owen's gas station they've converted into a Christmas tree store. We'll go there first."

"But you'll decorate it, right? Not sure I'm good at that."

Leah rolled her eyes. "I don't think it requires a degree, Garrett. Anyway, I was thinking of inviting Abbie and Nathan over tomorrow or Sunday night to help us decorate. We'll make a party out of it." She hadn't told Garrett of her new relationship with Nathan, which for the moment was a private treasure she protected inside her. She couldn't wait to tell Abbie, though, and let her know she and Nathan had finally had a proper date later that evening.

"You and your parties. We just had Thanksgiving."

"And it was a lot of fun, wasn't it?"

"Yeah, it was. I'll have to admit. I think you're getting on some genuine holiday spirit instead of the fake kind."

Leah splayed her fingers across her chest in mock amazement. "You noticed? I'm overjoyed. Yes, it's real. I think the fake cheer is a thing of the past."

"Thank goodness."

Two hours later, Garrett and Leah hauled the fragrant eight-foot Douglas Fir into the living room. Leah had already prepared the area in front of the picture window with the stand where Garrett labored to slide and adjust the tree.

"Thanks for your help today, Garrett. I appreciate your holiday spirit." She cast him a sly expression. "And maybe the idea of decorating with Abbie contributed."

He shrugged but said nothing.

"Are you and Abbie becoming an item? Or am I being too nosy?"

"I'm used to nosy. No, we're not an item. She says she's my friend, but nothing more since I'm not a Christian."

"Oh?" Leah fell back into the worn armchair near the window. "What do you think of that?"

"Seems logical that if it's so important for her, she'd want me to think the same way."

"But you don't? I mean, you were raised a Christian. Is there anything that, I don't know, calls you back sometimes?" She'd never had this kind of discussion with her brother. Perspiration broke out on her neck, though at the same time, she was grateful.

"Yeah, once in a while." He didn't look at her. He shoved his hands deep into his pockets. "She explains things pretty well, not in a churchy way, either."

"You know. . . you can talk to me about it if you want." She waited for his reaction.

He turned to her then. "Honestly, Leah, I never wanted to talk to you about it because you always had your pat answers, your clichés. I always felt like you were judging me, and there you were with your fake joy."

Leah's mouth dropped open. "Really?" For a moment, she couldn't think of anything else to say. Her chest felt heavy, as though someone were stepping on it and her eyes stung. "Oh, Garrett. I had no idea. I'm so sorry." All this time, he saw her as a hypocrite. Easy answers. Judging him.

"It's okay. It just didn't attract me back to the church or to faith. Don't get me wrong, it wasn't just you. It was a lot of other people too, and circumstances. Abbie's a friend, but she's genuine. I'm not saying yours isn't genuine, but. . . I've said enough, I think."

Leah jumped to her feet. "Garrett, I didn't know you felt that way. I'm so, so sorry! Will you forgive me?" She took his arm, as though she were a beggar pestering him for a coin.

"Leah, there's nothing to forgive. That's the way you live your beliefs—"

"No! Not anymore, Garrett. I did, but I'm changing. Don't you think I'm changing? I'm trying to grow. It's a daily process. I'll disappoint you and get on your nerves occasionally, but you will too." Her voice held a pleading tone.

He shrugged. "Yeah, I guess you're different. You're less fake, so that's good."

"What I *believe* is real and always has been. I'm the one who had other issues under the surface, like lies I believed. I thought after losing Dad and Michael, I had to suck it up and act like I had faith, but inside I lived in a state of hopelessness. I didn't even *know* I'd stopped believing in God's goodness. And his good gifts."

Garrett stilled and was quiet for a long moment. His face had softened as he stared at her. "I understand. But loss happens to everyone. You think I was happy to lose Dad? Then to lose Angela? She dumped me in a cold way after three years together. But life goes on. We move ahead, not behind."

"Yes, we do." Wisdom from the mouth of her pagan brother, bless him. "I do hope you'll forgive me, Garrett."

"Don't worry, Leah. Like I said, there's nothing to forgive." He swiped the air, as if he were embarrassed by the drama she was creating. "So, don't beat yourself up. You're lots better and easier to live with than you were before." With a grin, he left the room.

Leah wept for several minutes. What damage had she unknowingly done to her brother's soul? All these years, she assumed he was hard toward faith, oblivious, content living in the world. Maybe he was, but she hadn't presented a joyful alternative. She'd dishonored Christ by being fake happy as a veneer over hopelessness. He'd seen right through her fake Christian joy as easily as her fake Christmas joy, and he hadn't wanted her version. Though he too had been difficult in his own way, she fully understood his attitude. She'd have run away from that too.

Instead of chastising her for misrepresenting him, God had lovingly opened the door to the real thing.

ೞ ೞ ೞ

Nathan hovered at the doorway of Seasons at ten o'clock Saturday morning. Though he wore gloves, he rubbed his hands together and pulled up his collar. No sign yet of Brian Prokovich. He wondered if the man would show. Part of him hoped he wouldn't.

Five more minutes and he'd go inside to wait. Temperatures had dropped overnight, though the previous evening it had been mild for late November. He'd hardly noticed the forecast that evening. It had been his first actual date with Leah, and he'd been caught up in the wonder of holding her hand across the restaurant table, talking in complicit tones, gazing at her in the candlelight. He'd wanted to pinch himself and still did. Was it real? Yes, finally.

He guessed they were now an official couple. The last thing he'd expected returning to the Falls was to fall in love with Leah Albright.

Or into the process of it. That might add tons of confusion to his already complex life.

Or clarity.

He couldn't stop thinking about her. And when he did, a warm gush chased away the thirty-something temperatures of that frosty Saturday morning.

A car pulled into the empty parking spot several feet away, interrupting his thoughts. A fiftyish man emerged and walked toward him. "Nathan?"

"Yes, you must be Brian." Nathan shook the man's hand. "Come on inside. It's gotten cold."

"I expected it up here," the man said with a smile. "I live in Atlanta, so it stays mild until mid-November."

Nathan smiled politely. "Sounds nice. Maybe one day I should move down there." Of course, *that* would never happen.

He held the door open, but Brian had stopped and was scoping the front of the building. He jotted something on a small spiral notepad Nathan hadn't noticed before.

"Just a minute." Brian held up a gloved finger. He took a few paces backward in the parking lot and took several photos with his phone. Nathan still stood holding the door.

"I'm ready to see inside."

They walked into the darkened dining room. "Can I get you some coffee or tea?" Nathan asked him.

"No, thanks. I don't have much time today. I was in the area and wanted to get a first impression. Your broker informed me that your financials won't be ready until after the New Year, and that's fine. But I wanted to know whether I should move on sooner or wait it out."

Made sense, though Nathan didn't like Seasons being on display like a maimed dog in a show. Where had that image come from? Brian's attitude was predictable. And normal. What did Nathan expect? Maybe he wasn't cut out for business if he already felt protective of his disabled and tired-looking restaurant. He'd show Brian what he came to see and let the chips fall where they may.

"This is, of course, the dining room and currently, it's open for meals, whether a show is scheduled or not. Carley may have told you that my uncle, the previous owner, was ill so he couldn't maintain the programming like before. We'll be doing a Christmas event to see how people respond and how much they'll be likely to frequent the place in the future." Nathan realized he was saying too much. Anything he said to the man could influence his final decision. The less said, the better, especially since Seasons wasn't in a stellar position to bring a good profit. "I think you're aware of the town's growth in the last two years, and its projected growth."

Brian merely nodded and continued to make notes. Nathan wasn't even sure the man had heard him.

"You see the stage there." Of course, Nathan was presenting the obvious. "Productions can take place there all year round, though we haven't done many because of my uncle's illness." Redundant, but he didn't know what else to say.

"Would be better if it were in the round." Brian narrowed his eyes as he considered the stage. If he were to become serious, he'd want to see behind the curtain, the storage room under the floor, everything. "That way, you'd have seating on all sides of the stage and could accommodate more people."

"Maybe with renovations, that would be possible." Not really, short of tearing down the entire building. Which reminded him, he should talk to Mayor Faulkner to see if there were any zoning limitations on what could happen to the building, as well as how far he'd go as mayor to protect the historic Seasons building. *And if it was even officially designated as historic*, other than in people's minds.

Again, the man didn't respond, but continued taking notes. He pulled out his phone and took several more photos of the dining room and stage, without asking Nathan's permission.

"Can you tell me a bit about your vision, Brian?" Nathan crossed his arms over his chest.

"Certainly." Finally, the man turned directly to Nathan and spoke. "I have three dinner theaters in the southeast. One in Florida, one in Atlanta, and one in Virginia. I was interested in this location because if I have one in Pennsylvania and then another in New England, I'd cover the east coast. No one would have to travel too far to come to a production and it would be a draw for tourists, you know, like Branson or Dollywood, but much smaller. People are willing to travel a few hours by car or chartered bus, I've found, but not if they have to fly."

"I see. Do all your buildings have the same look inside and out, or are they all different?" Were they talking tear-down even if Brian kept it a dinner theater with the same overall mission?

"Generally, yes. Though, in this case, I'd see how sound the building itself is before making that decision. A lot can be done with the exterior if the bones are good. Clearly, the building is outdated, and who knows what kind of deferred maintenance it has hiding." Brian's voice was matter of fact, his expression opaque.

Nathan bristled, even though he knew little about Andy's maintenance schedule of Seasons. He made a mental note to find out. He himself had called it a white elephant but didn't want someone else to do the same. Especially a potential buyer.

"I'd like to see the kitchen." Brian turned abruptly and walked in that direction before Nathan could respond. He hurried to catch up.

"There's a small staff here already to prep for lunch and dinner." Nathan wouldn't tell the man they'd stopped serving evening meals during the week due to low attendance. Nathan had briefed Paul in advance, so he wasn't surprised when Brian strode into the kitchen as if he owned the place. The other employees stopped for a moment in alarm. Nathan introduced Paul and Brian to each other.

Brian asked Paul several questions about kitchen equipment and serving capacity. Nathan could guess what was roiling inside the manager, but outwardly he remained calm and friendly. Always the professional, contrary to so many raging chef stereotypes.

"I'll get out of your way now, Paul," Brian said, as if they'd known each other for years. "Just wanted to get an impression." He took a few photos of the kitchen, again without asking permission. "I'll eventually need to know the number of covers per week, month by month. But this is fine for now."

The visit took only about twenty minutes, but Nathan felt exhausted. Likely mental tension. And defensiveness. Why was he defensive? Didn't he want to sell Seasons? Why did he feel like he was giving away his firstborn for adoption by a stranger? Nathan shook his head. He was definitely not cut out for business. Too emotional, too subjective. And he kept thinking of Andy, along with the faces of people who loved Seasons, including Mayor Faulkner. Another thought entered his mind. What about the people employed by Seasons? Were their jobs in jeopardy? Why hadn't he asked Brian what his plans were for the staff if he were to buy Seasons?

There must be a way he could keep it.

After the taillights of Brian Prokovich's rental car disappeared around the corner, Nathan took a deep breath of cold air. *What should I do, Lord?* He hadn't been asking lately, and really should. He'd learned... then forgotten. Time to learn it again.

He pulled his phone from his pocket to dial Mayor Faulkner's number, but remembered it was Saturday. He'd talk to Leah. She'd listen and help him reason it out. She'd help him untangle the mess in his head.

The following day, Nathan found himself at Leah's small church plant, seated in a row of folding chairs in a rented space the size of an average shoe store. He had a clear view of Leah as she played her violin. The church members nearly filled the area, people of all ages. The room held an energy he hadn't felt in a while in larger, more established churches.

Usually, his eyes went magnetically to Leah, beautiful, talented Leah, while she performed. Now that their relationship was real instead of hoped-for, his feelings for her felt more grounded. Wherever that might lead.

That day, however, it was the lyrics that drew him continuously. *I will take the load from your shoulders, open your mouth wide and I will fill it. . .*

Was that a Scripture put to music? He had to find it. Must be a Psalm. Subtle fingers of truth were kneading into his tension, unlocking the hard core he'd been carrying around for what felt like years. Something pure and eternal was finally reaching inside to forcefully clasp his heart, since he hadn't yielded in the gentler way of a true follower. He *needed* God, and it wasn't a sign of weakness. It was a sign of tremendous strength. He needed wisdom, direction, and plenty of forgiveness.

When the music portion ended, Leah set her violin in its case and sat next to him. They exchanged a smile, and he brushed her hand with his fingers.

She clasped his hand. "I'm so glad you're here to share this with me."

"Me too." He didn't trust himself to say more. His throat tightened with emotion, and the sermon hadn't even started yet.

After the announcements, a thirty-something man with longish hair and glasses stood up from where he'd sat on the front row and took his place behind a music stand.

"Good morning." He greeted everyone with a warm smile and joked for a few minutes about how much they'd eaten during Thanksgiving and about an antic of his three-year-old daughter. "I have a word for you today. I was thinking about how busy and burdened people get at this time of year, when it's supposed to be a time of quiet recognition. So, here's what the Lord gave me for you. I hope you'll let it sink in. *Now I will take the load from your shoulders. I will free your hands from their heavy tasks.*" He paused and his eyes swept the room. "Do those words speak to anyone during this time of year?" A few people chuckled, and others lifted a timid hand.

Nathan stilled. *Yes, they speak to me.* How did this pastor know all he'd been dealing with? Of course, it was God. He knew.

The young pastor continued. "Consider dropping your burdens in his strong, capable hands. Then reflect on the baby in the manger, God's good gift. The little baby who became the powerful Lion of Judah, Savior of the world." He blinked. Nathan saw the pastor's own eyes glisten as he paused.

"It's not about our shopping, or our food preparation," the man continued. "All the things that, well-meaning as they are, distract us from the main thing."

Nathan's shoulders dropped involuntarily at the words that brought comfort. Permission to be weak, to need. To ask for help.

As Pastor Todd continued, the persistent impression that the message was for him alone tapped on Nathan's chest, his mind. He whispered to Leah, "Are you sure you didn't tell Pastor Todd *exactly* what I needed to hear?"

She grinned and shook her head. "He didn't know, but I know someone who did."

His heavenly Father spoke in words that shook Nathan from the inside. The Father could carry any burden, big or small, all by himself. God had already met the needs, provided everything, and quietly waited for Nathan to discover the provision. He'd met so many needs so far, even when Nathan hadn't asked nor humbled himself to unload his burdens. He already saw where that could lead. Anxiety medication. He didn't need that again. Clearly, God had another destiny for him.

One that was indisputably good.

Chapter Sixteen

Leah hardly felt the chill that laced the early December air. A veil of contentment enfolded her like a fleece blanket as she walked along Warren Street beside Nathan, her arm linked through his. Though she vibrated with joy over her new relationship with him, a wider sense of peace and enjoyment of the season, real instead of fake, invaded her heart. Might be the first time since her father's death that she'd enjoyed the Christmas season.

Every historic brick building along the sidewalk sparkled and called to passersby with shiny decorations, garlands, lights, and merchandise strategically placed to attract them. Garlands woven with tiny white lights topped each doorway and window display. Everywhere, she saw lit Christmas trees of all sizes with glittering or homey ornaments, inside shops and on sidewalks. Holiday music spun softly into the air from hidden speakers on the main street. It was mid-week, but crowds of shoppers hurried like bees in a hive as though it were Saturday morning.

Rehearsals at Seasons and at church and her music lessons filled Leah's evenings, but during the day she had swatches of time here and there for simple pleasures, like taking a hot chocolate break with Nathan. Stealing a bit of time during the day was about all they had together until the Christmas events were over.

"Oh, that's nice. Look." Leah pointed to a whitewashed box on legs with poinsettias flowing over the top. "I can see something like that at Seasons, can't you? Maybe at the entrance."

Seemed much of their conversation drifted back to Seasons. . . either the current holiday event or the future fate of the old establishment. He'd filled her in briefly on his meeting with Brian, but he hadn't seemed optimistic. Relief ribboned inside Leah, though she tried not to show it. Still, she wanted the best solution for him and didn't know what that might be.

"Lindy, one of the waitresses, did all the Christmas décor Monday," Nathan said. "There was a lot of stuff in storage that Andy used to put out every year. I'm sure Lindy wouldn't mind adding some new touches though." A moment of peaceful silence enveloped them. "Is everything on target for the church program Saturday night? I can't imagine the pressure you must have while trying to prepare two programs at one time."

"I'm a little surprised I'm feeling so peaceful about it all. I consider it as two parts of the same job, I organize myself each day, communicate well with everyone, and it's been coming together. It helps that they're all doing their part. It isn't just me. Lots of people at church are involved in making it a success. Almost all the members have some role, in fact."

"Can't wait to see it." He squeezed her hand through her mitten.

Soon, their destination came into view: Sophie's Coffee House. They ducked inside as the cold seeped through Leah's jacket and gloves. They found a café table by the window. "Hot chocolate or tea?" Nathan asked her since he already knew her favorites.

"Chocolate, thanks. Extra hot." Would take at least that to warm her up. She removed her mittens and rubbed her icy hands together. The line at the drink counter extended four deep. While she waited, Leah observed people coming and going, waving at those she knew. She liked her current life, with music students, music projects, and of course, Nathan. And her renewed focus on real faith, instead of forced joy and fake cheer. Made all the difference in the world.

Yet, her new occupations weren't financially sustainable. Doing what she was designed for wasn't going to pay her bills. Seemed she had to choose between dull but financially secure, and a career that made her anticipate the day ahead. An unfair choice. There must be another way.

Leah let out a frustrated sigh. The present was ideal. Right now, she had it all, or almost. But it was a small window that would close after Christmas. After the holidays, she'd have to become realistic. And Nathan would too.

Minutes later, Nathan placed two steaming mugs on the table and sat across from her. "You look pensive. Everything okay?"

"Yes, fine." She gave him a reassuring smile. No sense in talking about her fears of what would happen to them, to him, to her, after the holidays. She was learning to trust God more. She should apply *that* to the near future. Otherwise, it wasn't faith at all, was it? Maybe authentic joy and peace came from growing deep roots of faith during uncertainty. And she wasn't very good at that, especially since she felt on the verge of grasping what her heart always longed for yet feared it would slip out of her hands.

"I don't believe you." Nathan swirled his teabag in the paper cup. "I bet you're worried about Seasons and about us."

She had to chuckle. "How'd you know? I've been so happy lately that every now and then, I think, how long will this last?" As if to prepare for the inevitable crash, her eyes roved over his smooth, manly face, well-shaped lips that had kissed her the previous evening, his intense green eyes always observing, listening, showing kindness.

"Leah." He gently pulled her chin up, leaned forward, and placed a soft, lingering kiss on her lips. "First of all, don't worry about us. I don't know what I'm doing with Brenner Falls, with Seasons, or anything else. But I'm. . . I'm serious about you. Whatever happens, remember that. We'll figure this out together."

She blinked, and a slow smile curved her lips. Together. Yes, they'd figure it out. And he'd kissed her publicly. That was proof of something, wasn't it?

"I'm serious about you too, Nathan." Her smile stretched into a grin. "Usually, you're the one worrying about everything and now you're calm and peaceful. *I'm* the one worrying." Because in her heart, she still didn't believe in happily ever afters. She thought she'd changed, but maybe had more to learn.

"God spoke to me in church the other day. Your church. He lifted a burden from my shoulders, Leah. He spoke directly to me that day. I've felt different since then. I still have to bring to mind the truth day by day and whenever I'm tempted to be anxious. I remind myself every minute, just about. But I think it's taking root."

"I can tell. So, you liked the little church plant."

"I loved it. I'll keep going there as long. . . while I'm here in the Falls."

Something fell with a clang inside Leah. "As long as you're here? Are you still planning to leave?" Her voice was soft and felt papery thin.

Nathan swallowed. "No, not planning. I'm going to find a way to stay, try to. Even if I sell Seasons."

Leah grasped his hand, which rested on the table. "That's wonderful news. Maybe continue your job remotely? That seems to be working better for you now, since you found your rhythm to balance work and Seasons. I don't want to pressure you, but I'd love for you to stay here."

He sipped his drink and met her eyes. "I've had a big shift since I've been here. You're part of that, of course. But I had to make peace with my past. I think that's happening."

"No one but you remembers your past, Nathan. And your past is good when you think of Andy and your mom instead of thinking about your dad. Your dad doesn't define your past." She tilted her head. "Didn't you say something like that to me once?"

"You're right. It was clearer for me that time. My dad doesn't and didn't define me. I let myself feel shame, but it wasn't my shame. I had nothing to outrun, but I spent my life doing just that."

"Maybe coming back here was a way to say it's okay to. . ." She groped for words. ". . . to be who you are now with the unique past that was part of it. We all have baggage. You understand enough now to embrace it, whatever it was, and move on."

Nathan ran his thumb across her fingers, still cradled in his. "I'm getting it. It's coming." He held her gaze for a moment. "On another note, this morning I got an email from Brian Prokovich, the guy who came to see Seasons."

"What did he say?"

"Not much. He didn't say a lot when he was here either. But he mentioned deferred maintenance and the need for renovation both times, during his visit and in his email. My guess is he's going to make a low-ball offer and is preparing me by pointing out all that needs to be fixed."

"What's your overall impression of him and his potential as the new owner of Seasons?"

Nathan just laughed and shook his head. "I'd rather keep it. He's not worthy of Seasons." He stopped. "Did I just say that aloud?" He laughed again, and she joined him.

ଓ ଓ ଓ

Nathan decided to take Friday morning away from his *cell*, as he called it. Meaning, his home office at Andy's house where he worked on marketing for his company. Instead, he hung out in the kitchen at Seasons, observing what everyone was doing, asking questions about the process. It had been a long time since he'd worked there summers during college. He'd forgotten most things and remembered a few. Like how pressured things could get during a busy lunch or dinner rush. And how calm Paul usually was as he patiently explained what each chef was to do and when.

A noise just outside the kitchen door startled Nathan. The door swung open, and Paul rushed in, his face twisted with frustration. "What's up, Paul?" He'd never seen the man like that. Maybe there was an especially irate customer.

He speared Nathan with a glare. "There's a man outside who says he's planning to buy the land. Who is he? You didn't say anything about him. Now we have a parade of buyers every day. I can't work in that context, wondering what'll happen next week, if I'll have a job in a month."

Nathan's mouth dropped open. "I don't know who that is, Paul. Is it the guy who was here last week, Brian Prokovich?"

Paul shook his head and began pacing in front of Nathan. He dropped his gaze to the floor as he took a breath. "No, it's not Brian. It's someone else. Says he's a developer you found through your broker. I know this is your place, Nathan. I have no right to be angry if you sell it to a developer or whoever you want to. I'm just surprised, that's all."

Nathan put a hand on his arm and lowered his voice, aware of gawking employees nearby. "Paul, I swear to you, I don't know who that is and wasn't told anything about his coming today." After two months of silence, all the prospective buyers were showing up at the wrong time. "I was told three months ago about a developer who was interested in seeing the place. I thought he might want to tear everything down and build a strip mall, so I never even expressed interest. The only potential buyer I talked to my broker about was Brian, because he wanted to keep it as a dinner theater. Now that I've met him, I've lost interest. There's no one else who's a candidate, Paul. I'd tell you, wouldn't I?"

Paul regained his calm. "I apologize for jumping the gun, Nathan. The guy was so sure of himself, I thought it was a done thing."

"Where is he now?"

"I just spoke to him outside. He's walking all over the property."

Before the words were out of his mouth, Nathan dashed out of the kitchen and through the front door of Seasons. He saw a man on the edge of the property taking photos and making notes, as Brian had done. Made him think of a vulture.

"Can I help you with something?" Nathan called to the man.

The man's chin jerked up and dark eyes met Nathan's. He was younger than Brian, probably in his late thirties, with brush cut hair and prominent cheekbones that made his face almost skeletal. He approached Nathan. "Good morning. My name is Skip Kaiser." Carley Romano told me about your place here and I thought I'd stop by and see."

"Nathan Chisholm." Nathan shook the man's hand. "I'm the owner of Seasons. It would have been helpful to know you were coming, Mr. Kaiser."

The man waved the air dismissively. "I like to pop in to see the place first, so I can get an idea. I've been driving around the town as well, and things are hopping here. Or about to."

Nathan quelled the anger that simmered at the guy's nerve. "Yes, they are. I grew up here and it's changed a lot. Did you speak with the chef here a moment ago?"

"Yes, just briefly. I told him I was interested in buying the place."

"Without speaking to me about it first? That seems odd. At any rate, you'll have to wait until after the holidays to talk further about it. It's possible I'll take it off the market, but I won't know until after the holidays."

The man seemed unaffected by Nathan's statement. "Fine. I'm not that interested in the building, but the land has a perfect location. Right in the center of town. I guess that's City Hall over there?" He pointed to the imposing building across the street.

"Yes. What would you put here, Mr. Kaiser? Just curious."

The man stepped back and scanned the property from one end to the other. Then turned toward the intersection behind him. "Over there you have a nice park and a town square." He pointed across the roundabout circling the fountain. "Lovely. Small-town charm but up-and-coming. I like that. So, I envision a building right here—" He held up his hands like a frame in front of Seasons. "A horseshoe shape." He motioned with one hand. "Shops on the ground floor with two floors of apartments on top, like they do in Europe. In fact, that style is more and more popular in growing cities across the nation. I'm sure with the increasing population of this town, it'll be a desirable place to live and shop. There could be another fountain there in the middle too, if the parking's sufficient."

"Sounds like a nice concept, but I'm not sure this is your place." Nathan drew his shoulders straight. "You could do the same thing on the other side of town, and it would be just as attractive to people or more so. For one thing, it would be closer to our river. Have you talked to the mayor about this?" Mayor Faulkner would surely be against replacing Seasons with a row of shops and apartments.

"Not yet, but that's a good idea. No, I like *this* location for the project. I'd make a very generous offer, of course. I'll be happy to send Carley a portfolio of my previous projects along the east coast, as well as a mock-up drawing of what I envision here."

"Like I said, I can't discuss it until after the holidays." Why didn't he just say no to the man? Words stuck in his throat. After what he'd said to Paul and to Leah, what if, despite his best intentions, he simply couldn't keep Seasons? What if it wasn't workable for him financially or in any other way? What if it came down to selling? Would it be so bad to have shops and apartments here?

After the man gave Nathan his card and a promise to send his portfolio, he drove away. Nathan let out a deep sigh and returned to the kitchen. "I talked to the guy," he said to Paul. What could he tell him? That he hadn't told Mr. Kaiser to leave and never come back? That he was keeping his options open, despite all he'd told Leah, Paul, and himself?

"I knew you would, Nathan. You've told me all along that you wouldn't sell to a developer."

Discomfort gnawed inside Nathan. He might not have that choice.

Nathan drove to Seasons to attend the rehearsal that evening. Better than staying at home after two more hours of work while his mind ricocheted all over the place. His encounter that morning with Skip Kaiser remained under his skin like a splinter. The man seemed serious about wanting the property and being willing to pay top dollar. That was tempting, only because if Nathan found himself stuck with Seasons, he'd have a lucrative way out.

But what about his burgeoning desire to stay in town and make a go of it? To keep Seasons?

Despite the support of Mayor Faulkner and the town residents, despite Leah's and Olivia's giftedness for the theater area, and Paul's for the cuisine. . . despite all the apparent advantages, keeping Seasons could still be a business nightmare that would bleed him dry. He had a healthy savings account but hadn't planned to pour it into a failing business that might never yield a return. Seemed like he was being pulled in a tug of war between sentimentality and smart business. And the woman he loved wasn't neutral.

Yes, he was falling in love with Leah. What he'd told her that morning was true. Whatever happened, he didn't see himself being without her. And frankly, he didn't see himself returning to Philadelphia either. If he couldn't continue working remotely, maybe he'd have to find something else.

But what if he had to sell Seasons and the residents of Brenner Falls were unhappy with his choice? Was it still such a small town that he'd become a pariah? Would he and Leah have to leave town together? Could he do that to her? He couldn't. She loved Brenner Falls and showed no signs of wanting to leave.

Nathan let out a long, soulful sigh as he parked in front of Seasons. There were a few cars in the lot, those of cast members there for rehearsal. He scanned the area where only that morning he'd had a terse discussion with Skip Kaiser. The man who was now the only serious buyer on his radar. A man he couldn't like, no matter what burden he'd remove from Nathan's plate.

After rehearsal was over, Leah was coming over. She'd help him talk through the current crisis. He'd feel calmer after spending the evening with her.

He walked inside. This time, he sat farther from the stage. He didn't want his presence to distract anyone. And he was in a dark mood. May as well sit in the shadows, away from the stage lights. The rehearsal was underway. Leah didn't see him at first, but when she did, she gave him a limp wave. There was a strange expression on her face. Maybe she was just tired. She was working a lot of hours between Seasons and her church. And her students, who had multiplied. She'd told the parents their children couldn't start lessons until after the holidays.

Some of the cast members were missing. Maybe they had time conflicts, but it wasn't ideal, so close to the performance. The first one would be in just over one week. A wave of dread flowed through Nathan. Maybe it would be a deciding event. It would show him, as Leah had said, which way he needed to go, keeping Seasons or not. And with only one prospective buyer, was Mr. Kaiser his only choice?

No. He could relaunch with Carley after the holidays. Or give it more time and find a new broker in six months. Or a year. As Leah had suggested on Thanksgiving, he could sell it anytime.

Something wasn't right during the rehearsal, but Nathan couldn't put his finger on it. Less energy, less enthusiasm. And one of the missing members was a man who was supposed to sing the final duet standing in front of the sled. Brent was his name. Or Sean. Nathan couldn't remember. Another guy had to fill in and didn't know the lyrics.

Finally, the rehearsal ended, and Leah came to his table. "Hey," she said, but shadows hooded her eyes.

"What's wrong with everyone, Leah? Something's up."

She sat across from him at the small table for two. "We lost three cast members today, only a week before the performance."

Nathan pulled forward on his elbows. "What happened?"

"There's a rumor going around that you're planning to sell the whole place to a developer as soon as the holidays are over. They say the guy wants to tear the whole thing down and put in apartments." Her brows knotted. "Is it true, Nathan?"

"No, it's not. The man showed up this morning completely unannounced. He was one of three names Carley gave me three months ago and I'd never even had a conversation with him." Nathan heard a thread of defensiveness in his own voice. He gentled it. "I'm sorry, Leah. It's been a tough day. First, Paul jumps on me because he thought I knew about this when I didn't. Now you and the cast. I didn't invite the man and I don't know him. He just came, like the other guy. At least Brian called first."

Leah's face softened, and she reached for his hand. "I'm sorry. I should have known you weren't planning anything and keeping it to yourself. That wouldn't be your style."

"No, it wouldn't. I've been open with you from the start about that. I wouldn't sell to a developer unless things got to a point where I had tried everything, and it was the only solution."

She sat back. "But you'd still do it?"

Nathan frowned and blew out a puff of air. "I wouldn't *want* to, Leah. But imagine for a minute I go all in at Seasons, use my savings, quit my job, and it still fails. What choice would I have? I wouldn't want to sell to a developer but might one day have no choice. That's just reality. It might happen that way. There's a reason there aren't many dinner theaters left in the country. But at this point right now, no, I'm not planning to sell it to that guy."

"Okay. I feel better. I hear what you're saying, that one day, you might find yourself stuck in a corner and that might be an escape hatch. I understand that. I don't know where the rumor got started that you were for sure going to sell to him."

Probably went through the kitchen that morning when Skip came snooping around taking pictures. Gossip traveled fast.

"Between you and me, I'd consider if, and only if things get hopeless." It was tempting to get out from under the pressure once and for all. But then, he'd go back to . . . his lifeless job and townhouse in Philly.

Nathan fought a billowing frustration inside him that threatened to shoot out like a geyser. He stood. "I think I need some alone time, Leah. It's been a long day."

Leah had a stricken look on her face as he pulled his coat off the chair. "I'll call you tomorrow."

Before she could respond, he turned and left Seasons.

Chapter Seventeen

Leah spent the night tossing in her bed, tangled in her sheets, reliving her final words with Nathan before he wearily left Seasons. The memory of his angry, hurt face was branded in her mind. She'd slept little and finally slipped out of bed at four-thirty.

She'd failed him. She should have said she'd stand by him whatever he decided. Instead, she temporarily forgot that Seasons wasn't hers. It was his. Though she loved working there, her relationship with Nathan didn't guarantee a future role there. She'd let that become more important than the man she was growing to love. *Oh, Nathan, I'm sorry.*

Leah stumbled into the kitchen to put on a large pot of coffee. It was Saturday, and her one student had cancelled. There was still a Church rehearsal that afternoon and the big event that night. Up until yesterday, she'd enjoyed the rehearsals in both places, but had to admit, it was an exhausting schedule that she could maintain only a little while longer. She didn't know if she even had the strength, physically or emotionally, to get through that day.

Maybe he'd texted, though it was still early. While the coffee dripped through the machine, she scrolled through her phone. Nothing from Nathan.

She sank into the chair at the kitchen table, hollowness bringing a sting of tears to her eyes. Nathan thought she didn't believe in him or trust his motives. Had she doubted him, even after the time they'd spent together, in spite of how well she thought she knew his heart?

The real issue wasn't whether he would end up doing what *she* thought he should do. It was his establishment and his choice what to do with it. She'd watched him straining tirelessly to make it work, to please everyone. When he arrived two months earlier, he'd simply wanted to get rid of it as quickly as possible and go on with his life. Since that time, he'd made a one-eighty turn in his attitude about Seasons. And yet, the numbers still might not add up. It would be unfair for anyone in Brenner Falls, including her, to expect him to take a losing financial proposition simply to maintain their nostalgic sense of tradition. Business was business.

Leah didn't know much about business, but she knew that much. It wouldn't make sense to Nathan to follow everyone's desire and lose his own livelihood. She texted him. *I'm sorry, Nathan. I do believe in you, I hope you know that. And I miss you. I'm here if you want to talk. I hope you were able to get some rest and peace last night.*

He'd have her message when he woke up. Maybe he'd respond then.

She put creamer and sugar in her coffee and returned to the table. She read some Bible verses, willing her heart to lift, but it felt anchored in place, roots encrusted in the mud of her own stubbornness. Was it really true that all things worked together for good, as she'd read so many times? Did God really have good plans for her future? Was it good somehow that all this had happened? When she lost her job, it was good in some ways because she had time to invest in Seasons and in the church Christmas event. Maybe losing Michael had been good because God had someone better for her, hopefully Nathan.

Leah stared out the window where the street still huddled in darkness. *Faith is seeing where you lead and believing it's good, Lord. Even if it doesn't seem good. Your promise is that you're bringing all things together.*

Her job was not to judge God for her past dreams that hadn't turned out, but to trust him that he was weaving together something beautiful in her life and in Nathan's. So what, if Nathan was forced to sell Seasons and it got replaced with housing. Might be sad initially, but people would quickly get over it and enjoy the restaurants and shops that came in its place. So what, if she had to eventually leave Brenner Falls in order to be close to Nathan in a Philadelphia suburb. Wasn't he more important than her enjoyment of her little town? Did she want to grow old and alone there, just because she liked it? Or could she trust God with much more if she let go?

Slowly, the fog lifted from Leah's heart as the darkness outside gave way to a thin strip of sunlight pushing through the horizon. Surrender, not in resignation, but in joyful anticipation.

At nine o'clock Leah decided it was late enough to make a few phone calls. "Good morning, Sean. I apologize for calling so early. I wanted to give you some good news." That would pave the way to hopefully undoing the damage that the rumor had caused.

The sleepy-sounding man on the other end of the phone seemed to perk up a bit at her words. "What good news? I could use some, Leah."

"Well, I learned that what you heard yesterday about a developer buying Seasons is a rumor. Nathan himself told me that he hadn't invited that guy and had never even talked to him. I know you were frustrated by that and quit the Christmas production, but I'd like to ask you to reconsider. It's happening in just a week, and we need your talent and participation."

"Then after Christmas, the developer will come back and Seasons will be back on the block, eh?"

"No, not at all. I do know that Nathan wants to make a go of it. I can't guarantee that it will work long term, but he's trying. Will you give it your best shot, Sean? Please come back to rehearsal."

The man grudgingly agreed. "What time is it again?"

"Six o'clock Tuesday evening. Thank you, Sean."

Leah made a second phone call and had less luck. Violet Jensen had already made a new commitment elsewhere and couldn't participate any longer. "Thank you anyway, Violet. At least now you know that the sale of Seasons was a rumor." She could also call a few people at her church to sing in the chorus.

What if things didn't go well and Nathan had to sell it anyway? Leah shook her head. She couldn't worry about that right now. If she could help Nathan in any way at all, she owed him that.

ಌ ಌ ಌ

Nathan sank into the armchair near the picture window in Andy's living room, a stoneware cup of tea burning his fingers. It was nearly ten in the morning. He never slept that late, even on weekends, but he hadn't slept well. Not after the tumultuous rehearsal at Seasons and his terse departure. Not after seeing the distress on Leah's face, a mental image that followed him all the way home.

How had things gotten into such a mess? When he returned to Brenner Falls, his plan had been simple. Selling Seasons as quickly and efficiently as possible and returning home.

One thing was sure, there was no way to please everyone. He'd been playing to the crowd, doing what people expected for a long time. He'd even convinced himself that he enjoyed it there, saw potential in Seasons for the future. Who was he kidding? It was an outdated concept with deferred maintenance. It would take a fortune to bring it up to date. Why was he even considering it?

Yet, he knew there was more to this than practicality. More than numbers and profit. *What should I do, Lord? Please guide me as you promise in your Word.* Though Nathan was backslidden, he remembered that much. And he hadn't forgotten how God had spoken to him during the sermon at Leah's church the previous week. *I will take the load from your shoulders. . .* One thing had become clear that day, that God was for him and didn't want him to go it alone.

He took a slow sip of the hot beverage. The turmoil inside stilled a few degrees.

What do you want, Nathan? The thought came to him as if out of the blue. Was that God's voice, or his own? No, it was a question Nathan hadn't yet asked himself. Was it legitimate to ask what *he* wanted in all this? Were both choices neutral? What *did* he want? Had God already planted in Nathan's heart something he'd love, and he just had to find it?

Nathan took another sip and set the mug on the end table. He closed his eyes. How could he picture his future? *Guide me, Lord. Help me to know what I want and especially what you want.* Pictured himself at his desk at his old office building in Philadelphia. Pictured his boss, his typical day, his colleagues. His compressed lunch half-hour.

Time for honesty. Did he like his job? Or as Leah would say, did he love it? As he pictured his old job, a heavy layer coated his stomach. The stress was the worst. He liked marketing a lot as a career activity. But he could do that anywhere.

Even in Brenner Falls.

Okay, that was one answer. His enthusiasm meter for his old job was barely hitting fifty percent. Nathan closed his eyes again, still praying for guidance. This time he pictured himself at Seasons. Overseeing renovations. Changing up the menu. Doing marketing for it in the town and surrounding region.

A vibration began deep inside him and fanned into a thread of. . . excitement. Vision. Enthusiasm. He remembered the words of Brian Prokovich, who wanted to bring people from several hours driving distance to see a show. To have an experience. Maybe have a weekend away. Could Seasons become like that? Probably, with the right kind of changes, marketing, and improvements in programming. And time. On top of that, the town of Brenner Falls was a destination in itself. It drew people from bigger nearby cities to get away or discover a slower pace and outdoor beauty. Mayor Faulkner's projections for growth were optimistic and he had proven himself a proactive and visionary leader. The mayor would be a good man to have in his corner. Nathan could ask his advice about things, tap into his knowledge of local resources.

There was a way through the fog, one step at a time.

And then there was Leah. He'd been wise not to consider her first but rather, after he'd settled what his heart wanted in a job. If he let his feelings for her alone steer his decision, he'd be in trouble and quickly. But he knew that with or without Leah, he could easily invest in Seasons and enjoy the work.

Now he could think of Leah, and the resulting delight was tainted by guilt. He'd love to put his arms around her right then, share with her what he'd learned, what he'd discovered. He missed her already. She'd said the same thing in a text message she must have sent in the middle of a sleepless night.

He'd been hard on her. He'd blamed her for having legitimate questions, as if he deserved unflinching support regardless. Had he earned that yet? No, he was only getting his feet wet. He still had to prove himself, but he didn't feel driven, as he had growing up. Rather, it was a challenge he aspired to, like that of winning a medal or a race. People fought for less. He'd only begun to fight.

Peace stole over Nathan. He could do this, with God's help and only then. And Leah beside him. After the New Year, he'd ask for an extension of working remotely and offer to come back for meetings every two weeks or so if needed. And gradually, he'd let it go.

He slid his phone from the end table and clicked on Leah's number. His chest and shoulders felt feather light. He smiled in anticipation of hearing her voice, of repairing the fissure between them.

"Nathan, I'm so glad to hear from you. I'm so sorry."

"*I'm* sorry, Leah. You didn't do anything wrong."

"I'm sorry too. I wasn't supportive enough and I didn't stand up for you. I knew you weren't doing anything secretly. I can't even imagine that."

Her voice was a balm over his frayed emotions.

"I *might* do something secretively," he said. "If it were, say. . . your birthday."

"Oh, Nathan," was all she said, followed by a soft giggle.

"Listen, I've been talking to God and, well, rather, he's been talking to me. I started to ask God what he wanted me to do. Then he asked *me* what *I* wanted to do."

"Really? That's cool. Kind of fits my recent realization that he cares about how he's gifted us and that ties into what we should do."

"It *was* cool. Because I'd been doing everything others wanted me to do and didn't even *know* if it was what I wanted for my own life. Then, when I examined the whole thing for myself, I realized I *did* want to take over Seasons, to carry on Andy's vision and legacy. I wanted to give it my best try and live here in the Falls. I wanted to give our relationship my best try too. I wasn't simply trying to avoid disappointing people. I *wanted* it myself."

"Oh, Nathan. That's wonderful." Wonder laced her voice. "So, you feel at peace about that decision?"

"I do. I did a mental imagery exercise. I pictured myself at my work and noted how I felt about it. Then I did the same thing with Seasons. I tried to do this without letting you be a factor."

"That might have skewed everything. At least I hope it would." She chuckled.

"Definitely."

"What did your mental imagery tell you?"

"When I imagined myself running Seasons, I got kind of excited. Suddenly, I was imagining what it could become, not focusing on what it currently is. So, what I'm saying is I want to settle here. I'll have to keep working remotely if I can. The income won't be there for a while. Not sure about the renovations. That part puts a lump in my throat."

"One day at a time. We'll figure that out together."

"Yes, we will."

He had much more to tell her but preferred to do it in person. After kissing her soundly. "Leah, your church program is tonight, isn't it?"

"Yes, at seven o'clock. I have a final rehearsal at five thirty."

"Okay. I'll be there. I know you'll be tied up right after and probably exhausted, but can you come over afterward for a little bit?"

"Yes, absolutely. I can't wait to see you."

"Me too. I'll pray for the program tonight. Not just that everything goes smoothly, but that people will be touched by the message."

"Thanks, Nathan. I'll see you tonight."

He disconnected the call and rested his head against the chair. In that moment, his world felt complete. His questions were answered. The grinding in his stomach had ceased. Peace flowed in its place.

Phone still in hand, he scrolled to his calendar. It was Saturday. In one week, the first of two Christmas performances would take place at Seasons. He'd been monitoring ticket sales. They were nearly sold out for the first performance. Not bad, but he'd prefer a sold-out crowd. He'd covered all the social media channels as well as taken out various forms of advertising in town. Even the kids of the Olivia's book club members and Leah's students got on board taping flyers all over town and putting them into mailboxes.

The kids involved in the snowflake dance had a following as well. Maybe he'd schedule a regular gig with them. Nathan grinned. That's what he was made for. Ideas that would make things grow and catch on. He'd thought it was marketing, and well, maybe that was part of what he was good at. But marketing for a bigger picture that was all his own. . . that fueled him in a way none of his clients' goals had done. Though he always did his best for them, he hadn't been able to care as much as he did now.

What would he do with his townhouse when he moved permanently back to Brenner Falls? He could likely rent it out, and that would provide a bit of income as well.

As for Leah, once he was financially able, he'd give her a permanent job running the theater along with Olivia. She'd have what she always dreamed of. A career that allowed her to use her talents and organize music events to entertain the people of Brenner Falls. That thought caused a wide smile to spread across his face. He stood and took his teacup into the kitchen, his thoughts still bouncing from one possibility to another.

He entered the kitchen and encountered a mess. In fact, he'd neglected the whole house over the last couple of weeks and Leah would be coming over later. His dwelling no longer resembled that of a tidy man, as he'd described himself to her the first time she came over. Seemed like years ago that they sat in his office and phoned Olivia. He laughed aloud. How fast things could change.

For the next hour, he bustled from room to room tossing clothes into the washing machine, putting books and papers away, and dusting surfaces. He grabbed a handful of unopened mail from the coffee table, a sweatshirt hanging over the dining room chair, shoes, socks. . . he used to be so neat.

He tossed the clothing and mail on the bed and a letter caught his eye. He picked it up. The return address was the county department of revenue. Must have been tucked into some sale flyers and he hadn't seen it. He took it with him into the kitchen and set it on the counter, then finished emptying the dishwasher and wiping the counters.

Nathan poured a glass of cold water from a pitcher he kept in the fridge and went to the couch with the letter. He hoped it wasn't bad news. It was addressed to Andy. He frowned. Little mail came anymore for Andy since he'd been gone for three months. Nathan opened the envelope and scanned the contents. His eyes grew round, and his mouth went dry. His heart thumped against his ribs hard enough to shake him.

It was a tax bill. An overdue tax bill on Seasons going back three years, about the time Uncle Andy had first gotten sick. The amount due was over twenty thousand dollars. The buoyancy he'd previously felt bled away, replaced by an iron fist clutching his throat. Just when he'd decided to stay in Brenner Falls, to give Seasons all his effort and even some of his savings. Just when things had finally gotten clear for him. Just when he had a way forward. Now this.

His eyes stung. *Why, why, Lord? I thought I heard you. I understood you were leading me this way. Why this?*

This changed everything. He already needed thousands of dollars to renovate Seasons. He hadn't planned on paying that amount in back taxes. Andy must have either not had the means to pay them or had been too sick to take care of the bill or even know about it. Nathan couldn't bear to reread the paper, like a weapon pointed at his heart.

Now he didn't have a choice. He'd have to sell Seasons.

He wasn't sure how long he sat in a stupor on the couch, unable to organize his thoughts.

Unable to face the new dreams he'd embraced only three hours ago which now lay at his feet like a heap of ashes.

Chapter Eighteen

"Josiah, after we finish singing Silent Night, I'd like you to continue softly playing the guitar for an entire verse." Leah stood next to the teenager perched on a stool with his guitar on one knee. "That'll be perfect for peaceful contemplation, don't you think?"

"Good idea, Leah." Josiah had combed his unruly blond hair away from his eyes in honor of their performance that evening. Leah had scheduled the final rehearsal an hour and a half ahead of time. The musicians practiced each song with little need to stop and tweak anything. Their rehearsals had paid off. "Great job, everyone," she said to them with a heartfelt smile. She glanced up at the door as the first guests arrived for the Real Faith Chapel Christmas Festival.

Between rehearsals at the church and those at Seasons, Leah was exhausted, but convinced it would soon bear fruit. In the weeks leading up to that moment, the members of the small church met numerous times to pray that many people from the community would come and hear the true message of Christmas, as well as get acquainted with the startup church. Anticipation for the answers to those prayers sparked through the atmosphere.

A pine wreath embedded with tiny white lights hung in the center of the stage. In the middle of the wreath was a wood carved silhouette of Joseph, Mary, and baby Jesus. Thick candles on brass floor stands lined either side of the seating area, casting dancing orbs of mellow light onto the aisles.

For two months the children had made decorations. Along with glowing traditional ornaments, their handcrafts adorned the lofty Christmas tree in the corner of the room. Along the back wall sat a long table with a festive tablecloth where they'd offer hot cider, chocolate, and home-baked treats after the production, along with gospel tracts and flyers about the church.

The first to arrive at the community center were the church members themselves, as well as quite a few from the parent church, Brenner Falls Faith Community.

Leah felt confident in the quality of the music for the evening and the worthiness of the event itself, but her mood dragged. She'd been scanning the front door for Nathan for fifteen minutes and he hadn't arrived. Probably something had delayed him. She glanced at her phone between songs during rehearsal, but there were no text messages.

Her spirits lifted when Abbie and Garrett came in together and sat on the second to the last row, probably at Garrett's request. He'd never sit near the front, but at least he'd agreed to come.

Leah nervously glanced at the wall clock. No Nathan. The event was about to start.

Pastor Todd's wife, Janelle, took the role of emcee for the evening, opening the program with humor. She had a gift for putting people at ease and instigating laughter by intentional quips and or unintentional gaffes. She gave the audience a thumbnail summary of the church, its beginnings and vision, and invited those present to get more information and refreshments after the program. At least if some people left before the end, they'd know about the church.

The evening launched with an interpretive dance by two high school girls in flowing white gowns and sparkling headbands. A chorus standing behind them sang *Do You See what I See*. Behind them was a six-foot star, likely loaded with all the glitter available in Brenner Falls. Then the audience stood and sang two carols.

A variety of activities unfolded, a drama followed by another song, then a duet, but all maintained the same thread of God's good gift, which led to a short message by Pastor Todd.

The lights dimmed and more candles were lit as he stood behind a music stand and addressed the audience. "We love to give gifts at Christmas," he said. "Especially those we know our loved ones want. We love to see the looks on their faces when they realize, *Hey, they were listening. They got me what I wanted.* But what if they don't know what they *need*? It means even more when they realized how very much they needed it. That's like God's gift to us. We didn't know we needed it, but it was what we needed most. I'll explain what I mean." He left the podium and sat on a stool, Bible in one hand, gesturing with the other. Like a friend using simple, everyday vocabulary, he explained man's problem, his separation from his Creator and God's solution.

Leah wondered how Garrett was receiving the message but couldn't see his face since he was several rows behind her, and she too faced the stage. Soon, the message absorbed her attention as Pastor Todd unwrapped how Jesus changed everything for a person's life and his eternity. Her eyes stung, and she embraced anew the gravity and joy of what God had done in giving his *good gift*. She almost missed her cue to return to the stage as the message closed and the pastor gave an invitation to respond.

She rose and nodded to the music team, who seemed just as absorbed in the message as she had been. Quietly, they joined her on the stage near where Pastor Todd prayed a closing prayer and, with another nod, they began a musical introduction to Silent Night. She started with a violin solo, which cut the stillness with simple notes of the melody. Josiah strummed his guitar gently and a small chorus sang, leading the audience in the beloved carol.

Leah's gaze roved over the audience and narrowed to the back row where Abbie and Garrett sat and saw her brother's head bowed. Abbie's face tilted toward him, and he turned to her with a shy smile and with his fist, wiped. . . tears? Her brother was crying? Joy stirred inside Leah at whatever was happening. *Lord, I pray he understood.*

She returned her violin under her chin and played the musical bridge between verses. The audience took part along with the instruments, creating a full, rich sound. The candles flickered from either side of the room, bathing it with a golden glow that reached into each darkened aisle. Leah lowered her violin and glanced again at her brother, who whispered something to Abbie. Her gaze drifted down the row, and she locked eyes with Nathan. He'd come. He must have arrived not long ago. When he sent her a gentle smile, the tension inside her unlocked and fell away.

ଔ ଔ ଔ

Nathan slipped into an empty seat on the last row a half hour after the program had begun. He was far enough in the back that he doubted Leah would see him, but it had been one of the only seats available. Encouraging to see the room so full.

The unwelcome mail he'd received that day had so tangled his thoughts and emotions, he'd been paralyzed with grief and confusion to the point of physical pain and shortness of breath. He knew he couldn't attend Leah's Christmas event.

Then thoughts of Leah won out. She wouldn't understand why he wasn't there and would worry, which would distract her from her purpose, her ministry. He couldn't do that to her. Aside from that, he himself needed to be there. To hear truth. To know that it would somehow be okay. He hoped that somehow the program would pierce his blanket of despair.

God had confused him that day. Saying something so clearly. Then only three hours later, circumstances made a mockery of Nathan's weeks of transformed desires, brand-new commitments, and heartfelt goals for Seasons.

Despite the heaviness and disquiet inside him, he drank in the message, both clear and inviting. The portion of the program he'd seen was touching, amusing, top-notch at different moments. But his desire to support Leah raised the stakes even higher. Would she notice him there? He longed to talk to her, to hold her, explain what had happened, hear her wisdom. Share his burden.

Then, she glanced up and they found one another across the sea of people between them. Her face spoke everything they'd said to each other on the phone that morning and more. Soon, they'd be together. He needed to feel her arms around him. He sent her a gentle smile. She smiled back.

The final song of the evening was Leah's solo. She stepped toward the microphone as the room hushed. Piano notes began a soft melodic introduction. Her voice was clear and rich, a trained talent that no one would deny, yet it was the lyrics that pierced straight down to his marrow.

If God had been whispering to him over the last few days, even amidst his confusion, he might be shouting then, but with insistent love, a love and an unconditional acceptance that filled him completely yet battled with his dark questions.

When she'd finished, she stepped back into the shadow as a hush fell over the room while the piano continued softly. The lighting brightened and an attractive thirtyish woman took center stage to give a poignant conclusion. She thanked everyone for coming and directed them to the back of the room for refreshments and discussion.

As everyone rose and began moving around, Nathan slipped up the aisle against the current of people who headed for refreshments. He waited near the stage as Leah gathered her instruments and spoke to her fellow musicians.

Once her small band had dispersed into the crowd, she hurried down the makeshift steps and stood in front of him. "You came." Apprehension shadowed her eyes. "I was worried."

"I'm sorry, Leah," he said. "There's a reason I was late, which I'll explain to you when you come over. It's. . . it's good to see you." He reached out and grasped her hand, certain it would be inappropriate in that setting to pull her into his arms and kiss the words right out of her.

"It's okay, Nathan. You've had so much on you. I've missed you. . . only since yesterday." A delicate flush colored her smooth cheeks, whether from excitement, her bashful admission, or both.

Nathan gestured to the crowd. "It's a good turnout. The evening was wonderful. I was really moved by it all, and such quality in every category."

"I'm glad."

He touched her cheek and ran his finger along its smooth contour. He dreaded what he'd have to tell her but for now, he'd lock this moment in memory. "I know it's been a long day for you. I want to see you tonight but just know you don't have to stay a long time."

"And I want to see *you*."

Her smile lit up her face and brought a streak of sunlight into his darkness.

"I'll be over as soon as I can get away. Might be an hour, though."

"No problem. I'll be up. I just need to see you and reconnect."

"Me too." She blinked and reached out to squeeze his hand again. "Nathan, I think Garrett may have made spiritual progress tonight. He seemed moved by the sermon and the music. I can't be sure until I talk to him or to Abbie. I certainly don't want to rush him."

Nathan scoped the room and saw Abbie and Garrett still seated on one of the back rows, talking with their heads close together. "I hope so. They're still talking, so maybe she's answering his questions."

"I'd have to wait until he comes to me, I think," she said. "I don't want to hover. Making a step with God is such a personal thing. And I'm his pesky sister, so I'd probably be the last person he'd want to talk to about it."

"You'll know. I'm heading home. See you soon."

She smiled, and it melted his heart. "I'll be there as soon as I can get away."

Nathan returned home and tried to focus on the message and the songs that evening. *Lord, I hope there's a plan here, because I'm really confused about this. I don't see a way out, and I'm sorry for doubting. Still, I'll try to give it to you.*

An hour later, there was a knock at the door. Leah. Like an old man, he pulled himself up from the couch with a groan, one that came not from his bones but from his heart.

What did this mean for them as a couple if he sold Seasons? Would it become a test? It shouldn't, but after her reaction the day before, he wasn't sure. But she'd apologized.

He opened the front door. Leah stood there, impossibly beautiful, flushed with excitement from her evening. It took his breath away. Despite his terrible news and the feeling of being knocked to the floor, he pulled her into the house and wrapped her in his arms. They stood for a moment locked in place like a puzzle. He kissed her gently at first, then the hunger took over. She responded eagerly, slipping her hand into his hair as a soft groan emerged from her throat.

He pulled away and allowed his gaze to roam from her clear blue eyes with a smudge of mascara, to her soft pink lips and back again. That evening they'd talk. And it would be a defining moment, one direction or the other.

"That was quite a welcome," she said in a husky voice and with a tantalizing smile.

"It's *so* good to see you, Leah. I'm sorry."

"You said that before," she said. "It's over. I'm sorry too."

"Let me get you something to drink. I have juice or hot tea." He was already moving toward the kitchen. Putting off the inevitable, maybe. Hoping she wouldn't notice the desperation in his eyes. Not yet, anyway. "I'm sure you're thirsty after playing the flute and singing all evening. And maybe hungry."

She joined him in the kitchen. "No, I had a small plateful over there, only because people were talking to me. And I was hungry. But I really wanted to see you."

He pulled down mugs and put on water to boil. While he waited, he placed his hands on her hips and drew her close.

Her eyes searched his face. "What is it, Nathan? That burdened face is back. I hadn't seen it in a while."

Nathan hesitated. Should have known he couldn't hide anything from Leah. "Let's take our tea into the living room. I have to catch you up on something."

They took their mugs back to the couch and set them on the coffee table. Nathan let out a deep sigh. "I just opened this." He handed her the letter.

Her eyes widened, as his must have done a few minutes earlier. She turned stricken eyes back to him. "What'll you do?"

"I think I have to sell it."

"Oh, no. Not after the revelation you got about it. Maybe God has something else in mind."

Nathan fell back against the couch and gazed at the ceiling. "I don't know how this can work, Leah."

"What was the deadline on the payment?" She scanned the paper again. "It's overdue, but maybe they'll let you break it down month by month, since it isn't your bill but Andy's. You can send a death certificate, so they know the circumstances."

An idea he hadn't thought of, but wishful thinking. He owned the place. He'd inherited the tax bill. And making payments would gobble so much of his meager profit that he'd still have to sell it. He'd be behind, in debt, defeated before he even began. Whatever vision he'd had for Seasons had fled when he opened the envelope.

"Why don't we put this whole matter in God's hands right now and focus on our event next week?" Leah said. "We have to see that through first, of course. Then you'll have more clarity to decide."

His gaze found hers and he drew strength from it and the way she'd said *we*. "I can do that. There's only so much we'll earn from the event, though. I doubt there'll be enough money for both taxes and renovations." Let alone everything else he'd daydreamed about ever since deciding to keep Seasons. His short-lived decision. His chest felt like twenty bricks sat on it. "I don't see any way to avoid selling."

"Let's pray about it." Before he could respond she grabbed his hands. "Lord, you see the situation Nathan is in. Please provide clear guidance for him so that he can be at peace and see what you want him to do. We trust you, Lord. We wait for *your* solution. Amen."

"Well said." Nathan couldn't add anything. He didn't have the words, the energy, nor the heart. He sighed. "The show is in a week."

"Don't lose hope, Nathan. Let's go into this as if we never saw that tax notice, okay? We give it our all. You do the maximum with marketing and overseeing everything. Then we'll trust God to give a clear answer. Okay?"

He nodded. His faith had only begun to grow again, and the test he faced was huge. Was that fair? Shaky or not, he didn't have a choice but to walk through the challenge and expect an answer afterward.

One way or the other.

Chapter Nineteen

The early December chill cut through Nathan's cheeks that Monday morning, even though his collar reached past his chin. No one in his right mind would be out walking for pleasure on a day when twenty-five-degree temperatures would lead to a dusting of snow. But pleasure wasn't his aim. Sanity was.

He'd spent three hours already that morning on his marketing job, which helped only slightly in diverting his thoughts from his unwelcome mail. The mail that had upended his joyful revelations of only a couple days ago. Finally compelled to escape the computer screen, emails, and phone calls, he grabbed his down parka and headed outside.

Returning to work after his hopeful fantasy was an even greater drop than he'd expected. It was time to get real. Time to grow up.

The punishing cold almost felt good. Harsh enough to match his mood. Christmas decorations adorned many of the trees and bushes of homes he passed, though they sat pale and dormant during the day. He thought about what Leah had said before she prayed for him Saturday night. Give Seasons his best shot and reevaluate afterward. But honestly, what would change? They'd make some money that would pay the cast and restaurant staff. It wouldn't make a dent in the tax bill. Was there any solution that wouldn't leave Seasons stuck indefinitely in its current state? At least he hadn't cut ties with the developer, Skip Kaiser.

He knew he was holding God at arm's length because he was confused and angry. Why had he experienced a clear answer about his next steps only to have either a cruel test or an illogical solution?

After a barely tolerable walk once around the block, Nathan's house came into view. Just in time. His toes were going numb. In his pocket, his phone vibrated. A phone call, not a text. He couldn't catch the call without removing his gloves, and nothing could be that important.

Back inside, the heat was like heaven. He rubbed his hands for a few minutes until feeling returned then checked the phone. His boss had called, so he listened to the message. "Sorry I missed you, Nathan. It's Jeremy and it's important, so call me back, please."

Nathan frowned. Very unusual. First, his boss didn't call him often. They checked in by email or did an online video meeting once in a while. He sat on the couch and dialed Jeremy's number. "Hi Jeremy, what's up?"

"Hi Nathan, is it as cold there as down here?"

Nathan narrowed his eyes in suspicion. Though Jeremy was a likeable guy he'd always respected, surely, he hadn't called to talk about the weather. "I guarantee, it's colder up here than there." He waited.

"You're likely wondering why I'm calling. I don't know how closely you've been following the merger negotiations, since you're up there and out of the hub of things. We've tried to post things internally, but it's been changing fast."

"Yeah, I only know that discussions are happening or will happen, though likely in the spring, and that some of us'll lose our jobs. Is that pretty accurate?" He wasn't sure he really cared. But maybe he should, since he'd still need a job, regardless of when Seasons sold.

"We're in the midst of discussions and they're moving along faster than we planned. After the New Year, we'll have something firmer, but I can give you some good news. Now, this is completely unofficial, but I'm certain enough to give you a heads up. There will be layoffs, but your position isn't in danger. So, that's the first good news."

"Okay, good. Is there more?" He propped his feet up on the coffee table. He'd definitely need some tea after his ill-advised walk in arctic conditions.

"Yes, not only will you *not* lose your job, but I've recommended you for a promotion. A supervisory role. You'll work with a team handling bigger campaigns, but your staff will execute everything. With your interpersonal skills, you'll be great at that."

Nathan knew he should say something, but rational thought had fled his brain. "Thank you for your confidence in me." He should be happier. Six months ago, he would have been. No more dealing with people like Chuck. He'd have a team to do that. He'd be the visionary leader, a role he'd probably enjoy. But his whole world had shifted in the last three months. He shouldn't indicate to Jeremy he was eager to take the position but needed to buy some time without burning bridges. He needed to think it through.

"So, after Christmas, we'll get you in for an interview for the position. The other company, A. S. C. Marketing, wants to interview in person."

"I can do that." Nathan's voice sounded dull to his own ears. He hoped Jeremy didn't pick up on it and wonder what was going on. "Can you tell me a little more about the position?"

"First thing you'll enjoy knowing. The salary is eighteen to twenty percent more than you're making now." Jeremy quoted him a salary range.

"Really? That's quite a jump. Is the increase because it's a supervisory role?"

"That plus the kind of campaigns you'll be working on. We're talking Fortune 500 and the like. Some of our biggest accounts."

"I'm honored you'd think of me, Jeremy. I've been out of pocket for two months, so I never expected this." It might be an answer to his most recent problem. His salary was good, but the new salary could do so much more.

"And since you'd be supervising a staff, it would be an office position."

"You mean—"

"You'd come back to Philly. You can't do this one remote because of your staff. Makes sense that you'd have to be on site to supervise. But think of the new challenges, which I think you'll love, plus the increase in salary. There are stock options too."

Back to Philadelphia. Back to his townhouse. Back to the office. He swallowed. "It's a lot to take in, Jeremy. I have several commitments here coming up to the holidays, but if they're willing to interview in January—"

"Yes, of course. No one wants to interview this close to Christmas. I just wanted to give you an early Christmas present. And I guess New Year's too."

"Thank you, Jeremy."

"I'll be in touch."

He disconnected and remained still, as if in a trance. He stared out the front window where Leah had hung a shiny red Christmas star, claiming he needed something festive.

Leah. She'd prayed for a solution to the tax problem. Was this the solution? Going back to Philly to work again at the office? He'd only see Leah on weekends. Some weekends. He'd couldn't have an active role in Seasons either if he wasn't here.

They'd get through the separation. Lots of couples did. And it would be short term, until he got the taxes paid and some capital built up for Seasons. That is, if he didn't sell it. Several options still sat on the table. At least returning to his old office in a new position wouldn't force him to sell Seasons. Not yet, anyway.

He rose from the couch and went to the kitchen, his heart numb. He did manage to murmur a prayer of thanks for the solution provided so quickly. He hadn't had to wait too long. He should *feel* thankful. That would come later. Maybe.

While the water boiled for tea, he stirred the chicken breasts in the marinade he'd made the previous evening. Since Monday and Wednesday were the only nights that week Leah didn't have rehearsals, he said he'd bring dinner over. Usually, he couldn't wait to see her, even if he'd seen her just the day before. But she wasn't going to like the solution God had provided.

At five-thirty, he knocked on Leah's door, a Pyrex dish in his gloved hands. Temperatures had dropped further, and snow flurries swept through the air like aimless fairies.

Leah opened the door and ushered him into the warmth. "Come in, warm up." She took the casserole from his hands and went to the kitchen. He removed his coat and hung it on the hook. When she returned to the hallway, she went into his arms. He held her for a long moment. Tears stung his eyes, but he blinked them away before she could see them. He stared into her face then kissed her, unable to get enough of her. Stocking up for whatever was coming after the New Year.

They pulled apart. "My, that was a friendly greeting," she murmured with that flirty voice he loved.

"Well, I'm a friendly guy. Especially with you." He smiled. "The chicken's ready to eat if we just heat it a little bit. I don't know how hungry you are." He wasn't at all. Hadn't been for days.

"*Really* hungry. I'm doing a lot of lessons this week, since some of the kids are out of school already." She led him through the dining room toward the kitchen. "And of course, Monday night I try to stay free for my tidy, urban veggieman." She grinned.

Nathan leaned against the island and crossed his arms. "All my nicknames at once. Maybe you should just call me Superman. Save yourself some time." He managed to return her grin.

She laughed. "Good idea. In my opinion, that's a perfect fit."

"Hope you don't mind if no one agrees with you." He pulled two plates from the cupboard and silverware from the drawer while she heated the chicken. For a moment, it felt like they were married, having dinner together after a day at work. The image cheered him only slightly.

They settled at the dining room table with his chicken dish before them. "How are your students doing?" he asked.

"They're coming along." She poured them chilled water from a pitcher. "Today I had one on violin and my friend Blair's son on piano. They're both cute little guys."

"Should I be jealous?" He winked at her and served them some chicken.

"Well, maybe. Blair's son is such a cutie, I could gobble him up."

"So, you don't want chicken?" He couldn't help it. In spite of the weight inside.

Leah laughed aloud and threw a scrunched napkin at him. "You're in rare form, Nathan. What's got you so humorous?"

"Nothing." His fake good mood fell to pieces then. Words stuck in his throat. Suddenly, Leah saw what he'd tried to hide.

Her smile dropped. She reached out to touch his arm. "What is it, Nathan? More bad news about the taxes?

"No, good news, actually. Depending on how you look at it."

"Oh? I'd love to hear some good news. But you seem like your best friend just died."

"Well, since you're my best friend, you shouldn't worry about that." He let out a long sigh. "I think I got an answer from God today about my tax situation."

"A good one, I hope. Though by your face, it isn't good. Tell me." She leaned forward.

She wasn't going to like this.

"My boss called me today. There's going to be a merger with another company and some new positions are opening. There'll be layoffs too. So, he's recommended me for one of those positions."

Leah's brows knit together. "Go on."

"The salary is twenty percent above what I make now, and I already make a decent salary."

"So, you think God wants you to take that position so you can pay the taxes? I thought we were going to trust him for his provision."

He grabbed her hand and leaned toward her. "What if this *is* his provision, Leah? I got the tax bill on Saturday, and I got this news today. Forty-eight hours later."

"That doesn't prove it's God's answer. Might just be coincidence and you think it's God. I suggested we give it more time, remember? When I prayed?"

He released her hand. "I have different solutions available. This is one of them. Another one is selling Seasons." She flinched. "Taking this job would be a way of *keeping* Seasons. I could pay the tax and have enough money to save up for renovations." He shrugged. "Or I could sell it whenever I find an appropriate buyer."

"If you took this position, would you still be able to do like you do now, work in the morning and some in the afternoon, but go to Seasons in between? Or would you have more on your plate?"

"No." He had trouble speaking the words. "It's an office position because I'd be supervising a team. I'd have to go back to Philly during the week."

Her eyes grew round, and her pink lips dropped open. "You'd do that, Nathan?"

"I might have to. My choices are getting more and more limited, but here I am offered a promotion and higher salary. All in the midst of this mess. Don't you think it could be good news?"

Her gaze dropped to the table. "I. . . I don't think so."

"Lots of couples only see each other on the weekends. I'd come here most weekends, and you can come there sometimes. Couldn't that work in the short term?"

"It's not only that. You're right, a lot of couples do that. But for you to have this powerful revelation about Seasons and what a fit it is for you—which you said was from God—then have you turn and go back to your old office in Philly—" She shook her head. "I don't know how you're thinking."

Nathan pushed his half-full plate away. "My thinking is that I might not have a choice."

"But you also said you had different options, and this was one. Did you pray about it, to be sure this is God's answer?"

"I. . . I thanked him." Had he prayed? Maybe not. "It's a good opportunity for me. I'd be supervising other people." His voice dropped. He wouldn't plead with her. She had to see that he didn't have a choice. "So, you're not proud of me, that I earned a promotion?" He raised his eyebrows. What was he doing inviting her praise? Sounded like a spoiled kid, focused on himself.

She frowned. "Of course, I'm proud of you, Nathan. I'm sure you're good at what you do. But I'm seeing a bigger picture here. You told me God asked *you* what you want to do, and you realized you wanted to work with Seasons."

"We're going around in circles, Leah. Financially, I can't swing it." His voice had risen. Why couldn't she understand? "I don't want to be scraping by and shouldering a tax bill for years, barely making it. I want to build something that can be a viable business, even capable of providing for a family one day. I've built my career for years and here I am getting ready to walk away from it to take on a failing dinner theater."

She stilled. Blinked. "Is that what this is about? Your career? What happened to passion?"

"I'll tell you what happened. I had to grow up. Sometimes you have to do what you have to do." He hated to say it, but it was true. It was a golden opportunity. She'd come around. She'd understand.

Leah avoided his eyes. "Have you made up your mind? Is it a done thing?"

Her voice was quiet, and it chilled him more than the air outside. "No. There'll be an interview in January. After that, I don't know. Nothing immediate. That'll let us get through the Seasons shows first."

She didn't respond.

Nathan felt like a Jekyll and Hyde who'd changed personalities since spending time with her only one day ago at church. He didn't recognize himself. She likely didn't either, and questioned if she really knew him.

After a long, agonizing silence thick between them, Nathan slid his chair back. "It was a wonderful thought, me working at Seasons." His voice was calm, dry. His insides were dying. "Renovating and updating, bringing it back to vibrant life. I would have liked to do that. It just didn't work out. And no one, including you, seems to understand the pressure I've been under all this time. I'm done trying to please everyone. It just isn't possible."

Nathan stood and went to the door. She didn't stop him. He put his coat on and let himself out into the cold.

He'd wanted to tell her it would be okay. But he couldn't make that guarantee.

ଔ ଔ ଔ

Leah listened to the front door close. He hadn't slammed it, but the quiet click was just as bad. Tears began. They flowed down her cheeks and dropped onto the wooden table where not long ago they'd been eating, joking. She wept until it seemed she'd emptied her reservoir of despair yet hadn't reached the bottom.

Finally, she stood and cleared the table. She saw her phone on the kitchen counter and snatched it. "Abbie," she began, but the tears choked her voice.

"Leah, what it is? What's wrong?"

Leah muffled a sob. "Nathan and I had a fight. I need to talk to you. I need some perspective."

"I'll be right over." Abbie disconnected and minutes later, she knocked on the front door.

Leah flung the door open, and Abbie encircled her with a hug. Leah cried on her shoulder for a few minutes as her friend patted her back, cooing, "Oh, Leah. I'm so sorry."

Abbie pulled back. "Let's sit on the couch. First, you need a cool rag for your face. I know where they are, sit tight." She disappeared toward the back of the house and returned with a moist washcloth. "Put this on your eyes. You have to calm down so you can tell me what's going on."

Abbie's presence settled Leah, so she was able to speak. Where to start? She described Nathan's revelation a few days earlier about working with Seasons, and how peaceful and happy he was once he'd decided. Then the tax bill came followed by the job offer.

"Wow. That's a lot in a short time." Abbie looked reflective as she took it all in. Her eyes met Leah's. "I'm not taking his side, but

I do understand how he's reasoning. He doesn't think he has a choice."

"That's what he told me. But he does have a choice. He can wait on God like we talked about. Instead of taking the first thing that shows up."

"Leah, listen to me." Abbie's voice was soft, her face full of compassion. "Nathan wants to be your hero, everyone's hero. But he feels he can't. The numbers aren't adding up. Men need to earn a living and he's getting scared. He sees himself letting a sure thing go and having what? Seasons, full of debt and repair needs. You see what I'm saying? And my guess is, his faith is still growing. He can't see beyond the crisis." She took a breath. "Give him time, Leah. Give yourself time. This all just blew up today, right? Take some time to pray for him and for the situation. Ask God for his answers, though he won't necessarily give them on *your* timetable. Get through the Seasons event, through Christmas and New Year's, then re-evaluate. See if Nathan will agree to that much. The pieces will start to settle into some kind of direction."

"You think they will?" Leah's face turned to Abbie. "Oh, I hope they will."

"You have to be open to what God shows you, and so does Nathan. Don't predict God's will. Hear me, you both may need to compromise." She fell silent, still holding Leah's gaze. "What's the worst thing that could happen?"

Leah filled her lungs in a deep draught. In an instant, she knew the answer to Abbie's questions. "The worst thing is that we break up."

"That's the worst thing because. . .?"

"Because I love him." Leah's mouth dropped open. "That means I want to be with him whatever he decides." Hadn't she already learned that lesson not very long ago? The second time, it struck her with a force that gave her courage for whatever was coming.

Abbie smiled. "Doesn't that already give you some clarity?"

Leah managed a weak smile. "Yes. Yes, it does. I love him. I'm in love with Nathan. Not Seasons, Nathan." She blinked away a few fresh tears. "He's doing the best he can in an almost impossible situation. Of course, he doesn't want to embark on a financial nightmare. He wants to be able to provide for a family one day. That's honorable, whether it's with me or someone else."

"Yes. It's not the end of the world if he goes back to his company or even if he sells Seasons. You'll get through that. Trust me. But if you're meant to be together, you need to be."

Leah laid her hand on Abbie's knee. "Oh, Abbie. He probably thinks I'm putting Seasons before him. That's not what I'm doing. I'm so convinced that he's made for it, and I want the best for him."

"And why are you so convinced?" Abbie's dark brows lifted.

"He seems to like it and be good at it. But I guess that's not proof. And his feeling that God was telling him to do it. That could just be him trying to please others, or even please me, and interpreting it was from God. Oh, Abbie, I'm so confused."

"No, you're not. You told me you love him, so that's a given. What you're confused about is what he should do. And that's not for you to know yet. That's what you need to wait for."

Leah slipped her arms around Abbie's shoulders and squeezed her. "Abbie, you're so wise. You're the *best* best friend ever."

They leaned back and Abbie wiped a tear from Leah's cheek. "You'll get through this, and you'll see, it'll be good."

Chapter Twenty

Nathan pulled into his driveway and sat still, his breath puffing clouds into the car. His heart still pounded. And it ached.

With a soulful sigh, he got out and headed into the house. He slid off his jacket and threw it on the wing chair. He was empty-handed since he'd left the casserole and side dish on the table at Leah's when he'd stormed out. Along with despair, frustration flowed through his veins like hot blood racing. Frustration against Leah for not getting it. Against God for not opening the door in a better way.

He stopped and a humorless laugh escaped his throat. Yeah, now he was blaming God for not doing what Nathan wanted. No wonder he was in a mess.

Nathan took his phone from the table and texted Ben. *Pray for me, bro. Everything's hitting the fan.*

A minute later, his phone pinged. *I can talk in about an hour. Want me to call?*

No, just pray. Thanks. I'll call you tomorrow. Although Ben was a good sounding board, Nathan didn't want to talk to anyone.

Changing into comfortable sweatpants and collapsing on the soft couch in front of the fireplace did nothing for the discomfort inside him. The memory of Leah's downcast face passed like a movie in his mind. Her words also came back. *Wait on God*, she'd said. Did he do that? No. *Follow your passion.* Where else had he heard that? From God, maybe. And in his heart. But it wasn't financially sound. . . and so it went for the next hour as he wrestled with his desires against what was logical, mature, sound. Against the numbers. Who would win the wrestling match?

Finally, he stilled, whether from fatigue or from the tapping on his heart, as if someone were trying to enter. One thing was sure. Attempting to figure things out with his own brain was exhausting and highly unreliable.

He leaned his head against the back of the couch and stared up at the ceiling. "Lord, I need you to help me out here," he said aloud. "I don't know if this job was your plan or not. I forgot to ask you, but I'm asking you now." Silence filled the room. But he'd begun.

"Maybe I shouldn't have assumed it was your will just because of the timing. Leah said that, and she's right. I need patience to wait on your direction. I hope you'll show me. I shouldn't assume this is the only way you can resolve that tax bill and the bigger problems with Seasons. I need to make some decisions and I really need your guidance."

Hadn't he learned anything? *I will take the load from your shoulders.* The words which had struck him so powerfully that day at Leah's church returned to caress his tormented mind. A thin layer of tension lifted from his chest and drifted away.

What about his own declaration to himself? Running Seasons is what he was *made* for? Those were his words. Had he been carried away on the moment, or was that what he truly believed? Strong words, but were they from his heart? "Lord, please show me. Did you bring me here to take over Season, to begin a new life in Brenner Falls? To start a life with Leah? Is this your leading?"

As he prayed and his throat ached with grief, something stirred inside him. He wasn't sure if it was God or not. But he knew he had to fight a little longer and not run prematurely back to Philadelphia. He needed to fight for Leah, too. In the end, God might show him the new job was his plan. Maybe he was leading Nathan and Leah back to Philadelphia together to start a new life there. Or not. One thing was sure. Nathan wasn't the boss of his own decision, God was.

He was willing to wait, as hard as that was.

One thing he *couldn't* easily wait for. Reconciling with Leah. Holding her in his arms, telling her that no matter what he did or where he went, he didn't want to be without her. But it was after ten-thirty. He'd have to be patient.

☙ ☙ ☙

The next morning Leah had woken up surprisingly rested. After her conversation with Abbie, a whisper of peace had stolen over her. She got a glimpse into Nathan's mindset and dilemma and had new compassion for him.

Through the living room window, a blue winter sky spilled warm sunlight on Leah's blanket-covered legs. An open devotional book lay in her lap, a full coffee mug steamed beside her, and Theo cuddled against her thigh. Normally, she loved mornings like this. That day, despite her insight and new commitment, a cloud of uncertainty hovered over her head.

She could let go if she had to. Let Seasons go, even Brenner Falls. Or she could let Nathan return to Philadelphia and only see him on weekends. It wouldn't be easy, but for Nathan's sake, she could.

Now if only she could tell him, and he would listen. She'd never seen him angry before, and the memory of him walking out the previous evening still made her shudder. Though he was probably working early that morning, she'd risk texting him to test the waters. She hoped he wasn't still angry. She reached toward her phone on the side table.

"Good morning." Garrett came into the doorway of the living room fully dressed with his hair neatly combed.

"You're up early. It's only nine." She picked up her cup instead and took a sip.

"I have to meet a guy about a website in an hour. Business is picking up."

She smiled. "I'm glad. See, I told you they'd snap you up. Maybe not the same ones you expected."

"Yeah, funny how things turn out, but differently than you think." He turned and disappeared into the kitchen.

Leah sipped her coffee as she rewound his statement. *Funny how things turn out, but differently than you think.* Things would turn out. And probably differently than they expected. God was faithful and everything would be okay, as long as she and Nathan didn't hold too tightly to their own ideas of what was best.

She set her mug on the table and reached again for her phone. What would she write to Nathan? As she stared at the darkened screen, a text message from him popped up. *Can I please come over at nine to talk? Is it too early?*

Hope leaped into her chest and a smile tugged at her lips. It was already nine. When had he written this? About one minute ago.

Yes, please come over. I'm up and it's not too early. Should she say more? No, he'd be there—

Someone knocked on the door. It was too soon for it to be Nathan. Leah stood gingerly to avoid disturbing the sleeping Theo and went to the door.

Nathan stood there in a parka and knit hat. Green eyes from a solemn face blazed into hers.

"Nathan, come in. How'd you get here so fast?"

"I texted you from my car. At the curb. I had to see you."

He shrugged out of his coat, and she hung it on the hook. Just like the night before when everything had gone sideways.

They stood for a moment of awkward silence in the foyer. Garrett entered the hall from the dining room. "Oh, hi Nathan."

Leah turned to Garrett. "You were just leaving, right? Sorry if that sounded rude. Nathan and I need to talk."

"Yeah, I got that vibe. So—" he ducked into the dining room and returned with a backpack. He snagged his coat from the hook and brushed past Nathan. "See you guys later."

By the time the door closed behind him, Leah had gathered her wits. "Nathan, I'm sorry—"

"No, *I'm* sorry. Leah, I just—"

Then she was in his arms. She didn't know what he'd been about to say, if he'd decided to take the job in Philly, decided to stay. It didn't matter, because his arms were around her shoulders, warm and strong. Her head pressed into his chest.

When she lifted her head, he brushed her lips with a soft kiss.

"Let's talk," he said.

"Tea?"

He shook his head. "Let's talk first. Not that I even know where to start."

"Me either."

He followed her to the living room, and they sat on the couch. "Nathan, can I say something first?" She offered a half-smile.

"Sure."

She shifted nearer to him. "I see the kind of choice you have to make and how hard it is. I really do. I want you to know that." She watched his face. Swallowed. "I also want to tell you that whatever God leads you to do, whether you stay here or not, I'll support you. I'll leave with you if you want me to."

His brow furrowed. "You will? No, Leah, you love it here."

"I do, but...Nathan, I love *you*. And I'm so sorry if you ever thought Seasons was more important to me than you and what's best for you."

His eyes caught hers. "Leah—" He blinked a few times. "Aside from Seasons..." He smiled. "You love me?"

She nodded, her gaze glued to his.

"I love *you*, Leah." He took her hands. "Remember when I said *before-Leah* and *after-Leah*? Since I ran into you again at Andy's funeral, my life hasn't been the same."

"Leah part two." A tiny smile tugged her lips.

"Yes, exactly. But this is so much better." His gaze dropped to their joined hands. "We still need to talk about this. I assumed the job was God's answer. Well, you questioned if it was *God's* answer. I agree with you now. I thought about it after I stormed out during my tantrum." He gave her an adorable half-grin.

Leah squeezed his hands. "This job might be the right thing for you. And it might not be. I'm not going to pressure you either way, because you've been living this Seasons situation for three months now. You know the facts and the finances and whether it's feasible. And if you let God lead you, that's all you can do."

He fell silent as he considered her words. "I'm not here today to tell you I changed my mind and won't take the new job. But I'm not saying I *will*, either. I'm also not saying I'll never sell Seasons. I may have to. I'm only saying God hasn't shown me yet and I'm waiting on him."

She broke into a grin. "That's all I wanted to hear, Nathan. Let him show us. You know your options. As you said last night, you have several. God will show you which is the right one in his time. And you know what?"

"What?"

"I trust you. I know your heart. And I know you're smart and thorough. But especially, I know you want what God wants."

"I do want that."

His eyes roved over her face, to her eyes, her lips, back to her eyes. He reached and stroked her cheek with two fingers, leaving them there for a moment while his gaze locked with hers. "Leah Albright, I love you."

He pulled her toward him then and kissed her.

Chapter Twenty-One

The completion of the church program did nothing to lighten Leah's schedule since the Seasons event was only days away. Rehearsals and numerous errands and phone calls filled any gaps, and layers of fatigue accumulated each day. She wouldn't trade it for anything, though. She knew it might be her last chance. The future of Seasons was still hanging in mid-air. A sale might become inevitable. But her future with Nathan stood on solid ground.

That night would be the climax of two months of preparation. She'd supervised a dress rehearsal in the late afternoon, then had given the cast a break until an hour ahead of the opening of the front doors. The guests would enjoy their meal with only piped-in Christmas music until they'd nearly finished the main course. Then the program would begin. They'd break again for dessert and complete the program.

Leah glanced at her watch. The meal would start in thirty minutes. She had time to catch her breath before the intensity ramped up again. From where she stood on the stage, she surveyed the dining room as a steady flow of well-dressed couples, individuals, and families streamed in through the front door. Each party showed their tickets to the hostess, who escorted them to a table covered in seasonal fabric tablecloths and adorned with small glowing candles surrounded by sprigs of pine.

"What are you up to out here by yourself?" Olivia's normally pragmatic voice behind her sounded perky.

Leah turned and smiled. "Just savoring the lull. I'm also enjoying watching everyone come into the dining room, you know, the fruit of all our efforts over the last two months."

"Yes, it's encouraging to see the crowd." Olivia crossed her arms and viewed the scene. "Back in September, I agreed to help Nathan just this once. But I'll have to admit, I'd be disappointed if this were the only event. I wonder what he'll do next."

Leah swallowed. She felt the same way. "There may be a next time, but he's waiting to get through this one first." She couldn't say too much. Not only was it Nathan's place, not hers, but even he didn't know what the outcome would be after the two performances. Then, adding the tax problem. . .

In the previous few days, her optimism for Seasons had plummeted, but still flickered like a tiny stubborn coal glowing in the dark.

She knew one thing. Regardless of what Nathan decided, she'd be on his side. He'd never again doubt her support of him. He'd told her before he wanted to stay in the Falls, but now she knew it was no longer a given. In the week since the tax bombshell and job offer had hit, she'd reflected and prayed about her life and decided there were many places she could live and be perfectly happy, if she could be with Nathan. A new door could open for both of them. And it was a season for miracles. Maybe there'd be a way for them to stay right there in Brenner Falls.

Olivia touched Leah's shoulder and left her side to disappear behind the curtain. Leah had appreciated the older woman's commitment, experience, and friendship over the recent few weeks. Without her, the event wouldn't have been possible. It had been a successful partnership. If only it could continue. She wouldn't let her mind go there.

Leah knew things could change quickly. Garrett was a perfect example. Joy flooded inside her when she thought of him—her brother—the new believer. He'd taken a first step of faith that night during the church Christmas production and had begun meeting with Abbie and Pastor Todd. He'd made Todd's acquaintance at the end of the program, and they'd hit it off right away. Garrett had even asked Leah a question or two, which she considered a minor miracle, evidence that maybe she'd risen from the pious fake joy category in his mind. And he had already become less surly and more cheerful.

As people took their seats around the warmly lit tables, Nathan was in the midst of them circulating around the room with greetings, welcoming them to Seasons. Leah couldn't stem the flood of pride in him she felt. He was a natural. His place was here as a pillar of Brenner Falls, just like his Uncle Andy had been. Not cooped up in front of a computer doing marketing for faceless customers in Philadelphia. Though it might be important work, his talents were wasted there. But she'd hold those thoughts with a loose grip. God would show him, and she'd accept that.

Mayor Faulkner and his wife came in and spoke with several people clustered in the doorway. He and Nathan exchanged a warm greeting with an obviously friendly rapport. Nathan, who'd always felt like an outcast, was now friends with the mayor of Brenner Falls. She hoped he recognized the significance of that and released his unjustified shame for good.

She'd given Nathan's situation to God in prayer twenty times per day. She'd even asked Abbie and Garrett to pray for him about the tax situation but swore them to secrecy. Garrett had shown surprise. *You mean you can ask God to help with something like that?*

Abbie and Leah had laughed. "*Of course, you can,*" they'd said in unison. Garrett was learning a lot already.

That night, they had a sold-out performance. Though she knew it would be a high-quality program, nerves jangled inside her. She wanted everything to be smooth as glass, not only for Nathan's sake, but for the sakes of everyone who'd worked so hard for weeks, including her and Olivia.

Olivia had agreed to be the emcee for the opening. Nathan would close the evening, and the songs would proceed one to the next with no announcements or introductions between. Leah liked smooth transitions, and she'd handle these herself from backstage. With that goal, she prayed everyone would remember their parts, gestures, and the order of things. A lot was riding on that evening.

ତ୍ର ତ୍ର ତ୍ର

"This cheesecake is fantastic." Ben's girlfriend, Colleen, licked her fork. "And I love the almond topping." She looked across the small table at Nathan, who'd finally been able to sit. "Is this a part of the regular Seasons menu?"

Like the other guests, Colleen had dressed in elegance. Long gold earrings glinted through her dark blond hair. She and Ben made an attractive couple. Though he'd been dating her for over a year, he didn't appear in a hurry to move to engagement. When Nathan told him after Thanksgiving that he was dating Leah, his friend had glowed with smug satisfaction.

"No, it was special for tonight, but we can certainly adopt it on the menu," Nathan said. "I'll tell the chef how much you liked it." His gaze roved around the room. That was a first for him, to act like a restaurant owner, solicitous of everyone's enjoyment of their food and surroundings, rather than simply enjoying the time with his best friend. He was sure that hadn't been lost on ever perceptive Ben.

"Well, Nathan, everything's been perfect so far. Good food, great program." Ben lifted his wineglass to Nathan as his dark eyes sparkled. "To the Seasons entrepreneur." He turned his head to Colleen. "Isn't that right?"

"Absolutely." She lifted her glass and clinked Ben's. "I loved the variety of tonight's program. I've never been to a show here before. Never really wanted to, to be honest. The place seemed kind of rundown." Her eyes widened and her hand flew to her mouth. "Oh, I'm sorry, Nathan. I forgot for a minute that you own it now."

Nathan smiled with tight lips. "Don't worry, Colleen. I'm sure many people have thought the same thing." It's not like he didn't know. The white elephant image remained, yet now it was a very expensive one. Over twenty thousand dollars.

"Since you're planning to stay in the Falls and dive into running Seasons, you'll change all that, won't you pal? I mean, it won't be quick or cheap, but little by little, it can be *transformed*." Ben splayed his fingers and spoke in a circus voice. "And you can add programs, you know, a few at a time. Murder mystery theater is popular. You can do that, and of course, seasonal programs, birthday parties, concerts, cabarets. People can reserve it for their own events, like retirement parties, graduations."

"Even engagement parties, rehearsal dinners, or bridesmaid luncheons," added Colleen.

Nathan wondered if Colleen was dropping Ben a not-so-subtle hint. "Those are great ideas, guys," he said. He hadn't told Ben about the back taxes on Seasons nor the job possibility. He didn't have the heart to tell him he'd likely have to sell the place. He'd done the numbers, and even if he took the new job, it wouldn't make a dent on the numerous financial needs of Seasons. No reason to spoil his friend's evening or stem the flow of ideas.

"Here's an option." Ben's face was lit with enthusiasm. "If your cast gets tired or if you don't have something scheduled, you can always bring in an outside theatre troupe, from another town, or even locally if there are any. There are lots of ways to expand. Just start small and build, one step at a time."

"You should be the owner of Seasons, not me." Nathan took a long sip from his water goblet just as a staccato violin began a playful tune.

Leah. Every musical instrument she touched poured out her impressive talent. He'd watched her throughout the evening, though the guests divided his attention. His primary job was to survey quality and stay vigilant for all the details. Now, he sat back and let the tension flow down his spine and away as he listened to her play. She wore a white gown belted at the waist with a gold cord. She resembled an angel. Leah. . . She'd turned the Seasons nightmare into a blessing. Whatever else happened, he was thankful for her.

As she played, tiny figures in white scattered across the stage. Scatter was truly the best word, as the children flitted in, turning in different directions like snowflakes. The snowflake dance, which he'd anticipated. Just watching them stirred a chuckle in him, despite his gray mood. Several adults stood to take photos, probably the children's parents.

Nathan glanced around the room as the dance continued and other instruments joined the violin solo. People had stopped eating and leaned forward, delight on their faces. Several clapped and whistled. Everyone seemed spellbound by the dance, or rather, by the children themselves as they interpreted falling and dancing snowflakes. At the end, applause erupted in the room and many people stood, clapping vigorously.

"That was awesome." Ben clapped. "How will anyone top that?"

Nathan knew more amazing talent would follow. Next up, a quartet in colorful cardigans and knit hats of various shapes appeared on the stage and began singing Winter Wonderland. Olivia had rigged a way to have fake snow fall from the ceiling, though he hadn't convinced her to divulge the secret of how she did it. Leah had been wise to plan the quartet after the snowflake dance to avoid too solemn of a piece that might abruptly break the enchantment of dancing child snowflakes. One singer in the quartet was Sean, who'd quit the cast when the rumor of a sale to a developer came out. Leah had convinced him to return, that it was all untrue. Too bad it would probably be true after all, making Nathan a liar.

At least Mayor Faulkner appeared delighted, as if the whole thing had been his doing. He sat a few tables away next to his glamourous blond wife. Each time Nathan glanced in his direction, the man had a perpetual smile stretched across his face. A grave disappointment regarding Seasons loomed in *his* future as well.

As much as Nathan wanted to savor the evening, he couldn't staunch the flow of pessimism and self-condemnation erupting within him. Everyone in the room believed in Seasons and was convinced it would continue, but Nathan alone knew it was a false hope and he was a fake. At least he'd kept the doors open to Brian Prokovich and Skip Kaiser. He'd put them off until after the holiday, with the intention of turning both of them down. Now he was glad he'd strung them along. He'd surely need one of them to come through.

During the next three numbers, Nathan tried to focus. It was easier when Leah was singing or playing an instrument. She had more musical talent in her thumb than he had in his whole body. The final song involved a duet, a couple in nineteenth century costumes standing in front of the wooden sleigh which had been on the stage the whole evening. It had been hand-constructed by Olivia's husband and son and appeared nearly authentic, at least from a distance. The duet wound to a close and the fake snow resumed. Next, Leah led the guests around the room in four Christmas carols. Nathan couldn't bring himself to sing but mouthed a few of the lyrics so he wouldn't resemble Scrooge. The final carol, Silent Night, wrapped and closed the evening in a thoughtful, soft reflection on the baby in the manger. A fitting close to a successful holiday celebration.

Before the final carol faded, Nathan left his seat and waited by the stage, ready for his short speech of dismissal. After a moment of solemn silence, all the musicians who'd performed that evening returned to the stage and formed a semi-circle in front of the rear curtain. The audience responded with thundering applause that continued for several minutes.

When silence fell again in the dining room, the musicians bowed a second time but remained in place. Nathan mounted the steps to stand in front of them. He wasn't that comfortable speaking in front of a crowd but had had to do it a few times at his job, so he could pull it off if he had to. He forced a smile, hoping it appeared genuine.

"I hope this evening has helped prepare you all for a wonderful, Merry Christmas," he said into the microphone. "Thank you for joining us this evening and sharing these special moments of talent and tradition. My uncle, Andy, the previous owner of Seasons, would have been so happy to see you all here tonight filling this room. We know he's watching us now with joy and cheered for every talented musician in our program." He turned and gestured to the group behind him. "Join me in giving them another well-deserved round of applause."

The room erupted again in applause and Nathan joined in. When the noise died down, Nathan returned to the microphone. "Our performance was sold out this evening, but we still have some seats left for next week's show. Feel free to tell your friends about it. They can still order tickets online or buy them here with the hostess." Some lighter applause scattered through the room.

Nathan swallowed. He longed to be honest but knew he couldn't say everything. "When my uncle Andy passed away three months ago, I learned I'd inherited Seasons. I'll be honest with you, it was a shock. My first thought was to come here and sell it as quickly as possible." The room grew silent, tense. He swallowed and spoke more slowly. "But like you, I have many memories of this place. It was more than just a business, more than a building. I struggled with the question of whether to keep it or sell." His gaze panned the room. He thought he saw anxious anticipation on several faces. Mayor Faulkner was no longer smiling.

"But a few things won me over. My history in this town and the joy of coming back to it, all of you and your support, including Mayor Faulkner, and the heritage that my Uncle Andy left me. Reconnecting with dear friends also played a role." He turned slightly to spot Leah standing behind him and smiled. He scanned for Ben too, but his seat was empty. "I just want to tell you I will do my best. That's all I can promise now since I've never had a responsibility like this before. Know that my heart's in the right place, whatever happens. Merry Christmas, everyone."

After his heartfelt speech, Nathan didn't know what to expect. He'd revealed as much honest angst as he dared. Some people grimaced, as if they didn't know what he meant by his final words. Of course, they didn't know. Others began clapping and were joined by the majority of guests in the room.

He turned to leave the stage, but Ben had mounted the platform and stood beside him. He placed one hand on Nathan's shoulder and took the microphone in the other. "Before you leave, ladies and gentlemen, I'd like to add a few things to what Nathan eloquently said. Please remain in your seats for just a few moments more."

Nathan tried to catch Ben's attention to ask what he was doing, but Ben was grinning toward the audience and still held tightly to his shoulder. "Nathan here has been my best friend since high school. I can vouch for his integrity and sincerity. I happen to know he has a stellar marketing career in Philadelphia and could very easily return there. But as he told you, his heart was changed when he came back to Brenner Falls where he grew up. What he isn't telling you is even though his heart is here in the Falls and in Seasons, this wonderful historic establishment that has graced and entertained Brenner Falls for seventy-five years is in need of renovation. Andy Evans was sick, as you know, and unable to keep up with it. Nathan doesn't know what I'm about to say. This request is from my heart alone, not from Nathan. Inheriting Seasons means inheriting repairs and updates that may force its eventual closing. We don't want that, do we?"

He waited a moment, seeming to enjoy and feel completely at ease in the gameshow atmosphere he was creating. A surprising number of people called out, "No!"

Ben grinned. "I don't either. I want this fine establishment to continue being a beacon of Brenner Falls into the future. If you would like to help our friend Nathan with that objective, I invite you to contribute to the Seasons Renovation Fund. Every penny of your donations will go exclusively to renovations of Seasons. You'll find a round box near the door at the hostess stand on your way out where you can drop any contributions, or you can give online at Seasons Dinner Theatre dot com. Thank you in advance for your presence here tonight and for your generous contributions to restore and revive Seasons to its former *and* modernized glory. Good night and thank you."

When Ben finished speaking, he dismissed everyone, holding up a hand in a static wave as if he were an adored screen star or beloved monarch.

Nathan stood stunned into silence. "What. . .Ben?" was all he could say.

Ben turned to Nathan. "Bro, I hope you aren't angry at me. I just couldn't sit by knowing what an albatross this was when it really has so much potential. This idea just came to me about a week ago. I knew you'd probably balk at the plan, so I didn't say anything. Plus, I really thought it would be better if it were a total surprise."

"In that, you certainly succeeded," Nathan sputtered. From the corner of his eye, he saw the line of musicians disperse and move toward the curtain to exit. He wanted to snag Leah, but his feet were rooted in place. "I'm still amazed. I don't know how I feel." He looked back at Ben. "Thank you, I guess." They both laughed.

"So, Garrett was in on it and created a donation page on the website."

"I never even noticed. I'd been checking the stats and ticket sales for a couple of weeks."

"The page didn't go live before today, that's why you didn't see it. We didn't want people stumbling on it too soon."

As he spoke, Nathan's gaze wandered to the door where people were slipping money into the top of a large popcorn tin on their way out. He shook his head again. "I'm speechless. Hope it works." He'd need a lot of donations to do everything that needed updating plus pay the taxes.

A struggle tugged inside. In a very real way, Ben's well-meaning gesture might force Nathan's hand. It might close off the door of escape, since now people would expect him to stay in the Falls and make it work with their financial gifts. He no longer had the choice.

Suddenly, exhaustion filled his bones and he wanted to collapse. He longed to see Leah, but knew he'd have to keep it short. Otherwise, he'd simply fall to his knees and beg for rest, to escape for a few hours.

One more scheduled performance just like this one and he'd know where he stood.

Chapter Twenty-Two

Leah squeezed Nathan's hand, though she trained her eyes and ears on Pastor Todd. Felt good to be able to sit in church and listen instead of playing music. Especially sitting next to Nathan. The message found purchase inside her and drilled down to take root. Either Pastor Todd had taken an effective crash course in delivering sermons, or *she* had opened, humbled, changed. Or both. The little church had become her place of growth and ministry, a living organism she had the joy of watching develop and blossom day by day.

Despite all that was going on in Nathan's world, the uncertainties of Seasons and his future career, contentment engulfed every pore of her body. Nathan on one side of her while Garrett and Abbie sat on the other. Amazing. Garrett hung on Todd's every word, taking notes. Her throat ached as she watched him. *Thank you, God! You're so good and give such good gifts.*

Nathan nudged her shoulder. "Are you alright?" he whispered.

"I haven't been happy like this since my dad died." She kept her voice soft as a flood of emotion engulfed her. "There's so much to be thankful for."

He rubbed her hand and returned a gentle smile. For a moment, she was lost in his green eyes.

The service ended, and the four of them piled into Garrett's car. He drove back to his and Leah's house, filling the car with comments and questions about the sermon. Leah just grinned.

They entered the house and shrugged out of heavy coats and gloves.

"I'll preheat the oven," Abbie said.

"Thanks for the lasagna, Abbie." Leah touched her friend's shoulder. Abbie had dropped off a Pyrex pan covered with foil that morning before church, accurately guessing Leah would be too tired to prepare anything after her performance the night before and all the rehearsals before that. Leah felt too tired to remove her own shoes.

"We're also having a celebration," Abbie assured them as she popped the casserole into the preheated oven.

"Why a celebration?" Nathan wondered if she were being premature in her optimism about the donations to the Seasons Renovation Fund.

"Why *not* a celebration? There's a lot to celebrate. Just think about it." Abbie raised her eyebrows and sent him a grin.

Leah had heartily agreed, which she wouldn't have done a few months earlier. The glow that had settled on her at church remained throughout the meal despite the uncertainty of Nathan's employment status and Seasons. The four of them talked and bantered around the dining room table like. . . a family.

Nathan was quieter than usual, but she understood. In the living room sat the metal popcorn can of donations. They hadn't gone through it yet. Nathan had insisted he wanted to go to church and then have lunch first. *I just want to be sure my heart is right*, he'd said, *and that I'm submitting to whatever God wants. He's the boss from now on.*

"Whatever's in the can is up to him," Abbie agreed. "So, let's put it off a little longer. Seconds, anyone?"

ଓ ଓ ଓ

Nathan reached for the casserole. It was just the hearty home cooking he needed at the moment. Outside, the trees were bare, and a harsh breeze blew icy wind against the windows. The table setting glowed with cozy warmth. The sense of belonging and family rushed at him in a wave, despite the uncertainties in his life and in the metal popcorn tin.

Garrett sat across the table from him, looking relaxed and open. "Good job, Abbs." He served himself a second slab of lasagna. Because of Garrett's previous habits, his taciturn responses, and negligence in helping Leah around the house, Nathan had kept his distance from her brother. But even before becoming a Christian, Garrett had mellowed out, and his relationship with Leah had improved over the previous two months. Leah's brother was growing on Nathan, and he could almost envision a friendship one day.

Leah rose to clear the plates. "Tea anyone? Or hot chocolate? I have fruit too if anyone wants some."

"Are we avoiding the inevitable?" Abbie fiddled with a paper napkin on her lap. "It's like Christmas morning already!" she said with glee. "Let's see what's in there. Aren't you curious, Nathan?"

"Um, I guess so." Curiosity and dread wove together inside him.

"Let's go. Then we'll know what to do next." Leah's calm suggestion got them scraping chairs back and heading into the living room. Garrett placed the can on the coffee table. Everyone sat on the couch next to it and pinned their eyes on it as if it could explode.

"Feels like we're having a seance sitting around this can," Garrett said, which brought a peal of laughter from Abbie.

"I hope there's more inside than the ghost of Seasons past." Nathan met Garrett's gaze with a grin.

Garrett laughed. "You do the honors." He flicked his head toward Nathan.

May as well get it over with. Nathan pried the lid off the Christmas-themed container. Where had Ben come up with this thing? And the idea? Bills and checks covered the bottom third of the can.

"Well? What's in there? I can't stand the suspense," Abbie squealed.

Leah was unusually quiet.

"It's not empty. That's a good start. Here. You count the cash, Leah, and Abbie, you can count the checks. I'll hand them to you." He scooped out the currency with both hands and laid it on the table.

"And there's probably a lot more online," Garrett said. "You know people don't carry cash and checks around anymore. I'm surprised there's so much in there."

Leah and Abbie went to work counting everything, placing bills and cash into stacks. Garrett pulled out his phone. "I'll check the online balance. There's a special backend code I'll give you which lets you see the balance of donations. People reading the website can't access that part when they visit the site."

"You're brilliant, Garrett." Abbie sent him a smile and he shrugged. Nathan guessed Garrett must secretly enjoy her admiration.

"Okay, everyone. In cash, we have two thousand fifty dollars." Leah eyes shone with expectancy. "That's amazing. Like Garrett said, most people don't carry that kind of cash on them. They must have just emptied their pockets."

"And for checks, we have another forty-six hundred." Abbie pushed the stack of checks to the center of the coffee table.

Nathan's mouth dropped open. He hadn't been optimistic to begin with, but it was more than he could have dreamed.

"Six thousand six hundred fifty in all," Leah announced.

"And add to that seven thousand more online." Garrett raised his eyes from his phone. "Not a bad start, old man." He grinned at Nathan, who was still in a state of shock.

"Over thirteen thousand dollars." Nathan's voice was reverent. "It'll take more than that to renovate Seasons, of course, but it's a sign that people are behind it. They must love Seasons and want it to continue." Momentarily, he forgot about the outstanding debt and that the money he'd received wasn't even sufficient to cover it. The harsh fact returned to his mind like a punch in the gut. He wouldn't spoil their exuberance by mentioning it.

"And remember, Nathan, that's only one performance," Leah said. "We have another one next Saturday. If Ben gives the same speech next week, there'll be even more coming in."

"You should open a renovations account and put it in there until you get enough for a big project," Garrett said. "You'll be able to do small ones at first, or even if you want to get a loan for a bigger overhaul, you'll have startup money for that." Garrett's statement made sense, though the thought of a loan gave Nathan indigestion.

"There's also a letter here in the bottom of the can." Nathan reached in. He'd almost overlooked it, thinking it was a Christmas card someone had slipped in. The envelope was blank. He slipped open the seal and unfolded a sheet of paper. Mayor Faulkner's letterhead stared back at him.

Nathan's brow furrowed as he read, then he knew his face must betray a new level of surprise. "Guys, listen to this. It's from Mayor Faulkner. I'll summarize. He says he's aware of the tax payment due and the special circumstances surrounding it, meaning Andy's sickness. In view of the historical status of the Seasons building and its importance to the town, the town council of Brenner Falls has agreed to the city paying the outstanding tax."

He lifted his eyes from the letter. His gaze went to Leah, whose hand had flown up to her cheek. "Oh, my goodness. I never expected that! What an answer."

Nathan reread the letter to make sure he wasn't dreaming.

He turned to Garrett and Abbie. "Did either of you know about this? About the twenty-thousand-dollar tax bill?"

"I might have known a little something," Abbie murmured. "Leah told us about the tax situation and asked Garrett and me to pray about it. She swore us to secrecy, so no one else knew. You may know, I work at Mayor Faulkner's office, so I went to him to explain your predicament to see if there were any city programs of financing that could help you out. The mayor was very understanding but didn't promise anything except that there might be a way he could help. He said he'd look into it. So, I'm as delighted and surprised as you all are."

"But you were instrumental." Nathan felt humbled, grateful. "Thank you, Abbie. Seems so little to say. I don't have words." And he didn't. Once again, the burden had been lifted from his shoulders, and he could see clearly past the confusion into a well-lit clearing ahead. Maybe going through the agonizing tangle was part of the blinding relief of emerging on the other side.

"So, we prayed, and that's what happened," Garrett said in a matter-of-fact tone. He was getting an education already.

"Yes, God answered by moving the heart of the mayor to pay the bill. Wow. When does that ever happen?" Nathan couldn't stop the laughter that erupted from within him. He wanted to yell, *God is so cool!* But refrained. His normal personality was reserved, but he sensed a change was coming on, one he welcomed. "So that means I can use the full amount for renovations and not for taxes. That would have been a shame."

"A huge bummer," Leah agreed. "And all those people thought they were paying for renovations, but they didn't know about the taxes."

"Even Ben doesn't know about the taxes. Only you guys knew. And Uncle Andy up there." Nathan skimmed the paper again, then kissed it. "Thank you, Mayor Faulkner." Now Nathan understood why the mayor looked like the cat who'd swallowed the canary. He'd given Nathan a Christmas gift he'd never forget.

Abbie rose. "Now the excitement is waning, so anyone want to play Off Limits? We'll set up in the dining room as soon as Garrett and I, uh—" she sent him a pointed look. "—Do the dishes. We're giving you two the afternoon off."

"Thanks, Abbie. And you cooked too." Leah stood and gave her friend a long, tight hug.

"Thanks for the invite, Abbie, but I think we'll go to my place. That okay, Leah?"

Leah nodded and smiled at him.

"For tea, of course." Abbie sent Nathan a sly grin.

"Yes, of course." Nathan bowed toward her. "Thanks again for the delicious meal and for sharing this monumental occasion with us."

"Spoken like a real business owner." Garrett was already on his way to the kitchen. He must be in love to do dishes willingly with Abbie.

Nathan drove with Leah to his house, which took only a few minutes. "We'll get some quiet here." They entered the still house, which had returned to his habitual neatness, thank goodness.

Leah slipped out of her coat, and Nathan gathered her in his arms. They stood in silence, wrapped in each other's arms for several minutes. He felt the tension from the last two months ripple down his spine and out of his body as he held Leah close to him. "I'm still speechless, Leah," he said into her hair. "I might be very quiet today."

"Be however you want to be."

He pulled back and studied her face, then kissed her softly. "Want some tea?"

"Of course. Do you know how to make a fire in the fireplace? You can do that while I make the tea."

"Great idea." He winked at her.

Soon, they settled on the couch near the fireplace, a sputtering log just catching the flame. Nathan's arm hung over Leah's shoulder as they drank their tea in silence.

"I hate to ask this," Leah said. "But do you think the money Ben collected will change your perspective on the job promotion?"

Nathan took a few moments to think before answering. "It does. I have less incentive to do it just for the money. I think I'll ask to continue in my current position working remotely and turn down the promotion." He turned his head toward her. "That would enable me to stay here and oversee Seasons like before. *And* be with you, of course. Once Seasons is stronger, I can quit the job."

Leah smiled up at him and stretched her neck to kiss him. "I like that idea. I won't lie."

"Me too. Of course, the money that came in isn't enough to do all that I need to do there."

"But it's an awfully good start. You said so yourself. And it shows the commitment of the people, doesn't it?"

"Yes. I did say that, didn't I?" He took a slow sip from his mug. "Ben had some great ideas for new programming."

"Ben did? Maybe you should hire him." Leah giggled. "Though he probably already has a job."

"I'd hire you first. And Olivia. I might even request to work part time. And if my boss refuses, I'll quit."

"Seems like you've given this a lot of thought already."

"I've been thinking about it for over a month. I can do marketing anywhere. I can even start my own business." He smiled down at her. "That seems to be the trend these days, with you and Garrett. I could rent out my townhouse for income too. I'll be okay." He was on the cusp of an exciting adventure. And Leah would be right beside him.

"You will. Like you said in your speech Saturday night, you'll do your best with Seasons. And we both know you'll also trust God to lead you. From now on."

"If I've learned anything, it's that. So, how about if we talk about something else?"

"Like what?" Leah snuggled into him with her head on his chest.

"Like how happy I am to be here with you. Or should I say, happy to be here in Brenner Falls instead of Philly *and* happy to be with you. Doubly happy. In the New Year, I'll have to handle my job and my townhouse. But for now, let's just be together and celebrate. There's a lot to celebrate." He swallowed. "I love you, Leah." It had always been there, simmering in the background, even over the years of separation.

"I think I never stopped loving you."

Her eyes so blue and luminous, he could dive into them.

"What about that guy you were engaged to?"

"Michael? My love for you must have been in the background, waiting for the right moment. I thought I loved him, but I guess he was a temporary distraction." She frowned. "When it didn't work out, I thought I'd lost my chance for a happy ending."

"Ha! You had no idea just how happy you could be. Not bragging, but . . ." They laughed, and he wiggled his eyebrows at her. Yes, he was surely becoming more outward with his emotions and more playful.

He sobered, then leaned forward and kissed her, a gentle sweep of his lips on hers, then deeper with more heat. She curled both arms around his neck and melted into him as their tea grew cold.

"About that other guy," he said when he'd pulled his head away from hers. "They say when one door closes, a better one opens." He raised his eyebrows and thumped his chest as if to say, *you see? I'm the better one.*

Leah laughed, a musical sound even more beautiful than her singing, a sound he could listen to forever. "So much better."

There were good gifts, then there were better gifts. And there was no comparison.

Epilogue

Brenner Falls Times

Announcing the grand re-opening of our beloved landmark, Seasons Dinner Theater! After a two-month closure for renovations, Seasons is ready for its rebirth to a new epoch in Brenner Falls.

Come join us for a modern look, an updated menu blending innovative tastes with traditional favorites, and a sensational schedule of theater productions you won't want to miss!

To celebrate the Grand Reopening, reserve now for lunch and dinner specials from July 1 to 15. Make your reservations by phone or online. SeasonsDinnerTheater.com

Seasons' new owner, Nathan Chisholm, welcomes you to a brand-new era of Seasons!

I hope you enjoyed reading *Good Gifts*. If you did, please consider leaving a review at the online store where you bought it. It would help other readers discover my books and be encouraged by their inspiring truths.

Stay a while in Brenner Falls and enjoy **Book 2** in the series... **Custom Made.**

Blair McCartney's goal of becoming a fashion designer took a detour after an unplanned pregnancy. Eight years later, she's raising her son, Jake, in Brenner Falls and working in a clothing factory. Though she adores Jake, it's a far cry from the life she dreamed of.

Cooper Dawson, a contractor, still grieves the loss of his brother. He wraps up a housing project, then returns to Brenner Falls with his dog, Zipper. There, he wants to build his *own* dream house. In the meantime, he moves in next door to Blair and Jake.

What begins as a friendship blossoms into something deeper. Blair's rundown rental house presents its own challenges. Then, the sudden reappearance of Jake's biological father throws their lives—and budding romance—into turmoil, triggering old hurts, and testing the limits of faith and love.

Available on its own or in an eBook Box Set of Books 1-3.

Keep reading to discover Book 3...

Brenner Falls Book 3: **Embracing the Broken**

Physical therapist Amber Dawson strives to make life better for others. She'd love to leave the corporate atmosphere of her current job. If only she could buy the charming, abandoned house on the edge of town and open her own practice.

Ben Russo overcame a troubled youth and works as an engineer for the town of Brenner Falls. He's convinced the dilapidated house is historic and wants to prove it. Not only does he love history, but the discovery might also help him climb in his career.

When Amber and Ben meet at a wedding reception, the negative impression is mutual. But they later discover the little house they both have their eyes on is condemned unless they can prove it's historically significant. If the house is demolished, neither one will get it, so they decide to work together.

As Ben and Amber delve into the house's past, they encounter intrigue they never expected, and an attraction to each other they can't deny. But as they hit roadblocks to saving the broken-down house, they also come face to face with their own hidden brokenness and the grace that heals it.

You can also sign up to receive updates (and other goodies!) about new books at www.Kyle-Hunter.com where you'll *receive a free novella* just for signing up!

More romantic stories by Kyle Hunter

Romance in Provence Series

The Provence Series takes you with Bree and Lauren, best friends and business partners, to one of the loveliest regions of France. It's not always idyllic in the land of lavender fields and cliffside villages. Join Bree and Lauren as each woman discovers her unique journey. . . and surprising romance.

Prodigals in Provence (Bree's story) #1

Bree and her friend Lauren own Le Bon Voyage, a travel company specializing in tours to charming Provence, France. Bree battles anxiety before each trip, sure some detail will fall between the cracks.

Travis is a TV travel critic who crosses the globe to film documentaries. But he's been in a spiritual desert ever since losing his marriage and ministry five years earlier.

Between film projects, Travis plans to accompany his elderly mother on a tour to Provence, a long-term dream for her. Bree tries unsuccessfully to block him, sure he's coming to spy on the struggling company for an exposé article.

A diverse group of tourists arrives at the rented villa to spend the week and discover the spectacular villages, vineyards, and history of the Luberon mountain region of Provence. Amidst a series of problems and relational tensions, Bree thinks she has all she can handle . . . until she becomes attracted to Travis.

As Bree and Travis are drawn together, will their hidden wounds drive them apart?

A Promise in Provence (Lauren's story) #2

Lauren is at a turning point. If only she knew *where* to turn. Her long-term relationship with Mark is fading fast. Instead, she feels drawn to Jean-Pierre, an attractive Frenchman she'd met the previous summer. When she's laid off from her job as a chef, she decides to go see him in Provence, France.

Mark can't get Lauren out of his heart, even though it's been close to a year since she asked him to give her space. When she goes to France, he's afraid he'll lose her for good. That is, until he decides to go there, too, as a last-ditch effort to win her back.

At first, Lauren is angry that Mark follows her to France. But a joint desire to help a young refugee boy leads them to work together. Lauren finds herself torn between the two men. Worse, she's confronted with obstacles in helping the boy and even greater obstacles within herself.

Stand Alone Novels

One December

Nikki Mancini, a high school teacher in New York, has loved Mike Branagan for as long she can remember, though she was never more to him than his best friend's little sister. She claims to be a homebody, but secretly fears moving beyond her comfort zone.

Mike has his own emotional wounds to resolve, having lost his parents in an accident when he was fourteen. He's tried to escape painful memories by leaving New York and starting a new life on the West Coast, but years later, new facts indicate that his parents' deaths might not have been an accident.

At Christmas, Mike returns to New York for the first time in three years to visit and to chase down a lead in his parents' case. He and Nikki renew the friendship they had as children. Romantic sparks fly, but their mutual attraction takes an unexpected detour.

Nikki is shattered that she's lost her chance with Mike. She impulsively takes a one-year teaching opportunity in Paris to face her own fears and get over Mike.

Too late, Mike realizes what Nikki means to him. Time and distance should be obstacles, but are they?

"*One December* sizzles with romantic tension, taking the reader on a roller-coaster ride from New York to San Francisco, with a delightful detour in Paris. I couldn't put it down!"
      Elizabeth Musser, author of *The Secrets of the Cross* trilogy and *The Swan House*.

Circle Back Around

Hailey and her father haven't always seen eye to eye, especially in running the failing family textile mill. Frustrated, Hailey leaves the mill and her hometown in North Carolina to start a new life near her sister in Colorado. Only months later her father calls to ask a special favor. He needs heart surgery and asks Hailey to run the mill in his place.

Moving back would devastate Hailey's sister, Hope. Yet Hailey would have an opportunity to possibly save the mill, and at a time when her father needs her most. And maybe he'd even approve of her for the first time in her life.

Filled with self-doubt, Hailey returns to North Carolina and struggles to make a difference at the mill, facing more challenges than she bargained for. Her attractive neighbor, Alex, is almost enough to outweigh the difficulties, but she doesn't know that in the shadows lurks someone who wants to destroy both her *and* the mill.

Second Chance Series

In *The Second Chance Series*, you'll meet Marissa, Julia, Sydney, and Eden, four college friends who, twenty-five years later, renew their friendships as they find themselves empty nesters and single again. You'll love getting to know these women and following each one in her own book.

Marissa Rewritten (Book 1) A Novella

Author Marissa Thompson has had a writer's block since her husband died almost two years earlier. Her three closest friends are a comfort. Despite this, things are getting urgent as her career hangs by a thread and repairs on her historic home mount up. Prodded by desperation, Marissa heads to Wilmington, North Carolina for a Civil War research trip. She hopes for inspiration, but receives encouragement from a surprising source, a feisty character from her last novel.

Jarrod Lambert has already lost his wife. He's always been close with his college-age daughter, but she seems to be slipping further away from him. In an effort to reconnect with her, he makes an impulsive trip to see her in Wilmington.

Through an accident, Marissa and Jarrod meet and discover common ground. Will it be enough to overcome the obstacles standing between them?

Julia Redesigned (Book 2)

For the last three years, Julia De Luca has juggled her successful interior design business with caring for her elderly mother. Following her mother's death, Julia finds old letters from distant relatives in Italy. They remind her of visits she and her mother made when Julia was a child. Could these letters hold the answer to why their trips to Italy ended abruptly when she was ten years old?

These people whose names she's forgotten are the only family Julia has left on earth. How can she reconnect with them after so many years? Would it be crazy to try?

Her compelling desire to locate her distant family leads Julia on an impulsive trip to Florence, Italy. Along with savoring the sights and flavors of Florence, Julia discovers that families can be messy, that it's not too late to fall in love, and that there's more to Julia De Luca than she ever knew.

Sydney Rewound (Book 3)

Sydney Bennett's life is anything but calm. She's a high-school teacher and the single parent of a teenager. An unexpected event shakes her pressured but predictable routine. As she tries to regain her balance, she's drawn to a secret that even her daughter doesn't know. Nor do her three best friends.

Her private quest leads her to the beach town where she grew up, and her strained relationship with her mother. The last thing she expects is to cross paths with the man who once upended her life, a man she's never forgotten.

As Sydney's past collides with her present, she's forced to reveal her secrets and encounters the surprising power of letting go.

Eden Redefined (Book 4)

Eden Godfrey has been a widow too long. Or so her friends tell her. For the first time, she agrees, but she has a more pressing objective. Having sold the family business, which occupied her time and attention for over a decade, she now wants to find a bigger story where she can help people in need. Romance would be secondary. Especially since her brief stint with online dating didn't end so well . . . as she pushed away the only man with potential.

To the surprise of her friends, she decides to return to college to fulfill a long-term desire of finishing her degree. This will help her find her passion *and* silence the painful echoes of her past. Just as she discovers a cause worth investing in, she stumbles upon a suspicious scheme that overshadows it . . . and threatens to derail her dreams once again.

Can she finally grasp her dreams *and* find someone special to share them with?

Read Chapter One of all books (and/or purchase at numerous storefronts or eBooks direct from the author) at
www.Kyle-Hunter.com

Kyle Hunter is the author of nine novels of inspirational romance and women's fiction. Her relatable characters will become like close friends you'll cheer for and learn from as you join them on their journeys. Story settings range from Europe to small town America. As characters face challenges, the insights they gain are always relevant.

Kyle spent thirteen years in France, and she's intrigued by faraway places. Currently, she lives in North Carolina where she writes fiction, non-fiction (under the pen name K. B. Oliver), and the travel blog OliversFrance.com. She also teaches French to adults.

www.ingramcontent.com/pod-product-compliance
Lightning Source LLC
LaVergne TN
LVHW010312070526
838199LV00065B/5532